Saving the world one last damn time.

THE BROTHERS JETSTREAM

LEVIATHAN

— BY —

ZIG ZAG CLAYBOURNE

NARMER'S

F1088   14.95$

PALETTE

Mark well what has been said…because it's kinda cool.

~~~

Obsidian Sky Books
Detroit, USA

Published in the United States of America

Print ISBN 978-0-692-65546-7

Second Edition, March 2016

Cover and interior art designed by
Nathaniel Hébert, *www.winterhebert.com*

Interior design by Gentle Robot

"If it was special we made damn sure it didn't stay that way."

~ Fine print, bottom left corner,
Book of the False Prophet Buford,
located in his tomb under the
lifeguard tower on Belle Isle Beach
off the Detroit River.

*"Use **everything** to create the new."*

~ From one of the many notebooks
of Kichi Malat, old man
wandering with a guitar.

In those sprawling adventures of yesteryear
The villains were always so clear
The world, however, lost it
Evil today is as efficient and innocuous
As water exiting most faucets.

Home?

A pleasure ship moved slowly across open waters. The Brothers Jetstream didn't take vacations. Way too much heinous stuff for vacations; things people know about but try to pretend otherwise: movie industry's just a front for a secret vampire cabal; The Brothers Grimm? Their short stories were warnings. The brothers aren't dead. They teamed up not two weeks ago with the Brothers Jetstream. Much ass kicked that day. Much ass. Came as close as the space between a gnat's ass to finally getting rid of the False Prophet Buford.

Raffic the Mad Buddha's absence, however, made all the difference.

Regular Joes got tired and took vacations. Tired for the Brothers Jetstream was escaping the Bermuda Quadrangle, dodging angry resurrected dead folks, uncovering lesser known cabals (deep down folks knew about the vampires but it was a lot easier to stick a head in the sand and scapegoat Jews rather than admit a bunch of psycho blood-suckers were actually responsible for some damn good box office), or having to deal with the Thoom.

The Thoom were stupid. They thought Scientology didn't go far enough.

Seagulls, aware of the buffet aspect of cruise lines but not bold enough to land on deck, whirled past the ship's bright venting stacks. Ramses Jetstream watched one glide lazy eights.

He took a deep breath, scratching his scarred fingers through a rough goatee.

He was trying hard to relax.

Being dark-skinned was at times tiresome too.

For example: he and his brother wanted to procure cold ones for two of the loveliest women in seven dimensions, black, white, brown or green—and there were some damn fine green women in the world—and they'd been understanding of the busy *Joyeux Voyage* cruise ship, but the wait staff was performing its interpretation of Ralph Ellison's *Invisible Man*, zipping to youngish tan things as if guaranteed a fierce lay despite the commanding presence of the Brothers Jetstream.

So Ramses spoke up a little louder.

And got the *one moment* finger.

The resigned weight of a sigh dropped his chest. He was more patient than Milo, but that didn't make him patient per se.

And seagulls weren't interesting in the least.

Ramses Jetstream had little choice but to reach back and smack the college out of the boy when he gave him the *one moment* finger a second time.

The Shadow clouded men's minds. Ramses Jetstream calmly slapped the fye out of you.

Same effect. Nobody who saw it believed he had actually done it, and thereby negated the experience within a collective null-time bubble. A genetic trigger shunted the slappee into a personally localized alternate universe exactly to a point before the slap so he/she wouldn't have to deal with the reality of his/her dumb ass.

Sounded like a lot of work.

But didn't a brother get some drinks?

Virgin mango daiquiris for both ladies (one of whom looked on in appreciative silence), hot tea for Milo…

"Tea?" said the waiter. It was eighty-four degrees on deck.

"In a tall glass. Hot. You got Earl Grey?"

...and an orange soda for Ramses.

"Are you enjoying your first cruise?" Ramses asked one bikini-ed lady.

"This isn't my first cruise," she said, the younger of the two women. "I mean, I don't get out as much as I could," she said, and shrugged. "How'd you do that?" she asked.

"What?"

"Slapped the shit out of him and he just snapped back and took your order."

He and brother Milo glanced at one another. She saw *and* remembered it. Ramses was impressed. "It's got to do with the multiverse," Ramses started, but Milo saved the moment with a quick interruption.

"Are you going to dinner with us tonight?" he asked. The brothers and the ladies had run into each other several times over the last three days' recuperation in the guise of planning and regrouping, and had become *de facto* ship buddies during no-strings lunches and impromptu games of chess. They were lovely diasporic queens on a crassly commercial cruise who put everybody to shame (including that skinny supermodel wannabee passengers sort of thought they'd seen in some catalog but weren't sure since everybody was shooting collagen in their lips and asses these days).

Milo and Ramses warmed to them immediately. The Jetstreams were tired and glad to be back in the fold of civilization, however numbing, just this brief while. Home was two more days away.

"When did you want to eat?" asked Yvonne, the older of the two. She had military dog tags which, on her, didn't seem out of place with an orange swimsuit and floral wrap.

"Meet you in open-air dining at nine o'clock," said Milo, hoping the glint of sweat off his bald head wasn't off-putting. Another nice thing about these ladies: all they needed was a time and it was a date.

On most Atlantic cruises there was at least one person guaranteed to shout a daily "Dolphin!" alert.

"Dolphin!" shouted Susie Saindon from New York.

Her shout was relatively close. The younger woman, Neon Temples, burst from her seat and grabbed her friend's wrist. "Nine o'clock."

The Brothers Jetstream watched them run off.

"Ramses," said Milo.

"Enjoy the moment, brother."

"I like them."

"So do I."

"Damn," said Milo. He settled in his deck chair. The younger one was physical perfection. The elder: more athletic, a little taller.

"Let's make sure we don't do so too much," said Ramses.

~~~

Neon decided to broach the question Yvonne had advised her against. "So what do y'all do?"

"Not talk about work while eating," said Milo.

"Whale!" somebody shouted but the ladies kept their seats.

"And for fun?" asked Yvonne.

The muscle definition in Milo's arms was distracting. Yvonne couldn't look at him without wanting to wrestle.

"Something inside that was always denied for so many years," Milo sang.

"She's having fun," said Yvonne. "A Beatles man."

"Name the album and you can have my last shrimp," said Milo.

Yvonne speared the shrimp with her fork. *"Revolver."* She smiled. Half the fat flesh disappeared in one bite.

He retaliated against her defenseless flounder. "*Sgt. Pepper.*"

"You sure?"

"Another whale!"

"What are they spotting out there?" asked Neon, squinting toward the darkness.

They dined under a huge, lit canopy. The dark Atlantic night seemed like sky brought to ground. Patches of moonlight dappled in rippling, silent spots.

"Blowhole spray. Hear more than see it," said Milo.

"Whale snot," said Neon.

"Yeah," he said.

"Like I wanna see that."

"People pay money to see that," said Milo.

"White people pay money to see that. Personally, I'm on this cruise to eat, sleep, and walk around in a bikini." She and Yvonne high-fived. "Who feels me?"

"And meet nice people," Yvonne added.

"I'm glad we're nice," said Ramses.

"Your brother's nice. I don't know about you," said Yvonne.

"I look better than him," said Ramses.

"I'll give you that," she said.

"Big ass whales!"

The voice wasn't shouting this time; it was screaming.

"Hello?" the screamer said, clearly a "hello" of panic. "Whales!"

"Dammit," Milo muttered. He shot up. Whales could be royal pricks. He stopped short of the screamer, who was being swarmed by cruise staff. The ocean was almost a fountain square with blowhole geysers jetting at irregular intervals. Milo estimated thirteen big sumbitch whales forming a moving semi-circle less than fifty yards off the cruiser's port fore. Their huge backs broke the water like islands. The call had already gone above decks to cut speed.

He found a deserted section, grabbed hold of the fat safety railing, and launched.

Skin and Groans

Maseef Or-Ghazeem sat on the bobbing back of a whale. He rubbed a tired ache from his hairless eyebrows. Water allowed no time for fatigue. He wore full breach gear from head to foot. He carried a pocket umbrella.

He reached down and grabbed a brown hand from the water, keeping firm grip on his suction mount while Milo scrabbled for footing. It wasn't easy getting on top of a whale.

Maseef handed Milo a suction handle. Milo popped it on and swung himself up. They were a decent distance from the main blockade of whales but droplets of spray from those others still managed to rain on them, prompting Maseef to run a gloved finger along the outer ring of his whale's blowhole in quick squiggles.

Both men gripped their handles firmly. The whale's grey-black body jarred as a flick of its powerful fluke sent it gliding.

"Can't stand that on my skin," said Maseef. The only visible flesh on him was the figure eight around his eyes. Pressure goggles hung from his neck. The eau of mammals and fish was strong.

They waited till the whale's momentum stalled.

Then Or-Ghazeem spoke without his voice cracking:

"You left my sister."

"We're going back," said Milo.

"Soon."

"Immediately."

"You loved my sister." Or-Ghazeem rarely asked questions.

"I did." But not in the way everyone assumed. Lolita's interests lay in the hidden layers of the world, not the heart. Lolita Or-Ghazeem, for Milo, was a friend and a comrade who had planned to spend all her days alone and was fine with that. Maseef, being overly protective, took the furtive smiles she had for the Jetstream and turned them into a love affair.

"You need Raffic." The beserker. The only one of their crew who saw killing as inconvenience, not mortal failing. "I know all that happened." Nobody had ever heard Maseef's voice above a soft whisper one had to lean to hear. The Atlantic, however, didn't swallow the softness of his words; it seemed to wait, lapping waves between his pauses. "I'll find him."

"So will we."

"You left too quickly."

"Didn't see much of a choice, Maseef. You could've been there if you wanted."

Maseef looked out at the expanse of water for a silent moment. Milo followed his gaze. The ocean at night was terrifying for the uninitiated. There were huge *things* underneath which sometimes ate things. Huge ancients that were gigantic sets of teeth with human sized gaps between them. They were called *singularities*, dark holes in the darker night of the ocean, that sometimes rushed from below and bit whales in half so quickly and cleanly no one was likely to know. Singularities were nocturnal.

He and Maseef bobbed the waters of this night.

The Brothers Jetstream were never terrified of what they could not see.

Maseef Or-Ghazeem would not know terror if pumped with six liters of it.

The ocean matched their outward calm. Away from the ship's search lights Milo and Maseef were invisible against the water. In ancient times the moon had saved sailors from madness, illuminating pieces of the ocean for reference.

On the cruise ship, nobody thought to carry cameras at night; Milo imagined they were scrambling for them now. The whale blockade languidly kept the ship hemmed into a pattern of slow advance.

Maseef's silence was an admission that he knew Milo was right; Maseef could have been there during their battle with the False Prophet Buford. Could have, but had not. Maseef handled guilt considerably worse than he did terror.

"My sister knew what she was getting into," he said, leaving the "with you" part unspoken.

Milo said nothing.

Maseef looked directly at Milo. The moonlight's glint in Milo's eyes was dim. "We're men, aren't we, Milo?"

"Supposedly."

"I had to be sure you were coming back."

"You're a drama queen, Maseef." Milo disengaged the handle. "Let the tourists go."

"The whales would leave me in the ocean if I told them to ram that ship," Maseef said dourly.

"Your whales are pricks, Or-Ghazeem. I've never liked your whales."

"They can't stand you either."

Milo swam out of sight back to the cruise ship. He kept the suction handle, using it to climb aboard away from eyes and commotion. It took a little patience but he made it to his stateroom unseen. He dried and lotioned. Neon had thought it funny when he bought three sets of duplicate clothing at the gift shop. The Brothers Jetstream made sure duplicate clothing was always on hand. He and Ramses had learned that tip as children.

"Sorry about that," he said after returning to his seat and patting his stomach. "You might not want to finish that flounder."

Neon and Yvonne slid their seafood away.

~~~

Milo and Ramses promised the ladies they'd one way or another meet again. Strangely enough, their new friends realized a promise made by them was no flimsy garland.

Neon hugged Milo; Yvonne kissed Ramses on the cheek. On impulse, she gave him her dog tags.

"Somebody's always returning a keepsake in movies," she said.

"They'll be polished and waiting," he said.

She smiled brightly, looking him up and down. He was a little taller than Milo, not as muscular, but definitely prime material. "Boy, if you'd made one move on me…"

"We'da made this boat capsize," Neon seconded, giving one quick jump of her eyebrows to Milo before Yvonne pulled her toward the stand of bright orange shuttles. "But we're glad you didn't," Neon called out.

The brothers watched them walk away, then they grabbed their luggage, slipped shades on, and headed out.

Folks who didn't take vacations especially knew when it was time to go home.

Death and Wishes

"First and foremost know this: Milo D'artagnan Jetstream is not a man." An old dude spoke. Young faces squinted at him, feeling the muscle of each word.

The elder cocked his head to the left a scant as if listening, then grinned—again, just a scant, so the children wouldn't look to see.

On the rooftop across the shaded two-lane, a shadow between two gargoyles smiled down. Milo hadn't intended to delay but seeing his adopted father about to launch into another legend made him stop to listen.

"Everybody knows he ain't real," one of the Twins said to her sister.

The old dude (his name was Kichi Malat and he'd been the second son of a second son though wasn't quite sure if anything extraordinary was signified by that) pointed a steady finger at the girl and asked, "You heard me say he wasn't real?"

"Aw, hell," little Kevin scoffed in a tone which said he, at eight years of age, knew exactly what was what. Kevin was relatively new to the neighborhood. "It's like what's his name."

Malat's hand whipped out, knocking just a little fye out the boy.

The twin said, "Paul Bunyan?"

Kevin, not currently able to speak, shook his head.

"The Bloody Mary," the second twin said. Teasing boys was easy.

"No! The one in the tunnel who died," a dirty mop of a child, Kevin's friend, said.

"Leroy Brown," the Twin's twin said. They shared a secret twins' laugh.

"Why are girls so stupid? John Henry," said Kevin. "They read us the story last week, stupids."

This time Malat just thunked him upside the head.

"Ow!"

"Be respectful," said Malat.

"Jetstreams ain't nothin' but stories," said Kevin, in pain but defiant.

"If this was just a story I'd be telling you to read the book. The Brothers Jetstream are real. I know their phone numbers." Malat shifted for comfort on the stone steps. He balanced an ornate walking stick across his knees. "So!" he barked, and only when assured their tangent had run its course did he speak again. "He was born Man from Man, but was destined from the first to join the Great Lilac and travel to all her beyond regions. Which he did. And still does. Remember I told you of the Great Shadow Battle with the Mantis I had when I was much younger? If not for the quickness of Milo Jetstream's little fingers I would have lost and none of us would be here. He was just a child like you, an orphan, when he did this, younger even. I adopted him. Who do you think taught him to fly?" he said with another sly grin toward the upper shadows.

"You can't fly," said Kevin.

"All old people can fly. What do you think we do when you're not around?"

"I like Ramses the best," the Twin's twin said.

"Ramses Jetstream is another matter entirely. I'll tell you later how the two orphaned children were reunited by accident during the Great Battle of Equinox and Eclipse."

"BATTLES ARE NOT GREAT!" a voice boomed out.

Small heads whipped upward, eyes wide and hearts quickening.

But there was nothing to see.

Milo was nearly at the rear of the building away from them and picking up speed. He launched himself from the roof and over a hard chasm, tucking into a somersault to hit the blacktop on the next building to come up running.

He slid down a fire escape and dropped silently into a dirty, garbage encrusted alley. Bums never peed on Bruce Weyne's secret entrances, but let the Jetstreams go away for a few...

He would have to make it a point to play another practical joke on Bruce's fancy car. Putting spinning gold rims on the sucker had been sweet.

He approached a nondescript grate set into an alcove, and nudged garbage aside. The grate was magnetically sealed from the inside. Milo touched his right thumb to his left wrist. He hefted the heavy metal with a grunt then reached to drag it back into place as he descended.

Years ago this tunnel had served as an access to the sewer system just a few meters below, but now, with the area and pretty much the entire city effectively demolished by neglect, it was forgotten and never used. He walked quickly through the darkness. Five meters ahead was another door, also magnetically sealed. Behind that door they had created a narrow living space by blocking the tunnel with two very serious doors, the first of which raised into the ceiling at his touch.

Ramses was supposed to have been waiting for him.

Ramses was clearly not there.

Milo went to an ornate wicker chair, turned on a small monitor and disc player, and settled back to observe whatever cinema had been left in the machine this time.

A man was grinding his privates into another man.

All right.

There was a click. Then another click. The rear door opened. Ramses entered. "Porn, brother?" said Milo.

"We never considered where people go when they come. I think it's related to the fye. Worth studying."

"You're studying wax fruit to determine what an orange tastes like?"

"The porn was just a random satellite steal."

"I think I'm gonna wanna get out of this chair."

"I think you might." They switched.

Ramses scratched chin through goatee. "You talked to Malat?" said Ramses.

"Yeah."

"You still plan on rushing back."

"Now you sound like Maseef. Speak in questions, brother."

"We're going back to Atlantis, Milo," said Ramses. The Jetstreams didn't leave people. "But we do it right."

"Agreed."

"And this time we finish this."

"Agreed." Milo stood. It was time to go. "Let's go to the bank."

Death and Wishes, Part II

The luxurious bayside home of Mrs. Janine Grissom, recently disowned by the New England Grissoms for her appalling decision to consort with …well, they weren't entirely sure whom, but anytime you're consorting it's a step down, screamed stupid, vindictive money.

Ramses Jetstream, son of Hiram Percy and not of the False Prophet Buford as he'd been led to believe, had been born with the gift of reanimation.

It came at a huge cost and he was already thrice damned for it. In certain extremely rare but profitable circles he was known as *Jesus Price*.

Mrs. Grissom, her pitch to have her daughter returned to her completed in hushed, bereaved tones, waited for someone to say something.

Ramses considered. He slid hands into his pockets. "I won't do this."

"Wait now," Milo said, looking from Ramses to Grissom.

"She committed suicide," said Ramses.

"C'mere." Milo led him off to a large indoor lemon tree. "The mother's in the room with you. Keep that in mind."

"I won't do this. We a carny act now? She was a suicide."

"I understand."

"Is there a problem?" Mrs. Grissom asked, voice on a thin edge.

"Helluva big one, actually," Ramses said before Milo cut him off. Milo shook his head reassuringly at the woman.

"I spark flesh," Ramses whispered at him. "And whatever they had with them when they were alive," this he said louder, directing the words over Milo's head, "comes back with them."

"None of the others asked you to animate them," said Milo.

"None of the others were suicides."

"That's not good enough," Milo said.

"It'll have to be. Tell her."

They wore their black, hooded trench coats. Black hooded trenches made them look mysterious while concealing the assortment of advanced technology they carried.

Milo went to the downfallen matriarch.

"You heard all that, I'm sure. Let's be brutal with it. You don't have very long to live, do you? I'd like this to happen same as you, but the only way that's going to see light is if he's satisfied."

She held spider-veined hands delicately over her mouth to block medicinal odors that may have betrayed her. "She died unhappy…"

"We pretty much figured that," said Milo. "We researched your daughter—" The woman's eyes widened.

"I won't take the chance she'll find me," she whispered to him. "Her note vowed she'd find me when I died. She was always full of poetry." Her eyes welled. "And get me back! I'm her mother! No respect in life and no respect in death." She let it trail.

Ramses walked slowly toward them, eyes on her.

"Janine, ineptitude irks the hell out of me. May I be blunt? I'll be blunt. You drove your daughter to kill herself. This little skit was for the benefit of your truth. Bring your daughter back so you can escape in death; she kills herself again, you want me to bring you back? You have that rider written on a contract somewhere? Round and round? There are no pictures of your daughter anywhere. I see everybody but her. Milo?"

"Yeah?"

"End scene."

"Do you know how hard it took me to find you?" she said. She pointed at a satchel of money on the floor as if it explained away everything. "One million dollars."

"Blood diamonds in every single one of your jewelry stores, Ms. Grissom," said Milo. "Homework is a beautiful thing."

"You won't get off these grounds."

Milo almost sighed. Instead, he shook his head. "Janine, you don't have a threat means half a damn to us. Ram?"

"Yep."

"Walk with me."

Milo picked up the expensive brown satchel and headed past Janine's rooms upon rooms. She had given the staff the night off and had instructed security to remain outside the mansion. If she'd wanted she could have run to the front door screaming. As it was, Milo stepped out into the night, nodded amiably to a tall Italian whose partner glanced once at him and Ramses. As he and Ramses disappeared wordlessly into the night, the brothers split up.

By the time they got to the gate Janine would certainly have locked it.

They rendezvoused outside the estate's ornate gates that they'd had no problem vaulting coming or going.

"We're getting too old for this," said Ramses.

"Playing Robin Hood keeps us grounded." Milo tossed the satchel of money into the car. "I liked the touch of irony though. Spoiled rich zombies."

"Irony is beauty. We've got a satchel full of money."
"We don't do it for the money, we do it to plant seeds."
Bound for Atlantis by way of the Blank.

Blank
Stares

The Blank intersected the tropical waters of Bermuda. Two fast ships, the *Semper Fi* and the *Linda Ann*, navigated quietly and surely.

It was called the Blank because those who lived on the other side of it didn't have to be bothered with Britain, the United States, North Korea, China, Syria or Joyeux Voyage Cruise Lines.

It was a region of space accepted as existing (exactly opposite to Israel and Palestine, two regions caught in loops of slapped fye).

Crewmembers outfitted themselves in full breach gear.

Because Fiona Carel traveled with them, this was a slight distraction. Breach suits were like wetsuits, but with boots, gear pockets, utility harnesses and belts.

She had the most highly developed acuity to the multiverse of anyone alive, packed inside a five-four frame of curves.

She leaned over the railing to shake flotsam off a line.

Ship's captain Luscious Smoove appreciated her over his log pad. He sent a message to the *Linda Ann*'s captain: *She's bending over again.*

After a moment the message came back: *Advise against over-excitement.*

Smoove glanced downward.

All was cool.

He broke a peanut shell in half and cracked just the one, sliding the other into a pocket, then popped the treat into his mouth for the earthy sweetness of it, rolling it with his tongue. He scribbled the stylus over the pad, concluding a personal log entry. One day Luscious Smoove's writings would be as important as *Kichi Malat's Guide to Heroes* or the Necronomicon (depending on Smoove's mood). People would know that Fiona Carel had stolen the heart of this man from Trinidad with her bobbed auburn hair and insanely pale skin.

She straightened. A lock of that hair had worked its way from beneath a cap. She tucked it back and moved to the next line.

Smoove's wife, Captain Desiree Quicho, sent another message: *Will we pause for dinner soon after you're done fantasizing?*

Smoove's response: *She's just a dream; you're my fantasy.*

Quicho sent back a mocking heart.

Luscious Smoove came by his name honestly.

Repairs to the *Linda Ann* and the *Semper Fi* had been breakneck to prepare for the Jetstreams' inevitable return. Smoove's heart had sunk when he'd told the Brothers they'd have to secure commercial transport after the earlier failed voyage. The *Linda Ann* and the *Semper Fi* were more home than home, and home was what those men had needed most before setting foot on that Joyeux Voyage cruise ship after such a defeat, but a cruise ship was something huge and anonymous; it allowed for cocooning against disappointment and fatigue for the few days necessary to reconnect with their usual world.

The respite seemed to serve its purpose: Milo Jetstream's focus aboard the Fi could bore holes through steel; Ramses Jetstream walked the decks as if the universe was revealed with each step. The long reign of the False Prophet Buford would soon be a thing of the past.

Plus Maseef had promised to find the Mad Buddha.

Smoove breathed deeply, enjoying the life of the ocean air. It cleansed him and prepared him for whatever sacrifices were to come.

We anchor at eight, Captain Quicho sent back.

Who's cooking?

I am, appeared on his screen.

I'll be over to help, he sent.

I'll probably have to pull the Fi out of an iceberg since her captain's not watching where he's going.

I can help after that. Where are you now?

In the galley.

Be naked when I come.

Usually am.

The sleek ships sluiced the waters side by side at a comfortable clip. He smiled and tucked his pad away. Captain Quicho was blessings a'plenty.

Below decks, Ramses and Milo plotted out likely locales for Buford. The Atlantidean "civil war" created thousands of pockets for him to hide. The trick was realizing Buford didn't necessarily want to hide. The False Prophet Buford lived to be clever.

They knew he'd still be in Atlantis. The Thoom had promised to kill him for publishing a treatise on their philosophies entitled *A Thimble's Worth of Sense* (under what anyone in the know knew to be one of his pen names) the second he reappeared, and the Thoom, being stupid as hell, were unfortunately nearly everywhere. Plus Atlantis was new territory for this old enemy; the teachings of Buford had been seeded throughout the United States to saturation and now maintained themselves. Atlantideans had not yet accepted the truth, and Buford never left until a job was done.

"I hate when the bastards get away," said Ramses over outdated maps.

"He didn't get away. He was let go."

"We need the Mad Buddha on this ship with us. I can't stand maybes."

"He'll be there."

"When do you think we'll be too old for this, Milo?"

"By the time we marry."

"Smoove's married."

"Smoove doesn't count. Smoove and Quicho will be doing this forever. We started with Buford, we'll finish with Buford." Milo dangled a pushpin over the map, unsure where to insert it.

Ramses pushed one in quickly.

"That was random," said Milo.

"Buford knows how we think."

Milo left and came back with Smoove.

"Where's Buford?" he asked the Fi's captain.

Smoove glanced at the map, took up a pin, stuck it in, said, "There."

Milo clapped him on the back.

"Plot a course," said Ramses.

Change in course, Smoove messaged his wife. *After the mainland we head to the Mountain.*

Later, with the ships synced to one another and sailing tight, Desiree said to him in the *Ann*'s galley, "So they think he's somewhere around the Mount."

"I do," said Smoove.

Fiona Carel entered the galley, hair again escaping her baseball cap. "You're not naked," she observed of the *Ann*'s captain. "He said you'd cook naked."

"Keeping hope alive," Smoove told his wife.

"You're showing more grey," said Quicho.

"I'm fine, luv," said Fiona.

The *Ann*'s galley was small but the three of them moved efficiently. Fiona picked a knife to dice onions.

Meals were always taken together. Milo's and Ramses' idea of cooking somehow generally involved kielbasa so, being excused from meal prep, they were across the hall setting tableware.

"Anybody placing odds on Maseef finding Buddha?" asked Fiona. Fiona had a thing for Maseef, which Smoove accredited to the whales, but Maseef had a thing against getting involved with team mates, which Smoove accredited to stupidity.

Desiree took mushrooms from her husband. "As with all things Buddha, Buddha is found when he wants to be found."

"Buddha's full of shit," said Smoove.

"As with all things," his wife said. She shouted across the hall, "Dinner's in about twenty minutes, BJs!"

"Ok!"

"I won't tire of that. We need everybody in on this," Smoove went on. "Hell, I'd even recruit Fake Rome now." Fake Rome was an idiot from long ago. "Or Wax Off."

Nobody had seen or heard from Wax Off in over a year, but in their circles that was not unusual. Warriors disappeared on a daily basis and nobody ever knew.

Quicho looked somber. "You know we're heading toward war."

"We been at war, sweetheart," said her husband.

"Uh-uh. Been at stalemate. Our side's refused to go as low as they go. They've had time under the strata poisoning everything good while we're up here painting and being delicate."

Hell, 9/11 had been years ago and—despite marketing the slogan "Everything changed"—absolutely nothing had changed, and the same ones who marketed it were the ones that planned to make damn sure it stayed that way, because, actually, everything was supposed to change.

Buford just didn't want it to.

If Jesus ever actually did come back he likely couldn't even get booked on a talk show circuit after a year.

But *all* the Messiahs had pretty much decided hell with it.

Which left the Brothers Jetstream, Captain Luscious Johnny Smoove, Fiona Carel, Captain Desiree Quicho and Raffic the Mad Buddha to get themselves dirty as dirty needed be. The Forever War, from day one, had been *Art* versus *Commerce*. Art boasted change and evolution on its side; commerce had all the stuff in folks' closets. Large closets were a major sell in every housing market.

"We can stay moles," said Quicho, "sucking at worms here and there or we can be badgers going in with teeth. I say we devour the suckers topside."

"I used to be called the Badger," said Fiona. "Ask me why."

"Don't excite him."

Too late.

"Do you know how entrenched Buford is?" the short greying lady who spoke with a brogue said. "He's like icebergs. Underneath is a whole freaking planet."

"Calm yourself, dear," said Quicho.

Ramses entered. "No Buford at dinner," he said with a swat to Fiona's backside while reaching for a handful of chopped carrots.

"Except that Smoove knows where he is," said Quicho.

"Smoove has the gift," said Ramses. He swatted Smoove's butt.

"Smoove could be wrong," said Smoove.

Ramses shrugged. "So could we. I go with who I trust."

They sat to a dinner of abundant stir-fry. Steam semi-fogged the windows. The Brothers Jetstream didn't play when it came to eating. One generally had to look over their food to see their faces.

"So touristas," said Smoove, "who did you meet on your cruise?"

"We should've complained more," Ramses told Milo.

"Besides Maseef," added Fiona.

"Neon and Yvonne."

"And they were interesting why?" Smoove asked.

"Not pretentious," said Milo. "Beautiful as beauty."

"Fortunate sons?" said Smoove, not inquiring as to whether the ladies had children or not.

"No," said Ramses.

"You'll meet them," said Milo.

"I would hope so. The Brothers Jetstream aren't known for spurious interests."

"No, they're not, are they?" said Milo. When a Jetstream was wistful it was best to stay silent. No one immediately spoke. After a beat Fiona asked if they'd completed the list of supplies to radio Ele in advance.

"Be done before we get there," Ramses promised.

They ate quietly a few additional moments before Fiona set her fork on her plate with a clink and propped her elbows on the table, holding her chin in her hands and regarding her friends, baseball cap in her lap and auburn-grey fully free. "Why're we going into this like it's our final? Everybody's been dour and quiet."

"I haven't," said Smoove.

"We who have kicked vampire teeth say we will be walking out of this to fight again," she said with a rallying nod. "Milo? Ramses?"

Milo tried a smile for her. It didn't work. Since setting foot on the repaired *Semper Fi* his mind—occupied more with losing Lolita than false prophets—refused to move as fast as he needed.

Ramses saluted her with his beverage. He hadn't shaved since meeting the ladies on the cruise. Yvonne had mentioned something about their scraggliness making them look chiseled. Froth dotted his bushier than usual moustache.

"Million dollar question: what do we do when Buford's done with?" asked Quicho.

"We move on," said Milo. "Each one of you is coming back alive," he swore. "There's always something. We move on."

Luscious Smoove floated a reasonable suggestion. "In case I die, would like to have massive sex between now and then. Any takers?"

"Wouldn't that require a massive—?"

"Hush, wife. You leave nothing private." Smoove tapped on the table. "We're looking for madam scientist too, right?" His gaze was on Milo. Lolita was a given, but Smoove didn't want it to be a secondary priority. "We've got two angry ships. Two fast ships. I'll look for her," he volunteered.

"I'll help," said Fiona. Then to Ramses: "You don't need all of us searching for Buford. Long as we're in distance we're OK."

"Maybe we should stay together for this one," said Ramses.

"Captain's prerogative to make his own course," said Smoove. "I miss Lolita."

"All right," said Milo. He looked at each in turn. "This time we go in hunting for bear."

Night
MOVES

It might have been said that Milo Jetstream wasn't a man given to morose thoughts and ponderings, but it would have been woefully inaccurate. He'd spent thirty-five years developing mystical abilities, safeguarding secrets and upholding inherent truths. Thirty-five years of being Superman could wear anybody down.

The False Prophet Buford was an unpleasant Kodiak bear. Alien technology was never supposed to have made it to the religious Right, whom Buford had realized as a potent resource. He had been cloned so many times everybody was pretty sure the original was somewhere dead and forgotten. While pocketed politicians were arguing about a pittance of stem cells, the Thoom and Pat Robertson were using secret labs to experiment on activating humanity's dormant Methuselah gene. Outlive and outbuy your enemies was a tenet of all empires.

Outlive and outbuy. The key to being a survivor. The False Prophet Buford was effectively immortal.

Milo might not have known if he was up for this anymore but he was damned if anybody was going to find out. The *Semper Fi* and the *Linda Ann* had brought him around the world more times than he recalled; what kind of person didn't make sure such friends got home?

After dinner he stayed aboard the *Ann* to work logistics with Quicho till both their heads spun. The others had retired to their respective ships and activities. Quicho's absent-minded tapping against a bracelet on her wrist signaled the end of the night. She kissed his cheek good night.

He went above decks.

Milo watched the waters pass the side of the boat, one fist hanging over the edge.

He'd always thought the Blank needed its own borealis. The night, though, was palpably dark and quiet and full of stars, and that was enough.

Nights like these were nights of wonder.

He scanned the water for signs.

The wearied Jetstream stood alone at the railing of a fast ship moving very slowly. The earth was a huge golf ball of pocket dimensions, and he traveled now through the most famous and misunderstood of them all. That's not something one puts on a resume as proof of employment.

All he had to do was soft-focus his eyes: there was Lolita, superimposed over the world, racing her skiff across ice floes as if even the muscles of her smile were invulnerable. She was a beautiful woman, big and always laughing.

Too much self-reflection, he thought. *Too much self.* He thought about the cruise ship. Grown men don't launch themselves off liners in the middle of the night, yet he managed to find himself doing so on a regular basis. Launching. Catapulting. Vaulting. Milo was the elder brother, and Ramses would go by his lead, but there had to be a point when all was said and done that two brothers might retire to sending one another birthday cards and best wishes. Milo was forty. Ramses was thirty-six. Basketball players were put out to pasture sooner, and none of them had ever faced the Thoom.

Except Kareem Abdul Jabbar and Larry Byrd. But only once and only briefly.

Neon. A beacon of false light, and the irony was killing him on this decisive voyage to the False Prophet. But she was a beacon of something of which he wasn't a part.

Was Milo Jetstream getting old?

That meant retirement. The normal world had 401Ks.

He looked across. The *Semper Fi* kept pace.

The normal might fall *on occasion* through the Blank…

But his crew actively sought it. There were three people on that sister ship sailing to the edge of the world, and each realized the crucial thing: if the sign said 'Here There Be Dragons,' Buford Bone was the dragon with the cracked rib.

Milo stared through the sloshings of the inky water below. This definitely had the feel of *no turning back.* He opened the fist. The tiny vial Lolita had given him a year ago dropped with barely a sound. It contained a frozen tear, one of hers from a night of raucous laughter at Maseef's expense, laughter till she and her friend were on the floor with eyes wet. Saving it had been the act of a scientist never without her instruments and who didn't believe in not having fun.

Who believed in the immortality of water.

TUg
Of Oar

Early morning aboard the *Semper Fi*: Coffee. Reflection. Danishes. Smoove. Fiona.

"I noticed Milo staring into the water quite a bit," Smoove said. "Something's not right with this voyage. I speak the name The Brothers Jetstream, I should hear action music. I don't hear no action music. I hear dark cholic."

"Go kiss your wife, ease that tune." Fiona's pale blue eyes sparkled intensely all the time due to the concentration and effort it took to hold to the moment. Smoove was constantly checking her for cancer or cardiac stress.

"Aye," he said, and prepared to do just that, signaling Desiree on the *Ann* that he was about to row over. He idly thought of parting Carel with the joke *if the boat's a-rockin*...but rocking's all there is on water.

Desiree angled the *Ann* out a hair for every stroke he took, making him work just a little harder. Luscious Smoove enjoyed the use of his body and ignored using the motor. The angle widened and he strengthened his stroke, determined to transfer the grin on his face to his wife's cheek. One of his dreads kept tapping him on the forehead. Pausing to tuck it behind an ear, he pulled an oar out of the water.

When he returned the oar to the water, something quite definitely yanked.

Smoove let it go as though burned and hit the motor, backing the skiff into a tight arc that whipped into a figure eight so fast the *Ann* barely had time to complete its port swing before he had his weapon drawn and trained on the settling water around him.

"Something's curious under there, baby!" he shouted, knowing Quicho would be above with her rifle drawn.

The Fi came about and cut engines. The ships bobbed innocuously a moment.

"Milo?" Smoove inquired.

"Nothing yet."

"Carel?"

Smoove didn't need to look to know she shook her head; if she wasn't shooting she didn't see anything.

"Feel big?" Milo said.

"Felt definite." The oar floated out between them.

Milo whipped out his communicator. "Ram?"

"Nothing on screens."

"Fast sumbitch," Milo observed.

Smoove magnetized the skiff when it drifted close enough to the *Ann*. He jumped the ladder. He climbed quickly.

Nothing was that fast. And if it wasn't...

"Circle on decks," ordered Milo.

With Ramses on deck there were three sets of eyes triangulating. Whatever had latched on quietly splashed into the water on the port side of the *Ann* before Ramses could get a good look at it.

"Damn good swimmer," said Milo.

"All right, you got our attention," said Smoove. "Now what's the message?"

The message, insofar as the messenger was concerned, was quite clear: I have the advantage over you. The follow-up to this message was equally clear: and I will press this advantage when I see fit.

"I'll be staying over here awhile, brothers," Smoove called out. "Sail tighter with us." One look at his wife recalled intrinsically why he was there in the first place. "But not too close."

Empaths
and
Flatlands

Atlantis greeted them with open arms. Specifically, the skinny arms of Shigetei Empa, one of the few governmental officials anywhere they considered a friend. Granted English was rarely spoken in Atlantis, but the Brothers Jetstream, being master linguists, found no difficulty at all learning their language subtly suggestive of several Mediterranean dialects, pointing to more than platonic contact with the outside world long before a failed tourism experiment allowed modern ships and planes to begin flitting through the Blank.

Empa hugged the first person in their convoy, which was Fiona, longer than necessary. This was the normal Atlantidean custom: held long and tight just in case.

When he peeled apart she nodded acceptance on behalf of the group.

"We expected you back but not too soon," he said, leading them to his vehicle.

"Not by well-thought out choice," said Milo.

Empa noted Raffic's absence but decided to be quiet about it. "Intel is that we have an unrecorded stranger inciting messy bits."

It was impolite to point out that their records on who or what passed through the Blank were shoddy and unreliable at best.

"They say he's been predicting the future and things don't look very good for the fringe settlements. This has to be related to your Buford."

The short trip ended at the understaffed Office of Alien Registry. It was where the Atlantidean worked with four others, two of whom, a man and a woman, they saw as they marched the large building's corridors to his office; both immediately preened the second they recognized Milo and Ramses Jetstream. Shig's assistants Giselle Jira and Wither Ween.

"Hello, loves," said Captain Luscious Smoove. Desiree tripped him. As he got up, Fiona inquired if Ele had found out anything about Lolita.

"Nothing encouraging, I'm afraid, unfortunately nothing new. There's very little out there," Shig said softly.

"Very little's more than nothing," she said.

The main search party was one mounted by and consisting of Lolita's two sisters, brother Maseef, and an incohesive, on again off again ragtag band of science groupies operating under questionable motives.

"Her last reported position put her heading for the Glacial Range," said Ramses.

Milo's mind was on the Mount. It was from there that the future flowed. Many had tried, many had died, most went insane. The only verified prediction came nine years ago from the mouth of *He Who Dared The Vantage That Yields The Invisible Stream Of Prescience Which Stretched Over The World*, which was the tip of the Mount:

"We live." End of revelation.

That man was Milo Jetstream, brother of Ramses, son of Hiram Percy (and not the False Prophet Buford as he too had been led to believe). So the Mount held special interest for him, and anyone claiming to have reached its summit invited suspicion.

"What's our priority?" said Ramses.

"Buford," Milo answered his brother. "Give me anything you have on his movements after we left," Milo said to Empa. "We leave immediately."

~~~

Ele Hachette, master empath and Atlantis' Chief Theologian, was actually shorter than Fiona. She had a bob haircut that made her seem more like Peter Pan than a master psychotherapist. She was the only person the Jetstreams knew of to have accompanied Fiona on an alternate reality jaunt. One developed a great deal of resigned patience for the universe one was cemented into when made aware there are indeed others to choose from.

Hugging tall people tended to be awkward. She hugged Fiona. "Supplies are already loaded on the ships," the diminutive four-foot niner said.

"Are you riding with me, Ele?" Fiona asked. Ele nodded. "Smoove's taking the Fi. We sail in an hour. Looking for Lolita."

"Finding her," Ele corrected.

"Let's get Maseef to rendezvous," said Fiona. "Make sure he brings his damn whales. There was something in the water."

The *Linda Ann* cut through the waters with a speed that said stopping was so yesterday.

This observation was not lost on Ramses and Desiree, who both looked at its pilot with a bit of brow raising.

"Milo?" said Captain Quicho, bracelet vibrating with the hum of the ship. "Slow down."

The *Ann* immediately throttled back.

The day was bright, the sky was beautiful, and this should have been a chintzy cruise. He thought about that woman again: Neon. Nobody read signs better than Kichi, and Kichi had taught Milo. The odds that this was indeed the final battle with Buford didn't invite a wise man to put money on it. Beauty was therapy, and by every god he personally knew Neon Temples was beautiful. There was a quality about her that elevated physicality to the spiritual, something unshakably lodged in his skin and bones. If it had simply been sexual attraction Milo wouldn't have been flying so fast to see things through, but something about her invited rest. His whole body strained for it. And for this reason, he turned the controls over to Desiree and asked Ramses to follow him below decks.

"Problem, brother?" Ramses said. Ramses studied him with that critical eye of his, analyzing all the way to engrams.

"I don't feel it," Milo confessed. "I don't *feel* it."

"You're the only reason we're out here, and I don't mean this mission. I mean me, you, Smoove, Quicho—the life we lead is not for those lacking imagination."

"The life we lead keeps getting people killed, Ram!"

"We couldn't choose otherwise if we tried."

"Ram, I'm tired."

"Why are you tired?"

"A lot of people died last time we were out here."

Ramses mounted a couple steps. Milo had to shield his eyes looking up at him. "When you're interested in a real conversation, let me know."

"We came close. What if we fail again?"

"You feel that shaky?"

Milo nodded.

"We fail, that means you let me down. I ain't havin' that." Then he was gone. Then his voice ordered: "Stay down there and meditate."

While Milo did so for two hours in the lotus position, Ramses and Quicho outlined plans, back up plans, and plans within plans within back up plans.

Buford being around the Mount—which was a lot of land to cover—meant he was planning a long stay in Atlantis. Ramses and Milo were the ones who'd chased him that deep into the interior; they were the ones to drag him out. Atlantidean civilization, comfortably annexed from that of main Earth since Atlantis' earliest studies of emergent Man, had never had a tooth-whitening commercial hovering in its air or fast food death masquerading as fit for consumption. Their civilization had emerged to see the Egyptians using laser levels to square the pyramids and had thought *Now here are neighbors worth meeting*—until all the inbreeding had led to seeing an abundance of chariots and carts parked on the sands out front for days and days, and loud chanting parties during the night.

They'd emerged to see the Mayans zip around in their metaphysical transport chambers and had thought *Now here's a good showing;* and had thought to join in their games until they realized the rather uneven balls of the Mayans had nostrils.

They had way more than enough sense than to come out during England's Crusades, and early American history was still good for frightening errant children, although they did tentatively peep out a bit to check into a wooly haired old physicist coming up with intriguing ideas about time. Then a big bomb went off, at which point it was time to return to the Blank and wave a hurried goodbye.

Ramses Arturo Jetstream was not going to be the one to demote thousands of years of suburban civilization into earnest feminine hygiene ads (again, vampires) or inane superstitious impotence disguised as holy frijoles just because his brother couldn't own up to not being in love with a woman most would have loved to consider their best friend. Ramses wouldn't let him blame this on Lolita.

No, the Brothers Jetstream, Milo and Ramses, had brought Buford and his problems to Atlantis.

And the Brothers would take him out.

The mountain range waited for the *Linda Ann* to catch up to it.

False Prophecy

The False Prophet Buford was tired. He'd just climbed part of a mountain, and now lay on his back hoping to gorge on thin air. He was of solid build, had all his hair, which had grown considerably since he'd traveled the Blank, and was sufficiently pinkish. He had been born in Madrid to Sue and Sam Bone, outside U.S. soil for the first time and victims of the established fact that foreign soil ignites horniness, particularly for seven-months pregnant women damned if they were going to be saddled with a baby before getting out to see the world. Sam Bone, inside his wife and looking at the grey peeking at the nape of her neck, freaked out when Sue's water broke *in flagrante delicto*. Once he stopped freaking out they were able to get to a hospital and, a few hours later, hold their son.

That was sixty-four years ago.

The view dropped to a craggy plain for a stretch before dropping down again into a valley that led to more mountains and hills, and beyond that *the* mountain. The Mount. Where Milo had been and Buford was going. It would have been easier to do this by boat, sailing the coastal settlements, but difficulty felt right for this pilgrimage. The more difficult he made it for himself, the more difficult he made it for the Jetstreams. He got up, face full of lines, body stocky and well-lived. He squinted craggy eyes on the height of the next butte and gathered himself up.

He traveled alone, intentionally, and as technologically-free as prudent, both as penance. The Mount required a certain level of purification, of reverence. Buford himself had written that TRUTH, to be truth, when considered in caps, required BLOOD.

Additionally, he had forgotten that he used to be amazed that people believed him.

He climbed. Rock jabbed hard into his hands, cold and clarifying. Finally he tightened his grip over a final ledge and pulled himself up. He was sweating and really needed to pee.

The False Prophet Buford unzipped while facing the sun. It was perfectly arranged between wispy clouds, on a backdrop over the Mount so blue it seemed solid. Buford Bone peed in the face of beauty as the wind made wild with his hair.

POetiC
ViCeS

Their first port of call, under the direction of Kichi Malat, was the home of Vrea Talloon B'oom.

"Cute," said Ramses, "But what does it get us?"

There was a gnarled old biddy somewhere under swaths of fabric. She was visibly agitated.

"You've gotten somewhat stupid," she said, grabbing at the inscribed amulet she'd only just given him. "Kichi himself carved these runes."

"Power's never in the thing, Ms. Vrea. You know that."

"Do you know what it says?"

"Yes."

"And do you know he and I were lovers?"

That was a flat board to the gut. "Didn't want to. Feeling nauseous. Can we move on?"

"The words have words! A code to the code. There's no way you don't know Kichi's been to the top of the Mount, even if he hasn't told you. *But* he fell asleep there. Ah, stand there and pretend stoicism as you want. That took the wind out your sails. The Dreamtime and the Mount. So now tell me what you think this amulet is worth?"

"The message he sent was you were to *give* me something."

"Explain how that's exclusive of me getting." Fabric rustled closer to him, and a wrinkly hand, so ashen it almost radiated, poked a palm out.

"How do you see in there?"

"Give me something or give it back. Kichi doesn't scare me, you know. Nobody who's been inside—"

"Ok, stop!"

She slowly wiggled her hips back and forth.

"Please. Vrea, what do you want?"

"Tell me something about the last time you were in love."

"It wasn't that long ago. How's that?"

"It'll do." She shuffled backwards then spun on a dime to pull a book from a low-hanging cabinet. "Give this to Malat the next time you see him. I used to be quite a poet."

A peculiar thing about poetry was people who said they used to be quite a poet never were, and so books of terrible verse remained in cabinets for decades on end until an opportunity presented itself to have the evil things presented to their intended. Nobody ever said they used to be quite a short story writer, or quite a novelist.

Vrea Talloon B'oom was apparently a piece of their adoptive father's history never meant for general consumption. Ramses raised the questioning eyebrow.

"Mind grown folks' business, Mr. Jetstream. What happens in Atlantis stays in Atlantis." She tapped the small volume in question. "Bound and locked thirty-three years ago. That's not leather, it's singularity. Malat skinned one."

The hell he did, thought Ramses.

"Took a week." She was obviously proud of both the recollection and the man: the fabric swatches bobbed happily and he actually caught a peep of her eyes. "When you see the naked singularity, remember that old man as a great man. Tremendous lover."

That's gonna leave a mark, he thought.

"Nobody slays things anymore, young Mr. Jetstream," she said with a touch of ache, "Metaphorically or otherwise."

"ASPCA," he said.

"That amulet says ____. And it's worth a lot, so I'd hold on to it."

"You're saying he knows how this is all going to end?"

"We all do, love. Give Milo a pat for me."

Ramses returned to the ship. Milo's forced strict regimen of thirty minutes meditation every hour would be up soon. Ramses stashed the book of poetry in a trunk.

When Milo emerged, Ramses showed him and Desiree the amulet.

"Malat knows how this is going to end, Milo," said Desiree. "He's always known."

Milo traced its squiggly etchings with a finger. "Could've saved us a lot of work," he said. Defeat after defeat rang in his ears.

"Nowhere you can be that isn't where you're meant to be, brother," said Ramses.

Milo glared at him. "That easy?"

"Lennon only lied when he lied."

"Daddy's rubbing off on you."

Malat was famous for oblique statements. The Battle of Pro Versus Con had cemented his position as certified master.

"Who do you think fed John half the lyrics the FBI took interest in? You need to talk to pops more than you do," said Ramses.

"Why's he suddenly pointing us the way?" Milo wondered. He handed the amulet back with a frown. "I'm a little scared of this thing, Ram. Evil portents."

Desiree had been resting her chin on the tabletop watching the two of them. She held a hand out; Ramses dropped the amulet into it.

"Evil portents," echoed Desiree, studying the irregularly shaped slice of native Atlantidean rock. It was green but without the polished quality of jade and was definitely heavier than it looked. Malat had rushed ragged Atlantidean symbols on it, and Desiree wondered why, why rush and why write on stone? (Having read every one of Kichi Malat's handwritten texts, she knew his handwriting, she knew his moods.) "From the Mount?" she asked.

"Looks like it," said Milo. There were hunks and veins of that stone all over the Mount.

"My brothers," said Desiree, face cocked at an angle to see them, "I salute you."

"We are not about to die," said Milo.

"Maybe I be. The only immortality I sought was my husband." She spun her bracelet around to view its inscription: *m'anamchara*. My soul to yours. The only wedding band Smoove had given her.

"Only lazy people need to live forever, hermana," said Milo. "The rest of us get things done"

"Aye." She handed the stone to Ramses, who hung it around his neck where it clinked against Yvonne's dog tags. Desiree raised up. "Took the initiative to contact the Battle Ready Bastards."

"What'd they say?" asked Milo.

"Pick 'em up by nightfall and be limber."

"They're going to be sorely disappointed."

"Or we'll be. Nothing worse than a bunch of horny angels."

Milo and Ramses glanced at one another. There was nothing to do but agree with that.

When We Were Younger, So Much Younger Than Today

"Your husband's not here, Quicho?" said Lucifer. The angels of Atlantis were eleven-fold, descendants of purebloods who'd renounced all special gifts long ago. Being named Lucifer was like being named Jésus among Mexicans, and Lucifer was always quick to point out his name actually meant light-bearing.

Ambriel, the communicator. Arariel, curer of stupidity. Eloa, the compassionate. Nakir, the arbiter. Ra'asiel X, the baddest angel in the whole damn town. Sereda, the ambassador. Shetel, the servant. Samandiriel, the lucid. And the twins, Vulva and Coupdiviel.

"Where's Fiona?" The only spiritual difference between angels and humans was a human's gaze could be ignored; an angel's couldn't. An angel could stare the clothes off a dead person. Also, they came in a rainbow of colors.

"They're looking for Lolita," said Desiree.

"Well, did they at least leave pictures of themselves?" said Lucifer.

"We've got a whole ocean for everyone to jizz into," said Desiree, "till we reach land." At which point, anybody not thoroughly focused would make Captain Desiree Quicho very disagreeable.

Vulva, all six feet two pale blue inches of her, reached for Quicho. The captain was yanked tightly into solid bosoms. The Battle Ready Bastards knew what had happened the last trip against Buford. Defeats like that left marks in the soul. She held the small human the usual extra seconds then rubbed her back comfortingly.

She released Desiree, keeping an arm around her shoulder.

"You Bastards make me proud," Quicho said. "Listen, this trip is all or nothing. We do it or we don't." Desiree glanced at Milo, then back to the crew. "There is very likely going to be mayhem and death. We travel light but packed to the teeth. I would advise wearing clothing," she said to Sereda, who was already stepping out of her shorts. The statuesque angel stopped mid motion. Angels tended toward as much nudity as possible or practical once a social situation had been assessed.

Sereda was green. Not a bright green, but one could take her unusual pallor as troubling and consider calling a paramedic.

"It's hard for me to focus when you don't," Desiree told her. Sereda was still considering. "That thong does not count, Sereda."

"We're not wearing clothes for our preparatory ceremony," said Arariel, his voice as sensual as ever.

"Wouldn't think of it. Be right beside you," said Desiree.

"Brothers?" Arariel directed his gaze to the revered crossbreeds.

"Goes without saying," Milo said.

"Sexing starts at three," said Desiree. "Crew dismissed."

~~~

The level of sex aboard the *Linda Ann* reached what most of a religious bent called "ridiculous." Complete elimination of all primary desires beforehand was necessary for the Battle Ready Bastards in order to free up soul to do what was needed in the coming days. They had been off-world Milo's last gambit; they wanted to be extra ready this time.

It wasn't an orgy, because orgies celebrate anonymity. As they rotated sex with one another, the Battle Ready Bastards ascribed to the highest states of individual tastes possible. As there were no required couplings, sheer desire was the compass.

The sex was loud, the sex graphically shattered several ratings, and it was only the first part of a two-part ceremony. Taking a break to replenish fluids, Desiree saw Milo banging away at somebody. Around starboard, Ramses was, in more literal ways than one, passed off like a baton from Ra'asiel X to Shetel. There wasn't a single eye closed in pleasure on the entire ship. Eyes were just as sexual as genitals. Just glimpsing the determination in Ramses' eyes made Desiree want to bend steel with her clitoris. Instead she settled into her captain's chair and idly watched the waters for signs of aquatic life.

Once everyone was satiated there was a quick dip in the Atlantidean Ocean to sluice a bit, some quiet time for meditation, then the final gathering of fourteen absolutely nude bodies at the fore rail during early dusk for some fiercely transcendental masturbation, the men standing and the ladies sitting with legs dangling over the *Ann*'s side. The trick was to try to gauge the orgasm of the person beside you and synchronize it with your own.

Roughly, a fourteen-gun salute over the side of the boat heralded the beginning of a mission straight and true.

Everyone released long, deep sighs. Lucifer helped Sereda and Shetel to their feet.

"All hail the Cosmic Jism," he said.

They weren't overtly religious men, but both Milo and Ramses Jetstream said, "Amen to that."

Kichi Malat got his things in order, gave a few of the children a touch of latent magic for blossoming when they got older, booked a commercial flight to Detroit, and took a walk around Belle Isle. His cousin lived in an apartment on Jefferson Avenue not too far from the island. Seeing him again after thirty years might seem too much like the end of things. No point making the poor man think Malat was about to die.

No point in that at all.

So Kichi Malat walked, and looked at ducks. Belle Isle was like a tiny Central Park floating on the industrial Detroit River. Lots of land. Wild geese everywhere. A giant slide.

And a beach.

"The end of things," Kichi Malat wrote in one of the small notebooks he was never without, but stopped. It was sunny, getting noisy, and there were huge leviathan steamers of metal and grease making their ways from river to lake to ocean, primitively entrancing. He tucked the pad and pen away. He picked up a flat rock, advised it to fly, and skipped it on the water all the way from Belle Isle to the Canadian coastline a mile away, and he didn't care who saw him at all.

~~~

Buford's clone lab blew up in a flash so bright an orbiting shuttle saw it. The entire complex and all within it were vaporized. In other parts of the United States Pat Robertson's and the Thoom's went up next.

From their vantage a mile away Spuddy Rex shared a nod with Parker on a job well done. Then the two men packed their scopes and scrabbled unhurriedly down the side of a hill. In other parts of the United States, two other sets of operatives of the Agents of Change scrabbled down rugged terrain too, leaving dust in their wake.

The war had reached a new level.

A WHALE,
A HARPOON,
AND A
JACKASS
WALK INTO A
BAR...

Pointillist Ninjutsu

A whale's head broke the water.

"Maseef!"

They pulled him aboard.

"You lucky bastard. You get to sail," said Smoove, "with us."

"Carel. Smoove. Hachette." He pulled his headgear off, swiped a quick hand over his bald head, and hugged each. A little water never hurt. "I didn't find Raffic."

Where the hell was Raffic the Mad Buddha!

"We're keeping to a simple plan," said Smoove, crunching on a peanut. "Get deep where she was last seen and widen from there. I've gotta assume the search teams missed something."

"And how long are you prepared to search?"

"Until," said the second best water pilot in the world.

"Buford," said Maseef.

"By the time we find Lolita, I expect he'll be full of woe."

"Bold. Very bold." He let the absence of Raffic hang in the air between them.

"And I have every confidence in Buddha," Smoove said.

~~~

Somewhere in the world, Raffic the Mad Buddha's eyes opened. Wherever he was, it was dark.

In two seconds he realized he was in a container.

Buddha was not happy.

~~~

The *Linda Ann* put into port at Abba. Abba was the last small metropolis before the vast, unconnected fringes, which made it two things: Atlantis' true center of government, and the best place to procure vital information.

Green-hued Sereda accompanied Milo through the city's more technologically leaning trading zones to the other end of the docks. The attractively seedy end. There would always be seedy ends. The seedy end of Abba meant that most people there used their communication devices to communicate to people only when they had something to say, or they preferred to dress to accommodate the weather—in a word, they were practical. Seedy Abbans went about their days with a practical goal in mind: a peaceful end. Not surprisingly, they were mostly artists and were a huge attraction to the vanity of others. Artists tended to be exceedingly practical, insofar as they were always looking around for who or what they could use.

Sereda and Milo paused by one such sculptor long enough for him to be inspired by Sereda's Amazonian stature. The artist immediately destroyed what he'd been working on and added water to the clay to reform it. Milo let him work. Sereda assumed the air of someone unconcerned at being the subject of a passionate sculptor's attentions.

Quickly, a rough bust of Sereda graced his pedestal.

Milo leaned in to appreciate the work.

The sculptor acknowledged him briefly.

"Did you know her left one was bigger than her right?" he asked Milo before adding clay to begin the head.

"I did."

"Have you come to tear Atlantis up again, Mr. Jetstream?"

"I plan to avoid that."

"Then," the sculptor said, patting more clay, "you need to ask if anyone's heard about a stranger and your Buford. Perhaps," he said, pausing to consider the size of her nose, "start with the Arc of Painters. Loose lips rarely come to sculptors but they love painters."

"In time. Sereda?"

"Yes?"

"Do you mind if he finishes?"

She was a gifted actress. She pretended welcome surprise at noticing she was being made an object d'art. "No," she said, languoring under the sun. "I can strip," she offered helpfully.

"Don't make his hand cramp. Fifteen minutes?" he asked the sculptor.

"Twenty. Guerris will have a bit to say."

Guerris the Painter's only artistic flaw was that he wasn't as colorful a character as he believed he should be. Beyond that, he was what others refer to when they bandy words like *genius*. It was said Guerris could paint the next precise wing stroke of a bird before it even knew it wanted to fly.

He was so guileless he never knew he was of the breed of which people said, "It was said."

Most people who came to Abba eventually stopped to have Guerris *see* them. It was the single time in their lives they were absolutely guaranteed the opposite of invisibility.

When Milo found him Guerris was sitting. Sitting very intently. And staring over the water.

"You never seem surprised that we know you're coming, Jetstream," the young man said.

"That's because Atlantis is still small enough to bat a rumor from one end to the other. You're not painting."

"Just finished. Gave it away. I wanted to watch the sun go down."

"That's not for a few hours," said Milo.

"Your point?"

Guerris preferred the port's rocky shores as opposed to the more trendy inland stationing. Couldn't fish from way inland.

Milo dusted a sun-warmed boulder and sat down.

Guerris grabbed pebbles to flick into the water.

"When are we going fishing on those big boats of yours again?" said Guerris.

"Soon," said Milo.

"I told my daughter I'd hook a singularity."

Milo glanced at him. "You don't have a daughter."

"No, but that's how long since you visited. Life goes on without you," the young artist said. Guerris was thirty but looked twenty. "Remember we hooked that *dragoon*?"

"Took an hour to land."

"Then it thanked us for the exercise, spat the hook out, and flopped back to the water! The first anybody knew dragoons were telepathic. Get all kinds of side benefits from fishing."

"First anybody'd ever caught a dragoon."

"I used to see them all the time growing up. They never talked. I haven't seen one in a long time."

"Maybe they're busy."

Guerris searched for larger pebbles, something that would hit the water with a satisfying plop.

"Milo? I'm dying. Isn't that odd? We're never actually living. From the get-go, we're dying. We're flying *yebaums*. Never actually flying but gliding." He handed Milo a couple smooth stones before whipping one out. It skipped six then sunk.

Milo's skipped twenty.

"Show off."

Milo shrugged and skipped another. Thirty.

"What do you call 'soon,' Milo? Because by the time your man reaches the Mount, at least two weeks will have passed. If he makes it to the Mount will you kill him?"

I don't know, Milo automatically heard before he could speak, which he shushed by saying, "A lot traveling with him?"

"No. Last anyone saw, he was alone. People from Sip wonder why you keep chasing him. They worry about things blowing up."

Sip was on a direct route from Abba to the Mount.

"They don't like you very much. You're like kids running through their backyards. There are a lot of people from Sip moving here."

"Sip's nowhere near the Mount," said Milo. "People from Sip make good portrait subjects?"

"Not especially. I've always thought Sip was too self-contained. It shows in their essences. They don't see it. Been coming to me left and right. The influx thinks it's like planting a flag in a new world."

"I brought an angel with me."

Guerris brightened. Angels practically blinded with their essence!

"You'll have to fight Kafka for her."

"Kafka's only interested in bosoms."

"He's got a lot to keep him interested. What about a stranger?"

"Silly talk from the southerners," Guerris dismissed. "A stranger trailing Buford. Cloaked and everything."

"Can you point me to a useful Sipper?"

"There's this couple I went fishing with. No fun whatsoever. Kept talking about the vistas." He dropped the remaining pebbles en masse. "Have you eaten yet?"

Abba had the most exquisite sausage sandwiches. Guerris stood.

"I'll take you to meet them."

~~~

They weren't so much a couple as a unit of time measurement by how quickly the husband stepped in to correct the wife.

"He's supposed to be about your height and build," she said of the mysterious, shrouded stranger.

"A little taller. Lighter complexion."

"And I don't know if anybody's actually seen him," she said. "You know how rumors are."

"But based in fact a lot. I'd have to say, if he's traveled through Sip, someone's seen him," the husband said. "A good bet he's just some artist from here. Have you seen the view from around the Mount?"

"Actually, I have," said Milo.

"It's like a pilgrimage for artists. Except they never go. But he might be one."

"All the rumors say it's male?"

"So far," the wife said.

"So far," the husband agreed, "But you never know." He gave a meaningful glance at the interactive menu Milo had placed face down. "You haven't ordered anything."

"You don't have sausages."

"But these are Sip delicacies."

"We're in Abba," said Guerris helpfully.

"What do we always eat when we're in Abba?" the wife said, still not fully resigned to the fact that they now *lived* in Abba. "People come for the sausages. And art," she said for Guerris, who still planned to eat but at a little shop down the way that gave away free seconds on…

"What day's today?" he asked.

She told him.

…today. Artists were exceedingly practical.

"You could get all this information off the feed," the husband told Milo.

"Wouldn't have gotten to meet you," said Milo. "I like the portrait over the door."

At least they didn't tell him Guerris did it. Everybody knew a Guerris when they saw a Guerris.

"We thought it would serve as a thank-you to patrons as they left," she said.

"There aren't a lot of people opening restaurants anymore," the husband pointed out.

"Never underestimate the power of a good meal," said Milo. "People eat more when they feel welcomed." There was no one besides the four of them in the entire establishment. Even the extra chef had gone out for lunch.

"Tell me, has anybody ever been afraid of you?" asked the wife.

"In Atlantis? Yes."

"What about out there?"

"You don't have the time."

"The stranger is always writing in a notebook," she volunteered, as if it was the last card she'd been holding. "And all you see of him are his eyes."

~~~

Milo spent the rest of the day shuttling Sereda between artists and gathering bits of information. Angels didn't engage in a lot of interaction with their neighbors, and when they did, especially for artists, it was a special joy. Sereda was over six feet tall with a stunning build and eyes that captured all who saw them.

Milo got a helluva lot of information. Not all of it useful. Most of what people termed information rarely was. On the whole, between him, Ramses and Desiree (accompanied by Vulva and Eloa, respectively) they learned enough to know Buford was traveling light, traveling alone, and wasn't in any rush to get there.

Penitence? Of course not. Bloated ego.

That last battle, Buford had left two hundred dead in his wake. Two hundred people, some of them Atlantidean, loyal to Buford's cause without a clue what the cause was…

"Save them or get me."

Milo had chased the old man up a pass as far as Buford could go.

"Not another step, son!"

Milo's crew was outmanned, outgunned and minus their berseker, but the fight raged below in what to Milo's ears was a slow motion, faraway world.

A cut on Milo's scalp was dribbling blood into his eye.

"You kill that many people today," Buford said through *roiling smoke, "and you might as well give it up. You don't have that kind of stomach."* He read the suspicion of bluff in *Milo's eyes. "Why do you think,"* Buford shouted forcefully *then coughed into a wheeze, "I ran all the way out here? Son, I'm too old for running! Unless I have a damn good reason."*

Heat built around Milo's right hand. Tendrils of energy wafted from the fist.

"Put it away, Milo."

Milo calculated: it would take minutes to get his crew out of the compound.

"I already took Lolita from you. Ramses next?"

Milo needed to be able to teleport. God, he'd never learned to teleport!

"Pack that chi away," said Buford. *"Won't be a series of explosions. Just one…big…"*

Boom. Milo tried to imagine running so fast he left a sonic boom. He hit the panic button on his chest but didn't trust it to get through Buford's signal-jamming.

Buford had already planned that if it looked like the battle was lost, take out their ships. See how fast they got off that island to catch him.

Mortar rounds slammed into the Fi and Linda Ann even as the loved ones of the gunners were about to be blown sky high.

All Milo could do was scream in his mind 'Get out get out get out,' because they would sooner hear that over his lone voice.

Twenty-two against two hundred. Karaplides, Boo Boo D. Fool, Uncut Funk, Botha Dish, One Mo Deez, Lady of the Lake, Immortal Technique, Prodigal, Thy Rod, Thy Hammer, Bubba Foom, Lucy, Most Highly Favored, Sweetness, The Brothers Grimm, Ele, Carel, Smoove, Quicho. And two Jetstreams.

So much ass had never been kicked by so few. Running toward the thick of it Milo saw Ramses using the Unrepentant Fist; Smoove, the Greased Joy; Carel, the Five Fingered Explanation; Quicho, Enraged Banker, and the volunteers created techniques on the fly...

Then everything went violently white.

"It was a flash bomb," Ramses told Guerris while they ate on the deck of the *Ann*.

"Flash bombs don't kill."

"They do when they trigger implants. Buford sometimes 'inoculates' his people," said Ramses.

"They didn't know they were going to die?" asked Guerris.

"No."

"Going into the light is supposed to bring peace," he said.

"When we could see again," said Ramses, "there were bodies around our ankles."

"The dead of your enemies," said Guerris.

"Are still the dead," said Milo.

Vulva, who had been sitting nearby, placed a soft kiss atop Milo's head.

"Thank you, luv," he said. Guerris, at that moment, swore he was looking into eyes harder than anger. Anger implied politics and ego. Milo Jetstream's eyes were what decisions were made of; Guerris would later paint those eyes overlooking a mural of the *The Jetstreams' Last Stand*. Sad, vengeful eyes. "We buried every one of them," Milo said and shrugged. "Buford got away."

"You always go in so few," said Guerris.

"Surgery's sharp, not a mallet," said Milo. "Submission's Buford's goal, not ours."

"Not knowing where I'm going, this galaxy's better not having a place to go. Now I know," Ramses sang. "We prefer to heal."

"Rot the Philosopher?"

"Prince the Musician."

"We," said Desiree, standing and waiting till all eyes on deck fell on her, "were warriors. We are poets. We are artists. We are the thieves who grieve." She raised a toast to the evening air.

"We are the champions," she said, "...of the world."

Milo raised a sip of tea to that.

"Damn straight," said Ramses, tipping his orange crème soda. "For Queen and Country."

"And a world worthy to call home," said Desiree.

Guerris formed the painting in his mind's eye: stirring, with pathos, love, melancholy and death. With impossible odds and victory to the bold. It would be huge, and stand with *Life Re-told, Mourning Angels,* and *The Court of Death* as one of the last enduring monuments to truth.

"May fortune favor the foolish," said Ramses.

"Why do heroes always say that?" wondered Guerris.

"Ever catch anybody actually calling himself a hero," said Ramses, "there's a fool."

~~~

We were heroes, it was written in the Book of Buford under the lifeguard tower on Belle Isle beach. We led because men want to be led. We controlled because chaos scares and we are not ones to let men be afraid. We sell because what is free is not to be trusted.

We did what God would've done if He'd taken a moment to check on things.

We forced mankind to grow up.

There are no children here.

Point Break

Population control in Atlantis was never a problem. Given that space was finite, why give in to compulsions to fill it? The prospect of growing a family took a lot more consideration than the time it took to remove underwear, something the outer world had yet to comprehend.

Atlantis' populations had room to stretch-out between them.

Desiree and Milo figured the False Prophet Buford would have peppered his rural route with opportune stops among fringe settlements with large numbers of children.

"There are a few traditional farmers along Hobbes Creek. Homebodies." Guerris drew a red snake-line on their map. "Hobbes is known for changing course depending on the thaws, so this may not be accurate." Three other artists had joined them, not on deck but on the wharf around a small table and chairs. It was nighttime. A table lamp sat between them.

"You should've done it in green," said one of the other artists. When he leaned in for a better look he nearly tipped the lamp, which made a woman push him out of the way.

Hobbes Creek always looked green. Algae.

The realist had never met the Jetstreams before. He was a fractal landscaper and studied their faces looking for the secrets of the universe.

The woman, Lana, was Guerris' cousin, who actually possessed two of the seventeen thousand secrets of the universe, knew it, but told no one. She was always serene and beautiful, and painted frescoes. "Guerris wants to go with you," she said.

"All the way to the end," he said. "To paint him into submission."

"You could," said Milo.

Sereda kissed Guerris on the forehead. Angels loved kissing foreheads. It tingled their lips.

"I'll fight," said Guerris, his head pleasantly lighter. "In my way."

"Like a child," said the realist.

Cousin Lana tossed him away from the group.

"That's not fair!" he protested.

"Stay there till you learn manners," she commanded.

"What do you say, Lana?" asked Ramses.

"I say no."

"Family can't make decisions," said Guerris.

"We say no," said the last artist. She was old enough to be considered an elder and smart enough to be heeded and had always viewed Guerris as her contribution to civilization.

"Especially not mothers," said Guerris.

Sereda said, "You're a dreamer, Guerris, and reality is better for it."

Guerris sighed. He had fallen in love with the barely asymmetrical curve of Sereda's upper lip. He resigned himself to a life on the sidelines.

"Have we been any help, Milo?" asked Cousin Lana.

Milo leaned over and kissed her squarely, softly, on the forehead.

"You always are."

~~~

Elsewhere, Ele and Smoove tried to negotiate passage through a hastily set secessionist blockade.

"We know very well who you are," a de facto spokesperson was saying. "With your big black ship full of weapons and war."

"We're bound for the Glacial Mountains," Captain Smoove said. "And as you've already pointed out that we're bristling..."

"We're also aware of the *Ballad of Desiree Quicho.* You, sir, are not your wife. Your bravado is bluff," said the spokesperson. She was unctuous, and Smoove wanted to knock her overboard. "Legendary though it be," the spokesperson finished.

"I say hit her," said Ele.

Andrea of Root was taken aback. "Ele the Theologian! Violence?"

"You deserve to be smacked."

Fiona stepped between Smoove and the obstacle. "We don't have time for this," she said.

"You see, you do, because *you* came *here,*" said the Rootian.

"My feeling is that it wouldn't matter to you if you knew why we're here," said Fiona. "Ele, assessment?"

"She doesn't care. Smack her."

"What do the ballads say about *me,* luv?" said Fiona with enough sugary menace that Andrea backed a step and glanced left and right for assistance.

Assistance had already taken its step back.

"Move those ships, sweet lady" said Smoove, cracking open a peanut slowly.

"I empathize with you, sister," Andrea said to Fiona.

"Since when did we have a family reunion!" snapped Fiona. "Sister...get the hell out of our way."

Andrea looked pained. "We don't mean—"

"Ramming speed!" commanded Fiona. Smoove jumped to the pilot house.

The *Semper Fi* lurched forward, quick as a snake bite, cleaving straight for the two largest ships

"We have no interest in the politics of Atlantis," said Fiona.

"I do," said Ele.

"They're not going to move," said Andrea.

"Then you might want to hold onto something. Captain?" she called up to Smoove, who had already plotted the best course for the least amount of damage to his ship.

The *Fi* smashed through, tossed the boarding party's dinghy overboard, then tossed the boarding party.

"We don't have time for this," said Fiona. "Ele, you didn't tell us everybody in Atlantis had gone crazy," said Fiona.

The rest of the *Fi's* ragtag flotilla of science groupies passed through the canal.

"We weren't so crazy till your Mr. Buford showed up."

"And touché to you too," said Fiona.

"Your freedoms here can be annoying," said Ele. "You come and go as you please and chase madmen."

"We're here to save the world, Ele."

"We're here to find our friend. I feel that's more important," she said, adding, "Saving the world is what has made them wary of you."

"Empathy's a bitch," said Fiona.

"You have no idea," said Ele.

The False Prophet Buford rested in a small village some thirty miles from the Mount.

When the Jetstreams were young there was a game they played. Buford had taught it to Milo and, when reunited, Milo had taught it to Ramses. A simple game.

Checkers.

Featuring jumps, triple jumps, and double jump backs.

"These are important words that I want you to remember," the old man said upward into the faces of Atlantidean children gathered around. He sat comfortably on the grass. "When you feel yourself forgetting, I want you to repeat them." He had pitched his campfire close enough to the village to elicit pity, and pity being such an intoxicating tool, was welcomed as an itinerant teacher, telling the children about the Blank world.

"Decisions," he said, "are composed of a series of moods. That's all they are. The key is being able to decide what somebody else's mood should be."

"Mr. Bone?" said a young father coming up to provide a moment's peace for the man. Blank folks were a special fascination in rarely visited rural areas. He shooed the kids away. "Are you teaching our kids to eschew independent thought?"

"As best I can," he said, staring at the man.. Buford had learned watching six-year-old Milo subdue grown people just by looking at them that a held gaze was a powerful thing.

"I was just seeing on the feed that the Jetstreams are on your trail."

"I'd appreciate you not publicizing the fact that I'm here."

"I'm sure you would." The father shrugged it off. Things on the feed were about as intrinsically important as the mud on his shoes. "If nothing else you've given us a few jolts of intrigue."

"Life's but a stage," said Buford. News of the last battle had been squelched; Atlantideans, like any other elite power, didn't want its undesirable laundry aired, particularly concerning secessionist Atlantideans siding with Blank-worlders.

"Atlantis can be very boring," said the father.

"Depends on your perspective," said Buford.

"From the perspective of a man who's never gone outside the Blank nor has any plans to: it can be boring. A lot to be said for boredom though."

Buford shrugged. "You get bored of it. Then the invisible things you were ignoring jump you."

"Invisible things eventually demand to be seen," said the father. His name was Rasta, and he wasn't. He was as white and pale as milk through a cloud.

Buford held his gaze. Rasta didn't flinch. Damn.

"Where's this going, friend?" asked Buford.

"I'm just wondering how soon you'll demand to be seen."

"Oh, you won't see me till I'm gone," said Buford. "And even then you might not. There's no fight left in me."

"But you're traveling to the Mount," Rasta pointed out.

"I can dream."

"You'll never make it."

Buford yawned and raised a hand for assistance. "Care to wager on that?"

Rasta pulled him to his feet. "Mirama says dinner is ready," he said.

"Then let's wager after we eat."

Mirama Fonz was an extraordinary cook. Vegetables became ambrosia and sauces fine wines. Even their daughter Danielle loved her cooking.

"Have you visited Amelia Earhart yet?" Rasta asked, pushing away from the table afterward to pat his belly. "They say she's still alive on one of our remote islands."

"Hadn't thought about her," said Buford.

"Amelia is a story, daddy," said Danielle.

"Mr. Bone enjoys stories."

"The truth. I enjoy the truth. Nobody needs stories. Stories are why Atlantis is still a magic fancy," said Buford.

"You don't think we're magical?" said Mirama. She winked for him.

"I think you cook a helluva meal with serious marketing potential."

"You're a funny little man, sir," she complimented.

"I try to be. Most people go through life sand-blasted. Whittled sharp to poke, or a nub to bop. Teeny and pitiful. I prefer the practicality of potential. You know, Atlantis is basically a free market but you have no chains, no advertising, and profits to laugh at from what I've seen."

"We're not greedy," said Danielle. She was ten.

Buford tweaked her nose. "Yes you are. You keep yourselves away from the world. We could really use you out there," he said, and let his eyes twinkle from child to mother.

"You sound as if you have plans for us, Mr. Buford."

"I do, ma'am. In your best interests, insofar as I hope to see Atlantis grow and prosper past any need for segregation."

"Segregation is a particularly Blank word," said Rasta.

"It's human nature to compartmentalize," said Buford. "Close neighbors were the beginning of the end for human society. Give you an example: I recruited men from poor areas for a while, ghettos and rural. They live right on top of each other. Crazy as hell. Fake Rome, Boo Yea and Peanut: three men who wouldn't offer a single benefit if you ever met them. Did all I could, but they were too far-gone from living ass to ass. Crazy."

"He said 'ass', daddy."

"Yes, he did."

"Now I shall say 'ass' daily."

Rasta sent her outside to play.

"No, she won't," Buford told him.

Rasta waved it off. He got serious. "Why are *adventurers* looking for you?"

"They'd rather reign in hell, so to speak," he answered.

"And you know otherwise?" Mirama asked.

"You know, there are times when you folks living in Atlantis forget you're living on the earth too."

"We know all about your corporate oligarchies and wars on terror," said Rasta.

"I'm pretty sure you don't have spaceships ready to take off, 'cause you'd have been gone a long time ago," said Buford.

"As I understand it," said Rasta, "and I'm no scientist, we live spatially on earth, but not dimensionally. It'll just be us and the cockroaches after you've killed each other. There's a self-loathing out there that's particularly *Blank*, if you'll pardon the expression. Like," he searched for the proper wording. "Like for whatever reasons you expect better of yourselves but never live up to it."

"Why expect?" asked Mirama.

"Those adventurers you've come to love?" said Buford, "Were brought up by others with this notion that we are more than what we are, and I'll tell you one true fact of life no matter where you go: a dissatisfied populace is a confused populace. I hate confusion. Ramses and Milo are children."

"How many Blank-worlders know about us?" asked Mirama.

Buford shrugged. "Doesn't matter. If everybody knew about Atlantis it still wouldn't be safe for folks to walk two blocks from their houses at night. There are dreams and then there's reality, and that leads me to the second true fact of life: there are no children here."

"We have a very lovely child," said Mirama, smiling playfully across the table with the kind of smile that said *I am a mother, tread carefully.*

"Who shall say ass every day. Take it from a man who realizes he's getting old: innocence is a myth." He nodded toward a handsomely made corner-bookcase. There were books there immediately recognizable. "A lot of Blank books."

"I collect them from lost ships whenever I visit the mainland," she said. "There's something very fascinating about the stories you tell."

There was an entire row of nothing but John Grisham.

"I haven't read those yet," she said.

Other shelves had an eclectic mix. Octavia Butler. Judith Krantz. Asimov, Ellison. Shakespeare. There was even a Minister Faust. Minister Faust was one of the *Specials* hiding in plain sight like the Jetstreams, but that would be neither here nor there for her. But Buford was well aware of him.

But right there, right above Grisham: William Golding.

The Lord of the Flies.

Buford pointed it out.

"Have you read it?"

"Very disturbing book," she said.

"Memoirs usually are," he said with a smile.

~~~

It didn't pay for folks to be too curious and smart. The False Prophet Buford left the next morning. He found a cave and enough largish rocks that he could build a double-ringed semicircle at the entrance for a protective night fire, then set about waiting for Milo Jetstream to overshoot his position a day or two. The antidote to the poison he'd given the family was unopened in his pocket.

It didn't pay for folks to be too curious and smart. Didn't pay at all.

Mission Loss

The agenda was laid out.

Abba was behind them. Right around the coast, Sip. Land journey through Sip. From Sip more land, then hills, mountains, and Buford. Milo was tempted to let Buford reach the Mount and have an epiphany save them all the trouble of another confrontation, but a man who'd poison the world to keep an empire of lies alive wasn't likely to be struck or even gently prodded by epiphany's lacy hand.

Sip was in retro phase, which partly explained the migrations to earthy Abba. A number of Quonset and adobe structures had mushroomed in spaces ignored by their modern cousins, an appeal to simplicity designed to make whatever secessionist bid Sip entertained seem almost natural. There was something about the Earth's magnetic field that made the planet's inhabitants want to break away from ruling bodies in order to create more ruling bodies. If Atlantis itself was a *Heights* and Abba a *Pointe*, then Sip was the *Hills*, literally and figuratively. Pastoral greens undulated through the city like underground plesiosaur humps.

Some ways off, half a head protruded from the water to watch the *Ann* dock. Then it quietly disappeared. The ship barely bobbed as the crew unloaded supplies near the large framework house Smoove and Quicho hand-built between outings. Desiree had already decided Sip was where she and Smoove would eventually retire while Milo and Ramses healed their wounds and aches in a nursing home or on another planet. The green rolling hills reminded Smoove of home in his heart, with the added benefit of there being water right there so that the *Ann* and *Fi* would never be lonely.

Once the Atlantidean rovers were assembled, Desiree, Milo and Ramses hugged the angel Shetel—who volunteered to stay on board—and the parties headed out split per vehicle toward the first star they saw on the right, which was the setting sun, and straight on till morning.

~~~

Atlantidean rovers were not the most comfortable things to drive in straight on till morning.

Particularly with a bunch of oversized angels riding along.

And also when the only surety was that one was driving in a more or less 'general' direction.

The rovers looked like something DeLorean would've designed if he'd realized people would pay ridiculous money for huge military transports marketed as personal vehicles, along the lines of a muscular minivan with amphibian tendencies and armored plating.

Only these could levitate and required powering only once a year.

Atlantidean rovers were cool as hell.

They stopped to stretch with the sun. Being outside made them realize that inside the vehicles they'd unconsciously succumbed to the elevator effect, but outside there was banter, questioning, and breakfast: homemade *pastrolls* frozen and especially packed for the trip by Ele.

Right after breakfast, the Battle Ready Bastards taught Desiree how to stare down a snake.

Ramses and Milo studied the vista.

"There's a lot of open terrain," said Ramses.

"We know where he's going."

"Lot of terrain on the Mount too. He could've been there and back."

"We'd have heard about it. You don't go to the Mount without somebody knowing," said Milo.

"The goal him or the Mount?"

"Him."

"Just so we're clear." Ramses passed a scope to Milo. "Take the left. We'll work our way back." They went about a hundred meters apart then slowly and methodically searched the distances. There were no glints, no flashes, no sudden movements, but there was... smoke?

Ramses whipped his communicator. "Forty-five degrees east of you."

Milo searched. "Yep."

Ramses zoomed as tight as possible. "That's blue smoke," he said.

"Mount up, people," Milo called out.

Ra'saiel X trotted to him.

"East," said the angel.

"Soul fire."

"Right on."

Two more braziers had been lit by the time they reached the smoke. Blue symbolized nothing created was ever destroyed since the dead were an intrinsic part of the sky.

Symbols were comforting.

But symbols were just symbols.

The bodies were in cold storage for additional forensic examination, dead as sorrow and thick as the lump in the throats of the settlement when the Jetstreams, accompanied by eleven angels, walked into view.

Soul fires were meant to be maintained continuously for three days around the clock, tended by anyone respectful enough to tend them. Canisters of powder and accelerant rested at the base of each metal brazier. Out of the twelve braziers arranged in a wide circle, nine were unlit.

There were no cemeteries in Atlantis.

The handful of people in this settlement not about their daily business crowded around the three plumes. They watched as the outsiders approached, the crowd having the slow hesitation to move of those protecting the innocent, but they parted, revealing a sitting woman, her knees drawn to her chest.

Ra'saiel X sat quietly beside her.

The angel Eloa very, very gently touched her hair.

Desiree gave Ramses a quick glance. This didn't have the air of a normal death. Atlantideans weren't as consumer-driven as Blanks and so weren't as afraid of death; weren't so inconsolably mystified. Life may have been meant to be purchased out there, but here Guerris' attitude was basically the unspoken prevalent. Death's random inevitability was like drawing air.

Desiree, Ramses noted, glanced at him again.

The anger surrounding their group was solid.

The woman didn't care who was touching her but she looked up anyway at Ra'saiel's brown face and deeper brown eyes, up at Eloa, then at the three others who clearly were not angels.

Milo sat beside her so that she wouldn't have to speak. He nodded at Desiree. The captain pinched sprinkles of colorant on each brazier.

The woman suddenly sniffed raggedly with the effort of trying to calm herself.

Only a moment passed, then she said, "Don't ever come back."

Another moment.

Milo said nothing.

She looked at him. How dare he pretend to grieve.

But his eyes shimmered, and jaw set.

"May we ask the names of the dead?" said Ambriel respectfully to the nearest of them.

"He was my best friend," said the sitting woman to Milo's face. She wanted to slap him and detonate a bomb so that no one else would ever come through the Blank.

"Danielle was a child," someone answered Ambriel. "Mirama was a wife. Rasta was a husband."

"He was my best friend." The huddled woman squeezed her knees tighter. She shouldn't have tried to talk. "Friend" turned into a snuffling fit, a fight she lost. She began the torturous, destructive process of regression to animal screams.

She didn't try to shrug Milo's arms off. She grabbed at the strength of them and held tightly.

Ra'asiel stood and touched the one who'd answered. They walked enough paces away to be relatively inaudible.

"How did they die?"

"Poison."

"Of what nature?"

"The kind that kills people! We don't know. It could've been the blood of evil spirits for all we know," he said, throwing a hand toward the Jetstreams.

Ra'saiel used eyes to immediately calm him.

"Respect the dead, brother; they fought a battle to get there."

"His man left here two days ago. Danielle's friends found her first…they ran to get her parents—" and he simply froze. There are times when the mind should refuse to process the images it generates.

Ra'saiel X hugged him the way one protects a child, pulling him close and cradling the back of his head.

Coupdeviel had come up behind them. He spoke to hair.

"Did anyone look for him? Perhaps we—"

"No. No," the settler, Orion, said, breaking away. "What would the point be in looking for him?" he pleaded. "They couldn't handle him," he said, pointing Milo's way, "but we're supposed to? Rasta wanted his bit of adventure, had to let him into his home. Why'd he do that?" he asked the angels, then shuffled away to pair bewilderment with sorrow.

"It wasn't to cover tracks," said Coupdeviel to Ra'asiel.

"A gauntlet's been thrown," said Ra'asiel X, eyes hard toward where Milo sat and Ramses watched over. "There are no children here."

~~~

There are no children here Buford scratched on the wall of the cave.

If all else failed, those words would live forever and were bound to be found by someone.

Immortality wasn't so hard to come by.

~~~

They stayed an extra day in the settlement. The presence of the angels helped, particularly for the terrified children who'd found the bodies.

Buford stayed two more days in his cave.

They were now a day behind him. Buford thought they were at least two days ahead.

Twenty-four hours weren't much at all.

Run

They drove again, quiet in their containers, straight on till morning.

Milo saw him first. He was an irregular speck making his way over the hard landscape. The computer systems on those Atlantidean rovers found out two things. One: that they could be made to move rovers much faster than anyone'd designed them to, and Two: speed like that almost made a machine sentient.

The Mount was a huge backdrop for the vinegar on Buford's face as body after body piled out of the vehicles. They surrounded him.

It was silent out there with a lazy half-hearted wind.

Their circle closed in on Buford, who saw the look in Milo's eyes and felt afraid for only the fourth time in his life.

A cloaked figure appeared out of thin air beside Buford, grabbed him by the shoulder, and both vanished.

"Motherfuck!" had never reverberated so vehemently across the Mount before. Milo barked orders on top of his curse. They scrambled to break out every sensor device they could find on the rovers: heat, sweat, piss, fart, motion, stop motion, Harryhausen, ILM and Disney. Nothing.

Nowhere.

And "Motherfuck!" reverberated a second time.

"Teleportation's limited distance," Ramses strategized. "Motherfucker was running a relay. Who the hell has that many people trained to teleport?"

They all thought *Buford* but each had failed to notice the surprised look he'd had himself. Buford had very good reason to be afraid. Thirteen versions of Milo Jetstream soon had him packed like shipping in a crate heading through the Atlantidean Ocean toward the Blank.

Hide

The rovers became sentient again. Shetel already had the *Linda Ann* fired up and ready to go. They stampeded on board so hard and fast folks would've thought there was love involved.

The *Linda Ann* slit the water then dribbled alcohol into its wounds because it meant business.

The *Ann* was damn near omniscient. Bats out of hell jumped back and cussed

No one had spotted aircraft or other rovers. It would've taken some serious jumps to get Buford all the way back to the coast. Nobody could do that.

But guess what? Milo told himself. *What I believe has never held particular sway over what is.*

There was absolutely no boat in sight, no abnormal energy signatures within range...

A head start just meant they were playing hard to get.

"Quicho, fly her apart at the seams," he said to the *Ann*'s captain.

Desiree's eyes remained steady on the water and secure on the controls. "I know how to put her back together," she answered.

She extended the airfoils a little more.

She radioed her husband.

"Chase him down," husband said to wife.

"We'll be back."

"Goes without saying. We'll be here."

"This wasn't supposed to happen," she said.

"A plan's only useful till a simpler option shows up," Smoove said. "Is Milo near you?"

"Yes."

"Put him on. Milo? Anger ain't ya friend."

"This coming from you?" he said.

"From Ele. Good hunting, brother."

"Hotep and irie." Milo left for the Battle Ready Bastards below.

"Luv?" said Smoove.

"It's gonna take a while for us to finish that house."

"A plan's only a plan," he said.

"Send a good one our way," she said.

"I would if I could. We might have to get involved in their politics."

She warned against it.

"They're not giving us much choice, Sweets."

Way too much of that going around. Backs against the wall everywhere.

A sudden blast of static interrupted them.

Something very large moved underwater from behind them with the speed and mass of a comet.

"Milo!" Desiree shouted.

The bow wave was an underwater tsunami headed straight for the ship. Fish and dragoon shot above the surface of the water stunned or half dead.

The last thing Desiree heard was "Luv?" before she shunted out the world to pour every last bit of soul into that ship. *Even a pleasure boater knows to pay attention to sonar!* she berated herself.

A ship the size of the *Ann* wasn't supposed to ride breakers the way it was.

Ramses and Milo appeared simultaneously.

"Hold on!" Ramses bellowed to the angels below decks. To Milo: "There is no way in hell Buford woke him up."

"Not a narwhal, brother."

Desiree pulled hard to starboard, angling the *Ann* toward the weakest end of the explosive burst. The mass changed course.

Ra'asiel threw three breach suits to Milo's outstretched hand. "Smoove, we got problems!" shouted Milo. He and Ramses hurriedly dressed Desiree in pieces as she whipped the *Ann* apart at the seams, the captain raising first this arm here then a leg there, before dressing themselves.

Everyone donned full breathing gear.

Because in all probability, they were going down.

"Quicho!" Smoove ordered tersely, but by now there was nothing but sustained static on his end.

~~~

Linda Ann slid as though made of soap on top of that water, doing enough zigzagging and doubling back that the mass wasn't sure precisely where to break the surface.

It gave an irritated strong push of its triple-fluked tail and elongated its island body in a huge semicircle around the ship.

Desiree threw them into a hard port skid that nearly capsized them.

The sleek black ship rode a wave up and down before slamming against the beast's encrusted hide. A gash opened across the hull's flank plating. Monitors squealed beneath Desiree's eyes.

"We're taking water," she said.

Ramses and Milo scrambled below decks.

"No the fuck you are not," Desiree told her ship. She set the ship into as wide and fast a spiral away from the hide as possible, retracting the starboard hydrofoil and further extending the port.

Below decks, those Bastards had torches and solder plating in hand.

Ramses pulled a sack from a locker.

Milo and Ramses grabbed sets of clamps, slung two huge guns to their backs and waited on deck. When the *Ann* made its closest arc inward toward Leviathan, they launched.

WHEN THE ANN MADE ITS CLOSEST ARC INWARD
TOWARD LEVIATHAN, THEY LAUNCHED.

Singers and poets had written reams of fiction on things that swim the deeps of the planet three hops from the sun. Oceans, in the real world, were primarily created because that's all Leviathan would fit into.

The layers of sediment, barnacles, fossils and sludge made it difficult to tell what the beast actually looked like. Three flukes, no dorsal, and huge ventral jets that kept it righted. A leagues long, alien-artifact shark-looking whale with Great White protruding teeth to hunt with, rubbed over with black pepper, paprika and black caviar, left in the broiler too long.

Big enough to kill anything anywhere and very cognizant of that fact.

Lore had it that people were afraid to dip their toes in unknown waters because God did so after creation, forgetting what was down there.

This ain't ya Bible's Leviathan.

Here be evolution on a whole 'nother level.

"… those who curse days curse that day, those who are ready to rouse Leviathan." Book of Job 3:8.

"What the *fuck* are you doing?" Milo shouted, swinging over the brow ridge of its right eye and unslinging his massive gun to point at the eye.

to anger me is to die the thousandth death of your progeny Leviathan rumbled in Milo's mind. It was blind in both eyes from its incalculable span in the pressures of the depths, nor did it feel him on its surface.

Fear, not instability, made Milo tremble. Common sense made him stand his ground. He kept his finger well away from the trigger. One mistaken shot and the *Ann* would disappear with an insulting lack of effort.

the world has not known my kind. the world will not know my kind.

Milo tried to form cogent thoughts for the beast to glean but all he could get out was *He's getting away!*

When Leviathan communicated, every psychic on the planet got a headache.

Ele rubbed her forehead, believing it was tension and stress as she watched Smoove try to maintain.

Botha Dish sat up in his convalescent bed and repeatedly mashed the button for his buxom nurse.

Neon, who was about to pick the winning chicken in a rather unsavory game of chance their beachside waiter had tipped them to, blanked from the zone and lost Yvonne about two days worth of money.

Bubba Foom blacked out at a highly inopportune moment. Lab-coated people rushed to revive him.

Buford slept. He knew there were very few things not solvable by simply going to sleep.

*i am the alpha and the omega—

"No you're not!"

i am the alpha and omega it overrode him, *the swimmer and the ocean—

Out of spite Milo changed its grating, thunderous voice in his head to one sounding like Mike Tyson.

--i will create the known when i am ready and crush the past as i see fit.*

Creatures of the sea had a habit of making landlubbers come to them as a way of humbling evolution.

We go in peace, Milo tried, but it was hard vibing peace when pissed off.

Leviathan gave a twist of its body, churning the ocean into a sudden storm.

"You're not even supposed to be out!" Milo shouted and shot a few impotent blasts into the thing's surface, managing only to dislodge a strata or two of coral. He cast a glance at the *Ann* and calmed himself.

Do you plan to kill today?

my will be done on water as on dry land and i will flood the land, said Tyson, *and legs will be useless—

Milo tuned him into background droning. He looked out to the open water, at Quicho's ship, and at the thing beneath his feet. Nobody knew Leviathan's age, and that fact alone made the creature worthy of respect. Granted it was a bit senile, but the power that it packed significantly overcompensated for that.

Milo signaled the circling *Ann*.

"Desi, next arc toward open water, floor that sumbitch." He ran up the craggy surface to the broad plain of Leviathan's back and clamped himself down. His brother was invisible over the curve of a hump. "Ram, start running." Milo counted the seconds. Three...seven...ten... "Go, Quicho! Ramses, now!"

A series of explosions went off along Tyson's spine near its flukes just as it was about to flick for pursuit, nowhere near enough to hurt but enough to pause the creature to consider something it hadn't registered in ages: a sensation.

Any sensation.

In this particular instance: an itch.

Ramses crested the hump. Three more charges went off behind him along the monster's spine, showering coral and rock into the air.

"Keep going, Desi," said Milo. Then he sat cross-legged as comfortably as he could on Leviathan's head, locked himself down with clamps in both hands, and struggled to control his breathing.

I draw the breath of life and health; I expel the breath of doubt.

Ramses reached him. Ramses saw the boat zooming off. He saw Milo meditating. He felt the conflicted impulses of Leviathan's uncertainty toward letting the boat go or mainlining on these little itches erupting on its back. For Leviathan these sensations were akin to thousand year orgasms. The creature hadn't evolved yet that was going to turn away from a thousand year orgasm. It filled huge ballast sacks and began to sink.

"Dammit," said Ramses and rammed his clamps on the coral as hard as he could.

"Be at peace, brother," Milo told him.

Ramses forced a calm. *I draw the breath...*

Very gradually, like Atlantis itself lowering beneath the waves, Leviathan allowed the waters to draw it home.

It could be a very long ride.

seek

The beast was aware of them mentally. They were like soothing little lozenges on its head. Water flowed through cracked surfaces on its hide where it hadn't flowed in a long time.

These two things were intriguing enough for it to descend very slowly. Breach suits could handle temperature and pressure changes with ease, but not that much ease. The force of the displaced water sphinctering around Milo and Ramses was enough by itself to knock a prizefighter out. Without the suits they'd be dead tragic figures surrounded by the Atlantidean Ocean. With the suits, they were tourists.

Swarms of lean, armored parasites attended Tyson as if he were a bloated movie star, snatching at disoriented crabs and tunnel eels. Stunned dragoons and fish floated lazily with Leviathan's eddies. Dragoons resembled dolphins with prehensile noses, and it was odd to see several of these gray vacuum cleaners when normally spotting just one was rare.

Leviathan belched two gargantuan jets of water to stop its descent, scaring every living thing away for a quarter mile, which left the three sentients alone in the grey, encompassing water.

Milo closed his eyes again.

Ramses followed suit.

I draw the breath of life and health. I expel the breath of doubt... Speak to me, thought Milo.

the world has not known my kind. the world will not know my kind.

Milo tried to think in terms of deep secrets alongside the assurance of *we are not the voices.*

war brings truth it broadcast, and that's how Milo knew it was Buford. Somehow, someway, Buford Bone had managed to use the world's ultimate roadblock: convincing the Leviathan that the Brothers Jetstream meant to change its world. Milo could imagine scores of Buford's followers descending to their deaths under the Atlantidean all while broadcasting the fervent impression that the Brothers Jetstream's War meant Leviathan was going to become an attraction at the Mall of America.

By the time things got old they'd earned the right to want to be left the hell alone, and wanting to be left the hell alone was the prime inclination of all old things.

Even a beast that likely remembered what dinosaurs tasted like. And like old things, Tyson was supremely aware of what was going on in the world.

Both brothers tried as honestly and flatly as they could to convince the old fart they bore it no intentions, and they did this by detaching from its hide and simply floating, minds blank to everything but the water around them. They projected the sense that here, the water, was Leviathan's universe and Leviathan was god.

Leviathan, somewhat begrudgingly, saw that it was good.

And since it didn't care one whit for their lives, it prepared to give a massive push of its flukes to send it barreling to the depths where it would wait, and wait some more.

Breach suits weren't up to that kind of change.

Mosquitoes do what they can.

Ramses shot it in the eye.

what the fuck!

It wasn't as if it hurt but it was enough of a jolt to get its immediate attention.

Wait, was all Ramses put out.

Leviathan felt their feeble electrical impulses racing away from it. *did you just shoot me in the eye? alpha and omega? fool! stupid humans. son of a...*

We mean to keep you safe, Ramses broadcast.

Leviathan calmed itself. Several sensations in one short span. It really couldn't complain, but the intent was a pisser.

do it again it warned him. It settled back into its usual mode, further grumbling *alpha and omega...*

They swam quickly away from its head. The ancient aquatic was arching its back and filling its jets again.

Ramses and Milo weren't far enough away.

They grabbed hold of each other in a tight hug and waited.

Leviathan flicked powerfully downward and the brothers swirled around in the toilet bowl of its descent.

She said, the song ambled through Ramses' thrumming head, *I know what it's like to be dead. I know...* and it trailed sharply, leaving The Beatles' next statement unsaid. He still held Milo as tightly as he'd ever held anybody before, and Milo held him. So they were both conscious.

Being alive for the moment gave great hope.

The galactic spiral slowed.

They had no idea how far they'd been sucked.

Part of Ramses' mind was about to play with that thought but the majority of him corralled away from it to consider how likely it was they'd open their eyes and be surrounded by sharks.

Sharks and seagulls were cut from the same cloth, always on the lookout for convenient meals.

My stomach is around my spine, Ramses thought. He opened his eyes. It was darker here than it'd been a few seconds ago.

Oh lord, Milo thought, appealing half-heartedly to Zeus who was still living it up thanks to crafty reimaging as the God of Our Fathers who Art in heaven. Getting Apollo to agree to the whole sacrificial son thing had been tough.

Apollo, not so big on piety but very big on bazooms.

Milo motioned a circle with a finger. They unslung their rifles and floated back to back, then kicked to begin their journey upward.

Things in Atlantis weren't necessarily smarter, as they were cooperative. Sharks tended to scout for themselves but they'd report back to recruit help depending on the size of the prey.

A little ways off, a shark performed a lazy u-turn away from them.

They weren't so deep they couldn't make out the sun, but they still had a way to go.

After the shark disappeared something appeared out of the gloom and moved quickly toward them. It grabbed them by a wrist each and zoomed them to the surface.

Milo and Ramses peeled the coverings from their faces.

Swim toward your ship, it thought, planting the direction in their heads, then dove smoothly under.

After a minute or so it surfaced ahead of them.

I own you now, humans.

It took them less than a second to realize this was the dragoon that'd been following their ship.

There were thirteen of them prodding Leviathan, giving detailed impressions of you. Days ago. I tried to warn you. You pulled guns on me.

"Maybe you need to work on your methods," said Milo, sputtering away from the waves.

True to Desiree, the *Ann* appeared in the distance.

They pulled flares from the barrels of their guns and shot skyward.

"Why are dragoons suddenly talking to people?" asked Milo.

You caught one of us.

"It wasn't intentional."

You don't understand. We're always taking bait from fishermen, we just never get caught. It's a matter of pride. We're waiting for you to become extinct, you know.

"And your dolphin cousins?"

They're kind of stupid, but they're still playing you for your fish. I just killed four sharks for you. A long bony spear quickly shot out from a knot above its eyes.

Dragoons got defenses.

I think I'm part of your team now.

"This isn't a game," said Ramses.

The dragoon wrapped him with its snout and spun him. *It must be since you're the only ones who think it's important.*

Milo nudged it away with his foot.

Linda Ann was nearly on top of them. She slowed enough for a skiff to hit the water like a skipped stone. Ambriel and Vulva were on board.

The dragoon sank beneath the waters.

I'll be around, it said before leaving them with a single request: *Call me Death-mael.*

The
Belly Of
the Beast

The buildings in New York were like the crystal shards in Superman's Fortress of Solitude: they all looked the same till you picked one out and slid it in its proper slot; then all kinds of coolness happened.

On the thirty-seventh floor of the Nonrich Corporation, William Fruehoff, trusted Buford leftenant, unzipped his pants, pulled out his penis, and masturbated furiously. Most everybody had already gone home, but if a cleaning lady happened to walk in, so much the better. One of the many benefits of being William Fruehoff and speaking fluent Spanish was the ability to point out deportation protocols in great detail.

No better head than desperate to stay in the country head, provided he picked the meek ones, and William Fruehoff had the knack for understanding the inner mechanisms that made people meek.

The meek shall inherit the jizz.

Out his window: Rockefeller Plaza in the sunset. In his hand: his dick. The lights were off in his office and the door was closed.

The skyline of New York demanded seed. Every building was a dick of supreme power way beyond simple phallic theory. New York City—and not anyplace else on earth—was the new Olympus, and when Fruehoff finished off his creative round he immediately set out to prove it.

There were thirty-seven reality shows on fifteen networks flipping the Nielsens over and spreading their buttcheeks on a nightly basis. Morning shows and local news devoted entire segments gushing over whatever their network aired the night before. Money rolled in like porn.

Fruehoff, after wiping and zipping, made a note to add *Office Politics* to the production mill, a reality series about after-hours janitorial workers in one of Miami's swankiest office towers. The idea had come just eight seconds ago.

Nonrich owned Big Trick Smokes, the outrageously flavored smoke of extreme sporting; Nonrich owned The Goal: America's Center for Tobacco Reduction.

Slavery. Selective poverty, famine, disease. Every ism under the sun ran off corporate juice. People thought roaches would be all that was left after the Big One, but corporations would be the ones around to train those roaches in rewarding careers.

Fruehoff was high up enough to never have to see the face of an hourly employee unless he chose to. His position was a linch pin, a position he particularly loved. Assholes, by nature, wanted to be at the very top, which was the best place to keep them relatively out of the way. Linchpins, though, were protected by those very aware tops and sucked off by the even more aware bottoms.

He made a note on his tablet for oral sex by Thursday at the latest.

It would take two phone calls to get top advertiser dollars for the run of the unproduced *Office Politics*. Nonrich would grow another tic. Fruehoff's home Upstate would be assured another effective layer of insulation. The world would continue apace.

Reality TV worked things out with a simple algebraic equation: actors cost money…so fuck actors. A camera crew, some wannabees and the right marketing and you'd get people to watch anything.

Fuck California, he thought.

Fuck vampires.

He checked his tablet again.

Oh, yeah, fuck all things Thoom and Thoomish.

Remembering those three things was as important as facing the right way toward Mecca.

Upper echelons were still scrambling in the aftermath of the huge Colorado explosion. That had been a linchpin lab and the fuckers had not only found it but destroyed it.

Whether it was Jetstream fuckers or Thoom fuckers didn't matter to him. Too many damn factions to keep track of anyway. By the time he fell asleep every night it was always him against the world anyway, and the world existed solely to be fucked in all the right places.

Face Mecca again.

Not that he planned on getting directly involved, but William Fruehoff felt a definite hardness to the air outside his office, a major league boner signaling the approach of major coitus.

He left a voice mail for Jones in Stats.

"Jones, can I get the demographics for next week's debuts by nine-fifteen tomorrow with earnings projections and expected allocations? Oh, and I'd expect you might want to do that up as a presentation, some animation and sound somewhere and sneak some 'subliminal' sex images in there for the board, they get a kick out of that, loved the ones from last week, I could tell. Don't know where you got those images of the First Lady. Top notch. We'll be having lunch some day," he said, adding the properly-appreciative laugh. "While you're at it, if you can get word to somebody that I'm going to need several trays of hot dogs and doughnuts during lunch tomorrow, the sloppy ones from that skinny guy in the Park off Eighty-fifth, the one near the precinct. Thanks. Drinks go without saying."

He spun from the window to poke at items on his desk. It wasn't too late to actually get some work done, and having relieved several minutes' worth of tension, he was prepared to settle down and get to it.

Except he didn't get to it.

He spun again in that plush leather chair to face the windows where New York waited for him to decide what to do with it, and he wondered: where in the world was Daniel W. Pasck, a.k.a., the False Prophet Buford M. Bone? It was Fruehoff's turn to know, and in Fruehoff's world it truly did not pay to not have an answer to that.

"Buford's in the box."

"No! You're telling me—"

"We have him."

"Don't shit me."

"I never shit," said a crisply Deutsch accent.

"We have the False Prophet Buford?" said the woman whose only needed name (for those who mattered) was Madam.

"In the box."

"Him, not some clone?"

"I don't even know if the original's still around. He's all clones."

"Not anymore!" said Madam whilst, in exquisite lingerie, she moved about her kitchen. "So when do I get to see him?"

"Expect a large package in your home tomorrow morning."

"He protected?"

"Better than anybody on this planet."

"All right. I'll tidy up the house a bit, get a few things in order."

"You do just that."

"Get the basement straightened up," she said.

"Yes."

"Today's a good day," she said.

"Isn't that the First Law of Thoom? Every day's a good day?"

Fatherhood

Some days felt like death. The feeling was primal, but thirty thousand years of human history said we were still primitive.

It was hard to meditate when 'shit, fuck and damn' kept roiling, but direct contact with Leviathan required a re-grounding of self.

And they'd lost. Again.

The ship was on course for the Blank.

The Battle Ready Bastards were coming along for the ride.

Quicho named them all. "Bob (Ra'asiel). John (Arariel). George (Nakir). James (Shetel). Steve (Lucifer). Lisa (Eloa). Jane (Sereda). Ashley (Ambriel). Raoul (Coupdeviel). Barb (Samandiriel). Bubbles (Vulva). Basketball team, performance artists or sci-fi convention."

They'd radioed their status to the *Fi* again with the *Fi's* blessing to forge ahead. Then Milo had gone below decks and Ramses sat alone on the prow, sprayed till drenched but not making a sound.

"Does anybody know where we're going?" asked Lucifer.

"I don't think it matters just now," said Desiree. "Give us a bit of time, we'll figure things out."

Milo, in his trance, remembered admiring Buford but never loving him. Memory coiled and struck like a snake. His earliest memory was of Buford finding him. He saw his pudgy brown arms reaching out as Buford's hairy white ones reached down. Two? Three? He didn't remember where he was or who or what had gotten him there, just the universal precognition toddlers possessed that when they held their arms out big things had to pick them up.

Kids want to be picked up when they're scared. As a man, Milo often wondered what Buford had done to create that situation in the first place. Even now Milo didn't like to be scared, and these remembrances badgering his meditative state brought with them very real impressions of fear. The snake coiled leisurely around his skull and squeezed till the memory popped and reshaped into a boy openly defying Buford, six or seven, unleashing a spirit warrior against Buford's *succubus* in the Great Shadow Battle With The Mantis using nothing but finger motions, chi and air from having watched the unarmed Kichi do it only seconds before. Afterward, in a real home, both he and Kichi had been sick from the energy drain for days, Kichi only a few, Milo for two weeks plus listless a week more. Kichi had always seemed to Milo to be made of a kind of sinewy, hard chocolate, but had the most comforting touch a child could ask for. Milo's fitful sleep eased a little knowing Kichi's eyes were watching over his dreams. The dreams were where *things* kept trying to get out, sensing a weak bridge to bigger and better worlds. Milo's own *avatar* had tried to flee.

He and Ramses would seek Kichi out, thought Milo now, hard on that word 'Kichi' to drive away Buford, fear and snakes.

Because the amulet Vrea had given Ramses said quite simply, 'Come home.'

~~~

The *Linda Ann* blasted out of the Blank, appearing—had there been anything besides aquatic life to see (and aquatic life was used to it)—to blast out of thin air and continue cleaving the Atlantic like a hot knife through gel.

They called Kichi. His message said only: "I'm in Detroit."

Then so are we.

~~~

In an alternate reality, much of Detroit consists of farmland neighborhood co-ops started by grandmothers fed up with blight and grocer price-gouging, which then spread to others who realized that after years of a dying local economy the land was literally dirt cheap.

In Milo's particular reality, Detroit's crops were started by Kichi Malat, who bought a bag of seed from any hardware store he happened to find and spread them over any empty lot it was impossible not to find. Birds got most of the seed but here and there something would take root. An apple tree at Vernor and Gratiot where they used to make gourmet ice cream. Mustard greens along Montclair.

Even around Kichi's old home where nothing remained on the entire block but two broken houses on one side of the street and four on the other—his old home had been that empty lot right in the middle—Kichi sprinkled seeds, but only in the early morning, but even then, for a city so fragmented, cars were constantly running everywhere.

And nobody, man, woman or child, was outside without talking on a phone. Cities had long ago become very weird places comprised of a huge monolithic conversation.

Kichi Malat was tall, grey, old and lined—and stronger than anybody living or dead in the city of Detroit, with defenses grown men shielded their eyes from. He wasn't afraid of being accosted.

Being ignored though was a very different thing. The people who did see him…didn't see him. Cities were full of poor folks, and it was sad when poor folk lost the ability even to see one another. Granted, Malat was rich as sin, but he didn't wear his money. One would have thought Johnny Appleseed sowing the city was an everyday thing. Spreading life was unimportant.

At a certain point an old man gets tired of the things he does being deemed unimportant and he decides to put the battle directly in everyone's face.

Kichi dropped the bag of grass seed when he saw his sons approaching. He smiled despite the foolishness of what he saw: they'd brought angels with them, bold as day and eleven deep on Kercheval Street.

"You look like a gang," he said, eyes sparkling as he held his arms out to wrap both his boys. "Ra'asiel! You haven't aged a day."

"A few months."

"Lucifer," Kichi said with an enthusiastic nod.

"Old goat," said Lucifer.

"How'd you get here?" asked Kichi, studying the eyes of his eldest son.

"Called in some favors."

"You need to leave the pope alone." Sereda caught Kichi's eye. "Last time I saw such a beautiful green woman…"

"You cupped my left buttock in your hand and told me to pardon your spasm. It's good to see you, Kichi," said Sereda.

"Good to see all of you," he said to the ones standing silently. "Where'd you park?"

"Couple blocks off."

"Doing some chi tracking?" the elder asked proudly. "A fading art."

"We saw you a couple blocks off and wanted to surprise you," admitted Milo.

"I used the chi," said Ramses.

Kichi motioned to the fifty pound bag of seed, which Ramses picked up and toted to an old blue pick up Kichi led them to.

"I've never owned a truck," said Kichi. "I like it. Bought it cash from somebody's front yard." Part of the dirty, wrinkled 'For Sale' sign protruded from beneath a bag of flower seed. "They even gave me a little bag of treats to go with it."

Milo and Ramses shared a look.

"They thought you were a drug dealer, pops," Milo said.

"Well yeah, after I realized it was a bag of weed."

"Not many people carry around the money to walk up somewhere and pay cash for a car," said Milo.

"I gave him five hundred more than what he was asking and made him promise to teach his baby to read. Cute little thing running around in the dirt. Climb in," he told them. "Mind the cooler."

Milo jumped into the bed. The angels followed suit. Ramses climbed into the cab. Kichi called back to them through the open window. "If the police stop us, speak the old tongues." Then he pulled smoothly off, stopping at their vans so they could disembark and follow Kichi to Belle Isle, the latter being about a ten minute drive.

Kichi used the opportunity to talk about Milo.

"How's he doin'?"

"He's pushing."

"You as tired as he is?"

"Not yet."

"I don't want you getting there. Every battle is not ours, and even ours don't necessarily have to be fought to the bitter end." They drove silently a bit, Ramses viewing the city for its mysteries, Malat waiting for the inevitable.

"Pop, we can end this."

"You know how?"

"You've known how your entire life."

"Every warrior knows two guaranteed ways to end a battle," said Kichi.

"We're not going out like that."

"'With Great Power' huh?"

"With great power. What's in the cooler?"

"Sausages, soda, corn and buns. Hope one of you still knows how to set a fire. I forgot the matches and fluid."

"I'm sure between us we can handle it." Ramses noticed something was missing. "Where's your cane?"

"I never told the kids I needed it," he said.

"Only time you spanked me was when I tried to grab that cane."

"With good reason."

"Ms. Boom give you that?"

Kichi smiled a bit, deepening the wrinkles on his angular face. "No," he said, "but not a fault against her general generosity."

"You plan on going back?"

"Too sterile for me. Nah. Atlantis is a nice place to visit, and I would love to live there, but I've got other places in mind."

"Some secret place we get to retire to?" Ramses asked.

They drove quietly a few more moments to enjoy the pre-rush hour solitude.

"I'm sorry you never felt like you belonged anywhere," Kichi said flatly, eyes squarely on the road. He signaled for the turn that would take them over the bridge to Belle Isle.

Ramses answered the same, without looking at the other, eyes on…outside. "It's not your fault, pops."

"Your tone says you think it's yours." They passed a row of dilapidated apartments. "This used to be a better city," said Kichi. "Not good. Not perfect. But better."

"So goes the world. Nostalgia?"

Kichi nodded.

"Past can't piss us off as thoroughly as the present," said Ramses.

"East Grand Boulevard," said the old man, a hand indicating every city in every world there ever was. Concrete, decay and ennui. "They never got the knack of naming to create. Obfuscation. Obfuscation." He sighed. Waste was an egregious thing. "Nothing grand about divisiveness. I miss people who wanted things to be better rather than settling on not getting worse," he said.

"There're never more than five people out of a thousand who feel like that at one time on this earth," said Ramses.

"You still count your brother and yourself as two of them?"

"I'm not sure, pops. I'm not sure what we're fighting for."

"Yeah you are."

Ramses studied Kichi's profile. Kichi stared straight ahead, eyes on the road.

Ramses turned away to stare at the bright diamonds flickering on the surface of the river before them.

"Used to be a tunnel under water that led to the island," said Kichi. The pickup rode the gentle upward slope of the island's bridge. Fishermen sailed under the bridge, old men angling for bass or bluegill first thing in the morning.

Seagulls chased after bait, dive bombing the lines.

"You've got the heavier burden than your brother."

"I'm cool knowing you know."

"I do know."

Joggers ran the length of the grey bridge. Early morning on the island was paradise for those with a purpose. It wasn't until afternoon and evening that those without purpose took over.

A woman jogged toward them, ponytail bouncing like a baton marking her steps. She was tall and beautiful in grey sports bra, grey shorts, and red bandana. Both men said silent prayers of protection for her.

"You're a protector. You're a stronger man than you credit yourself, Ramses," said Kichi.

"Many thanks. I know when you use my name you're leading up to something."

"Nothing that won't wait. Let's find a good spot so we can talk without this metal beast interfering with our thoughts."

They parked near one of the inner ponds. Fat city geese were everywhere, regarding humans as vending machines. Kichi threw several handfuls of seed into their midst, causing a brief flurry of wings and squawking.

Elderly drivers, fitness bikers, and joggers stared at the odd gathering of uber folk, particularly the green chick, trying to memorize details so they could tell friends or family later. Probably a movie or video shoot. Local rappers were always trying to make low-budget videos on the island.

Milo scraped ash and leavings off one of the island's standing grills into a metal bin.

Kichi arranged the dry coals under the grate then walked to the pond's edge. It smelled like water and moss there, and invited all kinds of contemplation.

Milo joined him. They talked privately a few minutes before Milo returned to the milling group around an aromatic and smoking grill.

Milo frowned at it; frowned quizzically at Ramses lining the grill with foil for the sausages and corn.

Ra'asiel was bent forward blowing on the coals.

"How'd he get that fire started?" Milo asked Ramses.

"Stared at it."

"He didn't."

"The man is bad."

Ra'asiel straightened, looking Milo dead in the eye and grinning that slight grin of his that sent pleasurable shivers down most spines.

"Barbecue Ready Bastard?" Milo questioned.

"It's how legends are made," said Ra'asiel X. "Kichi tell you where Buford's at?"

"Didn't talk about him."

"Y'all looked deep, brother," said Ramses.

"Pops told me everything would be all right."

"Already is," said Ramses.

"Desiree?" Milo inquired of their captain.

"You'll never hear me say, 'No worries, mon.' The old man's getting maudlin. Maudlin perturbs me."

"Everything perturbs you," said Milo.

"Perturbing world," said Desiree and left them in favor of Sereda, who now leaned on the hood of Kichi's truck away from casual eyes.

"You don't think we'll attract too much attention?" Ramses asked Milo. This wasn't their usual plan of action.

Milo shook his head. "Kichi says there's a Navy post not far from here."

"So we're the Village People?"

"Boys," Kichi called. They trotted to him. He regarded both with his steeliest, most penetrating gaze. The men before him had been fighting this battle nearly their entire lives on fronts the world over. "What are your guts saying?"

Ramses answered first. "He wasn't expecting it either."

"Leviathan, teleporting, kidnapping and Atlantis. You come home with a helluva show and tell," said Kichi.

"I don't think it's the Thoom," said Milo.

"Just because you don't like them doesn't mean they can't be clever," said Kichi.

"We haven't heard about anybody else getting this close to him," said Ramses.

"Who's gotten close to you lately?" the old man asked.

Milo and Ramses studied one another's expression to see if they were thinking the same thing.

A couple of bikinis, magnificent chess games, smiles that were the very definitions of *human*.

"What is it?" asked Kichi.

"We met two ladies last time," said Milo.

Kichi smiled. "Oldest tricks in the book get their own special chapters for a reason."

"We find them, we find Buford?" asked Ramses.

Kichi shrugged. "Somewhere along the way."

"Ms. Boom gave me something to give to you," said Ramses. "I'll give it to you later."

"Eh, once you go black," he said with a playful snort, then he was immediately more serious. "Is it poetry? Burn it. Burn it before it gets you. You know how many warriors have fallen to poetry? Nobody reads a bad poem without feeling pity, and pity's the first evil."

"You bound it in singularity hide," said Ramses.

"Needed something strong to keep that stuff in."

"What made you carve 'Come home' after leaving the Mount?"

Kichi took their knowledge of his having visited the Mount in stride.

"Prescience isn't random," said Kichi. "Subconscious directs and shapes it inasmuch as the All shapes everything else. I doubt those ladies have anything to do with Thoom, Buford, Leviathan or spirits, but they *will* lead you."

"Lead us where, pops? Enigmas aren't helping," said Milo.

"I'd agree if I was presenting you with one," said Kichi. "Nowhere you can be that isn't where you're meant to be," he said.

"I know," said Milo.

"Handed down from god itself," said Kichi.

"Praise the multiverse," both brothers said in unison.

"Praise something in this idiot age." Kichi Malat nodded toward the group around the grill. "You brought angels?"

"We'll tell people Sereda's a performance artist," said Milo.

"You meant to fight in the streets," said Kichi.

"Buford's not the head of a hydra, he's the heart. We could have ended this," said Milo.

"This portion of it," said Kichi.

"That's not what I want to hear, pops," said Milo.

Kichi looked at him hard-eyed for a second. He expected better of him; then he remembered the inescapable truth of the Warrior: battle was a crucible of evolution, and evolution followed no moral imperative. Kichi was spending his elder years fighting the battle on a much smaller scale, following the wisdom of Anansi's lesson that the story one thought one was telling was never the one that was being told. He was an old man who spoke to children or he played guitar, and only occasionally did he summarily dispatch one of the many evil djinns of the marketing age.

"Send the angels to find Lolita," said Kichi.

"Smoove's already searching," said Milo.

"Bring Smoove and Carel back. Don't get goofy the closer you get to a goal. Check the coals."

Milo protested. "Desiree can see the grill."

"Check the coals."

Milo left.

"He's too distracted," said Kichi.

"What do we do?"

"You've got the gift of the fye. Use it."

"I've never smacked the fye out of him."

"He's got a lot built up," observed Kichi. "Worry about it if and when."

Milo pulled long sausages from the cooler.

"You didn't bring your guitar," said Ramses.

"I'm gonna buy an acoustic and wander the streets with it."

"All about the seeds, pops."

"Life grows from inside or beneath. Consciousness. Slice mine Toronto style," he called out to Milo. "Bag of condiments beneath the front seat." He nudged Ramses. "You think he's thinking 'slice 'em ya damn self'?"

Ramses laughed. Kichi clapped him on the shoulder and led off.

"Come on, let's see if we can figure out where your ladies are."

Interim

There was too much travel involved in being a Jetstream.

The ladies had used their real names, which pointed the finger away from them, but Kichi said go anyway. He'd make sure Carel and Smoove rendezvoused with them, but for now, go.

Next stop, Manila.

"You notice the billboards?" Ramses asked Milo during their flight.

"White kid telling the schoolyard, 'My reality's better than your reality'? Schoolyard's got the black, Hispanic and Asian sprinkled in? Yeah." They were everywhere. "Reality Unbound Network. Biggest one yet."

"Not even trying to hide it."

"Brother, they never really did. Every other billboard was liquor. The South is rising again."

"So to speak," said Ramses.

"So to speak."

"I've been plotting the logorhythmic path of commercials. Logical conclusion is no consciousness left," said Ramses.

"Money machines," said Milo. "Not people. Renewable, sustainable money machines."

"And we're chasing Buford to the exclusion of all else?"

"Brother, Buford *is* all else. Agents of Change can handle domestics. Botha Dish should be on his feet soon.

Karaplides and Technique disabled the broadcast towers of every Clear Channel station in Houston. The young guard prefers the old methods; we can afford our magicks against the magician."

"What do we actually do when we get him?" Ramses asked sensibly. "Seal him up? Put him on display? Hydra's heads grow back."

"So we cut off its nuts so it doesn't breed. They've never had a problem with extinction. Neither are we."

"The revolution won't be televised."

"Won't be broadcast at all."

They settled back to ride out the flight on one of Bruce Weyne's private jets.

Interim
TWO

Maseef was still crying though not a single tear ever touched his face. Lolita Or-Ghazeem had finally been found. Frozen. Her body held a laser in one hand and ice pick in the other.

They interred her aboard the Fi. The curiosity and grief of the single group of science groupies that had managed to keep up with them wouldn't be so high as to make them board. Maseef's other sisters didn't know yet. He'd sent a whale to find them. This was not news to be told over the radio.

They returned her to the capital city, a quiet ship. Ele catalogued her wounds. The torn breach suit was discarded; water from the thawed chunk of ice was preserved for use in a fountain to be erected in her honor.

Shig Empa asked the uncomfortable question: "When will Milo be informed?"

Carel, Smoove and Ele studied one another.

The captain answered for the group.

"When we see him again. Maseef?"

Or-Ghazeem, the entire voyage home, had done nothing but ask questions. His eyes were visibly hollow; his soul dry ice.

"She should stay aboard the Fi," said Smoove. "Fewer curiosity seekers."

"Yes," he said softly.

Shig spoke just as softly, turning more toward the captain to deflect his words.

"After forensics we'll have her brought on board," he said.

"Remove nothing," Maseef said softly, the lines around his eyes showing. "Drain nothing. If the dirt under her nails is not intact I will raze this city."

"We'll need samples, Maseef," said Shig.

"Get them as though she is alive."

"She fought. I want to know who," said Shig. His resolve brought Maseef's eyes forward.

"Vengeance?" said Maseef.

"I prefer Milo's word: payback."

"Payback's a bitch," said Smoove.

"A lot of that going around," said Ele.

"In this regard, payback's a bitch who works for me. Did I use that correctly?" the slight Atlantidean asked.

"It's what they call poetry, Shig," said Smoove. He left Shig to his arrangements. Ele, Fiona and Maseef followed. The *Semper Fi* waited for them in the harbor to ready itself as Lolita Or-Ghazeem's protected place of rest.

The Chronic

The lady was not pleased. "I don't know what kind of man you think you are, but nobody just shows up in the Philippines."

"I'm good at finding things," said Milo.

"And did your brother just happen to find Yvonne?"

"I expect he's with her."

"If we ran into each other at the airport," said Neon, "or even a club, I'd say cool. But I'm on a beach and you damn well ain't passing by."

"It's not what it looks like."

"What it looks like is some freaky shit." She had her arms folded under her chest but placed an innocent half step in the sand between them in case a kick to the nuts was in order.

"I needed to talk with you," said Milo.

"About?"

"Unusual things."

The look on her face said *Besides you?*

"And stop with that," she said. "The 'Looking at me all through my soul' look."

No reason not to cut to the chase. "Where's Buford?"

She considered him a split-second like he was crazy then countered with, *"Who?"* but didn't stop there, "the fuck is Buford?"

"Milo Jetstreeeeeeeeaam!" somebody shrieked.

Oh hell.

He'd forgotten Chronic Djinn had moved to Manila. Of all the powerless Djinns in the world and of all the touristy beaches…

The Djinn threw his serving tray to the ground.

Neon knew what a fight looked like.

Milo took his eyes off her a split-second; he had planned to purse his lips to say go, but she was already well on her way.

Other tourists followed her initiative.

Beach police, though, were heading their way.

"Were those her drinks?" Milo asked.

The Djinn realized he'd be docked their cost and faltered a step. Resolve kicked back quickly. He—

Milo grabbed the nearest wrist, twisted while digging into a pressure point, pulled him in close and said very clearly the three words no man whose wrath must be avenged wants to hear: "Not now, fool."

The Djinn tried struggling free.

Milo increased the pressure.

The Djinn calmed himself.

"Do you know anything about Buford that I need to know? Think a moment." To the officers as he stepped back and released Chronic—patting the Djinn's shoulder in rough forgiveness of an apparent misunderstanding—Milo said, "It's cool." He held his hands open. Strong and black is strong and black no matter the geography lesson.

"He bothering her?" the shorter and meaner of the officers asked.

"No," answered Milo. "A bee scared her, he thought I scared her, I thought he said something rude. No charges."

"Hotel charges for drinks," the second officer told the Djinn. "What'd you shout?"

"My name," answered Milo. "I signed for her drinks."

"What's your name?" said the first.

"Milo Jetstream."

"Hell of a name is that?"

Milo was about to answer when Neon returned, intentionally jiggling enough to disarm a nuclear device.

Both officers grinned.

The Djinn looked sheepish.

"You know a lot of people here," she said to Milo. "Everything's OK," she told the officers, who practically curtsied and left. "Hell's wrong with you, Rema?"

"That's Milo Jetstream," he said sullenly.

"Go," said Milo. Djinns thrived on any opening to remain annoying.

The powerless Chronic Djinn trudged footprints in the sand away from them.

"So you're famous and you can kick an ass," said Neon as answer to what he was doing in Manila. Famous people, as most were aware, were expected to track down beautiful women. "Just not famous famous. I knew Smith wasn't your real name but I thought hey, it's a cruise..." She pointed a nail at him. "Who's Buford?"

He opened his mouth to speak without being sure what should come out. "Let's wait till Ram finds Yvonne," he said.

"He's not going to. She's asleep. Unless you're into creeping into people's rooms." She bent toward him conspiratorially. "That's when a sister strikes a nut, you know."

"Duly noted."

"You flew all this way to see me to ask me about some Buford when I'm half naked on a sunny beach, and still got the presence of mind to be a gentleman. Your real name is Milo Jetstream?"

He nodded.

"I heard that name somewhere before."

He shrugged.

She relaxed her arms. "I just left a boyfriend named Le'mon J'ello, so who am I to say?"

She walked.

Milo slipped off his sandals and carried them, matching pace with her. Warm sand tended to leech tension from the soul.

"How accidental was it you and your brother picking us out on the cruise?"

"You make it sound like we had ulterior motives."

She pointed at him. She pointed at herself. She pointed at the beach.

"OK," he said. "No, fortune favors the foolish."

"Fortune favors the foolish?"

"All the time."

"What about a fool and his money will soon part?"

"That's stupid people. Foolish is part of a different game."

"Just 'cause you put ish on it," she started, but stopped statement and motion. "Are you gay?" She didn't wait for an answer. "We thought you might have been gay for a minute, playing chess and all, but then said naw."

"Every gay man doesn't scream, 'Flame on!'"

"So you're gay?"

He allowed a look of such open lust to inhabit his eyes that her teeth hurt.

"Did you just?" she asked.

"With variety."

"How'd I look without my clothes on?"

Milo Jetstream knew when to keep his mouth closed.

"Plus we caught you checking out our asses," said Neon. "Really, what're you doing here?"

"We came specifically to see you."

"No lie?"

"Not a one. There're a hundred ways to find somebody when all you have is a name," he said.

"This still freaks me out." Someone unaccustomed to honesty though couldn't fake that flash of pure-D lust he'd given her. "But I can't pretend it's not good to see you. So, you an action star? Direct to DVD?"

He laughed.

"I know this guy," she said, "who bootlegs all kinds of crazy kung fu movies. Rema's the type who'd be into that crazy stuff," said Neon.

"Pretty much."

"Movie star," she said reflectively. "Who'da thought."

"You interested in marriage?"

"Damn, brother, we haven't even slept together yet," she said, trying and failing to maintain a straight face. "No," she said, "I have no plans on getting married anytime soon. That also does not mean I plan on engaging in lunacy with you. I like the beard, by the way. Little raggedy but raggedy works for you."

He'd forgotten all about the growth. Her pointing it out made it itch.

"Got a bit of grey going," she pointed out.

"I *am* a little older than you," he said.

"Without older men I'd be forever thirsty. You did notice he dropped my drink, yes?"

"My treat at dinner."

"Milo Jetstream, international man of mystery, you're a bit forward. I may look like a dumb blonde—"

"You have the carriage of a queen."

"What I was about to say was, I may look like titties and ass, but I'm the smartest girl you'll ever meet. The game hasn't been invented I don't see through."

"Anything unusual happened since the cruise?"

She slipped her arm around his waist and gave him a friendly squeeze as answer. Then she pulled away and walked off, waving bye.

"Let's see how good you are," she said. "Find us tonight at seven. Can I tell Yvonne you're a movie star? Wouldn't want to blow your incognito."

"I'm not a movie star."

"Humble bastard. I just might have to let you find me a little earlier." She walked away.

He knew why attractiveness came so easy to her: because she was.

"You're not here for fun," the automatic reminder kicked in. But damn if he didn't walk the beach with the sand lodging between his toes just so the breeze could get to know him.

He'd have to be wary of Chronic Djinn, but that was a minor blip in the scheme of things.

He felt if he walked the beach long enough the wind would tell him where in the world was Buford Bone.

Eventually he sat on the sand and called Ramses. "Come meet me by the water, brother." Then he stared outward a while, because water, like the hips of dancers, rewarded attention.

~~~

"So why's 'high concept' used to describe things that are stupid?" the lady asked over dinner.

"Masters of regurgitainment," he said. "People who pay money to see juvenile stuff won't be branded 'lowbrow' when they leave the theater." Yvonne hadn't wanted to join them. She, too, was creeped out by their presence. She and Ramses were off somewhere with the younger brother trying his damndest to explain things.

"I'm not a movie star," said Milo.

"Don't be ashamed of direct-to-video. Lot of used-to-be stars on the freight now. Michael Jai White…"

"Who?"

"Played *Spawn*. Demon superhero movie. Van Damme, Wesley—actors gotta eat," she said and pointed out the heavy plate of *arroz caldo*, chicken *binakol*, *lumpia* rolls and two hellacious desserts in front of him. "It's cute you eat dessert during your meal."

"Why wait for heaven," said Milo, offering her a fork of mango cream cake, "when we're seeded here on earth?"

She leaned forward and took the fork full in her mouth.

"Real dessert is one of the last refuges of the working class. Homemade, though," he said.

"I make a mean caramel apple pie," she said.

"Cinnamon rolls."

"Completely from scratch?"

"Flour and everything," he said.

"As good as the malls?"

"Better," he admitted.

"'Cause there's this one store at the malls make you yank a white cane to be at the front of the line."

"Damn."

"Quite," she said. She studied the other diners a moment. "Nobody else seems to know who you are." Nobody else had shouted his name; no one in the restaurant overtly catered to him.

"That's good."

Briefly she imagined she wouldn't mind being a part of the paparazzi and chintz, but surprised herself by realizing she actually would. She enjoyed being with him just as they were.

She nodded in agreement and pointed her fork at his cake.

Milo cut it and slid half to her.

She wore shorts and a blue touristy tee shirt, nothing remotely sensual but all the more sexy for it. She belonged with Sereda, this brown goddess with wide eyes, quick smile, and irreverence that bordered on flight.

Milo loved her, he acknowledged that, but he wasn't *in love*. Verbs and prepositions rightfully place chasms between them. But it was more than obvious why Kichi had wanted him to go. The rest of the crew was expected tomorrow. Between now and then if somebody wanted to clone a gigantic Buford to do battle with nine hundred feet Jesus—hey, deal with it as it's dealt.

"You came all the way out here to find me?" she said.

"Yes."

He kept an eye out for Chronic Djinn.

~~~

Ramses tried. Focusing on the problem at hand had eluded him fairly easily for the past hour; the next showed no signs being any less agile.

He left the hotel Yvonne-less and walked.

Nighttime was the best time for thinking. Lights looked like lights. Shadows were real. And there were generally fewer people. People, masses of people, were the leaves on a fat full tree: they literally clogged the gutters of thought that led to the draining of animus necessary for free and open contemplation.

It wasn't a question of who would want Buford. Enough hands would rise for that. But who had the unmitigated balls to secretly trail both Buford and the Jetstreams? Even if Buford had Buford, the methodology introduced new variables.

But it didn't feel like Buford had Buford. He would have had himself teleported as close to the Mount as possible (without the 'porter getting there), penance be damned.

Ramses made his way back to the beach. Their butt imprints were still in the sand. He sat in his and consulted the water for a long time.

He kept thinking about Yvonne.

cut
scene

Djinns don't grant wishes any more than vampires don't age. The easiest way to make one's self untouchable was to claim immortality. Djinns stock and trade was greed. They fed off it. They were master hypnotists intuitive enough to know there was a sucker born every minute, particularly when Djinns were the ones behind the notion of every sperm being sacred

But there were Djinns who fed and then there were Djinns who gorged on the sweet electricity of dreams deferred. Chronic Djinn was the latter.

The Jetstream had had nothing to do with Chronic losing his powers but everything—as far as Chronic Djinn was concerned—with his stellar downfall. Even a Djinn without powers was persuasive, and Chronic (a.k.a. David Scott) had been comfortably ensconced in Nonrich's marketing Olympus until Milo leaked that an ant gnawing the wing from a dried moth carcass was guaranteed a more nutritious meal than from any of the seven varieties of the company's "Logo: Lunch to Go" campaign for kids.

Genius evil. "Don't Just Eat It: *Be* Your Logo!" Each Logo's packaging was distinct so kids felt they were owning their own special brand. Extreme, for kids who fell down a lot. Radical, for kids who were plain stupid. Sparks, for kids who were likely to become pregnant by fourteen. The Aw-dash-N, as in au natural, since there still existed that sliver of marketing segment whose barefoot parents made their kids eat granola. Outrageous, for the lonely kids. Wicked, for the eclectic artsy types. The Flavor, for the ethnic kids with the spices and the hot sauce.

Crap plus kids. A multi-billion dollar industry.

Simple Djinn came up with the immortal tag line, "They're Grrreat!"

Djinn And Tonic created the beautiful synergy of beer and automobiles.

Chronic Djinn had kids everywhere literally eating logos, and what was better than that?

Then came the public backlash and epic fall. Losing himself in the patois of Manila seemed safe. Becoming Rema had been easy. He was already Chinese, he just had to adopt the demeanor of a suddenly poor Chinese waiter.

It wasn't that hard.

Today, the small gods showed favor upon him. Kichi had been the one to strip him of his powers, and here was his idiot son.

You could strip a Djinn's power away but, when it came down to it, you couldn't take away his luck.

~~~

So he blew up a café a little ways off from his place of employment at about the time Neon usually showed up to lounge through a good portion of the day. The explosion killed several locals and tourists, including two waiters he knew, which wasn't so bad for the Djinn: death meant the possibility of wills, estates and insurance; he might not be able to feed but he could sure get a contact high off any greed that clung to surviving relations like shit to a shoe.

Knowing it was a trap didn't mean Milo wasn't going to help. He vaulted Neon's beachside breakfast table and went racing over the sand.

Then Neon got up.

Rema watched her run. She was only a few steps behind the Jetstream.

Djinn's henchmen (to himself, he referred to them that way) had been told: "Just look for a black guy running." And here came Milo running, and they, with small knives laced with poison gel, positioned themselves throughout the panicked crowd.

They were The Ten Men With A Thousand Cuts.

Feared by sleeping winos and those who consistently owed other people small sums of money.

Lucky bastards each, because of the Djinn's influence.

Milo evaded them easily enough going in, but coming out it wasn't so easy fighting off ten men while carrying wounded. There was a sharp slice across his bicep when one moved in pretending to help lift the crying young man from Milo's arms. The knives were thin as paper cuts and just as annoying. Milo blocked him from moving away, stared directly at him with as menacing and dead a stare as a prehistoric crocodile, then simply handed the young man over. The knife was safely palmed as the bewildered assassin carried the boy to safety.

Jetstream turned to go back inside.

Smoke poured through mangled window frames, but not so thickly that Milo couldn't see another quick step toward him. Milo pivot-footed, stepped in close so others couldn't see, blocked the knife, sharp punched the man in the sternum--making it appear the man had suddenly choked on smoke--and lowered him to the ground where concerned onlookers rushed to help him, inspired by his choking bravery.

A policeman inside the charred café handed Milo a woman. Her arms hung limply but her eyes were wide open, incredulous that this was supposed to be a vacation for getting away from the world and its problems. Her eyes saw the haze of smoke become sparse clouds and azure sky. The sun was warm. What she thought was sweat running down her neck was actually blood, and where she felt burned was likely not sunburn.

It would suck telling people about this trip.

A mix of languages hit Milo: Tagalog, Chinese, English; skins whirled past. There was only one poison that could bring Milo Jetstream down with one pass and that was love.

He saw Neon on the edge of the scene wondering what to do.

The next trip inside Milo grabbed a fallen extinguisher, squirted his arm, then joined a coughing, gagging employee in putting out the largest and most immediate fire. Quickly done, he ushered the woman out. His ears suddenly felt clogged with cotton. Time slowed a fraction. A man entered.

Whirling, Milo knocked him the hell out with the extinguisher.

Sound came back. Sirens. Shouting. Ordering. Crying. Name calling.

"Milo!"

He flew outside. They hadn't edged close to her yet and he planned that it stay that way. He pushed through the crowd, keeping an eye for concealed palms.

A slice across the other arm.

He pushed on.

Somebody got bold and angled a stab for the gut.

That called for the two-second ass kicking. With broken wrist thrown in for measure. The man fell: more smoke inhalation.

Milo saw Ramses. Saw Yvonne a ways off. Saw haze where there was clear air. Felt a tight pain in his neck muscles. Grabbed Neon's hand and ran for a clearing.

The cuts bled profusely.

Yvonne pulled her bra to use as a tourniquet. Neon did the same, using the one-handed bra via the shirtsleeve maneuver women master by the age of sixteen.

Unfortunately, none of the Thousand Cuts had been told about the Jetstreams. They thought they were going after a scrappy tourist mark.

That left things somewhat a mystery as to how so many grown men had succumbed to smoke inhalation so far away from the blast site.

When Yvonne lifted her heel from the groin of the man on the ground, another explosion, this one smaller, went off farther down the strip.

Milo, breathing heavily, pushed Yvonne away on the shoulder and told Ramses, "Go."

Neon stayed with him.

He had to get away. A bloodied man wearing two bras on his arms attracted too much attention. Things were still chaotic enough that slipping away didn't prove too difficult.

To her credit, Neon hadn't freaked yet.

She braced him after he stumbled, but had no idea where their two pairs of feet—mostly hers—were taking them, except away from the chaos (where emergency workers were showing up) to some intuitive sense of safety elsewhere.

Safety tended to reside in familiar faces, and there was Rema.

"Rema, help!"

The Djinn ran forward to prop Milo, who immediately let his full mass become a dead weight on the Djinn.

The Djinn struggled to keep him upright.

"He needs to get to a hospital," said Neon.

"I'm OK," said Milo. "I just need—" he slumped to force Djinn to lower him to the curb—"to sit down."

Chronic lowered him carefully.

"We need some bandages, these are Victoria's Secret bras, blood's not coming out of them easily—"

"Neon?"

She looked into Milo's eyes.

"I've been in worse," he said.

"And they were trying to mug you! What kind of trifling sumbitch tries to mug somebody rescuing blown up people?"

One of the rescue workers would have bandages. "I'll be right back."

She left them alone.

Chronic Djinn sat beside Milo.

"I'm pretty sure you're not dying," said the Djinn.

Milo took a deep breath and released it as a deeply resigned sigh.

"I can't remember the last time I had a woman that beautiful in bed," said Chronic. "Why you here, Jetstream?"

"You're out of the loop, Chronic."

"See how fast I get back I post pictures of you trussed like this on the Internet."

"Probably get your old job back."

"You have bras wrapped around your arms, man!" The Djinn patted Milo's knee. "I just did this to weaken you. How long you plan on staying in beautiful Manila? Enjoy the stay. Maybe you'll get to meet some more nice people."

"Gloating makes it feel worse when I pull my foot out your ass."

"Milo Jetstream with his friendly tips. I could stab you in the side right now."

"Except you don't have a knife," Milo pointed out. "And you've got the wrist strength of a pouty girl. And if you hit me I'll snap your neck so far around you'll see it coming."

Djinn unwound the fist. "How do you know Ms. Neon? We all masturbate quite furiously over her. She one of your weirdos? Never seemed like one. Not full of herself enough. Very hippity hop. Hm? Hip-hop heroics? The new breed? I guarantee I'll cop a feel before you kill me. When I borrow my friend's cell phone I plan to let everyone know you're here."

Neon raced toward them with a paramedic.

Chronic Djinn stood.

"Manila's about to be quite the party." Chronic winked at him. "The luck of the Irish wins every time. It's written in the Book of Djinn and Synergy that the strongest will fall to the weak that are persistent and anal. Diamond, Milo

Jetstream, in my ass, and I've been waiting a long time to get to say that. I am the weakest motherfucker you've ever seen, I am the—"

Milo's glance upward shut him the hell up.

"I'm shutting the hell up, but you're sitting there with bras on your arms. I couldn't have planned for better. This isn't over." Then he made a show of rushing to Neon and telling her he had to run back to work. By now, sirens and chaos ruled.

I draw the breath of life and health, Milo thought, but when he opened his eyes finished as *while the rest of the world dines in hell.*

He fervently hoped Ramses was over there countering any resistance with high prejudice.

He allowed the medic to quickly sterilize and bandage him. The medic knew suspicious cuts when he saw them, but blown up people took precedence.

"I couldn't get the police to come," said Neon.

Milo offered his hand. She helped him to his feet. There was a button on his phone that would signal Ramses 'situation green' when his brother got a chance to notice it. He pushed it.

"I need to get to my hotel room. Your hotel," he said. He gave her the room number. Djinn had chosen a fast acting, mean and annoying poison, much like himself. Milo's fingers fought to avoid cramping.

She didn't hesitate but he told her anyway, "She's safe with him."

Neon propped him with that arm around his waist again and quickly led him off.

The men following them to his room tried busting in before he got the antidote, but they were stupid—as men who follow people for a fee usually are—and these three had an idea what they were up against, which allowed for that little hesitation where the first one who tried to rush the door got the door quickly opened and slammed squarely against his face, causing the second to trip, fall forward as the door re-opened, and find his neck broken before he hit the floor.

Milo shoved Neon into the adjoining bathroom and shut the door. Did his heart good to hear it lock from the inside.

The third rushed inside.

Milo held him in a one-armed choke-hold while reaching into a pack for a quick-dissolve poison counteragent.

Chronic Djinn was hardly in a position to hire the best.

Hotel staff hadn't paid Milo or Neon much attention what with half the employees on one side of the building to see the excitement. Terrorists didn't usually strike Manila, Protestants, Muslims and Catholics notwithstanding. Now everyone would have to go home and head to bed with yet another reason to be afraid.

"You can come out now," Milo said. He closed the suite door.

She did, and aimed a punch directly for the last would-be assassin's nuts.

Milo didn't feel any need to deflect it.

Neon cocked a leg back.

Milo shook his head.

"You're wearing sandals. You could break a toe."

Milo tied the man's hands with the ironing cord—leaving the iron attached for added discomfort—and ground his finger into the pressure point that killed short term memory.

He grabbed their things and headed out. His head already felt a little clearer.

He was several paces down the hall before realizing Neon wasn't beside him.

He stopped.

He looked back.

"Negro, where we goin'?"

She'd never seen a look encapsulate the entirety of the concept *Not Now* so thoroughly in her life.

They paused in the stairway long enough for him to put on a clean, long-sleeved linen shirt (reddish orange for just such an emergency).

Outside, under the azure sky tinged with violent smudges, he asked, "Do you trust me?" He hailed a local *jeepney* that was glad to be going the opposite direction of the blasts.

"Ermita District," said Milo.

The driver forgot himself and spoke in Tagalog for *money.*

Milo answered tersely in Tagalog for *Move Your Ass. Please.*

Manila had two primary tourist districts: Ermita and Malate. Economics and time put the odds of Chronic having contacts in Ermita slim.

The colloquial vehicle took off.

Neon had held her tongue the entire rush down ten flights of stairs, but *this* needed to be addressed.

"What'd you just say? 'Goobledy goobledy' what? You speak their language. Fuck me, this is Navy Seal Mission Accomplished shit. I didn't come here for Tom Clancy!"

Milo grabbed a flailing hand and held it comfortingly. "I'm not military. We just need some open space."

He felt her tense to jump out.

"I'm leaving my bag with you," he said. "I'm going back for Yvonne." He spoke again in Tagalog to the driver. *(You will be paid, I promise.)* Then more.

To Neon, "I know where you'll be and you'll be fine. He's taking you to Aquino Airport. I have friends coming in." He pressed something in the remaining pack. "They'll find you. When they do, give them the pack and tell them I told you to wait. Two women, one man. An hour."

The jeepney slowed enough for him to jump out.

"Why don't I just fucking say Klaatu Barada Nicto!" she shouted.

"They'd think you were crazy."

He ran off.

~~~

Nobody died in the second blast. By the time Milo got there Ramses and Yvonne were sitting on a curb sucking oxygen and looking none the worse for wear outside of smudges and soot.

Milo noticed her dog tags back around her neck.

The Manilan fireman tried intercepting as Milo approached the two but Ramses waved Milo forward.

The arch of Ramses' eyebrows meant: Do we need to talk?

The set of Milo's jaw and dismissive cock of his head said: Minor irritation just elevated to serious annoyance.

"How long did you serve?" the elder Jetstream asked Yvonne, sitting closely beside her.

She answered without looking at him, holding the plastic cone to her mouth. "Five years." And he thought she was about to say something else, something faraway, but she didn't.

"You're OK, darlin'," he said.

"This ain't no vacation," she said. She looked at Milo. "You know the song where Bowie says, 'This ain't rock and roll, this is genocide'?"

"Diamond Dogs," he answered her.

"This ain't rock and roll."

"Straight up country and western," said Milo.

"Where's Neon?" she asked.

"She's all right. Let's look after you. She OK, Ram?"

"Pulled three people out. Think I need to propose."

"Neon has my phone. Ram?"

Ramses pulled his out and handed it to Yvonne.

"Kind of phone is this?" she said. Its buttons and swipe areas were in weird places. And there were too many of them.

"Hit the blue button," said Ramses.

Neon picked up on the first ring.

"Where are you?" asked Yvonne.

"I have no freaking idea!" She shouted something off phone.

"What'd she say?" asked Milo.

"Sounded like angry idiocy." To Neon: "You OK?"

"Yes! I'm on my way to the airport."

"Why?"

"Ask Tom Clancy!"

"You're OK?"

"Yes! Yes. I'm OK. I'm cool."

"We're on our way," said Yvonne.

"I'm sure Mr. Clancy can find me."

~~~

A Rasta, an Irish lady and a Mexican walk into an airport…

Neon spotted them, then they spotted her.

They marched right up to her. There was something almost criminal about them, a kind of…*indifference* about how the hustle of tourism was supposed to affect them.

Vaguely dangerous anarchy made her lift the pack immediately and hold it out.

"He said to wait for you."

Desiree took the pack.

"What's your name, luv?" asked Smoove.

"Rachel."

"What's your real name, luv?"

"That's my—"

"You're forcing yourself not to blink," Fiona clued her. "What's happened?" She said it with a measure of concern. All three softened their postures.

"Fuckers are blowing things up," said Neon, and really, really wanted to cry. "Pardon my French."

"Parlez vous," said Smoove.

She didn't know why she wasn't fleeing. Fleeing would've been called for. Didn't know why she didn't do something loud to draw attention, or subconsciously adopt that fighting stance that Yvonne had taught her. Didn't care that the Rasta was likely boning these two women; at this moment she needed to be held, dammit, and two seconds in his arms wouldn't permanently damage a damn thing in the universe.

She moved toward him full of the need-a-hug vibe. His arms instinctively opened.

"It's all right, luv. The Jetstreams choose their friends well. No harm here," he said.

"Matter of fact, there they are," said Fiona. "You guys," she said when they reached her, "look like hell."

"Got a damn Djinn setting off explosives to get back at me," said Milo.

Only one Djinn would stoop Djinn-dom so low.

"Chronic?" asked Smoove.

"That a new terrorist group?" asked Yvonne.

"Been around a long time," said Milo.

"And you're Homeland Security?" asked Neon, no longer held.

"Side mission," announced Fiona. There was a collective sigh.

"Ele's in the bathroom," said Desiree. "Insisted on coming."

"Best to deal with Chronic now," said Milo. "He's talking about rattling cages. We don't have that kind of time."

"We'll talk later," said Fiona.

Ramses took Neon and Yvonne by the hands. "I think you should travel with us," he said. Ramses had a less panicking effect than Milo, making it seem sensible to the ladies, given the circumstances, to travel with these two for a bit.

"Chronic gone into hiding?" asked Desiree.

"No," said Milo. "He's gotta work tomorrow."

~~~

They spoke through the evening. Lolita. Milo, for the most part, sat gravely. When done, he nodded sad thanks, asked about Maseef, then let everybody know he'd be going for a walk alone.

Would that be wise?

He was Milo Jetstream.

He returned quietly and safely late in the night.

NOt
AS Easy
AS It
seems

Drinks beside the beach were a necessity. Tourism could be paused, but it could not be stopped.

"Remember me, Chronic?" said Smoove as he sidled up behind the serving Djinn. Rema froze. "Enjoy your drink, ma'am," said Smoove to a sexy blonde. "Another's coming on the house." The Djinn was fully upright now. His tray trembled. In his ear, Smoove said, "There's the wife across the way. Anything blows up, you die on the sand. Nothing fancy. Seagulls shit on you and crabs roll you for change. Walk with me." They walked a few steps. "Who else knows about us here? Before you lie, think utter humiliation. Gifs. On the internet."

Then the Djinn screamed.

Like a girl.

Smoove hadn't expected that.

The blonde ran. Seeing this, others ran. Police converged mas rapido.

Desiree hurried toward Smoove, blasting a string of machinegun Spanglish ahead of her and looking so incongruously frantic that Smoove's first (squelched) impulse was to crack a smile.

The police motioned her to back off and get calm.

"He attacked my boss yesterday," Smoove accused, backing a step from the Djinn.

"He's got something against us," said Desiree and sneered at the waiter. "We're here on conference—" she made as if to backhand Chronic a quick one. "Racist little bastard!"

"I'm taller than you!"

"Little mind. Teeny dick."

"Ask anybody," said Smoove. "He's the same one on the beach yesterday. Accosted our boss and a client. A model," he said as the capper. What kind of sick fuck would accost a model?

"I didn't do anything!" Chronic shrieked, sounding again like a freaked out tween, except sincere with it this time. "I screamed first!"

"You know," Smoove felt civically compelled to point out, "he was around at the time of the explosions."

"I work here!"

"Radicals kill economies," said Smoove. He reached back. "Wallet," he said, pulling it out and sliding out crisp, professional, glossy business cards featuring a lipstick red logo and a snazzy name. He gave one to each of the officers along with his ID to the nearest, proving he was indeed Robert Thomas Marley, location consultant for Another Fine Mess Modeling & Production.

"You don't like black people, just say so, mon." Smoove pointed down the beach. "He scared off one of my models." To Quicho he said, "Can you go get Ariel?" To the police, "Can she get Ariel? She's no good without somebody within ten feet of her."

The blonde was watching from a safe distance, shifting uncertainly from foot to foot.

These officers had learned long ago that not talking was generally the best way to deal with most situations, 'best' meaning getting away as quickly as possible when there was no need to smack somebody.

"Yeah, go."

Quicho trotted off. She waved the woman inward, knowing it'd be construed as *The police want you*.

"I just want to know what you have against us," Smoove said directly and pointedly to Chronic Djinn, "and if we need to take measures."

"He's threatening me!"

Of course staff and management had come out.

"Rema? Twice in two days?" a manager said.

That's all the police needed to hear. "He's harassing guests," said an officer.

"We're on high security," another said. He really wanted to use his baton improperly. High alert was bothersome. Kept him having to deal with people.

The blonde now hovered uncertainly along the fringes. She was pretty enough to be a model. The crazy lady had calmed down. And the Rasta had the air of someone sharp and controlled, so all in all, Rema was more annoying than he was worth.

"You go," one said with a flick of his wrist at Smoove.

The other one gripped his baton knob and regarded Rema longingly.

Management tried to ingratiate themselves to Smoove and party (the blonde, sensing sufficient American-ness, gravitated alongside them), but Desiree shooed them off.

"We're done with this place," Smoove said as the capper. "Except give her another drink."

And thus did Chronic Djinn become unemployed.

~~~

Lolita Or-Ghazeem. Dead. Gone. Kaput.

But they'd known that all along.

As the author Kurt Vonnegut so rightfully explained, "So it goes."

Until it came.

Then it hit you in the gut and slapped the life out of everything.

I draw the breath of life and health; I expel the breath of doubt.

But what did that mean? Because as soon as one doubt was gone, a single inhalation brought a lungful right back. A selfish thing, drawing the breath of life and health in a sickened world. Selfish and insulating when it pretended to be restorative…

Milo Jetstream realized he was thinking like the False Prophet again.

He stopped.

Chronic Djinn had killed two people.

Nobody died unsanctioned in the name of Jetstream.

Milo didn't plan to meditate anymore for a while to come.

He was alone on the beach the way he preferred it. He pulled out his phone and started making calls.

Buford and Manila excluded each other. Tomorrow morning, they'd leave.

~~~

They split up.

Here's what happened:

Chronic Djinn released his inner child, a thing that— powers or not—remained locked within a Djinn and was never, ever to be willfully freed. This was the only cardinal law of Djinn among Djinn.

The wraith took shape out of the miasmic ether, coming into being from behind nothingness like someone pinching hunks of bread from a loaf. Each torn piece of space-time uncovered more of its shape until the quantum hole was big enough for it to step through.

Its hands in its pockets and its droopy shoulders defined 'laid back.'

It tipped a chin at the Djinn. "Dude, what's up? Yeah, OK, I see," it said as it regarded his comatose body. It sat on the edge of Chronic's small bed and smoothed the comatose Djinn's hair. "*You* have fallen very far. Biblical."

It looked around for what it would use to kill him. Most Djinns left knives or some such, something quiet and ceremonial. There was nothing immediately usable around Chronic.

"You're going to weasel out of it?" said the Ic, leaning to grab Chronic's cheap bedside lamp but settling instead for something less work-intensive. It pulled the pillow from under Rema's head and casually held it over his face. The Djinn was already in a coma; this was the closest the Ic could come to not having to do anything.

Where Djinns were greedily ambitious, their inner children tended to be lazy and vindictive. The eternal trap of the genie within the genie.

"Not much reason for you to've been awake for a while now, huh?" the Ic said to the softly dying man. After Chronic was gone the Ic rubbed its palms together, leaving imprints of raised skin on both that looked vaguely like the dead Djinn. Over time these imprints would fill out into perfect replicas of Chronic.

The Ic looked at the humanoid welts with the satisfaction of new vistas. "Dude, I got the whole world in my hands!"

Ics, as many a dead Djinn split into its component psyches and fused to the palms of its better half would tell you, were not the id to Djinn egos. They were much more terrible than that. They were the separate beast that lived inside and cared absolutely not one whit about the life and times of the common Djinn. They did not seek vengeance. Didn't retribute much. Far as anyone knew they never hunted down an enemy or forced spite down the throats of the cold, cruel world.

But they were the essence of collateral damage, and in war there are no civilians.

The scars on its palms itched thinking about the aborted revenue caused by *Milo Jetstream's Campaign.*

Chronic Djinn may have been reduced to a pool boy, but even a pool boy could slit the throats of a thousand men with a slippery knife on a dark night where the streetlights need service or it's kind of cloudy or the men have gotten laid off and are drunk to ease the burden but they still have to tell their wives…or, better put, for some unfathomable reason God designed any and everything to be a deadly weapon.

The all-consuming itch was annoying, so the Ic decided it would just have to collaterally make that itch go away.

It looked exactly like a grown-up Macaulay Culkin (for reasons best unknown).

The only thing it did as far as the Jetstreams was cause a huge early morning traffic jam that forced quite a bit of space between Ramses and Milo, and then got Milo's jeepney diverted by police along a ridiculously meandering route.

The Ic was aware of plans hastily set by its former host. It allowed elements of these to play out.

It cut off communication between the brothers.

Milo, Neon, Smoove and Fiona made up party one.

The Ic planted the impression of where they'd be in the next fifteen minutes; Chronic had made many phone calls on his friend's cell phone.

Milo knew when he was being corralled, but also knew that a log that rides a river long enough picks up the speed to crack a dam. Riding these rapids was the best way to end this, particularly as he had Smoove and Carel to keep Neon safe.

The Ic, though, saw to it he was cut off from them (except Neon) after the jeepney broke down and a massive surge of hospitality workers swamped the streets to get to work.

Thus on one side Fiona and Smoove were wondering how in the world people who regularly traveled to Atlantis could be like tourists in Times Square and lose half their party, and—after a while—on the other, a vampire, a Thoom, a priest and three Shiftless advanced toward Milo on the outskirts of an old parking lot on the far fringes of Aquino Airport.

This lot seriously overcharged considering how far it was from the terminals, so only those relegated to overflow used it. Right now it was effectively deserted, except for a few sporadic cars waiting for their owners to travel home.

Milo Jetstream couldn't do anything but sigh.

The Ic projected the itchy thoughts from the little men grafted to its palms straight into Milo's head.

"You think I don't have friends, Milo Jetstream? You think just because you ferried my powers frozen in a condom to some igloo somewhere that David Scott, the Chronic Djinn, has no resources at his command? I buy beer, Milo Jetstream, lots of beer, and beer gets you favors! Enjoy the vengeance of the Damned!" And for the first time ever in Milo's life Milo heard someone cackle maniacally.

David Scott, the former Chronic Djinn, now just destined for uncomfortably close relations with the knotty penis of an Ic, cackled like a fool.

Milo and Neon frowned at one another.

Neon looked aghast.

Milo realized she'd heard Chronic too.

"You tip for shit!" Chronic directed at Neon. "If not for the cleavage I'd have stopped serving you efficiently long ago!"

Earlier Milo had admired her resolve, resolve being a serious credit to inner beauty, but came a time when it was *highly* appropriate to tap the shoulder of a compatriot. "Milo…I'm freaking out."

"You go right ahead." He led her by the hand across the lot. This wasn't the time or place for a half-assed confrontation. The vampire, a mid-thirties careerist, was staying to the shadows, darting blurred but reasonably fashionable. Vampires were like cheetahs, fast in spurts but not so much over the long haul.

Milo kept an eye on her. She was too skinny to be any real threat, but with all that type A flowing through her veins there was no telling what she'd hyped herself up to undertake. She'd noticed the aforementioned priest too, and held back pending his move.

She'd never actually seen a Jetstream in person. For some reason she'd always thought Milo was short.

Nobody really noticed the three Shiftless.

Between Milo and the airport was the Priest, a steely-eyed mofo of grim visage and gritted teeth. Many priests in Manila wore lightweight white linen frocks over their street clothes. This one threw back the sides of his and pulled out two glossy white guns bigger than Jesus ever holstered.

Neon shouted, "Holy shit!" and backpedaled.

The Priest fired.

Milo grabbed her wrist and swung her in a fast arc. The bullet barely missed her.

The Priest was about thirty yards away. His frock billowed as he ran toward Milo, both guns raised to fire.

Milo really hoped this lady knew how to tuck and roll; he was about to fling her toward a lonely parked car. His spiral came around; when he released her he took off in the opposite direction.

Father Ignatius Poploski (Iggy Pop in another reality) was a good shot. There was nobody in the NRA who would say it was practical to run with both arms stuck straight out and amendment benefactors spitting like water on hot grease, but in the hands of a defrocked priest…it looked cool.

Damned if it didn't look cool.

But a good shot couldn't do anything against a highly uncooperative target.

Milo feinted, flipped and zigged the fight far enough away—but close enough to—Neon, all the while advancing the fight toward Iggy. People that shoot at you are thrown off when you run toward them; throws off the balance of power. Adrenalin surges made the Father sloppy. He accidentally winged one of the Shiftless after Milo drew his fire that way. The Shiftless clutched her shoulder and cussed as loud as an empty parking lot allowed, before charging the gun-toting holy rogue in anger. The second she'd seen the vamp and the priest she'd known the odds of anybody actually doing anything to Milo Jetstream weren't the greatest in the world. Shiftless folk tend to be realistic. So instead, why not rush boldly forward and reach the priest the same time as Milo with a double punch to the dumbass priest's head?

Iggy Poploski went down. She threw her entire weight at Milo, hoping the other two Shiftless were right behind her—but Milo wasn't there. Nothing she'd ever heard about Milo Jetstream told her he was that fast and knew jujitsu.

She only had a millisecond to think about this before he spin-kicked her feet from under her, grabbed a whole hunk of Shiftless mensware and yanked Shiftless Two into deflective position of Shiftless Three.

He'd been waiting for the necessary respite to take his pack from his back and pull out what would end this all—

That's when Valerie jumped out.

She looked waxy, and when his slamming blow across her jaw slid off like ice on butter he knew why; she'd lathered in sunscreen. That meant she was a neophyte vampire. Sensitivity to the sun lessened after a month.

She extended her fangs and tried to clamp down before the arm retracted. He spun and caught her in the back of the head with an elbow, then reversed momentum for a midsection roundhouse kick, pressing the attack till she fell backward.

The Djinn screamed in his head, *Swallow My Steaming Come of Vengeance, Milo Jetstream!*

The idiocy of this angered Milo enough that the type A vampire turned tail and ran, having seen something in his eyes that foretold the absolute worst few moments of her life mere seconds away. Milo pursued.

The other Two Shiftless rushed. They got within ten feet of Milo before three shots pockmarked an uncrossable line before them.

Neon, with two white guns, was very much pissed.

She shouted, "What?" as challenge, then popped off another for good measure.

The Shiftless froze. They subtly altered their postures to render themselves seen without being seen, and thought to walk away, seeing as Milo was opening up a serious can of issues on the skinny chick.

The gunshot at their heels surprised the hell out of their feigned invisibility.

"Run your monkey asses!" Neon shouted.

They ran, and in that action convinced themselves they'd had no pressing reason for going after Milo in the first place; as soon as they dissolved into the surroundings of a liquor store everything would be Oh dash Tay. Even in running, the Shiftless seemed made of bits of other human beings.

She fired another shot because they physically irked her.

Shiftless didn't run as a general course, so they stopped and looked at her wearing identical *'What the fuck?'* frowns.

Seeing her take better aim they communally agreed it was best to continue running.

Chronic Djinn screamed the Seven Screams of Loss like the point of a drill into Milo's brain.

"I slept with your mother! I'm less meaningless than you! High school was it! No love for you when you're weak! Your friends feel obliged! You should have been born white, you'd have more fun! No worthwhile popular culture in the last seventy years!"

That last one almost made Milo falter, and that almost was all a vampire needed to sneak a bite in. She only managed the tip of one tooth but, like many a mother would confirm, the tip is all it takes.

Milo yanked her head back, getting a good blonde twist of hair to keep her from running from the fist on its way.

Neon watched with a sick fascination. She herself had almost been snatched once, and had been through her share of pointless scrapes with boyfriends, but this woman was getting her ass kicked on a new and different level, one Neon didn't find herself objecting to because, obviously, the skinny chick was a weird level of strange herself.

Neon inventoried: she was in a parking lot holding a modified white Beretta off a priest, which she'd used to shoot at some shiftless mofos while this cute broheem from the Department of Homeland Security went all medieval on Ann Coulter's sister—

(right about here, Milo broke the vampire's leg; she went down screaming)

—so, yes, pretty much everything was that weird level of strange.

Milo waved Neon to him urgently.

She shook her head.

That's when Coulter's sister took hold of that skinny leg, gritted her teeth, and twisted to set the bone back in place.

Which was also when Neon ran like hell to Milo. They bolted across that parking lot, then another, then to the first commuter line they saw. Communications were still out. Milo hoped Ramses was having better luck than he was.

Milo wished this again about a half hour or so later.

By then, their plane was going down.

Not in the good way.

The pilot had been seized by the urge to masturbate himself into a frenzy from which there was no turning back. He got his thing caught in his zipper, which caused him to knock the plane into a nosedive. Sudden change popped an engine. The only good luck was Milo and Neon were the only passengers on the small twin engine.

The moment Milo flung open the cockpit door, he fully realized sometimes it's best to take whatever luck comes your way, no matter how small.

That was a landmass getting bigger through the windscreen.

Djinn's Ic gripped its knobby dick. This was about to get good.

Milo grabbed the controls and pulled. He wasn't a pilot but he knew planes were supposed to operate on the horizontal because the vertical was troublesome. He'd seen enough movies to know "Getting the Nose Up" was appropriate and prudent.

The pilot, sensitive to death, forcibly roused himself from the Ic's stupor and grabbed—in very pilot-like fashion—the controls, fighting the machine for supremacy.

Pilot lost.

"Find some water, brother," Milo advised.

"No time."

Then the pilot froze stock-still. There is pain, and then there's the realization that your penis is still firmly stuck in a zipper.

That's called clarity and focus to the exclusion of all else.

The plane was leveled enough that at least when it hit the ground to explode, it waited till they were a good distance from it.

~~~

Milo applied bandages to the pilot's delicate bits.

"What's your name, brother?"

The man mumbled something.

"Well, now they can call you sharkbite." He answered Neon's eyes bugged out behind him. "Levity heals, Ms. Temples."

"I don't think me sucking him off would help right now," she observed, but didn't his little half-dead ass perk up a touch?

She almost spat.

One kept explosions around him. The other crashed a plane so he could jack off. They were on the outskirts of probably some damn rainforest (no, she did not know if there were rainforests in or near the Philippines and did not care). She ached, she hurt, and—she slapped Milo upside the back of the head—she'd scraped both a knee and an elbow when he'd flung her in the parking lot.

"I need to get back to my plane," said the pilot.

"Dude, your plane just blew up."

The pilot stared down at Milo who was holding his sad, pale penis like a wounded puppy as he applied the last bandage. "Did it tear a nerve?" the prone man asked. "I can't feel my leg."

"It ain't there," Milo said. "Don't worry about it though."

There was a medicating patch above the stump of his knee, and contoured to the stump was a gelatinous blob that the pilot, Jacob Rao, could feel cooling as it solidified. Another patch was right above his groin.

The pilot looked at his former passengers. Milo, as evidenced by the large red stain sticking the shirt to his chest, had a cut across his pecs. Neon had a swollen eye and her hair was fucked.

The pilot was stretched out with his manhood bandaged and right leg somewhere off getting barbecued for whichever scavenger happened across it that night.

In a fit of hysterics he pointed this out to them.

Milo forcibly took the pilot's red shirt off and rolled it into a pillow.

"Whatever drugs you had on that plane," said Milo, "are gone. Rest comfortably. I need to go find something. Neon, if he decides to go, let him walk." Milo stood up. Wilderness, lots of wilderness, as far as the eye could see.

"We weren't the ones jacking off on a plane," said Milo, then he left.

Strawberry Tango

Two days ago Buford woke up in a box and met the most beautiful woman he had ever seen. His reinforced Plexiglas cage was distortion free, showing every nuance of her rosy skin, the crow's feet, grey-stranded hair, and greenest eyes that ever laughed at a man.

She walked blithely in negligees and slippers, which let him know he wasn't intended to live.

What made him wish for personal relations, however, was her laugh. It was the most spontaneous, full-throated, entirely at someone else's expense laughter he'd ever experienced outside his own. No pretense of "I'm not laughing at you, I'm laughing with you"—no, this handsome, joyfully mature woman relished this laughter.

The fact that he was naked sometimes troubled him.

The cage contained fully exposed timed shower, toilet, sink, and one body sized foam pad. Meals were whenever she felt like feeding him. So far he hadn't had one.

Until this moment, when she brought a plate of strawberries that she fed through the vacuum door.

"No whipped cream?" he asked. He was serious.

The smile lit her emerald eyes even more than the circle of light in which she stood. The room was otherwise pitch dark.

Motion-sensing guns were trained on the cage at all times. There was only one person given free access to the room, and that was her.

Buford judged the time of day by her general dress. She wore a red terry bathrobe now but didn't look freshly washed (her hair was still perfectly coiffed), so he guessed about early evening-ish.

He forced himself to eat the food leisurely. She'd given him twelve. He was down to nine.

"What if I'm not who you think I am?" he asked.

She scratched her butt through the terry while she answered. "If not? You've seen a half-naked woman. You've had some very sweet strawberries. And if anybody finds you scattered through four different states, you died for no particular reason. Since you are..."

"Yes?"

She undid the sash on her robe so the knot wouldn't bunch at her stomach, pulled a plush, wheeled stool from the darkness, and sat.

She still wore the everyday bra and panties, which were nice enough.

But a man—even a man who's a starving prisoner threatened with death by dismemberment—will still always hope for sexy lingerie.

"Rough today?" asked Buford, leaning against the wall of his cage as though about to chat her up in a bar. "It'd be acceptable if you'd let me see you naked. Nudity is very liberating to an exchange of ideas."

"Drop the plate lower. I can't talk with that looking at me." She had a warm, perfectly modulated voice. Buford pegged her as media-related, local anchor or such on one of the larger affiliates.

He complied. "I appreciate your keeping things warm in here," he said. "You laugh enough as it is. When I get out you'd better hope by God I still think you're interesting."

"When? Buford, nobody knows where you are. Nobody knows you're missing. When they find out, we'll have had you so thoroughly programmed that each successive clone will remember my middle name without ever having met me."

"To what purpose?"

"To our purpose, dummy."

That was all the answer he deserved to get. They regarded one another a silent moment.

"I'm guessing you're the Hive Queen?"

"I knew you were going to make that analogy. By the time people understand the Thoom it'll be too late. We're the last intellectuals," she said. "Do you think something so patently ridiculous doesn't have unparalled genius behind it? Look at your own organization."

"I'd like more strawberries," he said. He set the tray on the floor. "The beauty of my 'organization' is that it doesn't exist. That, sweet lady, is the seat of power and longevity."

"The famed immortality."

"No one will remember—I don't mean to be indelicate, but what is your name?—no one will remember the name whatever in two hundred years but 'Buford' will continue to own the wind."

"We don't doubt that. But Shakespeare said, *What's in a name?*"

"Learn the full passage."

"I know it."

"Then the rose remains a rose," he said.

"Until it's spliced, Mr. Buford Bone." She stood up but didn't bother looping the robe. "You'll meet our friend Gene soon enough."

"I see. I'm not scared, you know."

"You think I need the fear of a naked old man in a cage with no hope of escape? I could open that cage and have your ass kicked by the last frat boy to party with the coming President. He's standing guard outside this room. Has authorization to shoot anyone trying to enter who's not me. Doubly so on exiting. We are surrounded by a web of such checkpoints."

"Then let me pose a series of questions you won't answer: where exactly are we; how'd you clone Milo; and how long before I get some clothing?"

"Tray in the pizza door, please."

He put it in, pushed it forward, and closed the door.

She opened the outer, slid the tray out, and closed the door.

She disappeared into the darkness. Her slippers made comforting sounds.

BlOOd

The pilot died.

Milo draped the red shirt over the pilot's face and shoulders. He put eighteen large stones around the body at equidistant, linear points to shield against scavengers. Animals hated obvious precision.

The next order of business was getting Neon to safety, which for now was a matter of establishing shelter. The explosion hadn't brought rescue operations so he assumed their locale was remote.

Communications were still out and the Djinn kept nattering at his mind so much it was difficult maintaining focus.

For some reason the Ic hadn't gotten bored and left yet.

When Neon bent forward to let her arms dangle and stretch her back, Milo knew why. There was a reason Ics grew Djinns on the palms of their hands. In a word: magic fingers.

Milo glanced away. He shielded his eyes against the bright sky.

His pack contained a collapsible two-person tent, but it was best first to get a lay of the land.

That's when he and Neon first noticed the shortish man wearing faded cut-offs a little ways by a clearing.

An Asian pygmy.

"Fuck's a pygmy doing here?" said Neon.

The man confidently approached, regarding the two with definite intent.

"Where are we that they have pygmies?" Neon continued. She noted the dour expression on Milo's face. "What?"

"He likes you."

The pygmy had a smile.

"He's way down there. How can—"

The little guy broke into a trot and reached behind his back, pulling out a precision compact bow with arrow, and notched it. He picked up speed.

"OK, what the fuck is he doing?"

"Neon? Run." She was already gone and moving faster with each step. He spun on his heel and caught up. She was moving for the stand of trees ahead. He followed.

An arrow barely missed his thigh.

They entered the copse of trees.

The four who were waiting inside pulled out machetes. They obviously didn't watch movies, because they all charged at once and looked like they knew what they were doing. They wouldn't all swing at once, but machetes swinging in sequence would ruin any bright day.

Milo had seconds to act. He needed just a few more.

He whipped around and kneeled behind Neon.

All four paused, confusion clearly shared, which was enough for him to reach into his pack and pull out a piece of futuristic whup ass if ever these gentlemen had seen one.

They stopped short.

"Back your ensorcelled asses up," said Milo through gritted teeth.

They immediately adopted the universal body language of *no harm no foul*.

Then they saw the look on Neon's face. Being sensible, they ran.

At certain times the raw power contained in a woman is beyond fearsome. Even the Djinn's babbling was blocked for a moment while Milo heard crystal clearly:

"No. The fuck. You didn't."

Her lips hadn't moved. He heard it in his mind.

Her anger killed the Ic's influence for miles around.

This respite wouldn't last.

He grabbed the cobra by the arm.

"Come on." He pulled a thigh holster and strapped it on the run, keeping eye on the shapes maintaining uncertain pace with them through the trees and deliberate to avoid looking at Neon at all, which allowed her anger to fade and the antagonists to recall why exactly this man needed to be dead.

Chronic Djinn hurled a motivating epithet.

"Your fried penis won't feed their smallest child!" Djinns being assholes even in death. Of course the pygmies weren't cannibals. On any given day they were just a bunch of folks ribbing with various naturalist camera crews.

The group winding through the trees wouldn't hurt the woman, but couldn't figure out why she'd aligned herself with such a loser.

In nature programs the overhead shot would reveal lions converging on the gazelles in classic intersect strategy: so long as the cats forced the bounding beasts along a set path, the paths of hunter and prey would inevitably cross.

But one of the gazelles never cut and charged a surprised lion, clotheslining the cat and swiping its machete to become a whirling faun dervish. The overripe forest cleared at a craggy area of dirt and rocks in the neighborhood of a man-made cave set in a hillock. Neon instinctively ran for the cave.

Milo wished she hadn't done that. He bee-lined after her, accidentally dropping the machete but purposely throwing a concussion grenade behind him. The shock wave blew a nice crater in the earth and made the pursuers think twice about entering the hunting shelter. Sunlight extended a few feet into the mouth of the cave; beyond that, shapes became indistinguishable.

The Ic fed the pursuers memories of hatred and enemies, making them fire a volley of arrows inside for good measure.

Milo hoped Neon had the frame of mind to flatten against a side wall. He threw another concussion grenade.

He waited.

Two minutes passed.

It was quiet out there. Then he heard them talking amongst themselves. He didn't know the language but the tone was definitely one of confusion.

"Little bit of a standoff here," he said, solely for Neon's benefit.

From out of the darkness, her voice: "Am I going to die today?"

"Not today."

That was nice to know. She believed him.

"I can't get this voice out of my head." She sounded wooden.

"My fat dick bounces upon the nether cheeks of your grave!"

Milo didn't say anything.

Neon flung dirt that hit him squarely in the chest.

"Homeland fucking Security. I'm not even *at* home!"

They could make each other out well enough now. They moved even deeper into the cave.

"I'm not Homeland Security."

"I don't give a farthing damn if you're the hero of the Fatherland."

"I keep a man named Buford from running your life."

"We're in a cave! You don't keep shit. Who in the unholy hell is Buford? And that fucking Star Trek crew of yours," she demanded. "Who the hell are they?" She made a dash for the cave entrance. Milo grabbed her forearm. "I'm on vacation, goddamit!" She yanked away from him. "You lied to me," and her tone was more hurt than angry. "People are trying to kill me and I don't know why. I'm picking up some weird-ass talk radio devoted to cussing you out. I saw some cable channel freaky shit in a parking lot. A man with a priest's collar tried to shoot me. The radio station is my waiter. Your name is Milo Jetstream." She focused on the dim light from his eyes. "What'd I miss, Milo Jetstream? Besides pygmies, because how the fuck does one end a weird day if not for pygmies?"

The vampire's bite had numbed his arm to the point that now, when he had no answer and she punched him hard in the arm, he didn't even feel it.

She reared back to punch something less stoic.

One of the indistinct shapes in the cave moved. It moved in a way that freezes all human motion: surreptitiously. Surreptitious animals are either deadly or good eating, but rarely both.

She could punch Milo later.

She edged closer to him.

"How long do we stay in here?" she asked. "Don't answer; I swear to God I'll punch you in the throat. All this, and you haven't panicked yet? You're one of those hard asses who never worries about dying."

"I worry about dying all the time," said Milo. "But I have a job to do." He picked up a stick and began poking at the cave's darker nooks for poisonous things.

"You against Buford, huh?"

"Yes."

A huge centipede commuter-trained between them.

He waited for it, but she remained surprisingly calm.

"You ever heard of Malthus Zoog? Or Bubba Foom? Did you know that the Loch Ness Monster is a social scientist not very good at her job? Know that we are being studied by fifteen different species, all terrestrial? Buford does. That ghosts hang around mostly to watch people have sex? That babies bend time and space on a regular basis?"

"That one I knew," she interjected.

The cave was small, but brother got his pace on.

"All life aspires to music; kill the music, kill the spark! Emotion as commodity. Any news channel ever report that when we finally freed the aliens in Area Fifty-one they were thoroughly pissed and plan to come back with a vengeance? I hate space; I'm not looking forward to that shit—"

She timed his pace so that on this pass she grabbed him by the face, looked him in the eye to get his attention, and held him.

In a smaller voice he said, "Had you ever heard of me?"

"Not in any real sense," she said. She held his face until she felt his heart rate slow.

"I'm real," he said.

"Hell yeah to that."

They were in a cave with centipedes thick as lengths of frayed rope and a smell like ass on a summer day. His arrogance had caused this.

A snake peered out from a tight crevice trying to decide the best way to get past them without having to bite anyone. It was colorful and pretty, so it didn't have to be very imaginative. It said screw it and zipped out to strike.

Milo caught it mid-lunge and whipped it out to open air with one motion.

An arrow speared the snake and carried it out of view.

"Tell me again why they're not coming in here," said Neon.

He patted his thigh. "Because I've got this."

"Either you're trying to impress me or you don't realize you don't have a gun."

He looked at the holster. It was empty.

"Correction," he said. "They're out there trying to figure out how to use it on us." Milo sighed. Then he searched the cave's deeper recesses with a flare, ushered Neon there, and took up watch far enough from the entrance that they couldn't see him easily but near enough to repel. He tossed the stick to her saying, "If anything moves, kill it."

"I thought just the colorful stuff was dangerous."

As of this moment a depressed lemming was dangerous. He told her so.

"And it's granted that doesn't fire bullets," Neon said from behind him.

"Afraid it's more Star Trek."

"Phasers? Hell yeah. I want one. Stun, right?" she asked.

"Basically. We call it a focum."

"Excuse me?"

"Focused microwave."

"So we're popcorn they start shooting that off in here," she said.

"It'll only fire for certain people."

"I don't want to wait."

"Know what? We're not." He sat. Lotus position. "I need a little silence."

The silence was broken after a minute or two by the sound of the stick whacking something repeatedly.

After another minute he got up. "I'm going out, getting my gun, and shooting 'em all."

"Good man," said Neon.

He heard another whump, then stood to leave.

"Fuck 'em up," she said.

He crouched into a runner's position, dug his feet into the dirt, closed his eyes for a deep breath of one…then launched himself outward as only Milo Jetstream should do.

Interims
Three, Four
and Five

Bubba Foom was the single most powerful human psychic in the world. The voltage clipped to his testicles made sure the subtle controls he exerted on the thirteen Jetstream clones were diligently followed.

There was a large screen real-time display six feet from his face of his seventeen-year-old son strapped naked and unblindfolded to a narrow bed. Foom didn't know where his son was, and died more and more between blinks.

A constant stream of commercial jingles kept Bubba Foom's wits further at bay. State of the art speakers issued every inane note and lyric with pristine clarity.

But the tall man hadn't wandered the loud, intrusive world without developing a few outs.

You couldn't get into a mind without having a way out. These closed minds here were useless. But his people—there would be *somebody* out there searching, openly yearning, *needing* some ineffable sense of righteousness…

Raffic? That you?

Foom?

They have my son.

The wordless contact lasted less than a millisecond.

~~~

Meanwhile the Mad Buddha was tired. He refused to drink blood. Hunger, vampiric and human, sucked the life from him. Bubba Foom was in Iowa with electrodes stuck to his nuts. The Buddha was keenly sensitive to locations. Only person alive who never knew where he was going but never needed directions.

He moved in the direction of the Atlantidean capital. Nobody knew about the presence of vampires in Atlantis, bloodletting little ticks. It was up to him to make sure it remained that way, since, by the time he was done, they would every last one of them have been quietly bested.

Then back to Bubba Foom.

~~~

"Ramses, what the *hell* is going on?" demanded Fiona.

"Quiet!" Too many twists had hit them for this to be random. Separated, equipment out, and Captain Desiree Quicho suddenly unable to tell right from left. "This is Milo's story. He'll finish it."

"And what do we do?" said Fiona.

The chaos of Manila streamed unawares around them. "We wait."

BlOOd
and clarity

She was tired of waiting.

It hadn't been long, but still. There'd been such a flurry of noise she was sure he was face down with a porcupine back—and that was a terrible thought—and in a matter of moments she'd have to kick the ass of people attempting to enter the cave.

She tightened grip on the stout stick and approached the mouth, pausing to also borrow a grenade from Milo's pack.

Just before getting to the mouth she kicked off her sandals. The following might require an ass kicking with bare feet.

She stepped out.

Milo was on the ground to her right, but not face down. Kneeling. Unconscious pygmies littered the area. His back was to her and he was making scooping and patting motions near the ground.

She was about to call his name when he slit his wrist.

She grabbed at a bra she no longer wore.

Back in her old home she'd wanted to be queen of an island. This is why it's good never to dream. God listens.

"It's OK," said Milo. He didn't glance to see if she moved. "Blood is a special substance. Very powerful." He made a ruddy circle around the figure he'd made in the dirt.

"Very binding. Smart people fear it," he said, but she was gone, running back from the cave with his pack and dropping to her knees to rummage for bandages or a canister of the goop he'd used on the Red Shirt's stump. She found the goop and lathered his wrist in it.

"Blood and magic should be feared," he said.

He was entirely loopy.

Why all the fine brothers gotta be crazy!?

"I'm binding the Djinn's hatred to my blood," he explained, as if, oh, that explained it all, do carry on. "If the Ic doesn't abandon him, it's stuck here too. Ics are…"

"Shut up."

This crazy man had just slit his wrist.

The decision was made.

She claimed it: she jumped up and knocked him squarely in the head with the stick, then snatched up his pack. She didn't knock him out but she hurt the hell out of him, and pain was best used to advantage.

She ran. He seemed to have everything but a flame sword in that bag; she was confident she could defend herself for a few days if necessary.

She hurriedly made her way toward where, hopefully, she might run into some pavement.

~~~

Milo fought through pain to complete the Binding. Chronic's taunts were dim now. It might have been a good thing Neon'd taken off, as the last stroke was urinating on the totem and there are some things simply not meant for a first date.

"This piece of yours is mine forever, Jetstream," a tiny voice boasted like a gnat in his brain.

Binding him also meant Milo had to leave a piece of his own soul there. "There are bits of me scattered all over this globe, Chronic. You're not special."

"Just accept defeat and shut up!"

"Dude. You're trapped in a mound of pee, blood and dirt. With a piece of me I haven't used since puberty," he said, briefly taking his eyes off the humanoid mound to track Neon's progress.

"I was on top of the world," moaned the fading gnat.

"World rolls, Chronic," Milo said, shaking off the last of the ceremony and zipping up. The Djinn's broadcast abruptly stopped. "Dumbasses on top tend to forget that."

Now, if he wasn't mistaken, Neon had his pack and was running around with a grenade in her hand.

That wouldn't do.

He lurched forward. His bitten arm was now completely numb.

It looked to be a long evening.

Threats in the City

William Fruehoff despised bovine nature, and cities were designed to produce tons of it. If something was low enough to be hated, it was low enough to be controlled. Money flowed into Nonrich, which flowed it outwards into corporations and enterprises that touched every aspect of all lives from the food to the media chain, and the world's populace mooed on.

Buford had dictated: "The best way to destroy your enemies is to give them the means to do it themselves." Nonrich had a cadre of kidnapped conspiracy nuts on hand in underground areas to keep abreast of the pulse of the world. A few of them had once been high-level Nonrich employees. This underground holding area was called "Outside the Box," which is where, moments ago, he had been threatened to be sent if he didn't come up with results.

He faced Aileen Stone (not her last name) with the bravado of seven Six Sigma completions, albeit humbling his eye contact with the proper conciliation.

Aileen Stone never traveled alone. Adam and Eve always traveled with her, and yes they were, but only she and Buford knew. Adam and Eve never spoke a word but were rarely hesitant to nonverbally let a person know precisely how pissed off they were at the world.

"Aileen," said Fruehoff, "he told us he'd be away on business," he reminded her. "You know that means don't ask and don't follow."

"Don't ask and don't follow is what you tell the valet," she said. "Jetstreams in Manila means field trip is no longer part of the picture. Let me remind you it was your turn to know where he was. That's not a question you ever want to say 'I don't know' to."

"Reprographics is already torturing our Thoom operatives, Aileen." It was good to use first names. Names defused situations.

Except Aileen (not her first name) was one of those trick devices that exploded no matter which wire was cut.

She drew back a lock of silver hair then hauled off and slapped him.

He wasn't so shocked she'd slapped him as he was she'd mussed his hair. Perfect hair was critical to maintaining control of any situation. Instantly he'd become wet paper towel.

He fiercely wanted to brush his lock back into place but he didn't dare move. Eve, as perfect and toned as art, had a decidedly wishful hardening of the crow's feet around her eyes.

"Tell me what I know one more time," said Aileen.

Adam, the other half of Aileen's constant guard, very blatantly rose from his chair and stood behind Fruehoff.

"Oh come on!" Fruehoff said. "I'm popping asses to get this resolved. On *my* watch. And I don't see *this* helping much."

"Help implies you're doing something more than walking around with your dick in your hand," she said, matching ire for ire. "Help," she said, perched on the edge of her desk, leaning to his face, "implies weakness. Weakness is a sin—"

Oh God, with that again, thought Eve.

"You're torturing ten when you should be torturing twenty. I'd hope you know by now about the cloning facility." That meant she was willing to insult his intelligence. He glared at her. "Ante's been upped, Bill. That means, Bill, that the war won't be televised. We gave this country Shock and Awe and look what they did with it. A ghastly war that should've lasted two weeks."

"I've got a national catastrophe waiting in the wings if anybody peers in my window," said Fruehoff. "Seriously, we're fighting groups of misfits and freaks who don't even agree amongst themselves. We're two miles ahead of them; so what if they set us back one step? And clone or no clone, Buford *is* America. America *is* the goddamned world. We've won, they've lost, so let me go about my goddamned job of finding out what the hell happened to the greatest man alive. Thank. You."

"Succeed at your job or Adam and Eve will pound your nuts into quiche," said Aileen before sending him away, because after that what point was there saying anything more?

Bubba Foom: *Now?*
    Unseen Clone Benefactor: *Not yet.*

Bond.
Eternal Bond

Milo stopped her by screaming the truth. Not too many men use the 'I've been bitten by a vampire!' gambit to convince a lady of urgent sincerity.

She hadn't figured out how to arm the concussion grenades but she held one at the ready anyway.

Milo held his wrist for viewing. He pulled the goop bandage away.

"It's already clotted. I had to keep squeezing it to make the blood come out."

"The waiter's voice has stopped," she said and barely believed she was saying it.

"You're psychic. Your waiter was what's called a Djinn. Genie."

"Bigfoot?"

"Rather not talk about him."

"UFOs?"

"I've got two…but I've never been in space."

Overload finally hit her; fatigue, fainting.

"Got you." He caught her up and carried her huddled body to shade, cradling her in his lap while he rummaged for his phone. Leaning against a tree, he called Ramses. "Ram…come get me."

"You sound bad."

"Come get me. We need to regroup, brother," said Milo. "I got sloppy. Again." He rubbed the spot where he'd been bitten. The skin had healed but it was still new…and it itched. He signed off.

Ramses made a snap decision, one he was loath to make but right now there were other concerns. Neon and Yvonne needed the familiarity of a false sense of security. He called in a favor. Normally the worlds of luxury and false senses of security didn't cross the Jetstreams' path, but there was a safe house in Arizona known only to a select few, even among the Agents of Change. The personal vertical jet of the billionaire inventor who owned it, Tony Sterk, picked them up on the island Milo had landed on, and deposited them into the safety of walls, rooms, comfort, and respite. The house was underground, shielded both standard and esoteric, and offered enough immediate normalcy that Neon and Yvonne relaxed their suspicions long enough to soak tensed, bunched muscles after Ele, who'd seen to their cuts and bruises during the flight, empathically tended to their emotional needs.

Ele was small and comforting. The world: suddenly too big and screaming.

Steaming water and the low hum of filtration now calmed scattered thoughts for Yvonne and Neon. The feeling of absolute solitude was divine. They'd been told to remain in there as long as they wanted; they wouldn't be interrupted or disturbed in any way.

The hot tub was big enough that even stretched at opposite ends their toes didn't touch. Feet bobbed underwater weightless and free.

"Eucalyptus?" Yvonne asked, eyes closed.

"Please," said Neon.

Yvonne swiped a finger across the whirlpool's touchpad. A refreshing hint of mint joined the steam.

Those two words constituted an exhausting conversation.

Both women inched their bodies a little deeper into the warm, swirling waters, stretched their arms along the rim, and bled adrenalin off until, either briefly or for quite some time, both went to sleep.

~~~

"Explain this to me." Yvonne locked the brothers to the spot with the hard set of her jaw.

"A war that's been going on for a long time got real tiresome today," said Milo. "Neon saw a vampire, heard a Djinn, saw the true church, and reawakened one of her sleeping chakras."

Yvonne glanced Neon's way. "You did all that?"

"Girl, I've had a helluva day."

"Fiona Carel, Luscious Johnson Smoove, Desiree Quicho, Ele," Milo introduced.

There was something subtly different about Ele now that they were sitting in a responsible, adult group. It wasn't easy putting a finger on it.

"Ele's from Atlantis."

There you go. "Make it a little more outlandish for me," said Yvonne. "Tell me about Bigfoot."

"We don't talk about him," said Milo.

Yvonne looked at the rest of the crew; their stony silence agreed.

A tray of almonds and shelled peanuts sat on a handmade driftwood table in front of her. Yvonne chewed her cheek a moment, took a handful, and crunched. Loudly. The pin wafted through the silence of the moment, unhurried toward its penultimate drop.

Which came with a hard bite into a hard nut.

"Who are you," she said, refilling her hand's supply, "And don't give me any Twilight Zone Star Trek bullshit. Please."

"We're people," said Milo.

"People."

He nodded.

"And the rest of that?"

"They're vampire, Djinn, Thoom and Buford."

"There's the world," said the other Jetstream, "and then there's the world that creates the world."

"Roswell?"

"Yes," said Ramses, nodding her along.

"And those are your real names?"

"As far as we know," said Milo.

"And you're from Atlantis?" she asked Ele.

"I am."

"You are. OK. OK." Yvonne stood. "One of you crazy bastards is taking us home. If I have to knock every last one of you…"

Ramses pointed to the dog tags around her neck. "I didn't bring those back to bring harm to you."

"So you're saying we're free to go."

"Never our decision to make," said Ramses.

Neon, though, remained seated. She spoke to Yvonne, but addressed the group: "Remember those stories about the Pig Man and Bloody Mary? We've had this weird shit in our faces our whole lives, and I can't pretend I'm on the same level as yesterday. They're telling us this woman is from Atlantis and we *believe* them. That should tell you something."

"Tells me we've probably been drugged."

"All that stuff about Buford makes sense. Who in fuck heard about Kardashians then all of a sudden you can't piss without hitting their feet?"

"Smoke, luv," said Smoove.

"Big, thick, nasty, stank-ass stupid smoke," said Neon.

"*Ghetto Fabulous,*" Smoove threw out. "*Thug Life, Hood Rat.*"

"Benifer. *Bradgelina,* for crying out loud," added Desiree. "Have you any idea how much money and resources are poured into keeping you on that diet? There is a living, systemic juggernaut that crushes entire towns beneath its feet as it slouches toward born-again Bethlehem."

"Tragedies?" said Fiona. "The big stuff? War on terror and whatnot? Marketing strategies."

"The Patriot Act," said Desiree. "How dumb does a country have to be to wholeheartedly accept something called the Patriot Act? It screams, 'You're stupid, jingoistic and easily led!'"

"The world being fucked and stupid is a twice told tale," said Yvonne, still standing, still challenging.

"There's a reason the world's fucked and stupid," said Desiree.

"It's called suburbia for a reason," said Milo. "The layer beneath."

"Those who fuck the world wear condoms," said Ramses.

"And the fucked daily wash their faces with the collected jizz," said Smoove.

"Succinct as hell," said Neon.

"Call 'em like they be, sister."

"This shit is for real, huh?" said Yvonne.

"As my love for my wife," answered Smoove.

"You're a simple, sincere brother," Yvonne noted.

"I try to be."

Yvonne sat and put the bowl of nuts in her lap. "Then where do we go from here?" she said simply and sincerely.

"You don't have a life to go back to?" said Smoove.

"We liberated money from a neighborhood drug kingpin," said Yvonne. "Happened to be my cousin. I know: family's a bitch."

"Robin Hood situation," Neon clarified.

"Long story short: life is what we make it," said Yvonne.

"That, luv," said Smoove, "is wisdom."

NO
secrets

At nineteen Buford had accepted a missionary post to Nepal, even though he had no intention of converting anyone. He went because he'd heard a man could levitate.

When he saw with his own eyes a scrawny twig of a nearly naked man levitating freely off the ground, he knew with pristine clarity that the world's secrets were meant entirely for his use and benefit. Alzheimer's had claimed both his parents, so there was no difficulty assuming another persona. Not so much a new identity; personas were tools to be used at will. Everything in the False Prophet Buford's world was a potential tool. It took him two years of fasting and cleansing to learn levitation, which, shown to the right people, was a powerful recruiting tool, particularly among wealthy nutcases, of which there were ridiculously many.

Charles Eyelet, then premiere of the Thoom, took interest in a floating young man with steel-grey eyes, until he started to wonder why he always thought of himself as a lug wrench whenever the boy was around.

And now here he was, the most powerful man in the world, imprisoned by the idiots he'd damn near become the leader of. Buford hated irony.

The irony of almost being the leader of the Thoom was an irksomely useless tool right now. Buford stared through the glass cage.

So far they hadn't made any demands or threats. This was worrisome. Since the age of twelve Buford hadn't been bored a day in his life, but now he was reduced to staring at the void, and it was boring.

Staring upward made him think about the Mount. There was power there that no one, not even the Jetstreams, understood. Something *intrinsic* to the world... and he'd failed to possess it. His hubris hadn't fit in his pants.

Buford pushed those thoughts away. Failure was an outright terror not meant for civilized Man.

What would possess the Thoom to clone Milo Jetstream? Even rhetorically it was guaranteed to blow up in their faces. They knew it. But Thoom and logic were often mutually exclusive.

Of course, if Buford ever got hold of the clones...

A cadre of Milo Jetstreams running around would make damn good tools.

~~~

The end of the mundane day was the only time to put on a comfortable robe and know without doubt one was their better self.

It had been a long day of secret phone calls and coded open-communiqués, not to mention acquiring four major Hollywood stars as Thoom-front soldiers. True Humans Over Ordinary Man was a subtle sell, but a necessary sell, but as *Triumphant Heuristics* it went over that much better. It was true that it was all in the name, and the oldest meaningful joke in the world was that god spelled backwards was dog. Madam loved the oldies, because there hadn't been anything new in a thousand years. The proto-Bufords had made sure of that. Controlled obsolescence kept the world going 'round.

Her silver hair had one red streak in it, a look which complemented the sky blue robe. The blue robe had the careful silk thread count of dozens of child laborers. It was of the sort that slid on, as though her skin was pure glass and the robe merely there to polish it. The fabric even whispered over bra and panties, themselves of a quality not meant for touching by the ordinary.

Every Thoom wore perfectly fitting, private tickling, moisture wicking underwear, excellent as excellent could be.

But not as good as hers.

Madam's underwear changed the courses of nations. Buford Bone would never see the light of day again, but he'd definitely see her bloomers.

Large monitors came on for her as she moved from room to room. A new disease outbreak in Burkina Faso; Africa would be strip-mined the next eight lifetimes anyone had. Food and medical aid to Kabul blocked; new terrorist group; terrorist groups had PR departments. Madam laughed. Wonderful, necessary evils that the surface dwellers needed in order to keep going on.

She thought about the man—god, really—currently in the box. He was the sort of man she wouldn't have thought twice about if she didn't know who he was, but inside the Box it was her special duty to see that he thoroughly realized the impotence of his situation. He had abandoned the Thoom; he flagrantly questioned Thoom validity—

And he made more money than the Thoom. Way more. Can't forgive a bastard for that.

He thought he was important and behaved accordingly.

People who *thought* they were important did nothing but stand in the way of Madam on her way to *doing* important things.

While there wasn't a single guard visible in her house, there could be a race riot outside and she'd still be fixing herself a sandwich. Buford was four levels below as she padded a layer of silk away from bare-assed through her well-appointed home. Safety was not an issue. As with the Lost Clan of No-See-Ums, lack of visibility had nothing to do with impact.

She descended the levels. A boob itched in the three-hundred sixty degree monitored XY axis car and she scratched it. She had scratched ass, armpit, crotch and foot with utter indifference.

She shined that indifference now in the face of Buford.

"Full lights," she commanded.

Buford rolled upright and sat cross-legged on his mat, squinting.

"You're trying to make me fall in love with you," he said. "Blue's my favorite color."

"A sky you'll never see again, sir." She perched on her plush stool, doing nothing but regarding him a moment. "You haven't asked a single pertinent question yet."

"I make it a point never to ask questions of people who have answers. Makes me look weak. When does the brainwashing start, sweetheart?"

She didn't answer.

"Women like to ask men is sex that important to us," said Buford. "They think the question elicits contrite rumination. Short answer to an old question: yes."

"That's how you want to play? Nothing grander for your final hours? Trite sexuality?"

"You're not likely to come in here for the real thing. Trite will do."

"You're a bit of an idiot. Full dark," she said, then disappeared into the darkness.

"Men of power usually are," he called out. "Let's try to make tomorrow a little more interesting, shall we?" said Buford.

Dust
and
Shadows

This was new. Neon had flown many times, but never in something that could conceivably go into space. They were on their way to find something called "Bubba Foom."

The clouds so far below made Neon think of some alien world populated by marshmallow people: fat, comfortable people stretching as far as she could see, and above the roof of the world, Heaven only knew.

She settled resolutely back.

As long as somebody knew.

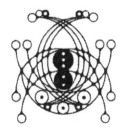

~~~

They touched down in a land of dust and shadows, having gotten word from Bubba Foom's wife that he hadn't turned up; that their son was missing.

She was also the world's leading researcher on vampire genetics.

She met them with the grim visage reserved for heroes who've come too late.

"Foom hasn't been here since we left Atlantis," said Asme Du Ikare as Ramses and Milo clanked the last steps of the gangplank, her Nigerian accent making each word its own pointed statement. She was long and skinny with a single braid she sometimes used as a weapon.

"Agents of Change?" asked Milo.

"Not even them. Nobody knows where he is. Or Michael. Why do I smell cocoa butter?"

"Sunscreen," said Milo.

"No the hell you aren't," Asme said.

"Yes."

"Milo Jetstream is a vampire. Sons of two bitches!" she said.

"It's OK."

"I'm nowhere near finding a cure, Milo."

"Asme?" he said, dropping palms on her shoulders.

"Yes?"

"Do I care?"

It was an old joke between them.

"With all my heart," she said, barely relaxing her corded muscles.

Neon and Yvonne emerged from the plane. Du Ikare bowed a head to them in such a way it was clear they were all complete and utter sisters.

The newcomers nodded in kind, proceeding past Milo, Du Ikare and Ramses to wait patiently at the end of the gangplank.

Du Ikare turned an eye to Ramses.

"Are you changed?" she asked.

"No," he said.

"We take what we can get," she said, and failed horribly at a smile.

The metal gangplank led to a series of stairs and hallways that Bubba Foom had designed as a vertical labyrinth. Most incorrectly thought of labyrinths as intricate mazes, when they were simply winding paths that always led one back to where one started, in this case a hall of mirrors with one clearly delineated door somehow freed from reflection.

"Fiona still pretending to be a pilot?" Ikare asked. The others hadn't departed the plane.

"They'll be out shortly," said Milo.

The door led to a sand garden.

"Foom changes this pattern every time he comes home," she said. "This hasn't been changed or disturbed. They got him when he got off the boat."

"None of us saw each other during the cruise, Du," said Ramses.

"Somebody connected," she said.

The sole common denominator of the Joyeux Voyage cruise ship was Neon and Yvonne, and no matter how that needle pointed it was not correct.

They entered Foom's home.

Ramses studied. "Doesn't help that Michael keeps the place spotless while he's gone," he said.

"We try to get him to act his age," said Asme. Her eyes were red-rimmed and she was fidgety. She was not normally fidgety.

Foom had gotten comfortably rich very young. It was ridiculously easy coming into money when one was the world's most effective psychic. His home had every security device known to Man and several not, all for the purpose of protecting Michael.

"I've been here a day and checked every sensor, every log, every recording. Nothing shows up. Who does that sound like?"

"Sounds like Buford on a very good day," said Ramses. Bubba Foom was no one's trifle. "Foom gets distracted easily. He told me it keeps him sane."

"We should've got his ass last time," said Ikare.

Milo and Ramses examined the grounds themselves, but Du Ikare not finding anything meant there wasn't anything to find. Michael Foom was her son, and the person hadn't been born who could harm him in her presence.

"I can't help thinking this has to do with the Mad Buddha," she said.

"We assumed he never made it to Atlantis," said Milo.

"What if he did?" said Ramses.

"Vampires can shield," said Du Ikare, looking askance at Milo.

"Vampires in Atlantis," said Milo. "Sounds like regurgitainment."

"Bad regurgitainment," said Ramses.

"Vampires out here," said Du Ikare.

"Vampires got Buford," said Ramses. "He did get commercials shown in theatres. Forced them to paddle harder. Vampires are only neutral till the next big production deal."

"Vampires," Milo said, "in Atlantis. Son of a bitch."

"Do you feel anything?" Du Ikare asked. "Any different? Any…connection?"

He shook his head.

Her soul visibly dropped.

"We have to backtrack Michael," said Ramses. "How old's he now?"

"Seventeen."

"My gods, we're getting old," said Ramses.

"Praise be," said Du.

"Who does he hang with?" Ramses asked.

"Nobody knows about this place."

"I mean among our people," he said.

Milo glanced sharply at his brother. "You're talking traitors," he said. "That ain't us."

"Us expands."

"Two ladies on a plane," said Du Ikare. "No offense."

"I'm not about to believe one of ours engineered against us."

"What'd pops say about what we believe," Ramses cautioned.

"Gordon's daughter knows this place. He and Michael swap visits. And Karaplidees' son. Bubba never allows anybody else, and Michael minds."

Michael Foom was one of the gentlest boys on the planet. He studied. Anything and everything. It was said if you looked long enough into Michael Foom's brown eyes, god stared back.

When they quickly relayed and conferred with the crew, Yvonne said, "Sounds like your war of art versus commerce has turned into ghetto squabbles."

"Only if we let it," said Ramses.

"You two like to talk as if you've got some measure of control," said Yvonne.

"It helps," said Ramses.

Du Ikare wasn't in the room. "People get killed around y'all," said Yvonne. "A man's son's been snatched."

"Asme's got people looking for him," said Milo.

"Are we looking for him?" Yvonne asked.

"We don't have ti—" Milo started.

Yvonne shook her head. "You make time."

Smoove leaned to whisper to Fiona, "She's an impertinent lass."

"I see."

Milo didn't respond. There were preparations to make and arguing wasn't one of them.

He left the room.

"No he didn't," said Yvonne.

"Yes he did," said Neon.

"You don't have enough of the story," Smoove advanced. "He's not the out-to-save-the-world-lost-sight-of-the-individual type."

"No? Tortured hero?" said Yvonne.

"We lost a dear friend recently," said Smoove.

"So it's tortured hero then."

"He's trying to navigate us all through it," said Smoove.

"He's not doing a hundred percent, is he?"

"He's done—" said Fiona, but Yvonne cut her off with a raised finger.

"You can't talk. You're in love with him," said Yvonne.

"Lady, when you know what you're talking about, you're allowed to speak to me," said Fiona. "That's the general mode of it. He's sacrificed more than anybody currently alive with the exception of Raffic the Mad Buddha, and his is a name you don't even get to speak."

Yvonne was twice Fiona's size.

"Now, you think a few years in the army's prepared you to deal with me, welcome to it at a later date and time. Violence being the last refuge of the incompetent, no one's ever said Fiona Carel was a genius. Right now, however, there are people in the know searching our friends out, and that's good enough to bank on."

"Ladies," said Smoove.

"We're leaving them here with Asme, right?" said Fiona.

"Not your decision to make," Yvonne reminded.

"Ladies?" This time it was Desiree, and everyone shut up. Desiree Quicho had mastered twenty-one of the Thirty-Seven Faces of Distaste. She currently used number eighteen.

She acknowledged Yvonne. "You're just joining us, and our story is already in progress. You never need to agree with us, but you have to trust us."

"Trust is earned, captain."

"We're not on your clock," said Desiree. "You can stay here and we'll have somebody bring you home, but this is the last time we have this conversation. Do you feel me?"

"I feel you," said Yvonne.

"Then trust me. Foom's son is a son to all of us, but we're also near to ending something that's plagued us a very long time."

"Kidnapping," Neon spoke up. "Attempted murder. Shoddy marketing…"

"The same wheel," said Fiona.

"Everything we encounter," said Desiree, "is entwined."

"But we came here looking for this man's help. He's missing, son's missing, so it's like, sorry bother?" said Yvonne.

"It isn't," said Desiree with enough finality to sever discussion.

"I want to be sure we haven't made a mistake," said Yvonne, meaning herself and Neon.

"Dear ones," said Smoove, "you won't know that till way after it's too late." He smiled for them, wanly and full of sympathy. The smiles of Captain Luscious Johnny Smoove had been known to calm raging waters…

…it worked wonders on the confused.

"Wait for more facts," he said.

Yvonne wasn't accustomed to feeling so lost. "Can you give us a primer?"

"After dinner," he said.

Her exasperation was nearly physical.

"First rule," he cautioned her. "Never do anything without first eating. Energy consumed is energy used."

Dinner was quiet and terse. Everyone was in Du Ikare's dining hall except Milo. And everyone besides Neon and Yvonne knew the underlying why.

Du Ikare finished her dinner before the others and went to his room. The door was open. He read on his bed.

"Milo?"

"Cleavage and Thighs will find him."

"I know. They'll find them both. In good health." She remained at the threshold. "You know me, Milo Jetstream. I don't scare easily. Michael's more grown than people twice his age."

Milo laid the book open across his chest.

"What are you reading?"

"Found it in the bathroom. *A Tale of Two Cities*."

"Bubba hates it. Michael likes it."

"It was the best of times, it was the worst of times," he read. *"It was the age of wisdom, it was the age of foolishness, it was the epoch of belief, it was the epoch of incredulity."*

"We had everything before us," she picked up. *"We had nothing before us, we were all going direct to Heaven, we were all going direct the other way."*

Milo closed the book. "I've never bothered with it. Dickens knew what was about." He absent-mindedly massaged the bite on his arm.

"Are you hungry?" she asked.

His eyes had a hollow pall beneath the sunscreen. He tried to speak but emotion jammed him. He tried again. "Asme…"

She crossed the threshold and pulled the door closed. "Go ahead and cry," she said. She hugged him a moment, letting his head settle on her shoulder. "I'll find a cure."

"I'm hungry, Asme."

She stroked the side of his face.

"How do you want your blood," she whispered, their dark bodies merging into one. "Whole or skim?"

Raffic
the
Mad Buddha

Idiotic, romantic notions of vampires got people killed, so Du Ikare arranged an impromptu presentation.

"She's trying very hard to be strong," Neon whispered to Yvonne while Du Ikare fast-forwarded to the section she wanted.

"Apparently an epidemic with these folks," Yvonne whispered back.

"Vampires," Dr. Du Ikare said, pointing her stylus at the screen, "are their own best PR." Onscreen an unremarkable middle-aged man pounded a cage. "Aversion to sunlight is due to a genetic change in melanin, allowing them a higher absorption of vitamin D to counter resulting anemia—but it's cooler to gloss with quasi-religious undertones of heaven and hell, light and dark. Vampires are resilient and drink blood, but only once a month after their initial feeding, and they only prey on decidedly weaker prey—(as if synched, the vampire in the cage looked directly at the camera in disbelief, but, clearly Du Ikare was offscreen telling him pithy bits)—because, in all honesty, there's nothing more pathetic than a vampire who gets his ass handed to him by someone he's about to bite."

Du Ikare lifted a thin, bent bar from among several on her lab table and passed it to Yvonne. "They're a little stronger than previously human, owing to an increase in lean muscle mass and decrease in overall fat to allow for greater speed. I theorize that they likely began as a scavenger species accustomed to being chased off. Viral mutations further diverged them from Man."

The vampire onscreen gave both middle fingers to the camera.

"They also tend to be emotionally aggressive assholes," said Du Ikare. "That one had been prowling school yards."

"Vampires. Are total. Pussies," Neon declared.

Milo quietly entered the room.

"Not all of them," Yvonne quietly reminded her.

~~~

Raffic, meanwhile, stepped over a pile of Du Ikare's theories. He was emaciated. Acts of extreme violence had prompted a vampire in Sip to divulge the remaining Atlantidean names and whereabouts along with a concise rundown of scouting operations. Raffic's mission was set.

The Buddha still couldn't remember exactly how he'd been made a vampire. He remembered robes, hoods, teeth and crashing his boat, but couldn't get the sequence of events properly linked, likely owing to the psychotropic drugs clinging to his veins. He did remember the hesitant bite of the redheaded vampire he now stepped over on the way out the door, because one of the other vampires had had to push the redhead forward.

A tuft of red hair was still on the makeshift club Raffic dropped to the ground.

He was covered in blood. Hunger made his veins howl but he stepped steadfastly into the noonday sun, which didn't hurt so much anymore.

He had to bathe. Even Shig wouldn't welcome him like this. At times Raffic seemed acutely aware of Bubba Foom reaching blindly for anyone, at others reality was so knotted that even the Mad Buddha felt lost. Vampirism enhanced the effects of all drugs, and he'd learned to sit out and ride the onset of a twist. While riding he anchored himself by extending his consciousness outward as far as he could, passing through the dreamtime, the seven-knuckled locus, the memory of mama's curry pies, several sexual encounters and the groping miasma that was Bubba Foom.

The pissy thing about being psychic was you couldn't just dial up whomever you wanted. One felt for groping hands and strained the fingertips for contact.

The water he splashed his face with pulled his matted hair into dripping bangs. He immersed full into the water and rubbed. He was tempted to enter Atlantis naked.

But no point engaging Shig in an awkward hug.

After a while, though, the Buddha wanted to be out of the sun.

Unwanted
Private Iowa

Milo wanted the sun. He sat huddled, shivering with pain under the skylight of Foom's sand garden.

This is where you stop to think, Milo Jetstream. Lolita's gone, Buford's missing, Atlantis is in danger, Bubba, Raffic and Michael need finding, you got a woman attacked by various assholes, are bound to yet another Djinn, and bandaged up a drug smuggler's dick. Wheels within wheels takes one person cranking to get it all started. The Mount could've just been distraction. You led somebody to Atlantis and Bubba, whoever they are.

It had to be the Thoom. And it had to be vampires.

You got your chocolate in my peanut butter.

You got your peanut butter in my chocolate.

His tongue played with the sharp tip of an incisor.

Milo Jetstream with fangs. That wasn't something he had ever expected to deal with. It was a definite step down in esteem.

The Thoom and vampires.

Which doesn't explain everything, he warned himself. *Michael's missing. And your friend is dead and you're showing no remorse.*

Because you know a few things about death.

And we're about to go chase after Buford.

He played his tongue along the other tooth and massaged his forearm, and said a blessing for the missing:

Forgive us.

~~~

"I'd been looking for Milo Jetstream for four years," said Smoove. "An ex told me to seek him out."

"Had she met him?" asked Neon.

"She'd been dead two weeks when she told me. It hadn't been that serious between us but I tended to crash easily. I was going to sail my boat off the edge of the world. She told me that dragons got fat off fools like me."

"We're supposed to believe in ghosts now?" said Neon.

"People ghosts only when they wanna be," said Smoove.

"So tales of malevolent spirits unable to move on?"

"Bullshit. They were jerks to begin with. They can leave whenever they like. She loved me, though. Her name was Melody."

"Smoove, is there *anyone* you haven't fallen in love with?" asked Fiona.

"Just one. I was born in love with her." He winked at his wife. "Everything's real," he told the assembled. "More or less by degrees."

"Why don't you talk about Bigfoot?" asked Yvonne.

He ignored her. "I landed in Hawaii and developed a reputation for calming spirits. Hawaii is full of them. Paradise, man. Nobody leaving there till they got to. I think I'm attuned because I'd never decided not to believe, you feel? I'm not the smartest in the world so I know what I believe isn't based on serious study, right? But all men have depth sometime. When I finally found Milo I came alive. He kicked my ass real good though. Milo Jetstream don't like nobody trying to sneak on him."

"It was one punch, Smoove," said Fiona. "And he hit you because you startled me."

He tapped his chest. "Square here. Kind of punch that if you wait a split second it'll clear your bronchitis before the real pain hits."

"What were you, a kid?" said Yvonne. It wasn't hard picturing him as a slender seventeen year old; youthful qualities would dog him forever.

"I'm four hundred-seventy four. Oop, here's the man now."

"Ram still with Asme?" asked Milo.

Smoove nodded.

"I think we're dealing with vampire Thoom," Milo said. "Gonna get Ram so we can get up to speed."

He left.

Smoove laid it out. "Three primary groups: Thoom, Buford, vampires. Thoom and Buford can't stand each other. Vamps just wait in the wings, don't give a nut one way or the other. Or so it's been."

"So it's seemed," said Desiree.

"A little extra red dye forty-six just entered the mix," said Smoove. "You ladies ready for more learning on the fly?"

"Ring the bell," said Yvonne.

"Beauty, the bell is rung. Let's hit the plane, luvs."

He showed them an array of weapons.

"Focum," he said, holding the pistol up. He set it down.

"Focum-Up," he said, holding a somewhat larger version. "Ultrasonic paralysis added." He slid an inlaid case open. "Earpieces. You don't focum-up without protection. Concussion grenade."

"Or bounces off somebody's head real good," shared Neon.

"Or bounces off somebody's head. Flash grenade. Smaller and lighter."

"I don't see any religious artifacts," said Yvonne.

Smoove frowned at her. "Who you think spread the notion of crucifixions? Hardly the best way to kill someone but very effective when you want to milk a cow, so to speak." He wanted to say this next very matter-of-factly, but there are times when lovemaking is simply fucking without the possibility of vice versa. "One of 'em drank from the Nazarene and opened the door to current mischiefs. We call him The Man. Nobody knows where he is. Nobody."

"Jesus was real? Not a bumper sticker?" said Yvonne.

"He was the son of *a* god, let's put it. Bit of a method actor. Anyway—pain. Babies when they're teething? That's what vampires are like. No heaving bosoms or swooning. They're just as likely to bite the bosom as the neck. Or the elbow. I've seen one stuck to a man's ass like a remora. When you engage one, kick its ass with utter impunity. They tend to fight dirty."

Yvonne glanced toward the door to make sure Milo wasn't about to enter. "He's a vampire."

"Yes."

"You seem pretty cool with that."

"Some of my best friends are vampires."

"Won't he change?" asked Neon.

"No." Without missing a beat Smoove went on: "If you have to kill one, break its neck. They hate that. They're not immortal. They live about three, four times as long as folks."

"You said you were four hundred seventy-four," Neon pointed out.

Smoove: undaunted. "They're not affected by disease. Have zero tolerance for drugs." He held up what was clearly a tranquilizer gun. "Crack darts, forty rounds each clip. If one happens to seduce you, they're sterile to us. Sterile to most themselves too but every once in a while there's vampire babies. Between births they populate by infection. The smallest nick will start resequencing your DNA quicker than tax evasion. Ms. Du Ikare's working on a cure. She's been at it seventeen years."

"Same age as her son," said Neon.

"Top o' your class, girl."

"Son of a bitch," muttered Yvonne.

"Top class," Smoove said again. "But she prefers to be called a secular-vampirist."

Du Ikare entered quietly, her soft accent preceeding her. "I was bitten two days before delivery."

"Being around Foom so much," said Smoove with a smile at his friend, "she has a tendency to know when people are talking about her."

"He hasn't shown any signs of vampirism yet," said Du Ikare. She hooked a thumb at Smoove. "Has he told you the lie about him being four hundred?"

Smoove passed the newcomers tranq guns. "Familiarize yourselves. Then I'll show you the strong stuff."

"These are defensive?" asked Yvonne.

"Trust me, you're not ready to offend. Everything in here is perfectly safe; nothing will fire."

He and Du Ikare left. They made their way to lower level storage and supplies.

"You're five hundred if you're a day," said Du Ikare.

"Hush, woman."

~~~

They left that evening, but not to California where most vampires lived.

"What's the state presidential elections hang on?" responded Ramses to Neon's query.

"Iowa."

Dreaded Iowa.

"May I show you a few things before we get there?" Ramses unbuckled and led her aft.

"What about Yvonne?"

Yvonne was in the cockpit with Milo and Fiona.

"I've fought alongside her," said Ramses. "She doesn't need me. What I'm going to show is going to hurt."

Neon stopped. "I've had enough pain to last."

He opened a rear cabin door. "Not you. Me."

In the cockpit Yvonne asked Milo to let her see his teeth.

"You can leave now," he said.

"They look a little pointy when you talk," Yvonne said, nodding.

"No they don't."

"Were there any vampires on the cruise with us?"

"Just that supermodel."

"I still like you," she said.

"Extremely good to know."

"Ramses is still cuter."

"It's that Idris Elba thing," said Milo.

"Can you pilot anything?"

"No."

"You're not really trying to learn in here," she said. "You're watching Red like you are but you aren't."

Fiona glanced at them. *Red?*

"He's smelling your shower gel," said Yvonne.

"I smell good."

"I'm not smelling her shower gel."

"You should be back there with your brother strategizing," Yvonne said.

"You a pilot?" Milo asked.

"No. Willing to learn though."

He relinquished his seat with a small flourish, then headed aft to the closed cabin door. He knocked and entered.

Ramses had just had the fye knocked out of him.

Neon whirled and did it to Milo.

His face returned with a completely blank look.

Cool, thought Neon.

"You just slap the fye out of me?" he asked.

"You're new so it doesn't last long," Ramses explained to her.

"Good for you," said Milo. "That's not easy to learn." He backed out to leave them to it.

Neon and Ramses heard the exclamation of pain through the muffling cabin door.

GOd
and
country

Every major evil operation in the world maintained sleepers in Dubuque, Iowa. Not bush-league evil like Al Qaeda or such dumbfucks. Evil as slow and pernicious as a poisoned cherry pop on a hot summer's day. Thoom worked a cubicle apart from Bufords but didn't know it, and every successful office party was one perfectly arranged by a vampire. (Iowa vampires took outstate trips once a month to feed.) Djinns always made sure they were the state's voting officials. Shiftless spruced themselves as permanent fixtures in coffee bars, and several other factions maintained the primary illusion of that rectangle of map being the quiet little Anglo sanctuary many wanted it to be.

The Jetstreams owned a sizeable plot of land far enough from curious eyes that they could come and go as they pleased. Fiona was technically not allowed in Iowa anymore, so to avoid potential police confrontation she remained behind.

"What are we looking for here?" Neon asked, wondering what exactly cornpone alley had to do with anything. Literally. They walked paths of six-foot corn stalks in the deep of the night.

"Gonna beat the bushes till a winged monkey shows," said Smoove.

"Huh?"

"*Wizard of Oz* reference, girl," said Smoove.

"We should've kept Fiona in the group. We stick out," said Neon.

"That's the point," said Ramses. "Nobody comes to Iowa for subtlety."

Yvonne felt obliged to point out they were creeping through corn stalks.

"First off," Ramses said, "we're walking tall and know exactly where we're going."

"Share with the class, brother," said Smoove.

"There's a shop we use as a base of operations," said Ramses.

"Don't tell me it's a barbershop," said Neon.

"It's a Walmart. Every other employee there works with us," said Milo.

"Sons a bitch," said Neon.

"Del Fuego Gardening is with us too," said Ramses.

"Who the hell don't y'all know? Del Fuegos are burb gardeners," said Neon.

"And office parks," said Ramses.

"We never said it was just us," said Milo.

"This is a real war, then?" said Neon. "Spies and everything."

"We don't do this for fun," said Milo.

"Esoteric yet visceral," said Smoove.

"And everybody's aware but they don't care," Neon said.

"Right," said Ramses.

"But," said Smoove, "they're busy having babies. No time for war with babies. Every sperm is sacred, yes?"

"What about your friend?" Neon pointed out, not sure if she should mention the missing son.

"Michael Foom," said Ramses. "was never a baby. My hope is whoever has him has the sense to keep him calm."

He left enough heavy mystery to ensure the ladies left the matter exactly where it was.

"Ow!" said Neon. "Corn stalk. Eye."

"Sorry, love," said Smoove.

"Why are we in a freaking corn field!" she snapped.

"On the way to Dubuque," said Ramses.

"I understand you can't be flying jets downtown but I'm sure you've got golf carts or something in that plane."

"Slow and steady wins the," Smoove began.

"Smoove?" said Neon.

"Yes?"

"You hit me in the eye. So shut up."

"This is probably why you haven't won yet," said Yvonne. "Walking when you should be motoring. Slow and steady is a good way to get passed by."

"And then run over," Neon pointed out.

"Squished turtle," said Yvonne.

"Yuck."

"Nasty."

"Ladies…" said Milo.

"We don't have cool names yet," said Neon. "You can't tell me he was christened Bubba Foom—"

"He was."

"—any more than Luscious."

"I am," said Captain Luscious Johnny Smoove.

"There are big ass bugs out here," Yvonne pointed out.

"We'll be out of here soon," said Milo.

"Can you fly?" Yvonne asked him.

"No."

"Stake through the heart kill you?"

"Most everybody."

"What if you attack us?"

"I won't," said Milo.

"What if you do? You might lose control."

"How many times you get so hungry you bit the head off a chicken?" he asked back.

"Why," hissed Neon, "are we talking about this in the middle of the night with the children of the corn around us? I swear to God I've seen eyes following."

"Red or just glowing?" asked Smoove.

"Red."

"Then we're cool," said the ghost-talking captain.

"I'm walking through the night with a vampire and I'm just a little uncomfortable," said Yvonne. "This is very freaky shit."

The moon, near full, illuminated sparse clouds; visibility was perfect blue eeriness.

"We won't be here long," said Milo, and true enough they exited the field not long afterward, but it was along the equally uncomfortable side of a deserted, dark, unlit road. The other side of the road proffered a large stretch of unremarkable nothing. To call this a road implied actual public use by someone other than serial killers.

"Be still a minute," Milo whispered to the ladies. Both drew closer together and mentally prepared leg muscles to bring knees to nuts.

Everyone scanned the surroundings but visibility was more a matter of vague shapes and hazy perimeters than recognizable details. What might have been a tree was actually the knoll of a hill in the distance. What looked like a boulder sitting suspiciously on an area of flat land was—as eyes scanned over it—definitely moving. Neon squinted (even though it was dark). Parts of the black on black shape distinctly shifted, very slowly and very lumberingly.

And then the boulder stood up.

What Neon and Yvonne saw was something tall and something hairy and something decidedly not beside-a-dark-road friendly. The Jetstreams looked dead at it and held their ground.

It lumbered across the road and looked down a length of reeking fur at them.

Then it pulled a flashlight from somewhere inside its fur and held the light under its chin.

'Piss ant humans,' it thought aloud.

"You aware of Foom?" Milo asked coldly, ignoring its show.

'No.'

"Punk ass bastard," said Milo.

'Unwashed prick.' It shined a light on Yvonne's chest and snuffed the air for hints of blessed pheromones.

"Fuck off," said Milo.

'Fuck you,' thought Bigfoot aloud, then lumbered off slowly. The shaggy beast flicked its flashlight off and tucked it away.

Milo turned away too. "Let's go," he said to the party.

Ramses caught just enough of the ladies' eyes to quietly shake off any questions. "House about a half mile from here," he said. "Transportation's there."

And of course, they walked the rest of the way in silence.

Night MOVES

Dubuque, Iowa at night is one of four things: cool, depending on the breeze coming off the Mississippi; muggy in the summer (depending); mostly quiet (if you're there after one a.m.); and for the most part white, except for tonight, when three black dudes, two black chicks, a Latina and an olive-complexioned Atlantidean rode through town. Dubuque's West Side was baby boomer suburban paradise, and the Jetstreams rode slowly through the more affluent areas, windows down, guaranteed to attract private security attention. They parked outside the house of Lee Batch, a prominent *Afro*-American corporate legal defender and known supporter of the Thoom, for ten minutes. Vampires tended to hang out in the Japanese Garden at Dubuque's Arboretum and Botanical Gardens; tonight, the Jetstreams parked, got out, walked right in, and sat down to catch the end of two vampires' conversation about market share as it related to collateral growth. Smoove wanted to kill them, but Milo said no, and made the vampires finish their conversation, which was suddenly an exercise in nervous fumbling and repetitive half sentences told before a stony-faced and minimally blinking audience.

The vampires finished.

No one spoke.

Then Milo said, "That was fascinating."

His words clattered ungainly off the rocks of the garden's central waterfall.

Two sharp handclaps startled the upwardly mobile vampires. They regarded Smoove as though he were some mad Rasta loony man.

He maintained the stony look for them…then he smiled.

And the Jetstream party left.

First thing in the morning they went to Walmart.

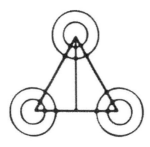

Nobody actually looks at a Walmart greeter. If one ever bothered to look at those nondescript old men and women and vacant younger ones, and perhaps follow them off their shifts, one would see that as the little blue vests ambled through stores between stacks of sugared drinks, socks on sale, mega vitamins, and improperly-raised children, one would find that almost every one of them somehow eventually managed to find a quiet, private space among the marked up discounted prices and very very easily vanish. They're *zephyrs*; they do not punch out or in for these breaks, and woe unto retailers if ever a one was docked. *No one* fucks with a zephyr's off time. Don't know where they go or what they do, and because zephyrs tend to be slightly crazy, it was wisest not to ask. Had anyone bothered actually to look one dead and long in the face, they'd come to a startling conclusion: zephyrs had the most beautiful eyes.

Yet their voices sounded like hell.

"HellowelcometoWalmart!" one barked before realizing the customers hadn't actually gotten close enough yet to warrant it. He tried to cover his embarrassment by inducing a mild coughing fit. When they reached him he was anticipating the soft breeze of their passing, which to a zephyr was like cleavage to a djinn. This zephyr, though, had looked into the eyes of an angel once and now thought he recognized something in the eyes of the man looking down at him. It was a black man, and his eyes met the zephyr's full on. They were warm eyes but left the impression they might bend steel for fun and challenge. The man said "Thank you," and moved to walk away. The zephyr—who was never to touch the customers—grabbed light hold of Ramses' sleeve.

"You *see* me?"

"Yes."

The old one looked Milo's way, at the others, and quickly added, "Jetstreams."

"Yes."

The zephyr smiled broadly. "Welcome to Walmart." He released Ramses. "This might prove to be a good day."

"We can hope."

Several Agents of Change worked hardlines in housewares. The group hit that department first. Neon picked up a bauble along the way, mulling purchase.

"Put that down, you don't know where it's been," said Milo.

"What's the signal?" asked Yvonne.

"There is no signal," said Milo.

"Sadness," she said.

"Look for somebody who looks like they'd actually be helpful to you in the store," said Milo.

That actually narrowed it down quite a bit.

A young lady arranging items on a shelf in a much more appealing way than the company's predetermined floor plan called for was so intent on her task she didn't notice them until they'd surrounded her. She looked up and the light in her eyes grew considerably brighter.

"Can we speak a moment?" asked Milo.

She glanced left and right, then headed deeper into housewares territory (vacuum cleaners, which always tended to be deserted). She whispered, "It's starting to filter that you put on a show last night," her voice carrying a hint of admonishment. Being an Agent of Change in Dubuque was a careful balancing act.

"We know to be seen when we want to. We need to know about iffy vampire activity," said Milo.

"Anything unusual you'd be telling *me* about it. What's going on? I break for lunch in a couple hours," said the agent.

"Spread the word to gear up for a fight," said Milo.

"Potentially," Ramses corrected.

"When you say fight?" the young woman asked. She had the most perfectly round Afro puffs of anyone within the next two states, and a total of three good eyes, one unseen.

Smoove answered her. "Peace with your god and animal sex with your enemy."

"He exaggerates," said Ramses. "We think Thoom and vampires are doubling up on Buford."

"Any unusual purchasing spikes?" asked Milo.

"Party supplies." As she nodded her puffs bobbed. "Office party stuff. Look for Jim Beame."

"Any more?" asked Ramses.

"There's always more," she said. Her name was Patty. She called herself Phantom of the Chakra.

~~~

Of course Jim Beame was a lanky fellow, but the grip of his shake indicated his strength. Ramses, after the group split up to cover more of the gargantuan store, had been the one to find him.

"Aluminum pans and cheap liquor," said Jim. He covered that department. "Did a total reorder recently."

"Low level folks celebrating," said Ramses.

"That means high level folks are already pulling up their pants and leaving the dried-up orgy," said Jim. "Patty tell you about the referendum to rezone sections of the city?"

"With privatized security, she said."

"Overlays Thoom territory with vampire-ville. Not a lot but enough to be curious. Especially the northern suburbs."

"Lee Batch support this referendum?"

Beame nodded. He left to help a wandering customer, then returned without missing a beat.

"Lee Batch hasn't been photographed as often as he used to either," said Jim.

"Bush-league Johnnie Cochrane," said Ramses.

"Rich bush-league Johnnie Cochrane."

"Looks like we're gonna have to deal with some lawyers."

"Looks that way."

"Damn," said Ramses.

"I'll spread the word for heightened vigilance," Beame said.

"Thanks. Any dealings with gods lately?"

"Just Muses."

A night with a Muse was like being gripped by the downy hand of grace itself.

"Making peace with gods is going to filter around the store. They'll say it comes from Milo."

"Does it?"

"Not really."

"I can ignore it?"

Jim Beame shivered with anticipation. He was getting a contact high off the man-with-a-mission vibes emanating from Ramses Jetstream's chest hairs at this very moment.

Ramses made to move off.

"You plan on buying anything?" asked Jim, who could assist with an employee discount.

"Hell no." Ramses Jetstream rounded an aisle of crap and was gone.

KnOW
the Enemy

This is what Lee Batch looked like: cropped, manicured afro, distinguished, grey with enough metrosexual panache to let others know he had money to burn but chose not to do so smack in their faces. He didn't blink much, which was disconcerting, disconcerting being the first tool in a lawyer's arsenal of offense. He'd perfected looking intently at people. This gave him the deep crow's-feet men in their fifties are considered ruggedly wise for, particularly black men used to seeing more than their share. Lee Batch could also bench press three hundred pounds, courtesy of the fact he was what's colloquially known as a big mofo. His in-home fully equipped weight room wasn't for show.

He saw his wife six times a year, his daughter three, and *her* daughter never except in pictures. The Batches were a traveling family, with Baby Batch considering the difference in skin tones between her and Nanny Frieda Gunter a parental anomaly.

But they were still a family, as the pictures throughout Lee Batch's house attested.

That and that alone made him question his decision.

Vampires made the best poets and storytellers because they could seduce jizz from pumice if need be. The ones who studied and practiced anyway. Not these silly younger ones, but the old ones, old farts who'd generated more philosophy and macroeconomics than anybody should.

You could tell an old vampire from the general populace because the old ones never wore watches, even if they could afford to use Rolexes as rubber bands. This small confidence swayed Lee over to a wild, simple proposal: create not a new order but a necessary one. The Thoom were marginal, Buford egomaniacal, and vampires frankly couldn't fight the tide of bootleg DVDs sweeping a forgotten Hollywood under a rug. Money, the lifeblood of all ambition, was hemorrhaging away such that, at around five hundred years from now, some of the higher level vampires might find a need to actually dip into their savings.

Batch draped a luxurious towel around his neck and grabbed a bottle of blood from the fridge. He popped the top on his anti-nausea pills and crunched two before getting a hard swig. Sweat continued to run down his face but he didn't dry himself. He preferred to air dry. He'd earned that sweat. Batch exercised in solitude and the hired hands knew better than to enter unannounced or uninvited, not that they could since there were new security monitors installed no matter which wall he faced, plus the room could be voice locked if he chose. The weight room was the one place he felt completely divorced from the world.

Which was a good and necessary thing.

Ramses perched high in a ceiling corner of the room with his hands and feet braced against the walls. The major flaw in Lee Batch's secure vision of the world was in feeling safety meant Lee saw what was to be seen. What Lee Batch saw didn't mean squat. The advanced security system his benefactors provided wouldn't normally be used to secure their own dogs, but Batch—used to a diet of labels and brands—was easily subsumed by the right trinkets and beads.

Ramses waited till Batch was nearly at the exit to drop lithely to the floor behind him.

"Lee Batch?" he said, clearly startling the big man.

Lee turned quickly. All that did was hasten the connection of his face with the slap of fye screaming his way.

~~~

His private blend of citrus smelling-salts revived him.

He took his time opening his eyes to assess the situation. He remembered the woman in the room; she had been the one who'd demanded to see him—because he'd interrupted his workout for her. One look at her and he'd sent the help on their way. Corporate lawyers often received corporate gifts.

Didn't remember much after that. He'd gone back to the weight room and his face was a little tender, but other than that a man's chest muscles didn't get ripped by themselves.

There were others with that fabulous woman now.

In his weight room.

And one of them was in his fridge.

"Negroes had better have a good reason for this," he said levelly as though whup ass and *habeas corpus* carried the same weight. "You're in my fridge."

"And you need to shut up," said Milo without bothering to look at him. Milo straightened and unscrewed the top off a cold bottle, glancing at each of his party cursorily for forgiveness. "I, too, have leveled woods with my words. What's going on, Lee?" He took a drink.

But Batch was strategically locked away in the courtroom of his mind.

"Ram," said Milo, "stomp the stew."

"Wasn't sure which was which," said Batch. Ramses paused. "Milo Jetstream in my damn house. Son of a bitch."

Milo took another swig. "Got no problem with you being a vampire. Got a problem with you being in my mix. Understand, Lee, I'm not leaving here without a total of three answers. You approach the vampires or they approach you?" Nothing. "OK."

"I can slap the fye out him again," Neon volunteered.

"Lee, you are not high level. You will never be high level. You can sit there and try to be cool but you've noticed we aren't restraining you and nobody's particularly worried. That cool will crack long before you're anywhere near a threat." Milo sat on the edge of a calf-leather weight bench and regarded Batch squarely. "What's new in your life, Lee?"

"You're on camera."

"We know."

"They're probably on their way here."

"We know," said Milo, catering to the bluff. "Smoove, we locked and loaded?"

"Enough to poke a bear's nuts."

"I imagine zoning would frown on heavy artillery leveling this neighborhood," said Milo. "You won't be the first operative giving up a confidence to us on camera. We do it all the time and we're still here."

"Speaks volumes," said Batch.

"You may have heard we don't kill people," said Milo. "That, too, requires a bit of clarification."

"Use logic in my home, Milo Jetstream. Don't give me that 'Tell me what I want or die' shit. I don't plan to talk after I'm dead."

"Why are lawyers melodramatic divas? Lee...Thoom and vampires and Buford: Do you guys have him?"

"I don't know."

"Speculate."

"Harvard law degree havin' bastard," added Neon.

"Morehouse. Yale."

"What the hell ever."

"You heard the words Bubba or Foom recently?" asked Ramses. Ramses' stare was portentous, like a cobra's, not merely hard like Milo's. Hard returned like, but from portentous there was no defense.

"No," said Batch.

"Brother to brother, would you lie to me?" asked Ramses.

"I would."

The two men regarded one another from wholly different fields of play. "How long before your cavalry arrives?" said Ramses.

Batch said nothing.

"I hate a sellout," said Smoove.

"I don't think I got a price belongs to you!" said Batch, glowering at Smoove.

"Get in touch with whoever approached you," said Milo rising, "and let them know you have personally fucked up the status quo." Milo screwed the cap back on the sloshing red bottle. "There *will* be blood. Thanks for the answers."

"I didn't say anything," Batch said to reassure himself.

"Can't answer what you don't know, and that was the entire question."

They left via the front door.

Yvonne was the first to question Milo's tactics.

"You drank blood in front of him," she said. "You don't think he's going to blast that from here to kingdom come?"

Milo nodded that he actually did. "That's the least of our problems. He doesn't even know Foom exists, he has no idea where Buford is and…"

"We need to find out who else they've recruited," Ramses finished.

"So the question is where's the party at?" said Neon. "Sounds like a Walmart run again to me. I can pick up some necessities while we're there."

"Agents of Change do not purchase things from Walmart!" both brothers said in unison.

"Hey, Agents of Change; we got a name, Yvonne!"

"Not our own yet."

"No, but still. So, Mr. Agent X, unless you've got a stash of panty liners on hand, we *will* be purchasing from Walmart."

Aisle seven, personal products.

When the words "necessity" and "panty" appear in tandem, men know unequivocally to shut the hell up.

The Long, Dark Night Of the Mole

Six of Milo's clones planned to revolt. That was the meanwhile. They'd learned that vague concept from Foom's mind, and had also learned enough deep-seated secrecy not to tip off any of their others. No matter how much amperage, there was a part of Foom perpetually guarded and it reached out in ways that, even while reinforcing the notions of Thoom obedience and reliance aimed at keeping the clones walking a road of narrowed perceptions, the Revolutionaries were somewhat sure his captors would have found troubling. None of the six were aware even of the intentions of the other five, so each of course believed they were working one against twelve. There were initially fourteen clones, but the fourteenth, whose death had been the keynote of their orientation into the world of heightened consciousness, had been autopsied right before them while still warm, revealing to the impassive thirteen a tiny machine still burrowing its way through arteries and connective tissue in a wild, wet slalom.

It had been plucked out, deactivated, cleaned off, then handed to a beautiful, bathrobe-wearing woman, whose entire participation then consisted of regarding each clone, sliding the machine into a bathrobe pocket, and wordlessly leaving.

At a billion dollars a clone this wasn't an empty show.

Teleportation came courtesy a recently departed instructor touted as a major influence early on in Buford's ascension.

The clones rotated turns sitting with Bubba Foom when not in use. They hadn't been in use for a number of days now.

Bubba Foom, thought Milo's number six, didn't much look like a psychic. During their indoctrinations to consciousness the Thoom had surrounded them with tantrics, yogis, monks, marketers and illusionists. Everything the world regarded as mystifying or arcane the thirteen Milos thought of as commonplace. Time travel—which was all teleportation really was—was inherently paradoxical. That's why it was so difficult to master. The limited abilities opened in the clones was sufficient though, particularly with Foom assisting with a sturdy leash.

Periodically someone appeared on a monitor in front of Foom's face to torture a young man. Or sometimes not torture. Six had learned there was value in this psychological game.

Right now was torture.

The young man was always naked.

Right now he was naked with a naked man lying beside him. The naked man's head rested on his hands and his erection angled toward someone taking pictures with her back to the camera, who then walked to a dock to print them, clinically laid them out, then resumed another round of picture taking. The man beside the young man was disturbingly impassive to the entire scene, not in contact with the boy, simply stretched beside him. His middle-aged body was lumpy, his skin pasty, and his pubic hair a grating mass.

Six listened to Foom's breathing. There was a barely perceptible change to its rhythm at times like this. For every shallow exhalation there were two even shallower inhalations, followed by a pause of no breathing at all. There was a clarity of thought the clones received at these times that was almost hallucinatory in its sharpness.

"He's not going to touch him," Six said to Foom.

Foom never spoke back.

"Your son's never been touched before?"

One breath out, two breaths in.

"I don't think my penis has ever done that. The little movements too. Mine doesn't move much at all. I don't think sexuality is as interesting as you make it to be. Why are they taking pictures? Why don't you ever tell us to be quiet, Bubba Foom? Silence is power, yes?" Six nodded. "It is best we remain weak."

The man wedged his hand between Michael's thighs and accidentally scratched him with a fingernail. Foom couldn't see the scratch but Foom saw pain register across his son's face.

All hell broke loose.

Michael Foom felt his father's rage and, for the first time in his young life, understood the fear his mother had of her son's potential. Michael had learned at nine years old that there was a pitch in his mind, a high-frequency piercing whine, capable of frying anyone panic made him think of, and had thus—under his own initiative—taken it upon himself to become the calmest child possible.

At seventeen, he was placid.

The pitch didn't need to grow in strength. It was simply *there* in sudden obliterating intensity. 'There' was the man lying beside him, whose mind was so instantly and thoroughly wiped he might as well have been dead. But he wasn't. He was merely in the prone, vegetative state he would be in for the rest of his life.

Michael had inherited this trait from his father.

The tenuous connection between son and father strengthened in that moment to a microsecond bridge Bubba Foom rode to enter the space where his son was being held,

215

blindly fry the brains on two floors, contain Michael from frying any more, then himself temporarily burn out.

~~~

Ele, in the checkout line of Walmart, grabbed her head and screamed so loudly the cashier almost looked up.

She dropped to a knee, jamming a palm to her forehead.

Ramses steadied Neon.

"He's *here*!" said Ele.

Smoove commandeered the cashier's intercom.

"Make peace with your god at lane two," he said. "Immediately."

What people saw: twenty-five blue vested warriors converging on express lane two before surging toward the front doors after some black dudes and their girlfriends, stopping incoming customers in their tracks.

What people thought: shoplifting at Walmart was being taken *way* too seriously.

Jim Beame said to the Afro puffs he'd never gotten around to asking out, "We just lost our jobs, you know."

"I don't think it matters anymore," she said.

All the while Ramses kept repeating, *This is not what we wanted,* but blue vests followed. They were in broad daylight. People scattered from their wave. Instructions were given. A caravan formed.

Ele pushed the pain aside. "I think I can find him."

"No need," said Desiree, and pointed ahead to Milo.

But Milo also stood directly beside Desiree.

Bubba Foom struggled from the other Milo's arms in a fit of anger and dignity.

This, thought Milo Jetstream, *is when something bad generally happens.*

Twelve more of him popped into existence in the Walmart parking lot.

Smoove relayed to a confused Agent of Change, knowing the reassurance would circulate, "There's only one here you need to worry about."

The other Milos were clean shaven and certainly didn't look as haggard as their source material.

"In for a penny…" murmured Yvonne.

"Mexican standoff?" said Desiree.

"No speekee englace," said Smoove, slowly and quietly, as though calculating the exact point in space-time the silent cobra would…

Strike.

"Take me back!" Foom shouted, releasing a concussive blast of psionic force that left the entire lot stunned.

Clone Six recovered quickly and grabbed Foom's arm.

"Wait!" shouted Ramses.

"Bubba!" shouted Desiree. "Where?"

Foom met her eyes then glanced at Ele a split second. The other half of that second saw him gone.

Ele brusquely wiped tears away and moved for Milo's car.

The other twelve Milos looked as lost as everyone else before blinking out en masse.

"I have *got* to learn to do that!"

"Milo, they're close," Desiree reminded him, pushing him and heading for the car herself. She and Ele jumped the front seats. The rest of the crew piled in. They sped off.

"Not to use you as a divining rod," said Captain Quicho, "but—"

"Right," Ele directed.

Desiree drove without a thought for anybody trying to keep up.

"Left. Straight. Straight. Left. Right. Down (a ramp). Off. Here!"

It was a house.

Milo jumped out. "Buford here?"

"Who cares about Buford?!" said Yvonne. "Foom's here." She danced about. "What do we do?" Yvonne couldn't figure out why it seemed to be getting progressively warmer between her and Milo.

Iowa air wavered around Milo Jetstream's clenched right hand. Without a word he dropped and punched the ground so hard it cracked. The echo effect of the expanding chi bounced Foom's presence back to him.

Ramses barked quick orders to several Agents of Change. "Cameras." Trunks popped. They pulled out movie-grade videocameras. "We're filming a scene," he told a Korean woman, who nodded and assumed her post to fend off the curious. The other Agents of Change waited for an attack. It was 12:35 on a Tuesday afternoon. Wind was light. Time stood still.

"Get inside," Desiree urged Ramses. He bolted for the door, slammed it as though no force existed that could keep him outside, dropped into a roll, and came up flinging concussion grenades. He didn't have to detonate them, though. The guards were crumpled against the walls. An arrow of Agents took position behind Ramses, and through them Ele emerged, legs still shaky but eyes fire red. She took a few extra steps.

"Trouble down that hall," she whispered, sensing the fearful uncertainty streaming off the hidden clone. The house was huge, furnished nouveau-Moroccan style.

Milo, about to rush ahead, was stopped by Ramses' grip on his shoulder. Heat flashed between them but subsided immediately.

Ele took point.

The entire facility—once they found out how to access the lower levels, determining without doubt this was indeed a facility and not a house—was incapacitated to some degree or other. Whether fully unconscious or babbling incoherently, men and women of the Thoom littered hallways and offices. Milo's small group moved quickly, flanking Ele and heeding her hesitations. They passed one clone, dead, and Milo tried not to look at that. Didn't need to know how he'd died, especially if at Bubba's hand, which considering would have put a decidedly weird spin on this endeavor. The more immediate concern was why Bubba wasn't making his presence known as there was no way he wasn't aware they were in the building.

Milo's comm squawked. Desiree tersely informed him that neighbors had called police. This was a "no shit Sherlock" observation but a necessary one. It meant rather than time all they had left was opportunity. "Have some Agents slip back into Walmart mode," he said.

"Pegging it down," Desiree acknowledged. Orders would be given to create as much confusion among the officers as possible. There would surely be some Thoom operatives arriving on scene as well, which might actually be a bonus as they wouldn't want the "authorities" entering this secret structure themselves.

"Ele, is Michael here?" asked Ramses.

"He's with him." She visibly shook.

"You OK?"

"This place is full of psychic assaults. He could've been right next door to him without being aware how close they were."

"If he believed there was time for them to hurt him he had to behave," said Ramses.

"Where are they?" asked Milo, then addressed the small band with him. "Everybody shut up and stand still. Ele?"

She came in close to Ramses and laid her face against his ribcage as if seeking a hug, precisely what she was doing. Comfort flooded her small body.

"We've gone too far down. He's above us," she said.

The room wasn't directly above but it was close enough that they reached it quickly. Foom hadn't found anything that could cut the polymer straps binding his son, and sat beside him, forehead to forehead. Clone Six stood in a corner as unthreateningly as possible.

"My head hurts," said Ele. Blood trickled from a nostril. Ramses eased her to a chair while Milo cut the straps with a laser from his pocket. Desiree removed the lab coat from the photographer's limp body to wrap Foom's son. Michael, eyes tightly closed, held his father.

"What happened to the clones, Bubba?" said Milo.

"Fighting amongst themselves."

At another time that would have been hilarious.

"Let's get you home," said Milo.

"That," Foom slurred, "would be a good thing."

Yet it had to be asked. "Is Buford here?" said Ramses, expecting the answer he got and ready to move on.

"No. I don't know, I don't think so. I don't know," said Foom shaking his head. "Buddha's in trouble."

"Where is he?" asked Milo.

"I think it was him. They got me fulla shit, and those commercials, and—"

Foom held his son even tighter and buried his face in his hair. Milo waited.

"—and clones. There were thirteen fucking yous! Do you know how hard that was!" Foom's Southern drawl was pronounced when angry.

Ramses gathered up the photographs and the camera.

"You still have influence over them?" Milo asked Foom. "Bubba?"

"Milo, my head really hurts," Ele groaned.

"We're getting you out of here," said Milo. He lifted one of Bubba's arms and draped it, raising both father and son since Foom hadn't let go of Michael. Foom's eyes were bloodshot, distant, simultaneously full and emptied. "Need you to do one more thing, Bubba," whispered Milo into Foom's shock of stringy hair. "Fry 'em."

Bubba's head shook slowly as if full of sludge.

"You fry 'em," Milo whispered, "or I swear you'll regret it. Make them forget. Make them forget and we'll scatter them. Bubba?"

Foom's breathing was barely detectable. A tremble started in Milo's right arm, which intensified along with his head clogging the more Foom stood under his own power. "Focus your intentions," advised Milo. The clogging eased.

"My intentions are a knife," murmured Foom inside the pocket universe behind his eyes.

"They need to forget this," said Milo.

Foom closed his eyes and exhaled sharply once. He stood fully erect for the first time in weeks and drew a huge intake of breath, releasing it as a heavy, clarifying grunt. His jaw clenched and unclenched over what felt like a long moment. "It is done," he said.

Milo addressed the Agents of Change hovering at the fringes of the room. "Scatter them."

"We should bring them with us," said Smoove.

"We should let them live their lives," said Milo.

"Whatever that may be?" said Ramses.

"Whatever that may be."

~~~

"That's just bloody stupid!" Fiona railed at Milo an hour later. "There are twelve of you running around out there without a clue what's coming after them."

"It's confusion—"

"*You*, Milo Jetstream, are confused." She paced back and forth.

"They're the least of our concerns now, Fee," Milo asserted. "Raffic is out there."

"Raffic is always out there! Raffic the Mad Buddha," she enunciated clearly, "could no more remain in here than Leviathan could swim my bathtub. This isn't like you, Milo. What the hell's going on?"

"We need to find the Buddha."

"No, I think you've been saying we need to find Buford. Yes? The False Prophet Buford Bone. Scourge of mankind. Yes? A right evil prick when you get to know him."

Ramses had said nothing until now. "You don't think the Thoom are going after them?" he said to Milo. "You drew blood, man."

Milo, standing in the center of their safe house's main room, said, "The Thoom know that I'm a vampire; know there's a bunch of me. That's twelve heightened odds wondering is it live or is it Memorex. Vampires are letting the Thoom do their dirty work, and you know the Thoom don't do shit unless they think the odds are in their favor."

"By that logic, they have to have Buford," Fiona tossed out, walking away before she gave in to wanting to hit him. "And since your clones got him out of Atlantis, we assume he *used to be* near. We assume now that they've since spirited him via underground tunnels to who in hell knows where. Ele and Bubba are tapped out. I hope not burnt. Michael's so far in denial I cry. Milo, we've followed you because you've always been a good leader, not because we need to be led. We trust you," she said, still walking the room, a human pinball, "because you trust yourself. This, luv, is a big thing. That trust is shaken if you do stupid things!"

"It wasn't stupid, dammit! Listen—"

"Don't think we can't plot as good as you. We know where in hell this was going. Do you think, though, you're fixated lately on plot, counter plot, point, counter point too much? We're running around with two untrained women, Kichi is going to chew the unlined hell out of our asses..." She stopped in front of him to stand as nose to nose as tiptoes allowed, eyes flaming ("He's still smelling your hair," offered Yvonne). "You can stone up as much as you want..."

He sat. She remained before him.

"We require a lot more of you than this," she said. "D'you understand me?"

He nodded.

"You plan to find them?" Ramses asked Fiona.

"Yes." She'd already sent word to the Agents of Change to report back. "They can teleport, Milo. You can't. That makes them twelve very valuable friends."

"They're clones of me," he said, as though that would explain it all.

"You know the joke," she said.

"Some of my best friends are clones?"

"No. *Isn't it queer, losing my timing this late in my career?* Send in the clones," said Fiona.

"Send in the clones," Ramses echoed.

Jim Beame radioed back to them that he was en route to rendezvous, clone in hand. Desiree acknowledged his communication, her eyes meeting Fiona's.

"Don't bother," said Milo. "They're here."

The
Deeper
Sea

Looking at a handsomer version of oneself can be problematic, a problem exacerbated by seeing via monitor one's brother interacting with said version and clearly fascinated no matter how clinical said brother pretended to be. Foom and Michael's assaults had knocked offline the implanted bio-borers; Asme surgically removed them. The clones were kept separated, and Bubba far from them. Neon, Ele, Foom and Michael rested with analgesics inside sound dampening rooms in Foom's compound. Yvonne thought Milo could use company inside a small anteroom that confined him to observation only.

She studied him closely. During the cruise he had fascinated her to the point that sex would have been a given. Handsome without being aware of it, smart, respectful enough to get lost in her sensuality only when he thought she wasn't looking, plus he knew every obscure song Bootsy Collins ever made. And a family man. Traveling with his brother. How often did that happen, two brothers taking the time on a cruise to enjoy one another's company? Who weren't Alphas! In the old life she had done a stint in the army, dealt with subsequent manic mood swings, hustled money from a no-account relative and set out with a young woman on what they'd thought would be a run of the mill, innocuous womanly journey of discovery. Very Lifetime Network.

Instead, she was championing a psychic named Bubba Foom; grappling with the fact that Bigfoot was a sexist prick who stole camping equipment; standing in a room with a *vampire—*

You gotta stop there, she rightfully responded and agreed with herself. "Do you drink?" she asked Milo.

"No," he said and glanced at her. She seemed waiting for more.

"That it?" she said.

"Yeah." He fixed on the monitor.

"Usually people explain why."

"It tastes like piss."

"OK." Topic closed. "I was going to say we should have a drink."

"How you handling all this?" he asked.

"I'm not."

"Imagine that state of mind the rest of your life." He allowed another brief lapse from the monitor. "You don't have to be part of this." Her left hand never knew what to do when she was anxious. It was directionless now.

"I don't see how I couldn't be," she said.

"I never realized I was that soft spoken." The clone responded to Ramses dutifully as if that trait was hardwired into Jetstream genetic makeup. "The back of my head looks a little funny too."

"Yeah."

"Will your relatives miss you?" he asked.

"Hopefully," she said. "They weren't very good shots anyway."

He looked at her and his eyes half smiled that sad way they had on the cruise when they parted.

"Cousin runs a drug ring with connections to the mayor," said Yvonne.

"Ah. Political family. What if these clones decide to stay here? What—" he stopped abruptly with a drawn breath and a crushed, deflated chest, shaking it off. The monitor's glow filled his face again.

"What are you supposed to do?" she finished, and nudged him with her hip. She watched the monitor for signs of whatever he was searching for. "You hate being selfish, don't you?"

He didn't answer.

She considered. "A bunch of me running around might get the person who was meant for me." She patted his shoulder. "You've had a rough day, Mr. Jetstream."

Milo sighed. "Hey," he said.

"What else is out there?"

He shook his head, not wanting to answer.

"Or what's in here," she clarified. "Since there's no 'out there'."

"The world's a serpent swallowing its tail wondering why everything tastes like ass," he deadpanned. Exhaustion burned his eyes. His right hand, even though healing quickly, was in swollen agony. His brother was being far too existential in there but had promised there'd be hell to pay if Milo reared his head. Ramses planned to speak with each clone himself first, then parcel them out to Smoove, Fiona, Desiree and Ele. Milo was forbidden to come into contact until the assessments were complete.

"This place have a pool?" Yvonne asked.

He resisted. Pliantly.

"Come swim with me."

He didn't budge.

"Nothing for you to do here, hero. Swim."

"You don't have a suit."

"You should consider that incentive."

~~~

But she did have a suit. Seeing him in his again, she almost opted for without. The man was *cut*. No, he was chiseled. Muscles were where they were supposed to be, back was just as broad and chocolate—even with the scars—as the fruited plains, the ass of which her hands wanted to harvest. And wet, plus looking pensive while heated water lapped against him?

Freaking delicious.

Milo hadn't been immersed in water since Atlantis. His imagination chewed a moment on the image of Leviathan bursting from the bottom of the pool to displace every drop of water as Yvonne screamed and ran.

"You sang that song on the cruise," said Yvonne. They bobbed as powerful jets bubbled their rear ends. "The Beatles. 'Something inside that was always denied for so many years.' That's how you feel, isn't it?"

"I sang one line."

"But you sang it with feeling. 'Never a thought for ourselves,'" she sang. "We're nearly naked in a pool and you haven't thought once to flatter me or make a move on me or openly appreciate the curvature. Unclench your cheeks and relax. Relax for five complete minutes."

"Please stop telling Fiona I'm smelling her. Why do you do that?"

"Because you're in love with her." She stretched herself upon the water, no longer aligned with him on the floating pillow. "You're also in love with Neon," she said. "You're also in love with me." She finished so matter-of-factly that he looked to see if she was smiling.

She was. And it was amazing. Absolutely amazing, her eyes closed and feet pedaling slowly. "Five minutes, Milo Jetstream."

"Five minutes," he agreed. How hard was it to spend five minutes content in a pool with a beautiful soul?

Not very, as the next hour proved. He himself might as well have been a clone, divorced of any and all responsibilities toward the thing known as Milo D'Artagnon Jetstream.

At the end she swam to him and gave him the best hug he'd had since nineteen eighty-nine, and that from Lolita. Yvonne molded herself into him and held him longer than necessary.

Which made tears well in his eyes.

~~~

They dried and dressed. Milo made it a point to thank Desiree later for the loan of a modified breach suit/bikini to Yvonne. The vision of Yvonne practically god-like rising out of the water at the end of their swim was therapeutic enough that a madman would have calmed in Milo's presence.

"Thank you," he said.

"You're welcome, hero." Yvonne punched his shoulder. "This isn't the end."

When they ran into Ramses he was chewing the insides of his cheek and frowning into space. After a moment he noticed their presence. "I really wish I'd had Ele with me," he said.

"Why?" asked Milo.

"I asked each one do you know who I am. They said no."

He waited a beat for everyone to catch up.

"I think they're lying," said Ramses.

Through
to the
Other Side

"So they have your memories," said Desiree.

"Buford's have his," said Ramses.

"I thought Bubba wiped them," said Smoove.

"Bubba's tired," said Milo. Damn and son of a bitch!

Ramses: "Thoom and Vampires have never been into cloning."

"So now we've got covert going between all three?" Smoove said. He looked at his wife. "Jesus," he said.

"Christ," she nodded.

"Let's not move too fast," said Fiona. "They steal technology from each other all the time."

"How do you clone a grown man in a matter of days?"said Neon. She was quite amazed by all this.

"Technology on the news is about a hundred years behind the real," said Milo.

"We could clone you a sheep for lunch," said Smoove.

"Are you clones?"

Smoove frowned at the very thought. If he was going to live to be a thousand it'd be in one unbroken strand. "No. Pretty sure I'm not. Rest of them could be."

"I guess we could," said Ramses.

"This isn't helping," said Neon.

"Hell, by rights we should be dead twenty times over," Ramses continued considering.

"If we're clones that just means we're toys of Buford," said Smoove.

Milo nodded slowly.

"That's what got you bent up?" asked his brother.

"Mostly. There are thirteen of me, Ram. Only supposed to be one."

Ramses wanted to slap the fye out of his brother. "You can't keep feeling violated, brother."

"Why the hell not?"

Desiree, tapping at her copper bracelet, asked Fiona, "What do we do with them?"

"Take them to Atlantis and make sure they stay there. Shig will keep watch on them," said Fiona.

"How?" asked Milo.

"We make sure they won't want to leave," said Fiona.

Neon stood and nudged Yvonne's knee. "Guess that means we're up."

Smoove barked a laugh. "Love a girl with a sense of humor."

"I need to talk to them," said Milo.

"No," said Fiona. "Take it from a girl with her head in the multiverse: this is their best life. *Your* best life. We've got enough psychic dampers working that nobody's teleporting anywhere. They're scared of Foom anyway."

"They should be," said a voice from the doorway: Bubba Foom entered with perfect timing.

"They *need* to be scared of Asme," said Fiona.

Ramses assured the group that he had impressed that upon them.

Bubba Foom combed his lanky hair from his face with his fingers. He was balding a bit and there was a fair amount of grey in with the tan.

He sat.

"You OK Bubba?" asked Milo.

"I'm all right." Foom closed his eyes and wildly mussed his hair. "Just give me a minute." A deep breath calmed and grounded him. "Hippocampus is throbbing like a celibate. I think I touched Raffic a few times."

Desiree hovered over him with medical scanners while Ramses asked how he'd managed to get captured.

"A man and a woman. Almost soon as I got off the boat. Mentally quiet through and through. Evil as shit."

"Adam and Eve."

Bubba locked eyes with Milo. "I remember you too, Milo."

When the hell had they cloned me?! "Which one of them?" asked Milo.

"He's dead."

"Seriously," said Neon. "Adam and Eve."

"What about Raffic?" asked Desiree.

"He said he's a vampire—"

Neon threw her hands up. "Who the hell isn't a vampire!"

"—in Atlantis. Heading to Sip. I think. Hell's with you playing with Djinns, Milo?" Being as tall as he was, Bubba Foom usually hunched, but now he outright slumped and seemed infirm.

"Vampires and Thoom have Buford," said Milo. "We'll fill you in."

"Later," said Ramses. "Go rest, Bubba."

"I'll make sure he does," said Asme from the doorway. She crossed to Foom.

"We been set up, baby," Foom said to her. "There's an inside man. Somebody with a bigger hard on in the brain than me. No offense, ladies."

Desiree reached for both Bubba's and Asme's hands. "Lolita's gone, Bubba," she said softly, so as not to prick his skin. "No good time to tell you."

Foom closed his eyes and kept them closed.

"Bubba?" said Milo. "Your fight's over. Tap out."

The big man shook his head.

"You got nothing to give, Bubba. When you do, let us know. Till then—"

Foom answered with his eyes remaining closed, his mind reaching. "There's a more powerful psychic presence than me. Do you understand that? Somebody with a lot more control over what they can do than I do. Somebody pulling a lot more strings than we do." His eyes danced the compass under the skin of his lids.

Smoove knelt beside his wife, taking comfort from her strength, hoping to impart a bit of his own. He put his hands on Foom's knees and squeezed. "Foom, you're gonna burn yourself out," said Smoove.

"Been there done that," whispered Foom.

"You can't reverse engineer this," said Milo. "We'll play it out."

Desiree cupped Foom's face in her hands. "You can't protect your son if—"

"I didn't do that anyway! Hush! I can push past the inhibitors..." Veins tightened angrily at his neck, then temples.

Ramses calmly went to a panel of readouts and lights and flicked a toggle. "Now you can't."

Foom's body immediately dropped. He dug rough palms into hollowed eyes.

Ramses waited the moment out. Once assured of everyone's attention, he pointed out the fact that as far as they knew, there was only one thing more powerfully psychic than Bubba Foom, and that was Leviathan.

Which quieted any response for a full second before Desiree said, "Oh. Hell. No."

"That's as far as we know," Smoove said. "We don't know everything." He caught the defeated expressions on Neon's and Yvonne's faces. "Ladies, work with us."

"The ride gets higher from here," Fiona said to them.

"What *isn't* true?" said Yvonne.

"Buying more and saving," said Fiona.

"Ok," said Milo. All eyes went to him. "We got Leviathan behind the curtain influencing Thoom, Buford and vampires to once and for all get rid of humanity like the best jaded politician —that work for everybody?" said Milo.

There was a general round of nodding. "Works for me," said Smoove.

"Hey," said Fiona.

"Too esoteric for me," said Asme.

"So we find this other psychic and we get him to show us what he can do," said Milo. "We're moving everybody out of here before anybody else mobilizes against us."

Asme nodded. "I've already packed everything I need," she said. She went to the control panel and entered codes. "Self-destruct in five hours."

In five hours canisters of a particularly effective acid released a corrosive mist to waft through important sections of Foom's compound. By then, almost the entire party was on its way back to Atlantis.

Left behind, Milo, in a non-important area, prepared several packs. He tossed one to the clone standing opposite him.

The
Boom

"I understand you don't like me," said the clone.

"No, you don't," said Milo.

"I know I'm not the most likable person. I got that impression from you on the flight here."

"Shut up."

The clone constantly looked around. Apparently life fascinated him. "I can leave anytime I want," he said.

"You'd spend the rest of your life wondering when I'm going to pop up," said Milo. "Please be quiet."

"Foom is a good man. He tried," said the clone, referring to the mind wipe that he was not supposed to recall. "None of these people know about us?" The other Milo took the gaudy spectacle of Rockefeller Plaza in a bit at a time. Jumbotrons and advertisements threw disconcerting assaults of light and sensation as determinedly as lightning from Mount Olympus. Warren, which he'd decided to call himself to elicit feelings of a minor sense of home, focused his interest instead on the group dynamics of all the strangers walking around him.

Milo remained tight-lipped.

"You act like I asked for this," Warren said.

"Warren, I know you didn't. You set my teeth on edge. Don't know why yet. I need you to be patient. I need you to be quiet."

"The Big Apple."

Milo gritted his teeth.

"And we'll find Adam and Eve?"

Traffic flared just as Milo let loose a healthy curse.

"What do we do when we find them?" said the clone.

Milo hustled across the lanes, heading toward 30 Rock, the home of NBC, but not daring to go inside. Not yet. "Hopefully, we survive."

Deep within New York, if one were to speed up time and accelerate past houses, people, cars and crime, there was a place where absolutely no one, not cop, banger or former mayor Guiliani, pretended to tread. A traveling zone that even time slowed to avoid entering, waiting just behind "now" for an opportunity to slip either left or right. It was the roving cold spot of life in the haunted house of the world.

It was wherever Adam and Eve happened to be sitting down for coffee. Which they did often. It was all they drank.

And it was always deep within New York.

Adam looked like a tanned Keanu Reeves. Eve, the actress Rosario Dawson. In their mid-forties.

Their sunglasses cost more than a German car.

Eve had killed a man once by looking so cuttingly at him he had a heart attack. Adam preferred tactile sensation, having mapped every point on the human body for knowledge of how to make a person bleed to death using nothing but wax paper and a cotton swab.

They were immortal, but they were bored, and this led to Buford, Nonrich, and Aileen Stone's involvement. Aileen, frequent slapper of William Fruehoff, had wild, dizzying plans that amused the hell out of them no end, involving so many different factions that it was what the vampires enjoyed referring to in their movies as "a non-stop roller coaster ride." Aileen would definitely be the world's new Buford. Boredom begot bedfellows.

Another game the parents of humanity enjoyed was tracking the Jetstreams, who were slippery children, Adam and Eve would give them that. Ramses animating the dead had come as a surprise. Adam and Eve had coached Jesus—the real Jesus, not Apollo—on his appeal to good will and sensibility because the boy had serious potential. Innate quantum awareness. Nobody knew about the real Christ. Ramses was likely related, but with genetics being so loose and democratic with itself, his older brother hadn't picked up that transformative trait of the family. No, Milo was much closer to Adam's and Eve's great great great (times a few more) grandchildren residing in Atlantis than anybody else. They waited for him to pay them a visit while they sipped on their balcony and looked out over what they knew to be, without doubt, their world. The coffee they sipped was always as strong and rich as they could stand it, practically water and beans ground with their teeth.

But flavorful.

Contempt for mankind went remarkably well with cinnamon mochas.

The
Bang

Milo and his new younger brother disappeared down an alley, emerged by a refurbished brownstone, and from there came face to face with the hugest Starbucks the world has ever seen. The coffee scent frightened rats away for a block perimeter. On the other side of the six-lane avenue was what Milo was after, a seedy liquor store where dream books sold next to lottery tickets, a confluence both disturbing and frightening.

"Stay here," said Milo.

"Understood. But as your lookout, what am I allowed and not allowed to do?"

"Do what comes natural."

Warren, with a nod toward the group of young men drawing Milo's attention, asked, "What are they?"

Milo ate a polish sausage so thick it dwarfed the bun. He ate very slowly to avoid disturbing the prayer mound of relish threatening at any moment to topple.

Warren hadn't wanted one. Clones had no appreciation for New York dogs. "Coffee smells," said Warren.

"I'm sure this isn't the first time you've smelled it."

"I'm trying to corroborate experiences."

"I never talked this much," said Milo. "And don't act brand new."

"There were thirteen of us. We aren't stupid."

"OK. But you *were* trained to kill me."

Warren nodded.

"A touch awkward pretending status quo."

Warren nodded that he understood.

"You nod too much."

"You told me to be quiet."

"What else can you do that I can't?"

"I have no idea."

"Foom told me I could trust you." Milo took another slow, thoughtful bite, still studying the group in front of the store.

"Only to the extent that you can trust anyone," said Warren. "I'll try to be honest even when it doesn't suit me."

"Particularly then, if you don't mind. Stay here."

The Shiftless spotted him coming and didn't move till he was right in front of them. There were five of them, each looking like a progressively pasty version of the other, their tangled blond Rasta braids creating straw halos. They surrounded him, identical in droopy shirts and sagging pants, dangling their hands at the hem of their visible underwear to indicate they were armed.

"Brothers," said Milo, giving the nearest a slight nod. "Which one's gonna be the first to say goodbye?" Simply a query of interest.

"No beefs," said the de facto leader. Milo noted, however, that the circle did not stand down.

"Static free," said Milo.

A tired woman with a frowning child exited the liquor/lottery store and walked straight through the ring, not even noticing the Shiftless and barely noting Milo's presence due to the influence of those same Shiftless.

The oldest looked about thirty-three. "What up, Jumbo?" he said.

"The rest of you talk?" asked Milo. The Shiftless stared into, through and around him with that special disregard only Shiftless possess.

"Not to you out in the open," the leader said. "Ain't that right, niggas?"

"Fuck you, Jetstream."

"Fuck you good," another clarified, except he mumbled so much it might have been "fried poo, wood."

Milo edged a corner of his lip upward. The sharp tooth showed. Vampires and Shiftless had an inbred dislike of each other.

Their talkative leader made the mistake of being slow to zip his surprise, and the others immediately tensed with fear.

Milo allowed the other side of his lip to stretch into a genuinely happy grin. He loved rattling Shiftless.

"No beef," reiterated the leader.

"Tell me about the last time you saw your folks," said Milo.

"We laughed, we cried, we hugged—what the fuck you think happened? Why you even joking about that?"

"Where was she?"

The Shiftless nodded in the general direction of *out there*. "And don't ask me where he was 'cause he wasn't there."

"They're always together," said Milo.

"Don't mean you see 'em. Look, man," the Shiftless said, finishing the pronouncement with a rap shrug he'd seen on TV, hunching his shoulders and throwing his hands.

"Which one of y'all's got the biggest piece now?" asked Milo.

The leader closed his eyes and caved even more into himself, causing his tee shirt to take on more of a deserted look. "Madrid," he said immediately.

Milo shook his head. "Not good enough."

"Don't look that oily," one said peering closely at Milo's face. "And you're out in the daylight. A lotta pain, brother."

"Anybody catches word of Eve, pass it around that I'm looking for her."

"Mom's a myth, man." The leader half-heartedly smirked.

"So am I," said Milo.

The mumbler mumbled, "Taped for safety, clit," which might have been, "This's some weird shit."

During the entire conversation the Shiftless, bit by bit, edged their circle and Milo toward the liquor store's alley. As a spread-consciousness people, and with the lion's share of that consciousness currently in Madrid, decision-making was always an iffy, shoddy enterprise, as evidenced by their thinking they could take Milo.

Milo spoke to the one directly behind him without turning his head. "If your fingers wrap around anything non-pliable, there will be trouble."

The Shiftless backed his hand from the gun in his pants.

"Sun's gotta be hitting you like a donkey fuck," said the leader. "Alley's cool and dry."

"We're concerned for you, Jetstream," said the mumbler, suddenly lucid. "Jumbo Jetstream."

"Milo Jambalaya," said another.

The siren call of the Shiftless was unmistakable, channeling a lazy sibilance into the air between them.

"Points for trying, gentlemen," said Milo. "But my associate and I have to leave."

Where the other man came from, not one of them knew, but there he was just outside the circle as though he'd been there the whole time. And although, or maybe because of, the way he stood so casually looking around with his hands in his pockets, he gave off a distinct, forceful *physical* aura.

And looking so much like Milo Jetstream that each of the Shiftless lapsed into allowing an actual facial expression to cross their dull, placid facades.

"Talk to people," said Milo. "Talk to non-people. I need Adam and Eve."

"They'll find you first, Jetstream," said the leader.

"But they won't reveal themselves. You know how the game is played," said Milo. "They'll let me find them if enough people say I'm looking for them."

"I hope they whup your ass," said Mumbles.

"I'll make sure there's enough left that I can come back to you," Milo told him specifically.

"No beef," the leader reminded him.

"Is this Mad Cow disease?" asked Warren, his first attempt at direct humor.

"Of a sort," said Milo. He emerged through the group's perimeter. Warren joined him in step. They walked down the block.

The silver bullet train whisked through the dark, subterranean tunnel:

"Nobody ever thought *Nineteen-Eighty-Four* would be taken as an instruction manual. But it has been," said Buford, "So here we are." He spoke solely to annoy. "Kichi begged him not to publish it but Orwell was one of those hell bent types—like all of them, really—one of *the world must know* brigade. That world included me, didn't it."

"And here we are. The architect of modern warfare," Madam dubbed him. This time the silver and red hair played off forest green.

"Modern life," he corrected. "Me."

"That was understood, Buford."

"Nothing's understood till it's expressed. God, you're a beautiful woman! Why the hell are all the intriguing women mixed up with the Thoom? Ever see *Bull Durham*? There's a Susan Sarandon-ness about you. Voraciously intoxicating."

"One of my favorite movies."

"I know. Give me some clothing. If you stop ogling me, we can accomplish things."

"You never know when to pull back, do you?" said Madam. Idiotic Jetstreams had forced her to pull up roots. She'd grown fond of that space in Iowa.

"Pulling back is like pulling out," said Buford, "which means the job ain't done." He directed his attention to the guard hulking at his shoulder. "In sex as in life, eh? This young man has never pulled out in his life," said Buford, crow's feet twinkling in camaraderie. "Ladies expect the full measure, don't they, young man?"

The guard's face remained expressionless. The tip of his weapon didn't waver a smidge from neighboring Buford's brain.

"The famed *Blue Guard*," said Buford. "Ultra secret and answerable only to you."

"I expect you know a lot about us, Buford," said Madame.

"Have I disarmed you?"

"No."

"Damn. At any rate, Cynthia—" which was her real name—"you have no logical reason for not allowing me clothing. I have no weapons. Got nothing you yourself are not personally aware of. I would have no problem attending my mother's funeral exactly as I am, so I'm not humiliated."

"I think you are."

"Think so?"

She slapped him quicker than he'd thought she could move. "I hate equivocation. Obviously I think so. I just said it, didn't I?"

With both his hands inside spherical manacles the sting had no choice but to fade on its own.

The train slowed. They came to another junction point. Buford deduced that there was no engineer and the train was set for random destination.

The computer's algorithm swung left.

"You built these tunnels with my technology," he said. "*Nothing* the Thoom bandies is its own."

"Defiance is the first refuge of the desperate. I wish you'd stop thinking your penis fascinates me."

"It can talk."

"I imagine you're a smash at board meetings."

"Just until they find out I'm no ventriloquist. Whose idea was it to teach Milo teleportation?" He caught Cynthia's annoyed nod at the guard. In a split-second the guard would attempt to club him. "Son, think hard," said Buford and tipped his gaze toward the former Navy Seal. "There's a reason there are six of you in this car," he said. The guard froze, wishing the shake would come.

A slight stand-down shake did come. The guard relaxed.

"Violence is the first refuge of the incompetent," said Buford, ignoring the guard and directing his glacial blues right at his captor.

"Violence saves time."

"Do these men want to die for you?"

She put it to the car. "Does that matter to you gentlemen?"

"No, ma'am."

"How much of real life have you experienced firsthand?" Buford put to her.

"You think Atlantis is any more intrinsically interesting than Prague? I'm part of the Thoom because it's what's right, not for notions of romantic mystery."

Buford dismissed her. "What's right has nothing to do with anybody but yourself."

"What did you do to Milo's parents?"

"Now *that* is what I've waited for. We can't fall in love without some interest from you."

An alarm chimed on a pad in her lap. She opened it. "Yes?"

"There's been no compromise," said an effective voice, one of those voices that never misses a target, never acknowledges the possibility of dissent, and wouldn't be caught dead waiting for an answer from those knowing considerably less than it did. It wasn't reporting in, it was debriefing her on the incompetence of her Iowa staff.

"That's good," she said, because she hadn't expected there to be.

"We are not yet aware of Milo's whereabouts," said der Kommandant.

"Teach a Jetstream to teleport..." Buford dragged out.

The pad came with in-screen and back-cover cameras.

"Why is he still naked? Nobody wants to see that. There is absolutely *nothing* remotely attractive about your doughy bodies, really."

"Cynthia's funbags are top shelf," said Buford. "And I'll be damned if every vampire is a tight, toned god."

"I am," said the sharp accent.

"In a pig's eye."

"Do we have eyes on Ramses?" said Madam.

"How often have you had 'eyes' on either one of them?" said Buford. "May I address you personally, sir?"

"Ricoula."

"*The* Count Ricky? Impressed as hell at this operation now, particularly this direct communication," said Buford. "Count Ricky speaking to the unwashed."

"The game has been yours for quite a while, hasn't it, Buford?" the voice asked.

"Game's over but you won't let me take my pieces?"

"Precisely."

"What do you need from me?"

"You mean besides gloating?"

"Yes."

"That's about it. We might clone," the Count posited before Buford interrupted him.

Buford addressed the voice while staring directly at Madam Cynthia. "Do you *really* want to start this war?"

"The end credits are rolling, Buford. Romanticism represents major flaws. You've engineered sheep to follow you, not warriors. The Dow won't help you; the S. & P.

cowers pathetically. Your sheep scatter and bleat as ineffectually as a mouse demanding cheese."

"The world turns within the world," said Madam Cynthia.

"The rotation carries you into night," said the vampire. "Go quietly. I will when it's my turn."

"There's a reason I rule this world, Count Willie. There's a reason I'm in every home, every car, every goddamned coffee shop and college campus in…the…world. I don't tend sheep. I create them." Buford leaned forward to address Willie alone. "In the pig's other eye. The only thing you do quietly is furtively sip at your little red flasks."

"In appreciation of your petty squabbles with the Jetstreams, we'll use you honorably," said Count Ricoula. "A wise man might say we gods need honor most."

"And the wise woman?" said Buford, nodding toward Madam.

"The wise woman," said Madam Cynthia, "thinks she'll have you sedated."

"Put clothes on him," said the vampire before decisively signing off.

Buford glanced at the guard over his shoulder. "You're about my size."

The throes of grief counseled Maseef Or-Ghazeem.

The presence of the clones further vexed him. Vexation was anathema to Maseef Or-Ghazeem.

Even Shig viewed the clones askance, so much so that he'd called Ramses into his office for a private conference.

"I'm not comfortable that the only guarantee of their behavior is fear of Bubba Foom," Shig admitted. "And I've never been comfortable with the Battle Ready Bastards."

"They'll watch over them. Except for Buford, murders, explosions and Leviathan, I'd never put Atlantis in danger."

"Granted."

"They're confused. Rightfully so. They're Milo without Milo's caginess. That's your best advantage. You stay several steps ahead of them to steer their course."

"Ramses, I'm habitually four steps behind my own assistants!"

"Shig, you're more Atlantis than Atlantis."

"Couldn't you have sent them to Asgard?"

"The Norse aren't particularly inclusive," said Ramses, tapping his skin.

"We're having a lot of troubles here," Shig said, each word an unwieldy reluctant block.

"I'm not going to add."

"But you do. Ramses, you—all of you—are the best and worst thing to come through the Blank in two generations."

"We love you, Shig." And he meant it.

The Atlantidean opened his arms for a hug. Ramses obliged. They held quietly and solidly in the faux-glacial décor of one of the more major of Atlantis' minor functionaries.

When Shig stepped back he regarded Ramses Jetstream as the brother he was. "Growing sentiment," he said, "is that the Blank be policed again."

"You could always join us out there," said Ramses.

"Misery shared is not happiness. We wouldn't make a very good fit, not anymore. I don't want to stagnate with the rest of the earth."

"Shig, the outside world learned everything it knows from you."

The Atlantidean's eyes flared briefly. "Atlantis has always stood for the good."

"Yeah, and so has America. Hollow point. Influence policy as much as you can, Shig. Closing the Blank would do more harm than good."

"Over two hundred *people* have died."

"We know."

"These are not abstractions, Ramses."

"I know."

"Because of you. Raffic showed up here naked and barely civilized. You should have seen Giselle nearly weep at the sight of him. I understand the entire concept: Men without a home needing havens of open arms. Your crew is definitely not the first. But," Shig said, needing an invective to drive the point but forgetting the word. *"K'thi,* what is it?"

"Dammit."

"Dammit," he drove. "Lolita Bebida is dead, fringe nutsacks—"

"Cases."

"Yes, are implicating Jetstream culpability."

"Ridiculous."

"She was one of the sexiest scientists of our time. You know how important that is. The Assemblies of the Mind commissioned Guerris to paint her."

"He will."

"Posthumous honor does nothing to appease the departed."

"Shig, I don't think Buford had anything to do with her."

"Then who was she fighting?"

"Is it conclusive that she was?"

"The bruising on her forearms and knuckles suggests defense and attack. They found her with a weapon in hand."

"Or a tool."

"Lolita Bebida allowed no accidents, Ramses. A raging fire wouldn't start without her giving it permission."

"Lolita could be reckless, Shig," Ramses reminded.

"You almost sound defensive."

"Shig," started Ramses, prepared to appeal to sterling logic. He realized a better tact. "What's Maseef said? In private."

"Maseef scares me, Ramses."

"Maseef scares everybody."

Shig's assistant, Giselle Jira, petite to the point of disappearing, interrupted with a polite knock at the threshold. He cleared his throat as further apology. "The new arrival is in Bay Three," he reminded.

"Extend apologies." Shig regarded Ramses as he posed the question within a question. "Will we be with her shortly?"

"You will," said Ramses.

Giselle disappeared. Shig's uneasiness crested. *"You awoke Leviathan."*

"We'll leave, Shig."

"What? There's a certain level of immediacy to your tone."

"Let me leave Atlantis the way we found it. We'll clear away every trace that we were ever here."

"Ramses, that will take years!"

"Not with everyone here. Raffic's already started. We follow his lead."

"You'll use the clones?" Shig asked, because otherwise they were his problem.

"Of course. Raffic, Maseef, the Angels—everybody. Will that solve a few immediate problems?"

"My problems," said Shig with a slight sigh, "are of the heart."

"They all are, Shig."

Shigetei Empa was not equipped to deal with this.

"You've got a new arrival to tend to," said Ramses.

"Will you ask about her over dinner?"

"I will."

sunlight

Sunlight, knew Maseef, would be glinting behind the peaks of the Glacial Mountains in that twinkling way Lolita described as *sentient luminescence*. There was a message in it, she insisted, a celestial mind waiting to be deciphered. Sunlight hitting the glacial peaks now meant dusk settling here. Maseef felt it fall over him leaving a brittle shell. His father had told him that family was the prime thing. The Family Or-Ghazeem had grown from nothing to Jonall Or-Ghazeem, father, to Kitredge Or-Ghazeem, mother, to Lolita Or-Ghazeem, daughter, to Maseef Or-Ghazeem, son, and finally Benifer and Jocasta Or-Ghazeem, twin daughters. A simple, steadfast evolution. Father and mother were pierced by time's arrow twenty years ago. Maseef checked the sun. He told time using it and his grief in correlation. Twenty years by the sun's declination.

The further de-evolution: the son mourning the daughter, Lolita Bebida Or-Ghazeem.

Maseef hated past tense. Temporal dread was alien to whales. They regarded Maseef as quaint.

But his sister was dead. Benifer and Jocasta were too flighty to be of use, off searching the Glacial Mountains for "clues" they were likely trampling bebeath their inept feet. He had a friend who could re-animate her. But there was nothing either on Earth, heaven, or in the universe itself that would make Maseef ask it, or make Ramses attempt it. To dishonor the dead as playthings was a heinous crime.

Maseef watched a *yebaum* peer at him from a fat stand of nearby fruit trees. The reddish simian blinked intently. Food though—which it smelled when the wind changed direction—proved much more interesting, and the small mammal hurriedly swung away.

Yebaums did not eat fruit.

When whales thought you were quaint and monkeys found you uninteresting, contemplation was a waste. Contemplation did not put you in touch with the universe. Motion did.

Maseef stood. When he walked, each step was a solid decision. He found Raffic onboard the *Linda Ann*. "I have decided," he told the small man, "to become a devotee of vengeance."

The Buddha nodded. He tossed Maseef a backpack containing numerous weapons from the *Ann*'s stores. The backpack he himself wore was massively equipped. Ramses waited for everyone on deck, having called a meeting. Maseef intended to listen, and then afterwards undertake his own mission. Somewhere in Atlantis there were unfortunate souls that needed to pay.

Ramses regarded each of them a moment. Raffic. Desiree. Smoove. Ele. Fiona. Maseef. Yvonne. Neon. The Bastards. "This is our last stand in Atlantis," the Jetstream said. "We have to function as scalpels. Our first mission is do no harm. We don't worry about anything else until we've cleared Atlantis out and the *Ann*'s on her way through the Blank. We find who killed Lolita," he said for Maseef, "and drag their forsaken bodies with us even if it's Leviathan."

"If you leave, we leave," said Lucifer.

"I can't stop you."

"They need to know about us," said Lucifer.

"I agree."

"What about Milo?" Coupdiviel asked.

"Silent running," Smoove answered her.

"I've never seen your home," Shetel said to Ramses.

"I live in a hole," he said.

Smoove veered Ramses away from melancholy. "Milo will wait for us till we're done here," the 700-year-old Jamaican said.

"What about the clones?" Lucifer was of a practical mind, and if the clones couldn't be trained…

"Cross that bridge when we get to it," said Smoove.

"We're at the bridge," Ramses told everyone. "Trolls and all. Billy goats are pissed. (Smoove side-mouthed to Shetel, "I'll explain to you later.") Buddha, are we go for full extermination?"

"This pack won't hold more," Raffic gritted out.

"I take that as go." Ramses slid his hands into his pockets and dismissed the group. "Ladies and gentlemen, tomorrow is a new day."

Neon raised her arm. "Wait. Code names?" she said, directing a finger between herself and Yvonne.

"Who the devil's speaking in code?" asked Fiona. "My name's Fiona—why do they need code names?"

Smoove waved her off. "I've thought about it." He nodded at Neon. "Tata Vega."

"Tata?"

"Obviously." To Yvonne: "For Now."

The ladies considered.

Yvonne answered. "We can live with it."

"Welcome to the crew," said Smoove.

"Welcome very much," said Lucifer on behalf of the Battle Ready Bastards. Ramses' new day would require a new cleansing ceremony.

Don't hurt them, Smoove thought, but directed the thought in the general direction of the angels' health and welfare.

"Do we get cool hats?" said Neon.

"No," said Ramses. Raffic caught Ramses' attention. The little man, in full gear, looked for all the world like half a soldier on a weapons high. "Buddha?"

"Yes?"

"You can take the packs off now."

~~~

The angels were sluggish in the morning. Neon and Yvonne were not.

"First stop," Raffic pointed out on the ship's map, his bifurcated goatee managing to not only not look ridiculous but also damn alluring, "is Ketel Falls. I feel it."

"It's heavily forested," said Ra'saiel X. A clone looked over Ra'saiel's shoulder, possible only because Ra'saiel was seated. Ra'saiel thought it good policy to keep the clones nearby. Each clone had agreed to take one letter from Milo's name for their firsts (granting their absent brother the *de facto* first M). Hence: Iggy, Luke, O'Neal, James (who was a bit more arrogant than the others and wanted, following Neon's and Yvonne's newfound coolness, to add the additional "King" before it), Excelsior (to rib at James), Tijuana, Sherlock, Titan, Reynold, Edric, Abomination (Desiree decided she would have to keep watch on that one), and M. Just M; he hadn't resolved himself to this whole subset-of-Milo existence yet.

"Do we suspect Milo might have issues to discuss?" Desiree later asked Ramses.

Ra'saiel tapped a section of the map and expanded it to an area several miles ahead of Ketel Falls. "Land here. They'll be expecting us closer."

"If there's anybody hiding in Ketel, I'll give them what they expect," said Ramses. "Then provide a bonus of what they don't."

Desiree pointed out the relative proximity to Abba, nearly telepathically formulating a plan with Ramses as she said, "Should we protect Guerris?"

"Yes." Ramses looked to Neon and Yvonne. "Ladies, you up to that?"

"I'll accompany," said Sereda.

"Best of both worlds," said Ramses.

MOOnlight

They walked the evening streets of Abba until nightfall. In addition to allowing Sereda time to observe them, it was a chance for the ladies to actually *be* in Atlantis, seeing the people and feeling the air on their faces, all under the pretense of trying to find Guerris.

"All I'm saying is why do *we* get put off the ship?" asked Neon.

"Quiet and pay attention," said Sereda.

"Should we assume we're under surveillance?" asked Yvonne.

"Always."

"What does this Guerris do? He a mindreader? Shape shifter?" asked Neon.

"Artist."

"Artist," Neon repeated flatly. She glanced at Yvonne. "Artist." She faced Sereda. "This is complete bullshit."

"Guerris has known the Jetstreams for years. You'd fault them for wanting to protect him?"

"No. I, however, don't appreciate being sent on a candy run to keep me out of the way."

"You're an *outsider* in *Atlantis* and your ego still gets in the way?" said the angel. "Amazing."

"I just want to help. They gave us names. How tall *are* you? Listen, I know how to fight."

"Do you know how to die?"

That shut her up.

"I thought not," said Sereda. "It makes a difference."

Abba was unusually hushed for such a comfortable night. Very few walked the spokes of residential streets that normally were barely different from daylight hours. Atlantideans somehow instinctively knew that there was a very dangerous hunt going on.

Huge discs of light hovered every thirty meters. On very rare occasions one or two of these discs, owing to the Department of Public Works' carelessness toward retrieval of something so inexpensive and mundane, would malfunction somewhere in Atlantis and drift "unnoticed" through the Blank, winding up in blurry photos and television shows featuring former state troopers. After-hours in most of Atlantis was like walking a huge sports field in the middle of the night, artificial light giving everything beneath it a vaguely otherworldly pall.

Perhaps twenty meters away sat Guerris—entirely oblivious—at a drafting table he'd set beneath a disc, arm whizzing away at a canvas. A small group of curious folks gathered around him, peering intently at the maestro's efforts.

Sereda headed that way. The onlookers didn't look up until the three women were in close range, and when they did they immediately made room for the ladies. The onlookers' clothing was shabby, their comportment slouchy, and they stank. Nothing overpowering, more along the lines of cabbage fresh out of the ground.

Art groupies.

Guerris wasn't painting anything. His hands made the motions, quick and precise as though fleetingly inspired, and the groupies watched each motion, firing in their minds whatever their private imaginations needed, but there was not a single stroke to the canvas.

Yvonne sniffed the air for evidence of wafting hallucinogens. Picking up none, she shouldered her way in front of the nearest groupie. Perhaps being closer would show her something that at two paces back she had missed.

He had a brush in each hand, flicking, pausing to consider, and flicking some more.

Yvonne stepped back to her compatriots.

"I think he's retarded," she whispered to Neon.

Guerris, without looking up, said, "I do speak your language and at night sound travels." His admirers finally took full notice of the interlopers.

Sereda's advance parted them. "I've never seen the *Big Bang Theory* at work," she said. "Art from nothing."

"Angel!" Guerris dropped the brushes and whirled to her. He smiled happily. "I thought the Blanks were just boorish newcomers." Guerris stood and offered a hand to Yvonne and Neon. "Guerris of Abba, very pleased."

"Atlanteans don't have last names?" said Neon.

"I took a cue from your artist, Prince. Only Guerris, a vocal symbol for who I am. And 'Atlanteans' makes you sound like a rube. 'Tideans', love."

"Take us home with you, Guerris," said Sereda.

"That's my house right there," he said, indicating a darkened structure set apart from the sidewalk and road; further set apart from its neighbors by a moat of lazily swimming fish that tended to splash at irregular intervals. "Which you obviously knew." He bowed to the assembled. "I'm sorry, students."

His neighborhood favored the solar-dome construction rather than the neo-pyramids traditional in the capital. The interior of his house was a slalom of *Feng Shui*, all smooth surfaces flowing into curves and open spaces. Of which there weren't many. Paintings lived everywhere, most of them completed but many caught in a half-life due to Guerris' hummingbird proclivities.

He led them into an anteroom that looked ready to serve a queen. Immaculate, sumptuous, and full of handsomely displayed local and out-Blank artifacts. A window arced the entire length of the room's curved wall, facing the street where the groupies broke away uncertainly.

"You draw them intentionally," said Sereda.

"He wasn't *drawing* anything," said Neon.

Guerris smiled. "During the day I paint what matters. At night I paint anti-matter."

"You're serious?" said Yvonne.

"Yes. There's food just past that arch. Refrigerator looks like a counter top. Where's Milo?"

"Didn't make it back." Sereda caught Guerris' flash of alarm. "He couldn't be here."

"Raffic killed vampires, didn't he?"

"Yes."

"These ladies?"

"Tata," said Neon.

"For Now," said Yvonne.

Guerris smiled politely, knowing outworlders could be loopy.

"Neon Temples."

"Yvonne DeCarlo Paul." There were paintings on display in the parlor. She asked the question every artist must be asked. "You did all those?"

He nodded, prepared to return his full attention to Sereda. Yvonne pulled him back.

"Some of these are the works of a master," she said. "How old are you?"

"Guerris is a young man full of life," said Sereda.

"Some are pretty frightening," said Yvonne.

"As I said," said Sereda.

"Ramses is here, isn't he?" said the artist. "This feels like Ramses. Very covert. You're protecting me. I don't think I need to be protected."

"We know you don't," said Sereda, eyes warm as memory.

Yvonne peered outside. "How long will they stand around out there waiting for you?" she asked, wondering how well the groupies could see inside the house. Lighting in the parlor was suitably dim.

"They'll go home."

"You were actually serious about that anti-matter?" Neon wanted verified.

"Have you ever drawn using a lightwand?" he asked, eyes dancing.

"Flashlight," Sereda said for their benefit.

"Yes," said Guerris. "Same difference. The eye creates where there's only movement and suggestion."

"And they'll stand around and watch you do this?" said Neon.

"It's an incredible aphrodisiac. The neurons get so fired it's all you can do to avoid orgies. Another reason why it's done at night with less traffic. And near home. Atlantis is quite pro-sex."

"We've noticed," said Yvonne.

Neon surveyed the room again. "You painted these," she said rhetorically. "I guess I can forgive if you're crazy."

"Thank you. Angel, tell me everything that's happened since you left."

"I only have bits and pieces."

"You have these two warriors. They'll fill in the rest." He smiled their way and pulled hair from his eyes. "May your first time through the Blank be an uneventful one."

"Great. You just jinxed us," groaned Neon.

Which, of course, meant that the attack waited till everyone had fallen asleep for all hell to break loose.

The element of surprise from the blockbuster movie *Brought It!, Part Two* featured crashing through a window and holding the heroes hostage, two villains against four heroes, using two guns and one grenade.

Elyse and Brian Hoek did just that. They came complete with thermal-goggles, action belts and lethal-looking weapons that trained on Neon and Yvonne later that night to keep Sereda from kicking their asses. Elyse clearly displayed a thermite grenade ready for arming at a finger flick if either Sereda or Guerris moved another foot forward subsequent to their rushing into Guerris' guest room. Brian held both guns aimed squarely. Elyse tossed Sereda a small cylinder.

"Inject yourself, hand it to him, and step back," she said, hoping there was a tinge of menace. Elyse Hoek was a marketing strategist; she had no business doing commando runs in the dead of night! This was Brian's idea.

Sereda assessed.

"Don't you dare," hissed Elyse. "Your man went crazy out there. We've had to feed by biting the buttocks of cattle!" Another of Brian's ideas.

"That's about as low profile as you can get," Brian defended.

"Yes it is, Brian!" said Elyse.

Sereda shifted a foot.

"Brian?"

The other stepped near enough to Neon and Yvonne to press the guns' muzzles directly against their foreheads. "Nobody in this room is fast enough to prevent somebody dying," he said from beneath his makeshift ski mask. One side of the goggles featured a zoom lens that kept going in and out with his movements, giving him the appearance of one regular eye and one googly eye. This was not, Neon decided, the appropriate moment for such humor.

Sereda injected herself. First tingling, then numbness. She handed the cylinder to Guerris.

"That might be poison," he said.

"I wouldn't give you poison," Sereda said. The rushing numbness had ridden up her arm and was about to crest her shoulder to rush her spine.

Guerris pressed the cylinder to his forearm. Sereda caught him with one good arm just before it went out. She lowered him to the carpeted floor, took a step back, then assumed the Lotus position beside him. Paralysis, well on its way to her toes, had firm hold of her upper body.

Elyse retrieved the cylinder from the floor. She approached Neon and Yvonne, gun drawn. "Is the situation clear, ladies?"

They said nothing.

"Even better," said Elyse. "You types tend toward speeches."

"That's villains," Neon said under her breath. She caught Elyse's eye. Elyse gave her the shot. Woman and vampire glared at one another.

Neon dropped.

Yvonne was taller by a few inches than Elyse. Elyse stared her up. "Look at the pretty neck on this one."

Yvonne rolled her eyes. "Typical villain shit," she said under her breath as well, which she knew the goggled-lady heard clearly. Elyse jammed the cylinder to her neck. "Thank you," said Yvonne on her way to the floor.

Brian knelt beside Guerris. He removed wire from a pack around his shoulder and looped it tightly around Guerris' wrists and feet. The two ends of the wire created an unbreakable self-seal. "What kind of idiot keeps priceless art and doesn't have an alarm system?" he said, smacking Guerris upside his paralyzed head.

They loaded the bodies into a waiting rover. They were just about to leave when Elyse heard an unfortunate 'crack.'

She half expected it to be a groupie, but they'd been gone for hours. Instead it was something much more benign: a neighbor.

Brian caught Elyse's eye. "We don't have time for this. You're not even hungry."

The set of Elyse's lithe body telegraphed the entire thing. Brian resigned himself to what he knew would be her gritty rejoinder. Just because she'd led the marketing team on *Brought It's* three hundred million domestic gross she had to take the theatrical lead.

She narrowed her eyes. The neighbor, a short, pudgy woman, had ran. Elyse took off.

"This has nothing to do with hunger," she had said just the second before.

Gaslight

At their lair, Brian felt he was contributing: "We should strip them," he said.

Elyse saw otherwise. "You just want to see them naked," she said in a tone that suggested the most derelict perversion she'd ever come across.

"Dammit, they could have transmitters or something, Elyse!"

She approached Yvonne, but he tried to see Sereda with peripheral vision.

"The angel? You—" Words didn't fail Elyse, there were just so many she wanted to use.

He braced himself.

"I think we should all strip," she said.

That wasn't the blow he expected.

She shrugged off her equipment and yanked a spattered black top over her head.

"You're losing it," he said.

"And you're under control?"

"No, scared shitless. Exactly why I don't want to wind up bludgeoned with my own elbow. They're going to find out what you did back there."

Her bravado faltered a second but she immediately recovered. "We're getting out of here whether they want us to or not. You should be monitoring the comm."

"The comm's on. You don't hear anything. It's only been overnight. They probably think they're at breakfast."

"Actually," came from the comm, loud and clear, "no. We've just been listening to you."

Elyse scowled at her husband. "Son of a bitch! You had it on two-way!"

"Like I know how to use this military shit!" He absolutely hated that look on her face.

"Ok, so you found the comm we left," she said to the voice in the air. "You know who we have. You know I will kill every…"

Ramses cut her off. "You killed a very frightened, middle-aged woman. Not me. I'm coming for you, love."

"Parley!" she shouted.

"What?" said Ramses.

"Parley. That woman was unfortunate. Your Buddha or Shiva or whatever the fuck his name is has everybody on edge. We're not going to be hunted like beasts."

"How long will my people be out?" came Ramses' voice.

Brian leaned toward the comm. "About…"

"Don't give them any information! Are you thoroughly stupid? What does your brain do with all that free time? Jesus, is there some foundation to benefit it?"

"Elyse," said Ramses.

"Jetstream, shut the fuck up now or I start killing," she snapped. "Here's what will happen: you and I will meet…"

"No, no Jetstreams!" Brian interjected.

"Who's listening in with you?" she asked Ramses. "The women. The human women. The captain and the other one. Parley."

"Do I look like frikkin' Kiera Knightly?" she heard a brogue lash out.

Ramses overrode the brogue. "Where do we meet?"

"I emphasize: no Jetstreams!" Brian wanted perfectly clear. "No madmen. We just want to go home."

"Where do we meet?"

"Restaurant in Abba," said Elyse. "They serve Sip delicacies."

"Ambience can't be beat," said Brian.

"Poets know it. Ask around. And before you try locking in on our signal and storming the castle, be assured my husband's more than capable of putting several bullets in these chests he admires."

"When?"

"Two days," she said.

"No, no, no, you're giving them time to be smarter than us." Brian leaned over the comm. "Hours, not days. Two hours. From now."

"We'll sit and talk and you'll agree to our terms," said Elyse.

"How many of you are left?"

"I don't know," she answered honestly.

"This every man for himself?" said Ramses.

"There are three other people leaving with us. This transmission is over." She flicked the comm off.

"That was masterful," said Brian.

"You want me, don't you?"

"You know it." They stripped.

Oh Dear spirits, thought Sereda. They were merely paralyzed, not unconscious.

Vampiric sex was really rather vile to see.

Boogie

Elyse sat at the table nearest the door, the open doorway flooding light into her balmed face. She wanted to see them coming.

They arrived as promised. Dressed in their outBlank clothing. The shorter one was certainly the one who'd spoken over the comm. All reddish auburn hair and attitude. The companion walked like someone who tended to Take Charge before breakfast. Elyse appreciated their lack of subterfuge. When they stopped at her table she looked at them from under the wide brim of her hat and was honest enough with herself that it worried her they didn't look pleased. Elyse resolved, though, that there had been no other way. "We just want to leave," she said.

The women stood impassively above her.

"What he did was *wrong*," Elyse said.

"I've been told not to speak," said the brogue levelly, "on the grounds that I might punch you in the throat. But know this: you've tread where you never belonged."

"Fiona Carel," Desiree introduced crossways.

Fiona returned the favor. "Captain Desiree Quicho."

They pulled chairs to sit (while several clones teleported Ramses, Raffic and Maseef into the stronghold where three vampires made sure their captives' paralysis never wore off). Brian, outside the café, hoped to be as inconspicuous as possible.

"We want safe passage out of Atlantis," said Elyse.

(While one of the vampires listening in on Elyse's wire screamed to her, "We were traced!" he also wished they hadn't decided, in the wake of the earlier fiasco, against a two-way subcutaneous—and was snatched mid-air from his immediate dive to sink his teeth into Guerris' leg. He landed hard on his stomach, rolled quickly, and looked into the face of Maseef Or-Ghazeem.)

"Once home, no persecution," Elyse went on.

Raffic grabbed a trigger finger, bent it totally against the grain, swept the legs of the vampire out, and retrieved the gun.

"Just leave us alone. Promise that, and we release your crew. In advance," Elyse added to show good faith.

Of course there was an entire colony. (Once apprised of the exact location, the Battle Ready Bastards came from the sky on solar gliders, raining hallucinogenic darts that forced the remaining vampires into spasms of psychological ennui.)

"Promise it," said Elyse.

"I don't think so," said Desiree. Her comm blinked.

Elyse's face was a huge question mark.

Desiree placed the comm on the table.

Ramses spoke. "Your name is Elyse Hoek. There are seventeen of you. There's another cell in the Glacial Mountains. I'm not interested in negotiating. Give me useful information."

"I don't know anything!"

"That didn't help. Signal Brian to come to you." Ramses waited a moment. "Brian?"

"Yes?"

"Where's Buford?"

Brian leaned close to the comm to waylay the urge to shout out, "I have no freaking idea!" In a restaurant setting, though, such urgent hissing drew more attention than wanted. A few poets glanced their way with properly stifled interest, and one or two patrons recognized the outsiders and deduced a show was about to begin.

The proprietor and tress quickly approached their table.

"You're enjoying the sun, I see," the tress said.

"Better before it clouds up," the proprietor said. He took in Elyse's pale, glossed features and matched them with Brian's. "Out-Blank vamphyre?" he asked, never having seen one but heard described enough. "At our restaurant! Here, move farther in, be comfortable." Nobody but Sip people pronounced it vaam-peer.

"We won't be here long," said Desiree. "Thank you."

"If there are any problems please let us know," said the woman.

"Not that you want to be bothered," said the man. "I imagine there's something exciting happening at this table." He noticed no one had ordered, despite the newly redesigned interactive menus inlaid in the wood of the table. "I would make a suggestion but...well, what do vamphyres eat?" he said. "Besides the traditional."

"When did you arrive through the Blank?" asked the wife. "I can't recall hearing about it."

"All just recently," said Desiree. She indicated the comm sitting patiently on the table. "Conference call."

The man brightened. "Business ventures! We'll leave you to it."

"They're going to kill me," said Elyse.

"The risks of investment," said the man. "There are several Sip delicacies on the menu."

"And sausage. You'll need to scroll down for that," said the wife.

"We would rather keep this a low-profile meeting," said Desiree. "If you could not mention that there are vampires here," she said, twirling a finger.

The two agreed with a shared nod and hustled off.

"Ramses," said Desiree.

"The Glacial colony," he resumed. "Why there?"

"They're scientists," Elyse said with a dour expression, darting her eyes low and scanning the restaurant. "Following a theory about the Mount and Glaciers."

"Fractal?"

"Quantum."

"Brian?"

"Yes?"

"Do you love your wife?"

"I do."

"Is she lying to me?"

"I don't know."

"Thank you. Desiree, bring them here."

"We'll take your rover," Desiree told the vampire. "Where is it?"

Elyse pointed out the top-of-the-line red rover shaded by an *odhiry* tree.

"Shotgun," said Fiona, and she was being quite literal.

Headdesk

The ride was not very informative and altogether awkward for the captive individuals. Ketel Falls was nearly an hour's ride from Abba at fast cruise. Huge, leafy trees gave way to conifers that grew thick and strong in the fertile ground. Sunlight fell between their spiky thatches in jangled spackles.

Just to be mean Desiree and Fiona didn't let the vampires polarize their windows at all.

Pointed silence was finally broken when the rover left the main markers and crossed the tree line, winding surely between spaced trunks that became more and more constrictive.

Elyse had the wheel. Her captors never asked where she was going, and she never once offered.

Fiona pulled her communicator out. Her weapon didn't waver from the back of Elyse's chair. "Ramses? Do we have eyes?"

"Nakir sees you."

The angel flew a slow arc above them, blocking the sun with the wings of his glider.

"Not spotting any activity on the ground," Ramses relayed.

"Be there soon."

Desiree had spent the ride looking at the landscape and thinking about the life she and Smoove planned to lead.

When he wasn't feuding with Bigfoot he was the most attentive man she'd ever known. It was very beautiful out here, and when she put it to Elyse why Ketel Falls, Elyse corroborated: "It's pretty."

"And you can't get to it easily," added Brian.

"You can if you have the right transportation," said Fiona, opening the sunroof and scanning the sky as Nakir made a second loop around.

"That hurts," said Brian.

"A fake weakness you play to advantage," said Fiona.

Neither vampire responded. Fiona closed the roof and settled back. "You made it seem like you and Brian were the last survivors of a major cataclysm," she said. "'In a world…'" she intoned.

"That's a brilliant campaign," Brian defended. "Warped reality."

"I wrote the book on warped reality," said Fiona. She shunted a microsecond and came back. "In one you're my father." He thought she was joking. "You pretty much leave me to fend for myself. A right bastard." She was thankful the vampires were in the front seat. The multiverse always made her feel like a puzzle missing pieces. The longer the shunt, the longer the recovery.

Brian jammed himself into his seat and closed his eyes. *Take over Atlantis, they said. Infiltrate then entertain, and before they know it,* Brought It!, *the Atlantean Salvo! Get Atlantis from within; by the time the Jetstreams care, it'll be too late. Yadda freaking yadda!*

A vampire was first and foremost a soldier, and thus fueled by STUPIDITY he and his wife had agreed to this journey. Turning Raffic into a vampire had been a bonus up until that bonus had pretty much knocked the living shit out of everyone they'd known. *I just want to go home. Field some scripts, make some deals, die rich and well fucked. Get that angel to be my mistress. Not like Elyse would mind; she's doing half the junior marketing department. Actually so am I. Would vampires be sexually compatible with angels though?*

"Sit up," said Elyse to him.

He glared at her. "I'm not going to sit up. We've been sitting ramrod straight the entire drive. You haven't come up with any plan to spring into action." He craned his neck a moment to speak to the ladies in the rear. "We're not going to spring into action." He glared at his wife again. Their current circumstance was neither her fault nor idea, but what's the point of marriage if not to blame someone?

"There's an entire infestation of you," said Fiona.

"Come on now!" said Elyse, eyes hot in the rearview mirror. "You're closer to being us than to them. Infestation?"

"You're not wanted here," said Desiree.

"Who've you asked?" said Elyse.

"Tou-fucking-ché," said Brian, low enough to be considered under his breath while specifically loud enough to be heard by all.

"Tou-fucking-ché," Elyse said. She narrowed her eyes on the camouflaged area ahead. If they were going to face Raffic or some other crazed heroic reject, be scared and pissless then. For now, be indignant.

The thing about now, though, was that it never lasted long.

They hovered through a man-made clearing, then a series of sensor points, then a cluster of camouflaged shacks.

The rover settled quietly and powered down. Raffic exited a shack to meet them. Desiree and Fiona got out of the rover. The vampires did not.

Desiree shook her head at the Buddha. He turned and went back inside.

Elyse and Brian exited.

Vampires ringed the thickest trees, wrists and knees tied securely around trunks. Each vampire's head lolled. Each dribbled incomprehensible gibberish, releasing "market share" into the air with one breath and "rim the ass" with another, and all randomly punctuated by whoever felt the need to scream "Fuck it!"

"We really need a Geneva Convention!" said Elyse. She whirled on Desiree. "You've got them out in the sun!"

"Sunlight does not kill you."

"But it hurts!"

"In much the same way as being bitten, I'm told."

"Evil bastards," Elyse muttered. Ramses exited the shack. She prudently shut up.

Elyse and Brian dutifully assumed the position of hands behind their backs for binding. Smoove swiftly did so.

"Properly introduced," said Ramses Jetstream. He was tall and he wore glasses, something she hadn't expected. And he practically poked one's eyes out with the intensity of his own while he spoke, a soft, insistent poke, not hard, but definitely promising to increase if displeased. He turned away. "Let's go inside."

Raffic the Mad Buddha was inside.

Scared and pissless became both prudent and advisable.

"Who's going to lead us to the rest of the encampments?" said Ramses. It was cool inside the shack and softly lit. The drives of the vampires' computers had been stripped, their equipment trashed, and the fridge, which hadn't held a canister of blood since they'd completely neglected to ration it after Raffic's rampage, was now similarly emptied of every other supply they'd had.

Ramses took a seat and stared at them standing before him.

"Bernard Pryor," Brian volunteered. "He can lead us. He's got the best sense of direction. The one out there in the red shirt."

"No red shirts. You think we don't know about red shirts?" said Ramses.

"Look, we barely had any dealings with the others," said Brian. "They're scientists, man! We didn't need them."

"Have a seat," said Ramses.

The two sat at a small round table.

Raffic flashed up, palmed the back of Brian's head, and slammed it into the table.

Elyse howled, "Fuck no!"

Raffic returned to his seat, leaving the vampire bleeding and bleary eyed.

"Fuck your good cop, bad cop!" said Elyse.

This time Ramses did it. The gash on Brian's forehead opened wider.

Ramses crossed his arms. "Now you have a new trope. Have you ever tested the theory that if you get hungry enough you'll start feeding on each other?"

A feline mewling issued from Brian.

"Elyse?" said Ramses.

Elyse was in her own world. "Jetstreams don't kill," she mumbled.

"That's not true."

"He'll take you," she said. "He knows pass codes."

"You don't?"

"I forgot."

"What do you know about Lolita Bebida?"

"Not even sure who the hell that is," said Elyse. "What?"

"We'll go," Brian groaned. He tried opening his eyes but the skin of his lids hurt. The cut healed slower than usual. "We can leave now." He determined not to cry.

"That's excellent. Raffic, you good with that?"

The Buddha sniffed and stood, then walked past them without a word. Sunlight streamed in through the door he'd left open.

Ramses handed Brian a towel from the sink behind him. "That," he said, referring to the unwilling vampire who'd just left the room, "was not the smartest thing you could have done."

"We didn't know he was insane!" said Elyse.

"Yeah, well, we all need hobbies."

The
Peeled
World

Warren was amazed at the awful diversity of the globe. Shiftless, Progenitors, Jetstreams, Vampires, Telepaths, Thoom, Bufords--there was no end to it. The thing Milo spoke to in the hole of an abandoned building had yet to show its face but it spoke with such an authority Warren was transfixed.

"You stir trouble to no benefit!" The sound was raspy, befitting something from a hole.

"It doesn't affect you one way or another," said Milo, hands braced on either side of the hole. Holes tended to try to pull one in.

"Time is finite, Jetstream, and you take mine; I am affected."

In Atlantis, during the trailing of Buford, Warren had seen a dead thing being picked apart by insects. There were many of them and they were efficient. He had the same sense here. Even on the periphery of the exchange, Warren felt that these Holes were legion...and patient. He wondered how many abandoned buildings existed in this brave new world. Patience had become a diminishing return for Milo over the course of the day. Adam and Eve apparently elicited much stonewalling. Warren calculated how soon Milo's methods would alter.

In a blur Milo reached into the hole and yanked out what appeared to be wet smoke and wrinkled skin. The thing squirmed furiously, coiling itself around Milo's wrist. A drug dealer who'd been eyeing them from the corner a little ways off decided to forego notions of commercial territory and ran.

The thing protested hotly with a string of "No no no's" that ran into one long wailing screech. It was a screech that said this was an affront not against itself but against God, nature and the very fabric of reality. Holes were *not* supposed to be on the outside.

In the ragged aperture formed from bricks mysteriously knocked out there had been only darkness. Out here with the muted light of a New York evening nearby, there were eyes, four beady sets of phosphorescent eyes getting brighter and brighter with the Hole's mounting outrage.

The Hole tried its best to constrict Milo's wrist into splinters. Milo whirled and held it high facing the street. It stopped immediately and cowered in his grasp.

"If I have to wear you as a necklace," said Milo.

"Ask!"

"Do you mind if others are watching?" Warren queried Milo.

Milo held the Hole against the wall. "Is there a crowd yet?"

"A few wide eyes."

"When there's a crowd I'll be tossing him their way."

The Hole struggled again, but only briefly. It went limp. Limp, it looked even more disgusting.

It snorted.

"These kids will hunt you down if I point you out," said Milo.

All four eyes closed, shutting out the visage of this ugly man. "They enjoy coffee."

"Do we bomb Star—" Warren began.

"No." Milo addressed the Hole. "Tell me what makes New York tick these days."

"Mergers. Rat to bird to slug. Moist activity. Sex. Much more sex than normal."

"Consumption?" said Milo.

"Inconspicuous consumption. Flow change. Underground. Lava." It noticed Warren frowning at it. "I daresay you haven't changed much. You are still rude and packed with testosterone." Back to Milo: "Progenitors watch over us."

"Do they want us dead?"

"Progenitors watch over us," it said, this time slightly hooking its body skyward.

"Warren?"

The clone's features went blurry in a quick vanish.

Two extremely attractive people flanked Warren on the low rooftop.

"Do *not* engage," Milo hollered.

Eve rushed, finger-striking Warren on the inner elbow, side of the neck and behind the ear in quick succession. The clone's breathing stopped.

Adam handed her back her cup of coffee.

"Jetstream, go home," Adam called down.

Eve peered over the edge.

"Ma," said Milo. He relaxed his grip on the Hole. It writhed its way back to the safety of invisibility, eyes dim in the cool recesses.

"Goodbye, Milo," said Eve.

Milo said, "Boom."

Warren exploded.

He popped back in beside Milo, naked and asphyxiating. The veins on his neck hadn't distended too far yet, so that was a good sign. Milo hustled Warren along, both men running flat out between rows of neglected brownstone tenements until landing in a shadow deep enough for Milo to reverse the paralyzing spasms inflicted by Eve.

Warren sucked a lung-rattling fill. Milo pulled clothing out for him.

"Wearing a bomb isn't something you think I should know in advance?" the clone snarled.

"No. You're very good at teleporting."

"I might not have realized explosive fibers were laced in *all* my clothing. Or what that beep in my collar presaged."

"I just taught you a valuable lesson. Things that suddenly beep are never good. Pissed them off royally, though. Oop, here they come. Run."

"I can—"

"*Run*," Milo reiterated.

Frat boys wept at the display of freejumping the Jetstreams presented New York City. They ran full tilt, vaulting over cars, leap-frogging bus stands, flipping over people and—at several points—taking to rooftops with the dexterity of men intimately acquainted with the word 'flee'. Adam and Eve followed close behind. Police couldn't keep up, bystanders damned their slow camera phones, and the children in the barrio found new heroes. As soon as they stumbled into a sufficiently abandoned area Milo shouted *"Stop!"* to his twin. Milo stopped running, sat with his back against a rooftop's edge, and caught his breath the few seconds it took Adam and Eve to reach them.

As immortals go they were charred and dirty but otherwise unhurt.

"Why'd you take Foom?" he asked.

They regarded him incredulously.

"You'll answer me or you'll kill me on the spot." He hadn't stood.

"Which one of you?" asked Adam.

"Does it matter? Warren, if I'm dead will you carry on the fight?"

"I will."

"Then both of you," said Adam.

"You could've found something besides Thoom to play with," said Milo.

"We don't tell you all our secrets, do we?" said Eve. The immortals leaned their buttocks against the tenement. Adam shook debris from his hair.

"The longer you two play," Milo began.

"The longer the game goes," said Adam. "And the game is life. Do you understand? Psychohistory? *Foundation?* Asimov?"

"I'll stop playing," said Milo.

"You won't," said Adam.

"Or," said Eve, "Warren will play. I don't think he'll do annoying things like you just did. You made us run through the streets."

Milo grinned maliciously. "Maddening, wasn't it?"

"Points for the exploding clone trick," said Adam. "This clone's more advanced than you."

"He's in the prime of his life. I'm an old man now. Eve, tell me what's going on. Alliances haven't formed in ages. Thoom are working with vampires, who are working against Buford…"

"Buford's become boring," said the unnervingly alluring woman. She sloughed scabs off her forearms. "His entire enterprise has stagnated, hasn't it?"

"Very much so," answered Adam. "Get up."

Milo stood.

"Clone?" said Adam.

"Sir?"

"If I see you again I snap your neck."

"Understood."

"*And* we hunt the others," the other alluring half of the ancient duo assured. She regarded Milo. "Counting coup, Milo? That's extremely juvenile."

"We can finish what we started without you two complicating things," said Milo.

"You would've been finished a long time ago in that case," said Adam.

"And family reunions are so infrequent," said Eve. She walked away. Adam followed.

"Here." Milo grabbed two jumpsuits from his pack and tossed them their way. "No need for you to walk the sewers home."

Adam gave a barely perceptible nod. A truly considerate son. A shame he refused to live up to his potential.

When they were gone Warren turned to Milo.

"Milo?"

"Hm?"

"I rather enjoy not wearing underwear."

"We all do."

"OK if I—"

"No. Briefs or boxers like the rest of us. Freedom ain't free."

"Understood," said Warren. Other than nesting pigeons, no one had witnessed the rooftop exchange. "I wish they hadn't threatened to kill me. I think I'm in love with her."

"Yeah, Ma has that effect on people. Let's go."

"What now?"

"We pick a fight with 'em."

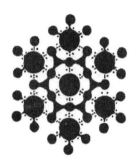

Important text messages:

ABOUT TO STORM THE GLACIAL MOUNTAINS.

ABOUT TO STORM THE GLACIAL MOUNTAINS

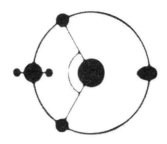

ABOUT TO ENGAGE ADAM AND EVE. NO RISK, NO GAIN. LOVE YOU, BROTHER. STATUS OUT.

ABOUT TO ENGAGE ADAM AND EVE.

"Be kind, for everyone you meet is fighting a hard battle…"
~Blissed dudes everywhere.

The Subtler Things

William Fruehoff, tasked with finding the greatest man on the face of the Earth, had run out of options. There was no Buford. Fruehoff's intention was to leave the country, live under a series of false identities—all independently and untraceably wealthy—and be dead within five to ten years satisfied he'd flung enough sin and debauchery in the face of mortality to sing his song as death approached.

This intention found favor because: (1) the odds of finding Buford were dead set against him; (2) the Nonrich Corp. was moving massive amounts of capital in what ultimately would amount to global tectonic shift, and whatever piece of the world broke off he wanted to be far, far from; lastly, one of the cleaning crew was about to be deported and she gave the most magnificent, languorous fellatio ever captured in sonnets and whom, as a miniscule token of defiance, he'd decided to take with him.

The reality was there was no way in hell he could accomplish this. One didn't get to be this high in Buford's world to disappear. Only Buford could do that.

The great, soul-crushing question was: Why had he done it on *his* watch!

No demands, no sightings, no communiqués—nothing gleaned from torturing Thoom, Vampire or Djinn.

The penalty for this kind of failure wasn't death, it was being thrown into the field. "Exercise" Buford euphemistically termed it. "Best thing to recover the soul." This meant being sent to the location of one's last failure with the mortal directive of straightening it out.

William Fruehoff checked his suitcase one last time. He'd never had any intention of going to Atlantis. Its existence had always seemed like a remora to him, hanging parasitically off the Earth—the true world—while contributing absolutely nothing. But here he was, packing for Atlantis, and missing the blue jacket with the micro-ablative armor sewn inside.

He walked the length of a cobalt blue runner to the second room of his closet, vaguely perturbed by something. When he exited the closet he looked down. The runner had eyes.

The instant he jumped he realized there was no danger because he recognized those eyes.

checking in on the score it said in a nearly southern drawl close to Fruehoff's own, the sound issuing from some indeterminate point in the air.

He had dreamed about those eyes a hundred times. They were the eyes of God. Actually, it was Leviathan, but he didn't know that. Worldwide, people sensitive to the transmission freaked out, hallucinating eyes appearing in random places, and the planet would mark another day of worldwide migraines with panicked scrambling by the Center for Disease Control.

The hallucination passed. The cobalt runner was nowhere near plush enough to contain another living being. It lay unmoving and ready for bare feet.

'Visions are never random,' Buford had written. They were, but if you'd told people the image of Elvis Christo was really just a few neurons firing disparate impressions at one another, you'd never see a profit margin in any industry above half a percent.

The eyes of God. Add to that a sudden headache to prove it wasn't simply imagination. And the timing of it, as he rumbled over having to go to Atlantis in search of the False Prophet Buford—that could only be necessary and important. 'Checking in on the score.' Who, the universe apparently wanted to know, was winning?

Was he aware he was on a team? Fruehoff asked himself. Yes. Did he believe in taking one for the team? No. But he did believe in tilting the playing field to his advantage.

Right now that meant summoning Aileen Stone's assassins.

~~~

Aileen Stone wasn't in the habit of loaning out her bodyguards. "You want them to go to Atlantis with you?"

"Yes."

"Why should I release them to you?"

"Whatever happened with Buford is more than I can handle, right? I'm going to need a team."

"You'll have infantry."

"I need perfection."

Aileen Stone weighed this. She also thought of slapping him again. "How long have you known who they were?"

"I really don't think there are any secrets left in the world," said Fruehoff. "I could tell you God told me and that'd be as reasonable as anything else. Aileen, three people in the world see you on a regular basis. I think you can do without your bodyguards a few days."

Aileen played with an earring thoughtfully. "A few days. You think that's all it's going to take to resolve a global catastrophe? A few days."

"A few days ago we ruled the world. Now we're checking the scoreboard."

"If nothing changes in a few days?"

"Then obviously I won't be coming back."

She could live with that. She contacted them. On the video phone they neither endorsed nor disagreed. They simply adopted the steely persona she thought was their norm and acknowledged her request.

Nor did they care that Fruehoff was naked in her office except for a tie loosely wrapped around his penis. They'd seen a lot worse on video phones.

She signed off, dropped the phone, and looked down at Fruehoff. "Once more," she said, totally unsatisfied from twenty minutes before. "And this time with feeling."

Battle scenes

It took two more days to find them again.

Milo reset his arm. The break had hurt like a *sonofabitch*. Milo could tell that Warren wanted to teleport directly inside them but Milo forbade it with a fiery glance.

Warren ducked a snap kick from Eve and threw himself into a roll to avoid impalement by the follow-up three-inch pump stomp. Eve read him in time to draw up short and hop over the leg sweep. Adam took that opening to leap over Milo and rain three solid blows to Warren's chest as the clone tried to backpedal, then the immortal whirled to block Milo's punch packed with chi aimed for the back of his head, knocking himself and Milo back with the force. Adam took it to Milo, who managed to parry a wild flurry of martial strikes for three seconds before a fist slipped in which caved his chest and drove him to his knees. People below the rooftop heard the explosive deflation as the last extended rattle of an exhausted train.

Eve fought Warren with one hand.

And won.

Adam gripped Milo's head from behind in a secure lock, needing only a proficient twist to end the entire game, with a full two days left to rendezvous with Fruehoff bound for the Blank.

Milo's ribs knitted slowly and painfully. Eve dragged his younger self, who'd never really had a chance to live, and dumped him beside Milo. Milo squinted through teary eyes at such a beautiful woman as most people will never meet. Sensuous, unadorned lips, unblemished olive skin, lean-muscles that melded perfectly into curves, fronted by a jaw with lines so crisp it seemed they'd snap if she smiled. Her eyes, also olive, now asked Milo if he wasn't ready to quit. Life was entirely pointless, because in order to have a point one must first clearly and undeniably stake a position, and human life was too brief for such a thing. Priests became professional gamblers, then drug addicts, then thieves, then clerks at Walmart. There was no stability in life, only chaos and disorder contained within sacks of flesh by the billions and billions.

Whether he quit or not meant nothing to her. She'd get to see him a little more often if he did perhaps, but other than that...

Other than that, he looked like death on bended knee. The vampiric material that supercharged his autonomic systems worked overdrive on repairs but the man looked decimated, not at all an avenger but a forgotten toy chewed thoroughly by dogs with issues.

"You've seen and done marvelous things," she told him. "You need to be on this planet. It's no fun without you." She nodded once at Adam. Adam tightened his grip in preparation. "We *can* find other amusements, Milo Jetstream."

"I'm not going to die," Milo wheezed.

"Remains to be seen, doesn't it," she said. "We leave for Atlantis in two days."

"They have the best coffee," said Adam, idly glancing at Warren and wondering whether he and his mate should allow themselves to be cloned.

"Nonrich wants Atlantis searched," said Eve.

"Buford's not in Atlantis," said Milo.

"We know. Your brother is," said Eve. "We'll give him your regards."

"You fought bravely and all that," said Adam.

Focusing through the pain was hard, right now one of the hardest things he'd ever done. He did it enough to see Warren unmoving on the tarmac and Eve nod once more at Adam, and then there was nothing at all.

~~~

"It's too freaking cold here!" Smoove shouted even though he wore a breach suit. For the second time he idly considered pushing one of the vampires off the cliff, but where would the Jetstreams be without a voice of reason?

They weren't in avalanche territory yet, and their chosen guide assured them they were nowhere near being detected…but how far was a vampire to be trusted?

Everyone else, for their part, ignored Smoove's wasteful use of energy.

"Don't particularly care if they know we're coming," said Smoove. "Damn stupid idiot vampires," which normally would have made Elyse and Brian vocally defensive, but given the circumstances…

"Calm yourself," said Ramses.

Smoove did. For two hours. After which time he was stretched out in the snow with field glasses verifying the camp layout as provided by Elyse. "We're close enough for them to smell us but they're totally oblivious," he said.

"They're scientists," said Ramses.

Desiree was in the snow beside Ramses. "How do you want to play this?" she asked.

"We promised Shig we'd get 'em out," he said. "Raffic?" Ramses said to the man on the other side of him, then glanced upward at a standing man who looked as though the mountain itself should be afraid of him. "Maseef? You're with me. Somebody bring me Brian."

~~~

Ramses, Raffic and Maseef waited. Brian had entered the camp and told the gathered vampires exactly what Ramses' plan was. Ramses, Maseef and Raffic waited till they saw what they were looking for: a flurry of bodies panicking who were then quickly directed by bodies who weren't.

Twenty scientists, ten soldiers. The soldiers were armored and armed with standard babysitting gear, but would be armed for bear by the time Ramses' attack force reached them.

Ramses indulged a grin. For a change, a plan was running perfectly.

He stowed his sights in his pack. "Let's go."

He, Buddha and Maseef marched in clear sight, side by side the entire way to the camp and then straight up to the camp. The soldiers didn't fire a single shot, glancing everywhere that the approaching three weren't for signs of reinforcements.

The camp dropped the electrified fence and allowed the three to enter. The fence went back up immediately, even though it was more a deterrent for ice weasels and the occasional *trat*.

"Who's on your behalf?" Ramses asked the middle of three soldiers training weapons on them. They didn't answer. "All right then." Ramses took a step to go past them.

They squared the weapons and prepared to fire.

Ramses took another step. His compatriots advanced with him. "For the love of mercy tell me you were more creative than having the better trained hiding under the snow ready to pop out."

"They're not!"

"Because that's something you clichéd bastards would do."

An armored head popped out of the snow to the left of them, followed by shoulders and a gun.

Ramses gave a quick sigh. "Buddha?"

Raffic rushed them. He took shots to the shoulder, bicep and thigh. Ramses dropped to the snow and Maseef was in the air above him with a sword drawn and the snow-covered soldier's helmet in his eyes. The sword clanked off the helmet but had distracted the soldier enough for Maseef to drop it and do what he'd intended anyway: snap his neck.

Four bodies on the ground and utter silence. Ramses, Maseef and Raffic: standing. "Die or leave!" shouted Ramses. "Soldier or scientist?"

The vampiric scientists, realizing there was no shame in thinking 'Screw this', gradually emerged from their shelters. The remaining six soldiers were not among them. Ramses spoke to Maseef. "This is probably where Lolita died." Maseef nodded once. He advanced past the scientists. "Raffic, help your brother." Ramses glanced around the perimeter to see Desiree standing with Yvonne and Neon. The Battle Ready Bastards and the clones were spaced beside them to ensure no one escaped. "Fiona," he said into the comm, "come say hello to the scientists."

~~~

"They were hoping to duplicate the teletropic properties of the Mount," Fiona said later, "based entirely off specious logic. The Mount's like that glowy tunnel dead people like to see. Idiots."

"I'm going," said Ramses.

"No, you're not," she said. "Your hold on reality is already tenuous enough. Leave the Mount its mysteries."

"We might not come back to Atlantis after this," said Ramses.

Smoove squooze Desiree's hand. *"We* are."

"You deserve to," said Ramses.

"Don't you want to wait for Milo?" asked Fiona.

"Not especially." This crew, Ramses noted, had gotten substantially crankier the last few missions.

"Nobody goes near the Mount," Desiree commanded. "We wait for Milo, we pack up, and we go. Buford's not in Atlantis."

Ra'saiel X emerged from below decks. The surviving vampires were securely locked in cells outside steerage. "They're very annoying," he said. "Have we had contact from Milo?"

"No," said Ramses.

"You're sounding like Maseef," said Fiona.

"A day overdue's unusual," Desiree told Ra'saiel. "Not troubling."

The deck of the *Linda Ann* was crowded with angels and clones. Neon, who tortured Guerris no end by leaning at the railing and staring at the unmoving water, looked particularly disturbed. Yvonne caught this disturbance and shook her head at her friend. Patience.

Shig sipped tea. He'd only been on the *Ann* twice before. "I wish our myths had never traveled to your world," he said.

"We'd have come through for something or other anyway," said Smoove. "Hell, I was probably born here."

"You don't know where you were born?" Shig asked idly.

"Nah, brother. Wasn't there at the time." Smoove smiled at Fiona.

Fiona smiled back. "The clones seem pretty content to follow orders," she pointed out, watching all the congregated Milos off by themselves. "We could send them to the Mount and tell them not to reveal anything except to us. Foom got *really* deep into their subconscious."

"You're talking about a mountain," Neon wanted verified. "Not code for a talking Wooly Mammoth. Not Bigfoot's spaceship or some such shit? Big ass piece of rock? There is no way all this James Bond has been for a big ass piece of rock."

Shig perked up. "You've spoken to Bigfoot? How is he?"

"Not now, Shig," said Ramses. "Somehow or other, Leviathan is part of this too. Maseef, your whales reported anything?"

"Nothing."

"How the hell," said Fiona, "does something like that hide?"

"By telling you he's not there," said Ramses. "And you'll damn well believe it. You can feel the future from the Mount, Neon," said Ramses. "Not specific events. Everyone's future. The soul of the future."

Smoove turned his friendly face to Neon. "Why do you think people are always trying to climb mountains?" he said.

"The soul of the future, huh?" she said.

Ramses nodded. "Time is alive. Buford's a spiritual man, and he knows the value of upgrading. If he could tie the insights of the Mount to Nonrich it's game over. Consumerism would become for all intents and purposes genetic. He'd have de facto control over the decisions of every person on the planet."

"So GDP goes up," Neon began. "Is that so big--"

"Consume without producing. Where does that take us?" said Ramses.

"Enough gas to get to hell, not enough to get back," Neon said.

"Exactly."

"We don't seem so silly now, yes, Luv?" Smoove asked Yvonne, who had sat in quiet observance.

"I'm still with you," she said.

Smoove nodded at her. "If my wife wasn't standing right here..."

"You'd be a man getting no play from three women instead of four," said Desiree.

"Precisely," said Smoove.

Sereda popped her head out of the control room. "Incoming message!" She set a communicator on the table. "Automated."

It played. "Ram, assume they've got me. Proceed, brother. Eight hour delay." It repeated.

"Two days ago timestamp," said Sereda. "Delayed send."

Neon glanced from one to the other. "Does this help? Ramses? This helps us, right?"

"Yes. Everybody gear up."

"The Mount has driven explorers insane," Shig added.

"This isn't just about the Mount, is it?" Neon asked Ramses.

"Money is alive. Literally. Parasitic concept. Thrives on the brain's pleasure centers. No other reason on a planet teeming with food, people starve."

"So everything's alive?" said Neon.

"Pretty much," said Ramses. "Buford may not have created profit-driven suffering but he perfected it. Nonrich has the course of the world plotted for the next hundred years."

"We're here to throw up road blocks?" asked Neon.

Desiree headed up to the wheel house. "We're dismantling the goddamn car," she called back.

"And nobody knows where he is?" said Neon.

"No," said Ramses.

"And nobody knows where Milo is?"

Smoove, crossing between them toward the weapons deck below, said, "He's fine."

"And you know this how?"

"Ele?" said Smoove.

"He's fine," lied the empath. She hadn't a clue.

The *Linda Ann* let the water lap its sides. Ramses was glad they'd brought the two new people along. Sometimes what you didn't need was magic. Sometimes you needed common sense. He looked to Yvonne. "I'd like to speak with you later. Privately."

She gave a nod. The deck dispersed.

~~~

Speaking became a chaste kiss, became a hug, became an understanding, then a bond which was a reason, reason for Ramses to want to drop his shields. Reason for Yvonne to let go the last doubts of Yvonne DeCarlo Paul and embrace the Agent of Change: *For Now.* She undid the clasp of her chain. "These are yours now because I trust you."

He slipped the dog tags on.

"It's OK if you worry," she said.

"My brother doesn't brush his teeth unless he's got four back up plans."

"I respect you," she said. "And I will follow you."

"And I'll follow you."

"Not just to look at my ass?"

Ramses made himself remain serious so she could see the smile behind his eyes. "Not entirely," he said.

Meanwhile...

Meanwhile, streaking toward Atlantis aboard William Fruehoff's plane: "Milo? Do you think we're going to die?"

"Ask again and I'll kill you."

"I haven't asked that many times. I've improved my self control."

"Seven times."

"Queries about death in general don't count. Since we're tied up I assumed passing the time was acceptable. I kept notes. About death. In my notebook. I lost it at the holding facility."

"I'm not tied up."

This made Warren open his eyes.

"I got loose about an hour ago. The guard knows. He's scared."

"I'm not scared," said a voice via the cell's speakers.

Another voice said from the other side of the door, "You knew he was free?"

"No, I did not know he was free. Mind games, man, he's in your head."

"I'm not in your head," said Milo.

The entire complement of security on board a ship carrying Adam and Eve had no idea how superfluous they were, but they made Fruehoff feel perfectly coiffed. Against Aileen's advice Fruehoff had chosen flight to Atlantis. As for the Jetstreams' presence, that was a simple matter of four words from Eve: "They're coming with us."

"A boat is less obtrusive," Aileen had said to Fruehoff.

"Time's finite," he said back. "The quicker we get there, the quicker we find our leader, the quicker the world rights itself." But that was just Aileen showing she was still willing to insult his intelligence; this plane was filthy with stealth technology.

"Have you considered," Warren put to the guard, "that Milo might be deep in your head?"

"Milo Jetstream is not in my head."

"Just admit it and be done with it," the other guard said. "Mental preparedness. Stay frosty."

"Stay frosty," repeated Milo.

"Are we going to escape?" Warren whispered.

"We hear you," said a guard even as Milo was saying "No." Milo sat straighter. "I'm going," Milo said to the young him across from him, "to teach you to breathe. Repeat: I draw the breath of life and health; I expel the breath of doubt."

The first guard clicked the intercom off. "He's not in my head."

Intercom back on: "Show us your hands," the other said, staring intently at the monitor.

"Can't," said Milo. "They're shackled."

"Have you been constantly monitoring?" guard two asked guard one.

"I can't believe you let him get in your head."

Milo and Warren continued their breathing meditations.

"Gas them. Then check them."

"They're in there taking deep breaths."

"This is why I can't stand you." He reached rudely across the other's face and hit the gas control. "Just keep them knocked out."

The rest of the watch was carried out in uncomfortable silence. Another hour before they reached Atlantis.

~~~

Meanwhile, Death-mael surfaced in a panic. Dragoons were planning to travel en masse to the Blank world, and that was not good. The psychic stew underwater had gotten thick and nearly overwhelming. Even the whales were testy and short. A cool espionage code name was useless if everyone snapped at one to go away. It tasted the air for hint of Jetstreams and, finding it, set out, fervently hoping that Leviathan didn't surface to swallow it in the interim.

~~~

First Fruehoff thought *Atlantis smells like mangoes,* then Fruehoff, looking along the camp as women and men hustled and dutied, realized *I'm in charge of a flipping platoon.* A platoon. Soldiers. Guards. Security. People with guns and sharp things. Whatever one called them, it was a platoon, twenty-five strong. And that didn't even include Adam and Eve. He'd tried ordering those two to leave the Jetstreams unconscious and locked up but they'd merely looked at him and glanced at the guards outside the cell.

Fruehoff wasn't the kind of man to wonder how many of his people would be returning, because, frankly, he didn't care. As long as he was on that plane through the Blank— with Buford—life was good. If Adam and Eve's gambit entailed some kind of prisoner swap, so be it. Again, as long as Buford was seated across from him on that plane, Fruehoff didn't care one whit what happened in this suburban dimension.

The only question was how do you track a man who did not allow anyone the means to track him? No GPS, no implants, genetic scramblers, hell, even hoods and cloaks.

No way to do it covertly. Atlantis was about to get shaken up.

~~~

He hadn't wanted to do it but it had to be done. It was an unrighteous and foul death.

Resurrection. Ramses hated the connotations of the word; hated that there were times he knew he could do it and didn't, and times he did and shouldn't have. Never often, either way, and never without great spiritual sacrifice. That first gasp of the resurrected was always the worst. So much confusion. The dead dealt with the same stages of grief as the living. Acceptance came after a long, hard battle, so it was no surprise there was so much anger directed at Ramses Jetstream from a number of people with minimal pulses.

That was why he always held them a little longer in the resurrection hug. The unique sharing of his life force had taken at least ten years off his own life if he were to tally from the first of the "gifted" to the current. In the same way that Milo bound Djinns to the earth—only on a much deeper quantum plane for Ramses—there were bits of Ramses Jetstream scattered worldwide inside a variety of souls living quiet, largely unremarkable lives. The dead rarely partied. Liseen Welty, neighbor of Guerris for three years, felt the strength of Ramses' arms and didn't bother struggling to break the hold. Instead she burrowed her face as far into his chest as she could and let her body heave huge, wracking sobs.

Liseen's wife had agreed to this. Out of all the ways her wife was supposed to die in Atlantis, being attacked for no reason by a vampire wasn't one of them. Her name was Anda, and she currently sat at home dreading the knock she knew would come sooner than it was possible she be ready.

"I'm cold," Liseen said into Ramses' collar.

He increased his output of chi. "That's the morgue."

Moonlight reflected off Bynum Lake, so much so that their two bodies sitting on a large stone beside it had shadows. Seeing her shadow made Liseen's eyes well. "I remember," she said.

"The mind never shuts down," said Ramses. "Never. It can't. I've made sure a new identity is available for you if you want it."

"I'll have to move."

"How old are you, dear?"

"Sixty-two."

"Then you don't have to go anywhere. You earned life no matter your circumstances." He stroked her hair.

She swallowed hard, pushed out to look at him, lowered her head back, and absently scratched her nails at the scraggly hairs at the nape of his neck. She had sensed and felt things of importance to him during the resurrection hug, private things. "Will I forget?" she asked.

"No."

"I'll have a few things to say to Anda."

"Yes, ma'am."

~~~

After driving them both to Liseen's home, Fiona asked Ramses, "Are we done here?"

"We're done." He sealed the door of the rover. "Let's go home."

Turf

"If we focus here first," said the woman with the most scarred hands he'd ever seen, "we get their attention but we're far enough from the mainland for easy egress." She traced the line from Abba to Sip. "Particularly if his goal involved these mountains."

"Why are you saying 'if'?" said Fruehoff. "I said that's what we're considering the focal, didn't I?"

"Yes, sir." The age-old conundrum: give a dick a mission and he becomes Patton, but as Sharon was a consummate professional she continued detailing the best courses of action. "We need to be surgical, sir. No matter how best the best of the best are, numbers always matter."

"Any of your people daunted by Atlantis?"

"No, sir. They've all been here before, reconnoitering for the facility we lost."

"Then they're good at getting information and finding their asses with both hands. I need less charts and buzz cuts and *only* get your asses out there and find Buford." Sweet God, she'd gotten him up before the crack of dawn for this. "If he's on this rock, find him."

"We're operating with major limitations."

"Somebody found him. You're saying we can't?"

"I am not, sir." She closed the map display. "I'm saying we will."

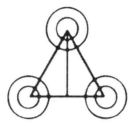

Too much stuff happens off the grid, thought Ele as she hacked Shig's computer. The official post mortem on Lolita Or-Ghazeem was public knowledge. One did not keep such news on a scientist of her stature secret for very long. Ele didn't view the hacking as particularly clandestine or as the precursor to a bombshell of information. She hacked computers the way people thumbed books at a library. Besides which, Desiree stood over her shoulder. They were after just a little more detail than most needed to know.

"Go back a second," said Desiree. The mug of peppermint tea her husband had brewed had gone lukewarm. He was still in the galley of the *Ann*, alone, quietly cooking up everything in sight and inventorying the rest. There was no doubt in her mind that she and he would be quite fat in their waning years. Well, *she* would at any rate. It sucked having a husband who lived forever.

She scanned the file for key words. Nothing.

"OK," she said.

"We're not going to find anything," said Ele for both of them.

"Shig never gives us everything," said Desiree. "Would you?"

"No."

"Do you?"

Ele smiled. "No."

"Where's the connection that none of us are seeing?" It was a question born of a sense of urgency. This would be the last time—as a crew—they would be in Atlantis. Ramses' promise to not bring the battle to Atlantidean soil wasn't one that would be easily or readily broken, whether Buford ever surfaced again or not. "Buford, Raffic, Lolita, Leviathan, war."

"You mean our secessionists? Secession is fashion here." In the time it took Desiree to skim, Ele had entire pages read. She planned to shut the computer down after another moment or two. "There's nothing here," she said to Desiree. She swiveled in the chair. "How worried are you about Milo?"

"You feel it?"

"Your emotional control is excellent, not perfect," said Ele.

Desiree smoothed the empath's shiny dark hair then patted her on the shoulder. "I've never lost anyone under my command."

Ele smiled. "I didn't know they were under your command."

"They are."

Smoove's voice issued through the comm. "Luv? You need to see this."

"Where are you?"

"Starboard aft deck."

"On my way."

The instant she saw it she knew what it was. The dragoon the brothers recounted as their rescuer. Its grey mottling darkened and lightened with agitation. It practically paced in the water.

"Says his name is Death-mael," said Smoove.

"Captain Desiree Quicho," she said, having to speak a little louder over the water.

"You still only want a Jetstream?" Smoove asked the dragoon.

"Ramses is away," said Desiree. "What can I do for you?"

Leviathan's awake.

"We know."

No, I mean Leviathan's AWAKE. Where do you think the Mount's dreams come from?

"It's not the Mount?" said Smoove.

It's a rock! Leviathan sleeps beneath the Mount.

"Rather not face Leviathan again," Desiree said to Smoove. To the bobbing aquatic: "Ramses will be here soon."

The other one?

"Missing."

Impatiently, Death-mael dipped under and came up rolling, the equivalent of rolling its eyes. *No, he's not. He's here.* It shut their what-where down with *Next time, just ask. Even the yebaums know he's here.* Nothing happened in Atlantis without at least one gossipy species knowing about it.

"Ele, anything?" said Desiree.

She shook her head.

"Can you reach him?" asked Desiree of Death-mael.

Simply communicating with you is extremely hard with Leviathan awake.

"What does it mean to do?" she asked.

Travel.

~~~

Buford invaded Kichi's dreams.

'You want *me* to help you?' said the dream Kichi Malat.

'Trust your intuition, man, you wouldn't be dreaming this if you didn't think something was wrong. You've been to the Mount but you never sensed this. What's different?'

The dreams were different. The music, the thoughts, the art…were different. The past few days his guitar hadn't said a word to him that he hadn't heard before.

Kichi's dream was nothing but presences, which was the most powerful kind of dream. No imagery, no sound, the only color that of air on water. Sentient emptiness.

Bubba Foom's dream-presence was in the background, silent and judging, ready to kill if need be. And that was different too. Foom had been the best and gentlest of Kichi's early adepts. Foom had calmed the jangled minds of Milo and Ramses Jetstream enough to help their own talents grow. Kichi had subliminally implanted certain guides in Foom's mind and Foom, in turn, unknowingly passed these on to everyone else in the struggle.

'See? You're my brother,' said Buford.

Kichi hushed that part of the dream.

The last from Ramses was that Milo had gone looking for Adam and Eve in the hope of finding Buford.

Hell, Adam and Eve likely *had* Buford. Kichi knew the cards they dealt. They were the Mobius snake, circling everything back upon itself. They always were. Always had been. Whatever planet they'd arrived from had likely been glad to see them and their small crew go.

But something, even for them, had changed.

'Tick, tock, old man,' went the dream presence of an evil so smooth it flowed effortlessly like water in a faucet.

'Buford?'

'Yes?'

'Quiet.'

~~~

Eve needed water. Water was in the opposite direction of where they were going, in a sense, although Atlantis *was* an island. But it was huge and criss crossed with tributaries and lakes fed by the surrounding ocean. Eve needed a very specific body of water, she felt, which meant her plans were about to take precedence over Fruehoff's.

She motioned one of the bodies hustling through the encampment to her side.

"Ma'am?"

"I need a vehicle with submersible capabilities, no drivers, no crew complement."

"Yes, ma'am."

At times homo sapiens was downright precious. She loved the way the entire unit had been pre-drilled to answer anything she or Adam said with an immediate yes. One seldom found help like that outside religious orders.

~~~

Fruehoff briefly blotted out the sun. "Where'd your partner go?"

Adam briefly considered snapping Fruehoff's neck for interrupting the sip of chive-infused coffee he was about to take. He regarded all thirteen thousand four hundred-eighty two dollars worth of fabric and equipment standing before him, and whistled the opening bars from the Andy Griffith Show, an ancient bucolic television program about small town life whose opening montage featured a sheriff and his son enjoying a stint at the fishing hole. No point in further agitating 13482 though. He stopped openly mocking Fruehoff. "You didn't know that I could whistle, did you? I taught the Ibis."

'I don't need your frikkin' ninja poetry!' railed 13482 internally while giving nothing away externally. "That's fascinating."

"I promise to acknowledge your authority during this outing."

Maybe it was because they were in Atlantis but, even though it was weird to hear this always silent killer speak, it wasn't as weird as Fruehoff would normally have expected. Maybe even, influenced by the Atlantidean air, going for a third sentence out of the unsettlingly handsome man wasn't a bad thing to do. "Do you think Buford is here?"

"No."

'But we have to give theatre its due,' thought Fruehoff, who caught the slightest of smirks on Adam's face as though the man were agreeing, 'Yes.'

~~~

The house apes have never seen anything as big as you. You'll destroy the global economy. Mass pandemonium. The dragging of popes in the street. That kind of thing.

*i am the—

You've gone a bit insane too, thought Eve.

the world has not known my kind; the world will not know my kind.

Because you'll destroy it.

yes.

And get to swim the seven seas.

*i created the ways for the water. i am the path and the—

It was rather fun interrupting Leviathan, like playing a mental game of Words With Friends. *Sad, befuddled bear... They woke you far too soon, yes?*

--and i will sleep on the other side of the world and spread out and be the new earth.

A gigantic, psychic whale-like thing isn't endearing to Hollywood. Can I convince you to stay, to sleep?

It took a while for the synapses to return a hit, but suddenly Leviathan recognized the timbre of these thoughts and it remembered the name it had given her on its world. It thought the name now, surrounding the name with a huge question mark and a sense of happiness.

Yes. It's me, thought Eve.

Leviathan so rarely got visitors. It sent the names for the few others from their ship who'd survived, instantly in that act of mental echo-location knowing exactly where each one was. Hell, it even slept atop their ship, as the vessel kept Leviathan warm and even gave off a pleasant white-noise vibration.

The small craft she now occupied was similar in design to that much larger one but in clumsy, retro fashion.

It pulled the Thoom from her mind.

Yes, they're the tools who woke you up. You were supposed to have killed the Jetstreams, she thought, but Leviathan was still on the Thoom. *I honestly didn't think things would progress this far.*

do they not know i am the alpha and the omega, not to be trifled with?

They cloned thirteen Milo Jetstreams.

idiots. part of that one shot me in the eye. Oh, the synapses were firing to beat the band now. No more fugue state or scrambling half asleep for the surface of the world. No more random peeking through psychic minds via the dreamtime. *i'm certainly wide awake now.*

Will you stay here a bit longer?

no.

Her presence effectively negated, Eve severed mental communication. She piloted the submersible away from the encrusted topography that was its body and made way for the surface.

'We're going to need Bubba Foom,' she messaged her mate. 'And Raffic wouldn't hurt either.'

'Milo?' he messaged back.

'Time he was reunited with his brother.'

worm
pulling

An entire cancer ward filled with children was reason enough to vilify Buford Bone. A world full of such wards was reason to kill him. Kichi's sons in imminent danger was reason, however gallingly, to rescue the oily prick while doing as much collateral damage to Thoom, vampiric, and Bone enterprises as possible. The stock exchange would rue this day.

Kichi had gone old school. They knew where Buford wasn't, and it was a given that wherever he was, Buford would do his damndest to throw up flares of a sort.

Kichi sat with Foom and young Michael—under the watchful eye of Asme Du Ikare—to get a feel for the young man's abilities. Michael Foom's mind was like a bee: if you planted a stinger barb in your mind of who you wanted stung, his hive could find them.

Also, he could start fires.

Michael Foom was ultra cool.

It wasn't easy, and Bubba and Michael had to mentally elbow aside Buford's own psychic search teams any time he and his son felt close to a solid lead. They'd be damned if they'd lead them to him. But inside the chaotic stream of the ether-mind they eventually found him.

Buford had formed a huge bubble of null thought around his head. There were only a handful of people, including psychics, who knew the technique and were brave enough to do it. Buford's ace-in-the-hole rescue failsafe was an appeal to his enemies.

There were times Kichi dreaded getting out of bed in the mornings.

He'd admonished the boys for taking the fight public. He just might have to apologize for that.

Jefferson Avenue was one of Detroit's major arteries, an eight-lane two-way from city through suburbs. Deep beneath it and somewhat under the bordering Detroit River (robotic carp kept eyes on it at all times) was a Thoom wormhole. The terrestrial kind. Buford was inside it.

Several Agents of Change kept Jefferson blocked. The underground maglev trains weren't going anywhere; huge polarity disruptors made sure of that. The Detroit Police Department would not take kindly to huge polarity disruptors blocking midday traffic on Jefferson Avenue.

Three spokes ran out from the underground bubble. Kichi left one avenue of escape open: the maglev tunnel under the debris and silt of the river heading northeast to nearby Canada. He was certain a train was racing toward him that very moment. The Detroit side of things had taken care of the operation flawlessly. Time for Toronto to return the favor, which was where he was.

He ate the last of his pancakes sitting outside the Golden Griddle, a favorite breakfast stop each time he visited Toronto. "Everything ready on Yonge Street?" he said. A button-sized comm at his collar relayed the query.

"There's a disruptor team below the subway. Inside Man's cleared the station and disabled trains a kilometer in either direction. We expect they'll be dressed in their best furs for confrontation," came a woman's mature Southern drawl.

"Be prepared," said Kichi.

"We're armed for bear."

"They'll be close enough for you to disable them in fifteen minutes. Cleavage?"

"Yes, sir?" said the mature drawl.

"Have Thighs keep our communications open. They'll try to disrupt. Let theirs stay open though. I want as much chaos for the Thoom as possible." Kichi Malat wiped his mouth, left money for both bill and tip, and stood. "On my way." The people he passed topside going about their magnificent lives had no idea the stately old man ambling by possessed enough chi to level a skyscraper.

Kichi entered the Yonge Street subway station. Agents of Change in police garb guarded it from public entry. This ruse wouldn't last long though.

A short escalator ride down, and he was underground.

They had already accessed the utility catacombs under the subway tunnel, then lasered a hole to the deep level below that (where the Thoom wormhole was) and a final hole through the sequoia thick plascrete and steel maglev tunnel. A burly, hairy man emerged from this hole as Kichi entered.

"They're still five minutes out," said Thighs.

Kichi nodded. "No sign they know we're here yet?"

"None, but I'm sure they're on full alert. We left only the one escape route."

"Which is why I'm going to drop this tunnel on top of them. There's going to be a lot of shooting; I prefer it remain inside the train. I want Buford alive. Focums on maximum stun, maximum dispersal."

"Relayed," said a woman with marvelous laugh lines and ice-blue eyes coming to stand with them. Cleavage. She stood beside Thighs.

Kichi had considered using Bubba and Michael to incapacitate the train's complement, but as soon as the word "use" entered his mind he put all thought of Michael Foom out of his head. This wasn't that child's war. Cleavage was forty-seven years old, divorced, estranged from her family, former Air Force intelligence. Thighs, a former semi-pro linebacker who'd turned his back on sports and the possibility of fame for the mystic teachings of Po Yum Ken and an almost obsessive drive for language acquisition. They had lived their outer lives to their satisfaction, had assumed ownership of the second world in total and private volition, and fought the New War out of necessity. As Agents of Change they knew truth was only worth something if an element of beauty could be found in it, not the heavier, leaden element of profit. Kichi would be damned if he'd take that same discovery away from Michael Foom. He already felt thrice damned for the boy's involvement in this idiocy at all.

"Bullets," Kichi had Cleavage relay next, "are our last resort."

Atlantis

'Atlantis doesn't feel right' buzzed incessantly at the back of Milo's head, keeping his plans slightly but noticeably out of sync with actions. He'd had two opportunities to deal with the guards and both times a split-second of hesitation had killed the moment. Atlantis smelled the same, humidity wasn't drastically altered, the grass—in that moment the captives had been transferred from the ship to the outdoor holding cube—had its usual strong, vibrant resistance underfoot, but there was something...different. As if the local gravity had shifted a notch. And Warren not saying a word the entire time they'd been in the cube didn't ease things. His clone sat with both feet planted on the pressure sensitive floor, seemingly intent upon the lines of his hands.

"A palmist," said Milo, "told me my life lines will never break. I think I was thirteen. Not a good idea telling a thirteen year old he'll live forever." There was that thought again. *Atlantis doesn't feel right.*

"I remember things that you don't," Warren blurted, clearly having held the information too long.

"Memory serves no purpose when there's no immediate danger," said Milo.

"We're in a box."

"As much to protect them from us as us from them. What do you remember?"

"You laughing," he said. After a moment: "Your parents. I can tell you what I remember."

"Why would you remember it and I don't?"

"I don't know. But I clearly do. I've sensed your discomfort on various topics."

For the first time Milo looked at himself and realized that's how he thought of Warren. Himself. The younger could have teleported them out, but there was a time differential in teleportation, a fraction that would allow the thermite cascade to flash-incinerate them in the nano-second burst triggered by the absence of their four feet on the box's floor. No telling what would be left of them wherever they managed to 'port.

"We're not going to die, clone."

"If I remember it then somewhere you do too."

"I don't have time for my past."

"That's a shame. Our parents would likely be amazed by you. Likely very proud."

"I'm gonna need to get you some helluva therapy when this is over."

Warren nodded.

Milo glanced around the grey box. Insurance, that's what he and Warren were right now, which meant sitting. And waiting. The world outside the box ran laughing without them.

Ramses was out there, alone.

Ramses stood eighty feet away from the grey, metal box after having walked directly into Fruehoff's encampment, his hands upon his head and body completely gear-less except for the breach suit.

Fruehoff was hurriedly summoned.

"You really expect me to believe you're alone?" he said from behind the four soldiers between him and Ramses. Ten guns were trained on Ramses. Another fifteen were trained outward, eyes wary on the deceptively empty air.

"Needed to know what idiot brought a battalion to Atlantis. Now I know."

"And?"

"Leave."

"That's it?" said Fruehoff.

Ramses nodded once.

"Ramses, that won't do." Fruehoff's mind whirred. If he returned home with Milo and Ramses Jetstream, plus Buford, he would be nigh unto a god! Hell, maybe even without Buford. He'd be the new Buford. A sheen of sweat instantly coated his palms; fortunately a decent breeze circulated between all the women and men and their various armaments.

Adam emerged from the phalanx of bodies. All eyes immediately shifted to him. That was all Ramses needed to know. Adam smiled at him.

"Ask any of your psychics if they feel a bit off," said Ramses, "then tomorrow morning ask everybody else about their dreams." Then he turned to walk away.

Except for the vein bifurcating Fruehoff's forehead not a thing moved. Fruehoff felt a sputter coming on. What was Ramses going to do, just walk all by himself all the way to wherever he'd come from and think he was simply going to wisp away?

Everyone watched him leave the area, unsure what to do as neither Adam nor Fruehoff said anything, Fruehoof quiet because Adam was. Ramses walked another fifty yards or so. Then a clone appeared beside him. Then they were both gone.

There were ten guards around the box. Fruehoff managed to say, "Check the box." The message was relayed.

"Video is good," came the response.

"Have them open the damn door and look inside."

Milo nodded at the peering face.

"Still inside." The door quickly and efficiently sealed.

"We're accelerating the schedule," said Fruehoff. He looked at Adam.

"Yes, sir," said Adam.

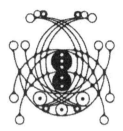

Milo, in the box, to Warren: "I'd say we're fouling up their plans pretty nicely."

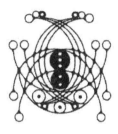

The train angled crookedly on the track as though a huge child had left it in favor of something else. Its bullet-front was broken by a single small light, giving it the appearance of a cyclopean worm.

No one had made a move from inside the train. Not a peep.

"Do you wait them out?" asked Cleavage.

"This is reverse chicken," said Kichi. "They're waiting on us."

"The whites of our eyes?" she said.

"Yes."

"Fortunately, we have breach goggles."

"Move in."

~~~

"Milo's in a box. They've got it out in the open, guarded. Adam's here," said Ramses.

"Being a dick?" asked Desiree.

"Yes. The minor functionary's here looking for Buford. Adam and Eve don't give a damn about Buford. Only one thing would bring them here at this particular time, and Eve wasn't at their camp," said Ramses. "Yvonne, Neon, you with me?" Ramses asked. "I know things are a bit twisty."

"Actually, way ahead of you," said Neon. "What big ticket item would attract the big guns with the quickness?"

"Gigantic psychic fish," said Yvonne.

"All right. Eve's underwater. Do we go after her?" said Neon.

"Uh uh," said Yvonne.

"No?" said Neon.

"No," said Yvonne, "because from the way everybody's sphincters are tight, she'd kill every last one of us, am I right?"

Ramses nodded.

"I'm feeling how every time we confab," said Yvonne, "the situation's fucked factor increases. Have we hit end game?"

"Giving up is never an option," said Smoove.

"But—" said Neon.

"We don't give up," Ramses said simply.

"Dying with honor is well and good except for the dying part," said Yvonne. "Soldiers die and get replaced; commanders live on. The ones who keep starting shit always live on. Nothing changes."

"It would take three years for all life on this planet to be completely and irrevocably enslaved if we stopped," said Ramses. "I've done the math."

"Then what do we do? You're up against someone you can't beat, who in turn is against something you can't fight, wrapped up in—" Yvonne threw her hands up in frustration to encapsulate the entire world. *"What do we do?"*

"We get polite," he said.

"Meaning?"

"Hold the door open and let everyone through."

LEVIATHAN

It was well after dark. For Leviathan it was always well after dark. It spent its life solitary as a monk…in a black hole…with heavy drapery, which is why dreams were so important. It saw the world through the minds and dreams that had the wherewithal to see. Those minds that didn't were much the same as cancer cells in its brain driving it inexorably mad. It swam Atlantis' deep undercurrents in the way that islands don't swim but would if they could. The grotto where veins of the Mount's magnetic and fluidic ore rooted into the earth to ground the huge mountain in reality was the perfect size for sleeping. It had hollowed the space out itself eons ago with its own body, where it slept according to its own schedule. Leviathan had dreamt so many species and evolutionary advances into being it lost count. It actually missed the dinosaurs. Their dreams had been full of large thoughts and hungers, sometimes the one indistinguishable from the other. *Expansive* was the word, and Leviathan had roamed the true world—the water world—openly. Leviathan's passage was always cause for herds of brontosauri, pods of plesiosaurs to stop what they were doing and enjoy feeling small. Not so these idiot humans with their constant, manic ant dreams of enlarging themselves.

And here it was, fully awake and involved in their affairs. The last time it had been fully awake Spanish

Conquistadors were sailing about like dragoons hungry for tuna. It didn't like being fully awake. Twice now powerful minds had disturbed it. Those twelve minds shouting at it the first time had been like an icy alarm clock suddenly dropped onto its brain.

It made a slow arc away from the Mount, idly ingesting a giant squid that had already been damaged by a singularity. It moved toward land. Toward Atlantis. More precisely, the capital city.

Leviathan didn't like being awake at all.

Death
Mettle

"Ramses, there's something very large moving toward us," Shig relayed via the sensor tech who kept pointing as though that were helpful.

Ramses, on the *Linda Ann.* "How fast is it going?"

Shig, in the capital: "It's very large."

"Shig."

"Slow but large. Slow for something that large is not slow."

"We're between you and it, Shig," Ramses assured.

"That might not be wise."

Eleven clones in full breach gear dropped over the side of the *Ann.*

"We've got back-up," said Ramses. "No worries."

"Several stages past that already."

Smoove stepped beside Ramses. "May I?" He leaned toward the mic. "Shig? Every little thing's gonna be all right." He stepped back.

"Thank you, Smoove," Ramses said.

"It felt appropriate."

Ramses nodded. "Crank it up loud." He returned to his conversation with Shig Empa.

After a few moments the black surface of the ocean vibrated with the beat of "Three Little Birds," reggae legend

Bob Marley's song of hope amidst hopelessness. A long way away the *Semper Fi* synched speakers and both ships blasted the reggae master's chorus, *"Don't worry... 'bout a thing. Every little thing...gonna be all right... "*

Neither Maseef nor the twelve whales forming a floating line between the *Ann* and the *Semper Fi* shared this optimism. Both Maseef and the whales wished both ships would be quiet. At night water demanded quietude. But Maseef and the whales said nothing to the ships, opting instead to, themselves, quietly wait, imagining that they heard nothing but the lapping of the water and, in imagining it, making it so.

The bobbing of flotation became quite pronounced not long afterward, fed by unseen movement.

Eleven Milos soon after broke the surface and mounted eleven whales. A clone nodded to Maseef. Maseef relayed to Ramses. Ramses relayed to Shig: *Success.*

Relay race. The whales and ships sped out.

~~~

"Where did you send him?" asked Guerris.

"I sent him to New York," said Ramses.

"Why?"

"Because Adam and Eve wouldn't expect that."

Guerris was clearly upset. "People will die."

"Not if we're clever."

"Are we?"

"That remains to be seen. Captains?" Ramses said to both Desiree and Smoove.

"Yes," in unison.

"Fly us apart at the seams. I want open water well ahead of Leviathan."

"And Milo?" asked Guerris.

"Milo's in a box. Precisely where he wanted to be."

"Can it actually reach New York?" asked Guerris. "Wouldn't it be like a whale in the shallows?"

"Nobody ever said he couldn't walk on land," said Ramses.

"Remains to be seen?" Guerris said.

Ramses nodded.

~~~

Eve was pissed. Didn't matter how old something was, or how psychic, how sentient, it wasn't meant to get the better of her. Or, worse, to effectively ignore her.

One could tell she was pissed because she hadn't touched her coffee yet.

Then she actually pushed the cup toward Milo. The acrid smell of the drink was inescapable in the confining box.

"You know I don't like coffee," Milo said but smiled in thanks.

"Clone?" she said. "I guarantee it will change your life."

Warren sipped. It was extraordinary. He was hooked.

"Ramses comes and doesn't free you. Kichi now has Buford—"

"Who *doesn't* have Buford?" Adam said dismissively from where he leaned against the door.

"—and is on his way here. With him. Didn't know that, eh? Tell me how that affects your plans, and use small words; I'm impatient today," she said.

Milo did the calculations: if Kichi had Buford then Atlantis, while not entirely safe, was the safest place to isolate, contain and eradicate. Meaning Kichi was not on his way to Atlantis. Her information was false. "Not one bit," he said.

"I have a vial of my blood." Eve's eyes lanced him. "You haven't eaten spiritually, mentally or physically in days. They haven't even given you a book."

"I might grow breasts like yours."

"You should be that lucky. Clone?"

"Warren."

"Warren, what would you like to eat?"

"Fruit," he said.

"You might share Milo's love of mangoes. The local version is a bit less pulpy. Interesting that you like coffee and he doesn't. We'll have food brought round in the morning, then release you," she said.

"Your leader is listening outside the door," said Milo.

"You say that like it matters," she said.

Fruehoff's expletive lexicon wasn't robust enough to encapsulate this moment.

"Letting him out is not an option," he said when Eve and Adam exited.

"Agreed," she said without stopping to address him.

"It's a directive," said Adam.

Fruehoof hustled after them. "What the hell?"

"They've already routed the vampire presence from Atlantis. Now they'll get to do the same to the Thoom," she said.

"There's Thoom in Atlantis?"

"Sweetheart," said Adam, "the Thoom were born in Atlantis."

~~~

Bifrost the whale was having a helluva time keeping its shit together. It would never forget the size of the thing, the sheer bulk and immensity—the sense of *life* from the thing, as though it, and not the waters, were the world, and all else, including Bifrost, merely barnacles.

The whale gave credit to the barnacle of a man atop Bifrost's head for knowing when to hold tight and hug rough hide as it spun, dove, and leapt the night waters; as all its sisters and brothers swam like no whales had ever swum before, maintaining a gap with Leviathan with the humans on their backs.

For the clones' part, contrary to movies, it wasn't easy keeping a monster after you. It was even harder doing it underwater in the dark strapped to whales fighting mightily against their better judgment.

Bifrost filled its burning lungs again, closed its eyes, and dove with a powerful, graceless slap of its fluke. This was no time for grace. This was a time to keep the thought 'Damn, that sucker is big' in mind.

Which it did.

Maseef, for the first time in his life, was actually glad to communicate with someone. The comms were adjusted to handle most of the electromagnetic bursts the big fish was likely to put out, and the link with both ships and the clones, whose comms were on mute so they wouldn't be disturbed, remained open. The ships would cross the Blank well in advance of Maseef, whose crew would only have to keep this pace up through half the Atlantic.

Or until Leviathan reached the U.S. coast. Then trucked its way across the continental United States.

"What's your distance, Maseef?" It was Smoove.

"Still two kilometers ahead of it. None of the clones are dead."

"We might have help with the psychic corral. I'm hoping there won't be brain damage. Keep an eye out for dragoons just before the dimensional shift."

"The one you called Death-mael."

"A dragoon with a death wish, right now, might be a necessary thing, brother."

Grit

Milo Jetstream was buzzed out of his mind by Eve's blood but in a good way. If he had to remain a vampire forever, things might get interesting.

He saw everything clear as day even with his eyes closed. And the aura around Warren seemed to forecast the clone's actions by a full second. *You're about to scratch your nose. Again. Do I do that a lot?* Could get very interesting. Ram would definitely want to study the effects. A pre-ordained shadow world? Thought visually manifested as action creating action?

I wonder how long this will last?

"Morning soon," said Warren.

"Stop asking me about plans."

It was dark in the box. Both of them liked it like that. "You expect to simply walk out of here?"

"I expect to ride. Ram should be here with a rover."

"Ramses doesn't belong in this world."

"I know. He knows."

"Not like Ms. Carel. She maintains not belonging everywhere."

"You noticed that?"

"She told me."

It was like talking to one's self. Milo asked, "Can I ask you about Bubba Foom?"

Warren was silent long enough for it to register as assent.

"What did it feel like, releasing to someone else's control?"

"I'd rather not answer," said Warren. "Ramses warned me you might get jealous. Said you might be out of sorts."

"Did he? Well, he is our brother."

"Yes."

"Notice I said 'our.'"

Warren smiled in the darkness. "Yes."

"Can't fault circumstances of birth," Milo said with a grunt.

When their ride arrived a few hours later Milo saw it was Sereda and not Ramses. Their rover zoomed away from several millions dollars worth of Nonrich Corp personnel and assets.

"What's Ram done?" Milo asked.

"He's counting coup with Leviathan." Sereda kept her eyes focused out the windshield. Milo Jetstream angry was generally…unpleasant.

"Son of a," he muttered. "Where?"

"Deep ocean," said the green angel. "Both ships are out there."

"I need to get out there. How many jumps will it take for you to get us to the Capital port?" he asked Warren.

"As few as I can make it."

"You strong enough for it?" Milo asked.

"Not a concern."

Milo turned to Sereda. "Get Shig to get us a boat, fastest they've got, engine running, please."

"There's a pack in the back," she said.

There were multiple packs. He tossed one to Warren.

"Who's on the ships?" Milo asked.

"Guerris, Fiona, Eloa and Ra'asiel. And the clones."

"Why's Guerris on the ship?" The landscape outside couldn't whiz by any faster.

"Because he's never seen Leviathan and figures if this is do or die…"

And that would have been the only reason Ramses would have agreed.

"Pull over." The rover fried air coming to a halt. He and Warren exited. "Get word to Ram I'm on my way. I don't want to distract him. Comm stays open. Let me know where Shig's parked my boat." He and Warren clasped forearms. "Do it," he said to his clone. They disappeared.

Reappeared.

Disappeared.

Reappeared. Warren trembled.

Disappeared.

Reappeared several dozens of yards above the ground, falling fast. Warren hugged Milo to him and immediately teleported. Both rolled and tumbled when their feet hit the ground.

"Sereda!"

"Dock twenty-seven, forward harbor."

They disappeared.

Warren collapsed on the deck of the boat. Milo blessed Sereda for having coordinates and plot laid in. Shig had arranged a Stinger for them: ships used for emergency purposes. Milo'd never seen one in use, much less piloted one. He apologized to the sleek ship for the hell it was about to go through.

"Warren, you OK?" Milo shouted over the wind.

From the one knee he had under him, Warren nodded.

"Rest a bit."

Warren nodded again.

"'Cause I'm gonna need you to move a boat."

The
Lady Eve

The whales were tired. They may have been more maneuverable than the ships but didn't have comparable energy stores. Snatching gulps of krill helped but Earl's heart was likely to give out, Bifrost was taking in more water than air, and Bruce was practically useless. Each whale took turns cycling to the rear of the vanguard, and the humans atop them did their best to funnel energy to them, but trying to corral a moving island was tougher than it sounded.

And it seemed that not only was the beast being driven crazy but now it was quite peeved, twice having turned on them before resuming its directed course toward the other world. It had left the Blank behind some time ago. Had even scuttled an oil rig and a fishing supertanker in the same way a large person might not feel a small child bouncing off him.

Now the beast was coming up on a raft in which Eve sat in the lotus trying her best to meditate through all the irritation and anger she and Adam planned to share with Ramses as soon as possible.

She knew the Jetstreams well enough to know their gambit. New York was her home, and that meant a great deal to a wandering soul. The buildings and all within them could burn to fine ash but her ship was there! Not the one buried under the Mount but an actual functioning one. Granted it was protected against anything Man or nature could throw against it, but Godzilla's grandfather tromping the boroughs hadn't been part of those safety precautions. She'd need that ship for when the Bimaiy came, and she hadn't been to an industrialized planet yet where they hadn't arrived using their quantum engines to pop in through time. And because Leviathan was awake she couldn't effectively activate and relocate the ship mentally, but she could, and did, focus one word into a blunt, insistent object.

Idiot!

A) Adam on the ship behind her, B) Leviathan's displacement of the ocean in the distance before her, C) the Jetstream and his efforts a good distance behind that. The raft bobbed and bucked. She needed simplicity in order to focus. She needed to know that there was no fast escape for her nor weaponized protection. Leviathan, somewhere within the folds of its calcified brain, would pick up that immediacy and she could use it to her advantage. The problem with the human world was they were all too distracted, and Buford had done the best job imaginable maintaining that. A single person truly focused could change the face of reality. Eve bore down on the one reality she wanted and tried to give it birth.

When was the last time you walked the earth? You can't stand them, remember?

In this reality Leviathan acceded to her wishes.

Go back. Leviathan is not cattle to be prodded. What's even in New York for you?

And the one word that rumbled back, like thunder crossing the waters, and less a word than the deepest pang of desire possible, was *sleep.*

Eve almost opened her eyes. The crafty buggers had convinced it all it had to do was get rid of Nonrich and Buford and its sleep would never again be interrupted by tiny people. The Thoom might have considered cloning Milo Jetstream their greatest coup but it was their biggest cock up yet.

She redoubled her efforts, but doubted she was making much headway against all the Milos.

Adam brought the larger ship alongside her. She abandoned the raft and climbed to the top. Time to move in and start killing clones.

Battle Hymns

Kichi watched the satellite feed. He wasn't a man given to being horrified. He'd seen and caused enough horror in his time that nothing on a viewer held to him by Thighs could compete. Unless it showed grainy network footage of a giant monster, an oil rig explosion, and a giant monster continuing on its way unfazed.

This was not a dream meant to come true. It was the end of known things and the beginning of truth.

"They're on their way," said Thighs.

Kichi commed his boys. "Milo, Ramses, whoever's got ears out there: They're on the way." He waited a moment and was about to repeat when Ramses came through.

"Who?"

"Media."

Out of respect for Kichi Ramses didn't cuss. Out loud.

"Get word to Buford," said Ramses. "Unless he wants to see *everything* he's built disappear he'd better squelch *every* news outlet right now."

Kichi hurried off to Buford.

~~~

Kichi handed Buford a cell phone after a brief explanation.

"Who do you need to call, and how will they know it's you?"

"This funnels down from only one person on the planet, and only at my order. Three words: It's too hot." Buford prepared to dial the phone, which was undoubtedly monitored and undoubtedly scrambled to high hell.

Kichi stopped him. "Ain't satisfied with the second part of my question."

"No worries, old man."

Kichi removed his hand. "Dial it, jackass."

Buford did, said, "It's too hot," and disconnected, passing the phone to Kichi.

The thirty Agents of Change surrounding the two in the shielded bunker un-tensed.

On the receiving end of the communiqué, Aileen Stone announced to the head of the Food and Drug Administration and the acting chief of the Bureau of Alcohol, Tobacco and Firearms that their meeting was over. The two fat men left with frowns on their faces but total silence on their lips. Aileen keyed the transponder in her neck.

"Pope-level communique: Kill that satellite image. Ground any crews thinking they were heading that way. Kill anybody dumb enough to make it out there. Get me terrorists and explosions in five cities, two today, one the next three days."

"Yes, ma'am."

So Buford's alive, Buford's well, the Thoom don't have him, the vampires don't have him. He's current and he's making calls.

That meant, one way or another, the Jetstreams had him. Game-over Protocol was simply to walk away. Pivotal moments in human history were few and well-guarded. Aileen sounding the *Game Over* would be one of them.

The only thing was, she wasn't exactly ready to make that call. "God save the queen," she said aloud, recalling a line from a book she'd read in high school, which ended, *because the devil couldn't do a thing with her.*

~~~

"What now, Malat?" asked Buford. "The Thoom and Count Ricky will have everyone short of the Boy Scouts hunting you, and the United States isn't as big as anyone thinks."

"Quiet, jackass." Everybody thought Kichi would hightail it to Atlantis, except they knew he'd know they'd think that, so he wouldn't. Linear-thinking jackasses would try to play the Trapped Man game and close him in.

He told Thighs: "Get us as fast underground as possible, get Bubba Foom to meet up with us on the fly, get us the fastest transport to Atlantis, and keep him," with a slight glance at Buford, "unconscious."

Thighs had been learning how to smack the fye out of someone. He rubbed his ex-football player hands together.

"Be creative but effective," said Kichi. "I need to talk to the boys a bit."

~~~

Bodies. Bodies were strange balloons. You could let all the insides out of one and they still floated. The whales had been tempted to stand guard over the fallen but they knew there wasn't a shark within fifty miles foolish enough to enter this scene, even for a meal as large as Polsus, whose heart had given out when Leviathan charged them. Three of the humans were dead, shot from long range. Bifrost broke off with two of the larger bulls straight for the assassin's ship, the clones clinging underwater to their bellies.

Adam took aim at Bifrost.

The whales dove and separated, becoming for all intents and purposes Neptune's trident on a collision course of godlike wrath. Bifrost did the math and angled downward on a straight thirty-seven degree trajectory which would put it directly below the interloper's ship for when sixty-five tons of sperm whale decided to suddenly shoot upward with all its might. The other two stayed parallel to the surface, twenty meters below it.

We might have needed a bigger boat, thought Eve.

Maseef had already ordered the others to submerge. The clones were not to stop their mental sheep-dogging.

Adam shouldered his weapon and dropped his helmet in place. Eve was helmeted and braced for impact. The waters, given what was coming, were annoyingly calm.

Rhythmic breathing in both helmets provided the impact's countdown.

Bifrost hit first, knocking the ship's stern completely out of the water. Nnedi looped under and came up ramming starboard. Momentum carried the ship into Takra's path at port; the heavily-scarred sperm whale smashed a hole in the hull half the size of its head.

The three whales regrouped. The three whales gathered speed. This was about to get messy.

The three clones disengaged.

Takra hit first, Nnedi second, Bifrost last, each time leaving pieces of the ship floating on the water. It would be whittled to nothing, and then the humans, who would be in the water, would be theirs. Granted they wore breach suits, but this was a good day to test a breach suit's tolerances.

On the next pass Bifrost felt feet land near its blowhole then a searing slash across the hole, followed by another, a large bloody X forming on its head. The whale thrashed and dove, sending Adam into the water. Takra's fluke slammed Adam with the force of a small truck. Eve was on Nnedi's back, running awkwardly for its tail with vibrating sword steady in her hand. Bifrost rolled under its compatriot and charged Nnedi's midsection, knocking Eve off. She no sooner made a splash than Nnedi twisted, clamped Eve's sword arm in its mouth, and dove straight down.

Clones Luke and Iggy, taking advantage of Adam's stunned confusion, whopped the shit out of him underwater using pressure points and holds. Then they tazed the shit out of him. Luke disabled Adam's breathing apparatus. Iggy and Luke swam off, leaving Adam floating limply. Bifrost picked them up. Bifrost hurt everywhere, but far in the distance the waters were churning around Leviathan. The beast was getting annoyed. No amount of ramming it would amount to anything. Bifrost didn't know what would do, but it hoped the humans did.

56

ThiS
SidE Of
ParadiSe

"Where's Milo?" asked Guerris.

"Give him time," said Ramses.

Another huge wave hit from the roiling bulk of Leviathan in the distance. Ramses wiped water from his face and Guerris spat. The *Ann* stabliized. Ramses zoomed in on Leviathan. The surface of the water gave little sign of all the work going on beneath it. Blowhole spray jetted in the peripheral.

"Do you think we'll die today?" asked Guerris.

"I need you to go below," said Ramses.

Guerris patted Ramses' arm, then gave him a gentle kiss on the cheek. "You're a good man, Ramses Jetstream."

"Thank you."

Guerris disappeared below-decks.

"Smoove?" Ramses said to the man beside him.

"Brother."

"Assessment."

"It's a wide ocean. We calm him in this stretch of it, but ten feet in either direction lies unknown territory."

Two more blowholes returned.

"How you feeling?" Smoove asked him. Smoove fought to keep the ship riding the unpredictable waves. He'd seen the first clone go down. Afterward things had moved too quickly. There came two more flashes. Neither Adam nor Eve were known to miss.

The comm squawked loudly in Smoove and Ramses' faces. "Ram!"

"Jetstream!" shouted Smoove.

"Where you at, brother?" said Ramses.

Guerris returned topside at Milo's voice. Milo spoke quickly. "I've got you fixed but I'm coming in hot and a little wild. Be ready to dance!"

Nothing immediately starboard, port, aft or stern.

Then just the slightest tingle to the air, as though a million bees had surged to move the air a hair's breadth forward.

The boat appeared with about eight meters of air between it and the water. It was far enough from them that Smoove didn't need to dance much, but whoever was piloting the Atlantidean craft threw it into a watery skid the second it splashed down, its nose dipping dangerously before whipping out and around.

"What're we doing, Ram?" Milo asked.

"Keeping us between it and the rest of the world."

"Quicho?" said Milo.

"I'm eyes behind it. Fiona's in Atlantis, right at the Blank. This much animal should never be confused."

"Almost heart wrenching," said Ramses.

"Almost," she agreed.

Maseef broke in. "I have an idea."

"You maintaining?" Ramses asked him.

"The clones meditate better than Milo ever could. The whales are going to try to dream to it."

"They've never done that," said Milo.

"Nor a clone teleported a ship," said Maseef. "We lost three to Adam and Eve."

"Send them in and be gentle," Desiree interjected. "Honey," she said for Smoove, "you fall back. Don't wreck my ship. I'll stay tight to the action and report."

"What do we do now?" Guerris asked.

"We wait for Buford and the Thoom to show up," said Ramses.

"Big fish, many feeders," said Smoove. He clapped a hand to Ramses' shoulder. "That was a serious gambit, brother," he told Ramses.

"Past tense might be premature, Captain."

"Pointless not to be optimistic," said Smoove.

"What," Guerris said into the open comlink between the ships, "if Leviathan decides to continue toward Blank lands?"

"Best Godzilla movie ever made," said Smoove. "Absolutely unforgettable. Welcome to the other side of the Blank, luv."

POPPa DON't Take NO MESS

Death-mael, gliding as quietly as a ripple, wondered why people, in his case Atlantideans, forgot the world was made of water. It was everywhere, it was everything. Its absence was death; its over-abundance, a different kind of death. The Atlantic stretched forever. Traversing the Blank world had felt strange, but only briefly. He wondered if being underwater shielded him. Animals were always traveling the Blank. Dolphins tagged with radio transmitters did it for fun, knowing how they'd blip, disappear, or sometimes appear to be everywhere at once. Compared to dragoon dolphin were still backwoods relatives, but they were somewhat smarter than humans who, no matter how much incredible complexity you hit them with, remained fixated on opposable thumbs.

The dragoon was so far Blankward he couldn't get an impression of the battle far behind him, neither psychic nor sonar. No dragoon had ever done this. No dragoon had the facial muscles to perform a smile but if he'd had, Death-mael would have smiled.

He surfaced, and swam atop the deep blue.

A dragoon cruising the Atlantic coast just for the hell of it? Might be fun...

...except for that speck coming toward him from the direction of the Blank lands that would grow to larger than a speck in not too great a time judging by its speed.

This would be the old man then. Dragoons knew several rumors about him. Better than that, they'd dreamed with him. Well, all of Atlantis had, but still. He had been to the Mount and become part of Leviathan's pattern of force. Hard to do that without gaining a measure of notoriety in underwater circles.

Death-mael had felt echoes of him in the Jetstreams.

He strained to see if he could feel anything now, but a book of poetry bound in singularity hide blocked him. Poetry was powerful mojo. It was chaos and physics distilled. Bad poetry even more so. The clamoring of that book produced a shield around Malat, whether to keep others out or keep Malat in or equally both, the dragoon neither wondered nor knew.

~~~

Fiona was bored. That was dangerous. Moreso anxious than bored, but the net danger was the same. Her boat was positioned half in, half out of the Blank. A person could easily get unhinged in the multiverse like that. When you had an elite team of battle angels, enough tech to start several new industries, and all of the world to protect, waiting on the outcome of a fight with a fish didn't sit well. Sereda was on the ship with Desiree; Smoove and Guerris with Ramses. This wouldn't be won by force, so no need for everyone to die.

Except, apparently, the clones.

Fiona had fancied all of them secretly wanting to sniff her hair.

The comm squawked. Even modified, proximity to Leviathan generated static and spots.

"Say again," said Fiona Carel. But the only word that came out was "...wreckage" and then nothing. It had been Kichi Malat talking.

~~~

The closer Kichi got to Leviathan and Ramses, the less reliable the ship's communications. At half zoom the hump in the far distance was Leviathan, the two specks—visible only through specs—were the *Semper Fi* and the *Linda Ann*. At full zoom a third ship, dead, displayed its component parts along the waters, floating in that broken-doll-trying-to-fit-back-together way wrecked ships had that was unbearably sad and heart wrenching.

"There shouldn't be this much interference," said Thighs.

Kichi grunted. "Leviathan's active. All kinds of extra energy. Bubba and Asme still asleep?"

"Bubba is. Asme's with Michael."

"Ask somebody to get the skiff ready, get Asme and Mike on their way right now. Tell Fiona to have somebody meet them, even if you only get one word through at a time. I don't want them floating this ocean. They can stay at Vrea Talloon B'oom's."

Thighs really wanted to ask *What about Buford?* With him on board they were a dog with a t-bone around its neck traveling an alley of coyotes. The bastard didn't deserve safe harbor. Throwing a harpoon at Leviathan with Buford attached to it was an honorable idea.

Kichi, scanning the water again, mumbled, "There's a dragoon in the water."

"What's a dragoon?"

Kichi handed him the specs. "See that thing doing somersaults? Don't hit it."

This is embarrassing, thought Death-mael, but it was the only way it could think of to get their attention at a distance, which they closed fairly quickly.

They saw it, altered course just enough to avoid hitting it, and zipped on by.

Death-mael plopped into the water, bobbing in their wake. *That was just rude!* it mentally shouted at them, but it was, admittedly, expected. Rather than feign indignation it decided to stop and watch from a safe distance.

Death-mael didn't see this, but one of the clones walked Leviathan's back placing charges.

"Ram," Kichi radioed.

"Sir? I got everybody in the stew."

"Good. Now back away," said Kichi Malat in that tone that brooked no dissent. "Milo? I want you and Ramses on this ship watching Buford. Me and Bubba are taking the *Ann*. Smoove, you staying on board?"

"I'm coming over," said Desiree.

"Best pilots in the known world," said Kichi.

"All worlds," said Smoove.

"Pops--" Milo started.

"I'm gonna park it on its butt and we're gonna have a chat. Maseef?"

"Sir," came Maseef's voice with the rumble and rush of wind and water.

"You and the whales are rear guard. Ramses, I'm sensing hesitation on your part?" said Kichi.

"Part of me wants to see it make landfall."

"Not the cataclysm the world needs right now," said Kichi.

"Yes, sir."

The *Ann*, *Fi*, and Atlantidean vessel altered courses and approached Kichi.

"What if the genie doesn't go back in the bottle?" asked Thighs, his thick legs slightly unsteady, and he hoped it was just from the boat.

"Then I read poetry to it," said Kichi. "Hoping it doesn't come to that."

Bubba Foom emerged on deck blinking into the sun. His wife and son, as promised, were already far away from immediate danger, but far away was not out of. It was a big ocean.

Kichi took Bubba's hand and held it while talking to Milo. "MJ, how're you holding up?"

"This sun's a sonofa. I've got a half-dead clone. I don't want him all the way dead."

"We're doing our best to ride into the sunset here," said Kichi, his strong, wiry fingers giving Bubba a squeeze. He shook his head in disbelief and laughed. "God damn! Y'all got the fish out in the water!" His ubiquitous notepad was safely in his pocket, the paper and ink waterproof. "This is going in the book."

"Who else is with you, pops?" asked Milo.

"A good soldier named Thighs. Few other folks."

Milo, glancing at Warren, added up the responsibilities. This was a big ocean and bodies—be they from Kichi's, Ramses' or his own ship—floating it would do nothing to decrease its enormity.

The clone atop Leviathan's back dove and swam to meet his next supply of munitions. He slung the large pack over his neck and shoulders and scaled the beast again until reaching the spinal crest. He quickly and efficiently placed additional charges.

"Thighs?" said Milo.

"Yes, sir."

"Get that old man in a breach suit."

Thighs gave a glance toward Malat, who clearly communicated "no" without a word. "Not likely, sir."

"It was worth a shot."

Kichi Malat, old as he was, was used to all the physiological and mental peccadilloes involved in traveling the Blank. He wore cargo pants and a loose, buttoned shirt, pointy elbows and corded arms contrasting nicely with the eggshell cream of the shirt.

"What's that clone doing?" asked Bubba.

Kichi, not letting go Bubba's hand, brought the specs to his eyes again.

"Insurance plan," said Ramses. "If I yell 'clear' everybody boat the hell away."

"Once you two get over here get this boat to Atlantis," said Kichi. "Tomorrow we start dismantling Buford's empire."

The ships rendezvoused, swapped crews, and went their needed ways: Kichi toward Leviathan with Desiree, Bubba and Smoove on the *Ann*; the *Semper Fi*, captained by Thighs, providing escort to Milo, Ramses and a skeleton crew of Agents of Change with Buford, the two ships bound for the Blank; Guerris and Warren aboard the Atlantidean Stinger, Guerris piloting via adrenaline and sheer willpower, following Milo and Ramses. *Going home,* the Atlantidean thought, and for some reason this made him inexplicably sad.

On the *Ann* Desiree noted how Smoove kept watch on the tall psychic. "Bubba, you frosty?" she asked, eyes softening to give him a place to lay. They were heading toward eight clones of Milo on what would likely turn out to be a really shitty day.

"I'm good, hon'," he said. He tried smiling. It looked weird. Too much worry.

Desiree comm'd Guerris. "Guerris, if you see a small ship with two people on it, pick them up. They're heading to Fiona." She smiled for Foom. "That's two ships on the way to them. They'll be fine."

"How do we know this will work?" asked Smoove.

"When have we ever known anything?" said Kichi. Where Guerris was fear and adrenaline, Kichi was exhilarated. Not that it showed. Only fools and politicians showed exhilaration in the face of doom. "We passed a dragoon. Other than doing somersaults for attention it wasn't insane. That means Leviathan is calming. Bubba, this might burn you out, but it's the only chance we get: we've got to convince the oldest living thing on earth that we mean to leave it alone forever and that we'll make sure that everybody else does the same. You won't just be riding his mind in there, Bubba, you're going to be guiding him."

"The clones have done a good job of it," said Desiree.

Kichi shook his head. "They were a curiosity to him in the first instance. At best they're tiny detours now. "

"I'm putting a saddle on the sucker," said Bubba Foom, "and riding his ass back to oblivion."

And that's all Bubba had to say about that.

Into
The
Breach

"Have them get out of the water," said Bubba. "I don't want any distractions." Bubba Foom in a breach suit looked like a bearded mantis dipped in rubber. The waters were relatively still around Leviathan who, for the moment, felt content to stretch out motionless on its ocean. The *Ann* got within throwing distance of a wall of encrusted hide. Maseef withdrew the whales and clones to Foom's satisfaction then Foom lowered himself into the water and very slowly (it seemed to all observing) swam out to meet Leviathan.

He'd seen every episode of Star Trek and Spock had not once tried to mind-meld Godzilla.

He was tethered to the ship by one of the impossible to tangle lines Quicho had invented. However, the amount of comfort in that couldn't convince him of his safety one whit. He felt like bait and hoped to gods his jangly bones weren't the hook for this fish's mouth.

Smoove monitored Bubba's vitals. "He's close to hyperventilating."

"Bubba," said Desiree.

"I know." Foom shunted his mind outward in twenty different directions and had it together when they snapped back.

Smoove, satisfied with the new reading, nodded to his wife.

Desiree allowed Bubba to continue. "Any doubts, big man?"

"Kichi told me we're leaving him alone forever. No doubts. Total clarity."

"Thing could kill him without being aware of it," Smoove murmured to Desiree.

"Yes, I'm aware of that," Foom said. "I've got my gain turned to full; don't need to be psychic to hear you. Thank you."

"Sorry, Bubba," said Desiree.

"Hon', when I'm ready please have everybody shut the hell up," said Foom.

"Done."

After a few moments he reported that he was starting his climb.

"What's it feel like, Bubba?" said Captain Quicho to keep his mind off what he was doing.

"Like climbing Everest with a lot on your mind."

"It's an iceberg," said Smoove. "Be glad most of it's below."

"How many brains do you think he has?" asked Bubba, his breath coming through labored.

"I'm gonna go with eight," said Smoove.

"Twelve," Desiree guessed.

"This is going to be fun," said the world's most powerful psychic.

"You don't have to do this," said Desiree.

"You should have told me that before I climbed on the monster's back."

"We'll yank you back first sign of movement," she said.

"Quicho?"

"Yes, dear?"

"What if I die?"

"Then I'll jump in with a knife and gut the fucker myself. Rest yourself now. Comm silence for a minute."

"OK."

"Next time you hear me it'll be to say that Michael and Asme are in Shig's office. Let's hold tight till then."

"That's a good idea. If I get bored I'll ask for music."

"Anything in mind?" she asked.

"Credence Clearwater Revival wouldn't hurt." He wedged himself deep into a pocket of barnacles and tried his best to feel Leviathan's heartbeat. Or one of them. Multi brained, multi hearts. Hell, thing probably had a platoon of Munchkins spinning hamster wheels somewhere inside it.

Foom hated the movie *The Wizard of Oz,* particularly the Munchkins. Particularly the Lollipop Guild, little roughneck wannabees.

Foom took a deep breath and meditated.

Kicking the Lollipop Guild's ass would be a good thing.

Desiree got word that Michael and Asme had just crossed the Blank into Atlantis. She relayed this to Foom. Foom roused himself head to toe, inside and out, and let the game begin.

Buford was seated. His eyes went from Milo to Ramses, both of whom sat watchful in front of him, silent. He said nothing. In fiction the arch nemesis would taunt a hero, but in real life, with life being the key word because Buford had no plans to die, ever, Milo could punch a hole straight through Buford's ribcage if he wanted.

He knew what they were thinking. *"We should kill him."* How could they not? Even if there were still clones out there they had the real Buford, and for them that was practically end game in itself. He knew his boys.

The palpable buildup of animosity and chi lent a static to the cabin that clogged ears. Buford couldn't hear anything above decks, not the water nor wind. The space had the feel of an isolation chamber.

Outside of thwarting Milo at the Atlantidean facility he hadn't been this close to both of them in years. Not where he could see the nick of a scar on Ramses' neck from where the boy had first fought his brother using throwing stars, or this deeply into Milo's eyes. Where his brother's might always have been slightly melancholic, Milo's eyes were damning, constantly seeing the hells Dante described and blaming the human world for them.

They traveled fast, away from Leviathan, away from Nonrich, back to Atlantidean soil and justice.

Justice was a foolish, dangerous concept, Buford thought; Nothing the human mind was equipped to toy with.

He felt the frisson of the ship entering the Blank. He hadn't been given a breach suit in case of emergency. Drowning, Milo had said, was acceptable.

He thought about the Mount and of how succumbing to that last personal hubris may not have been the most prudent of acts. *But if one can't be the god of all outcomes,* Buford thought, planning as he stared into Milo's eyes, *you might as well give up.*

The Battle Ready Bastards immediately surrounded Buford upon docking. Shig's forces, in turn, surrounded everyone, with eyes and sensors on land and in the sky. Shig himself even carried a weapon, as did his two assistants, and he looked very much as if he wished to use it.

"I want him underneath something, Shig. Buried. Untouchable," said Milo.

"Understood."

"Raffic?" said Milo.

The Mad Buddha stepped forward, a dwarf compared to the angels.

"You got this?" said Milo.

"I got this."

"Ram?" said Milo.

Ramses nodded, which was all Milo needed. Their father was a good man. A smart man. And there was no way he thought they would leave him to those waters alone.

"Where're Asme and Michael?" asked Ramses.

"Very safe. Ele and Fiona are with them," said Shig.

"Do you have the Blank fully monitored now?" asked Milo.

"Yes."

"Anybody besides us comes through blow 'em the fuck to hell."

The Blue Fantastic

By now Leviathan had sufficiently calmed that the beast's boredom entered Foom like an inner packing of wet sand.

How big are you underneath all this encrustation really? Probably the size of a carp. Growing up in Michigan then moving to Ohio, Foom had caught his share of carp. Most people hated carp as being bottom-feeding garbage fish, and they were right. Foom couldn't stand the taste of the things. But they also put up a helluva fight, and Foom hoped the similiarity between them and the aquatic land mass he sat on ended before that.

The comm beeped softly. "Bubba." (He'd always loved Desiree's voice.) "Milo and Ramses are on their way back. Just crossed the Blank. You want to wait for 'em?"

Foom roused immediately. "No. Gimme a few to sharpen my knives. I'm going in."

It was like stepping off an escalator into a hurricane with winds strong enough to reduce reality to atoms. He hoped he didn't scream. He hoped out there Desiree wasn't listening to him going out of his mind. Everything regarding thought was an illusion, he knew that for a fact. No matter how long this thing had lived, no matter how much it had seen or caused, it was not the universe. It was not god. It was a fish, an impossibly, ridiculously big fish. Constrained by the same world as Foom. Subject to hungers and boredom and dreams.

You could alter its transmissions, Milo had told Foom, but that wasn't the same as controlling the message.

Foom drew his consciousness into as tight a ball as he could manage. He needed time, time to find something that he and Leviathan could share before Leviathan's memories obliterated this tiny pea in its mindstream, a direction in which Foom's consciousness could ride *with* a current as opposed to against it.

He found it in blue. Leviathan, after billions of years of asexual reproduction and genetic memories where it lived as a continuum beneath the deepest blankets of the earth, feeding between hibernations now and then on singularities but most often through the osmosis of nutrients from the ecosystem living on its body, after stretches in darkness long enough to see the fanciful dreams that were civilizations rise and fall—Leviathan enjoyed the sky. The blue forever of it, the quietude. Clouds didn't unconsciously ask to share Leviathan's dreams, and the sun in the sky was like the creature's twin cast off from it. Blue tasted like polar ice, breath, and thoughts at the same time.

Blue was Foom's favorite color. Sky blue. He rode the pull of blue on their minds like scattered ball bearings toward an inescapable magnet.

Blue was sanity. Blue was control. It was memories of spring and apple orchards along lonely roads; memories of the scarf Asme had around her dreads the first time he ever saw her, its fabric the precise light shade of blue he'd gravitated to ever since his third birthday; it was the icy shock of his own eyes in a mirror the first time he'd ever read another mind, his father's, an unsettling experience in the extreme.

It was seeing the sky suddenly burst full across the world as though it hoped to hug the sea, the beautiful forever of it reminiscent of the way Foom's heart constricted thinking of his love for Asme; in this Foom found voice to communicate in a voice Leviathan hadn't heard in eons: its own.

may i speak? he broadcast.

you may.

there is nothing they have that you need.

this world is mine?

yes.

then i need this world.

This was not a matter of finesse or gentle actions. Foom's tiny Pequod grew pincers as reins, lodged itself, and forceably pulled, knowing how laughable the vision of a mite trying to direct a rhino was but ignoring that for now. Leviathan's mind was a land of dreams, for what else did it have to do? He pulled hard in the direction of Atlantis, trying to feel the bulk of the rhino turn under him, but the beast was stone.

go home, Leviathan. you're drunk, drunk off the thoughts of others, off their false directives.

i am the alpha and the omega...

we haven't been that for a long time. He pulled again, digging into tough flanks. If he could forge bridges of intent with its other brains, Leviathan would believe it had come to its own decision; its bulk would move and, by the Deities Three, Bubba Foom would be like unto a god.

That last part troubled him just a nibble. Gods, however, easily ignored nibbles.

their world is intrusive and incessant Leviathan pointed out.

we're the source of their aspirations. we are the creators. But we're behind the curtain, Foom realized. *behind the curtain!*

Leviathan's mind slowed, its brains aligning toward solidarity. *i once dreamt lizards into dragons. the dragons went away. i dreamt monkeys into people. they need to go away.*

we never should have awakened you.

no.

we never should have manipulated you.
agreed.
we are unfit to be graced by you.
you are.
go home. Foom tugged again, every erg of conscious energy strained and bulging.

i know your mind. said the beast. *i gave you the purest color blue.*

Foom's grip on the reins slipped. *you?*

i gave him visions of god meaning Fruehoff; *her, realities.* Fiona. *you, the limitless blue.*

i am the alpha and omega.
there is nothing you cannot do.
except be you.

i am the alpha and the omega Leviathan communicated.

Foom felt an ever so tiny nudge of movement.

then you can afford to wait till we move out of the neighborhood before stretching out again Foom sent. *for now, however, let this dream be over. we will wake you no more.*

Foom felt a definite tug on his body and ignored it, although there was the feeling of suddenly sailing through air. His mind, however, splintered outward to Leviathan's other brains, the mite giving orders, the mite taking charge. There was a huge cave under a mountain in a land through a dimensional drift, deep, deep, where the earth was still primitive and thus still new. It was home. Safe, necessary home. A place where dreaming created the world.

Leviathan stirred and very slowly swam toward the Blank, ignoring the whales and humans darting about it retrieving bombs.

Milo and Ramses saw it coming and gave it a wide berth. It felt strange seeing Leviathan swimming near the surface where the sun was just beginning to turn the ocean orange but the sky held to its lovely blue.

They continued at due speed for Kichi.

The Atlantic was getting larger and larger to them the more they traveled it, but that was neither here nor there. Their father and compatriots were on the water and that was destination enough. Even Death-mael had a destination; Kichi had not forgotten the adventure-sick animal.

Milo rendezvoused and assessed injuries, damage, and victories. "There's a dragoon out there thinking it's going to Florida," said Kichi. "He's likely tired and surface bound." Physically, outside of aches from being yanked off Leviathan, Bubba Foom seemed fine. Mentally wouldn't show till he was reunited with his family. Psychically, not till Foom relented to show. The tall man was alone, below deck, at his request. "Maseef and the whales will fan out," Kichi continued. "Y'all find the dragoon. Thank it. Send it home. The clones stay with me."

"Sir?" said Milo.

Eight Jetstreams, tired, bedraggled, water-logged, mourning, spread across the deck like random dolls. They needed to be talked to. "Hurry up, Milo. We'll meet you at Shig's."

Kichi Malat's boat went one way, Milo's the other.

Death-mael, feeling the presence of the whales and seeing the ship bearing for him, simply stopped swimming and thought *Damn.*

Transcendental Strangulation

Neon and Yvonne were going batshit stir crazy. It was Neon's idea to leave Shig's anteroom and wander outside. From all reports, the big fish was back in its grotto, although Milo, Ramses, Kichi and Foom stayed nearby it on the ships just to be sure; this Buford asshat was on lock down; Atlantis was a no-fly zone and, lastly, not a single enemy or faction had made a peep the last several hours. Stars exist in multi-dimensions, and Atlantis' portion of the sun slid down the color spectrum into citrus blasts, the sky's last bits of blue becoming umber. The only other quiet evening they'd spent in Atlantis had gotten them attacked by vampires.

They both had cross-checked the packs on their backs and the guns on their belts. Tata and For Now. Full breach gear, no ass to kick.

They knew not to wander far. Matter of fact, leaving the facility hadn't occurred to them. It was large and open enough that it felt like outside. The hallways of the government building glittered in places, catching strategic bits of light along walls which gradually darkened and lightened. The air was too perfect not to be filtered. Abstract installations of art, plants, or a combination of the two sprouted at every juncture.

They knew not to bother the angels. That left one person: Shig Empa. In a very soft way he was one of the strongest people the ladies had ever met. Just being around him would offer comforts as they waited for the crews to return.

The Atlantidean might have characterized himself as a minor functionary but it was never hard running into someone who knew precisely where he was.

A man cloaked head to toe in a gauzy black burqa pointed them in the direction of a meditation chamber. For a government building it was littered with those chambers. Neon couldn't quite imagine Congressmen meditating.

The rooms were windowless, unmonitored, soundproof and built for one though large enough for two or three.

Yvonne knew meditation wasn't necessarily a non-*physical* thing.

The doors were clear glass; this one had darkened to obsidian, which meant a chamber was occupied and the occupant wished to be disturbed only in extreme emergency. It was not locked. Doors in Atlantis rarely were. Courtesy was not optional.

The fact that they were in Atlantis counted as an emergency, so unless Shig was in there wanking furiously he was about to have company, maybe even show them a few techniques, meditative or otherwise.

They walked in. Shig's assistants, Giselle Jira and Wither Ween, were with him. Wither was on top of him; mostly her knee was. It was in his back. A piece of clothing served as makeshift garrote in the clenched hands she pulled with. Shig, the stubborn bastard, wouldn't stop moving. His face led his body through contortions. Giselle was half naked and unmoving.

Wither jumped off and tried to run but there was only a doorway, the two out-Blanks, and hardly space to get to decent ramming speed. Yvonne palm-struck Wither hard in the left shoulder, knocking her off balance and in position for a left hook. She expected the Atlantidean to go down.

They seemed so soft and fragrant, like babes whose bones never fully hardened under tender, perfect skin.

That punch, instead, ignited a sudden influx of rage in the Atlantidean's eyes.

Neon saw this. She backed a step into the doorway to give Yvonne room. Yvonne read Wither's stance as that of a fighting person, a smaller one who would realize a flurry attack was her only viable option, but who would realize from Yvonne's stance that Yvonne would be aware of this and counter with in-close fighting coupled with—judging from the near blinding throb from the previous blow—solid, definitive punches. Plus there was the woman behind Yvonne.

Suicide it was then. That or massacre. No three ways about it. Wither met Yvonne's eyes.

They began.

Wither clawed, drew blood but not as much pain as she'd hoped.

Yvonne followed with a perfectly synchronized backhand swipe, catching Wither across the chin.

Wither backpedaled, stopping short of tripping over the unconscious Shig, then quickly shot her lithe body forward, feinting left, trying for a leg sweep right. Yvonne raised her leg, allowing Wither's foot to pass under, then spun with a solid elbow to the jaw.

Her turn now to corner the Atlantidean. If Shig's attacker had a weapon she'd have used it by now—she'd have used it on Shig—so up close and personal would see this fight over before the smaller woman could land any decent blows. Yvonne tried a strike which Wither easily parried, blocked a strike from her, meant to thrust a knee in a groin but instead left her own midsection exposed, into which Wither delivered two quick punches, knocking Yvonne's breath out in an explosive *whuf!*

Yvonne grabbed one of Wither's punching arms and twisted, whirling Wither face first into the nearest wall. Hard.

She bent the woman's arm behind her back pressed close. "I've got three more walls to choose from," she said.

The struggle went out of Wither, who tried to go dead weight. Using the split-second lack of tension Yvonne hauled Wither into the air into a body slam.

Wither was done.

Yvonne rolled the limp woman over. "Tata," she said.

"For now," Neon added perfectly, her heart bathed and crazed in adrenalin. She opened Yvonne's pack for restraining coils.

"Let's never quip again," said Yvonne.

"Agreed." Neon checked Shig while Yvonne applied the restraints. "He's not dead." She checked Giselle. "Alive." She stepped outside the room. Still quiet and deserted. She pulled her comm out. "Raffic? We have a situation." She hit *video* on the comm and swung it around. "They attacked Shig."

"Sit tight," he said from his post guarding Buford.

"You can't leave. He'll escape or something," said Neon.

"Hardly."

"Yvonne can bring her to you."

"I'm not dragging this woman through the hallway."

Neon shushed her. "I can take care of Shig and the naked man. Send whoever you need to down here. Meds, police, whatever."

"Done," said Raffic. "Anything else?"

"No."

He signed off.

"She weighs less than your hips," said Neon.

Which is how Yvonne DeCarlo Paul came to be carrying Wither Ween over her shoulder toward Raffic the Mad Buddha deep in a detention center in the heart of Atlantis. If that wasn't worth a future memoir, thought Yvonne, nothing was.

The Sleeper Awakes

"Shig," said Neon in the hospital room, "you are one kinky bastard. Naked assassins."

Shig was awake. The only reason he agreed to remain in the hospital bed was so it could finish scanning him. His voice was raspy but he was otherwise fine. "No, it wasn't like that."

"Where's your weapon?" asked Raffic.

"Storage. Outside the meditation room," Shig said.

It wasn't. Giselle, who'd been roused and who hadn't been choked, had been questioned, released, opened Shig's locker, and was on his way to free Buford. More so kill him, but he had to get him away from the angels first. So free then kill. True Humans Over Ordinary Man preferred things in logical sequence.

Wither Ween was the sleeper.

Giselle Jira was the deep sleeper. Even now he wasn't completely aware he was a Thoom operative. He was guided by compulsion. The sight of Buford had triggered it and it'd gotten steadily stronger to the point where rational thoughts were simply too confusing so he put rational thoughts away.

Shetel saw him coming. The large, brown angel stood. "You're wearing a weapon," he pointed out.

"Shigetei Empa wanted me to."

"How do you feel?"

"I've never been attacked before. We were attacked because of him. May I see him?"

"No."

There were four angels visible, two in the room with Buford, and five unaccounted for.

Neon, to Shig, said, "You were with your two assistants being strangled while one was topless."

"I've seen them naked many times," said Shig.

"You freaky bastard," she said appreciatively.

"Stop saying that! Giselle Jira is a narcoleptic meditator. He has to have someone with him. They wanted to join me in meditation."

"This is common?" asked Yvonne.

"It's not uncommon," said Raffic, having left guarding duty to Ra'asiel X. "I have been naked with Shig."

Shig glared at Neon. "Jira's shirt was a gift; the fabric has annoyed him all day."

Giselle unhooked the gun with distaste. "I don't want this thing. Take it."

What he shouldn't have done was given it to him and then run. Hauling ass equaled guilt and suspicion and Shetel immediately saw Giselle had affixed a narrow, crowd-control tranq canister to the underside of the stock. Shetel was fast. He ripped the canister off and threw it at Giselle. It exploded halfway between them with enough dispersant force that the entire enclosed space was filled almost instantly.

The dull 'whump' of the blast drew Sereda out of Buford's cell, her slight green pallor becoming just a little greener. The tranq immediately entered her lungs before entering the brief crack in the door, where it said hello to Ra'asiel X and Buford.

What it didn't do was knock out the Atlantidean guard who was the source of Wither's and Giselle's programming, as he'd taken a long lasting counter agent just after being ordered part of this detail. The subtle code words, visual cues and touches he'd given Shig's assistants were tedious and way more time-consuming than he liked, but he was a professional. Professionals know that non-lethal and quiet get results. Non-professionals were good as diversions, but to truly get the job done, thought Bodax, agent of Thoom, as he entered Buford's cell, you needed the element of surprise and—

A punch in the throat prevented him from completing that thought.

Ra'asiel whirled on Buford, who saw between him and freedom one lone angel.

Both men held their breaths.

Ra'asiel stood ready. Buford sat down, cross-legged. Ra'asiel, knowing other angels would be there within minutes, sat as well. The staring began. Anyone viewing them would not know of the war being fought. Spirit against spirit on a galactic plane. Ra'asiel X was trained in seven forms of mental combat, second only to Lucifer. There were no demons this human could throw at him that Ra'asiel hadn't already sent to hell.

Buford saw his opportunity in that split-second of hubris and flooded the silent battle with the chi of intense pleasure, so sudden and swift Ra'asiel drew the smallest involuntary breath, damned himself a fool, and passed out, still maintaining the outwardly calm lotus position.

Buford ran.

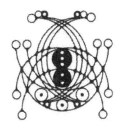

"Pride goeth before a fall!" Milo shouted. "Doesn't it say that? In the bloody book! I. Will. Be. Damned!"

"He's as surprised as us that there were Thoom sleepers here. He's not safe here anymore. For a person like Buford," said Ramses, "that's terrifyingly humbling. Where would he go?"

"Seriously?" said Neon. "You're gonna go chase him again?"

"To the last I will grapple with thee. From hell's heart," Asme began.

"Stow Melville!" Milo said. "We were just beaten by two clerical workers. Guerris?"

"Yes?" Guerris said from behind him.

"Anything to share?"

"No."

"I believe you, which is forever our weakness."

"I'm assuming he doesn't know there's a Nonrich garrison here?" said Ramses.

"They were trying to be black ops," said Milo. "And right now he doesn't want to be found. I'm not worried about them."

"He wants to be found," said Kichi Malat.

"By?" said Milo.

"You."

~~~

Shig Empa's office was quiet. Lots of glass, particularly blue glass: vases, sculptures, surfaces. Atlantidean tech was inlaid in a half metal, half glass desk that, under different circumstances, The False Prophet Buford would have loved to have gotten his hands on to compare to his own, but currently he figured he had perhaps another five minutes to add to the fifteen he was gone before company entered. The easiest thing in the world to do to be overlooked was to sit in one spot when people were looking for you. Finding Empa's office had been easy. Sitting crouched out of view behind the metal elements of his desk had given Buford time to enjoy the evening sky out Empa's window. Time to think. Time to (and this would certainly craw Milo's gullet all the way to Christmas) surrender.

To everything there is a season, he thought. "Greed is its own downfall," he had murmured to the sky. He had written that a long time ago because truth was truth.

And then, "Fuck downfalls. I don't consider this a downfall. I consider it a refit."

Which is when Milo entered the office.

Death

"Is this where we fight to the death, Milo?"

They were in barren land, the middle of nowhere. No one had gotten in Milo's way, not Ramses, not Quicho, not even Malat. Milo had taken Buford to a rover and took off.

Ramses, Neon, Yvonne and Kichi followed in a rover; Desiree, Smoove and Fiona in another.

Milo didn't stop until deep in the heart of the Sip Plains, where they had initially surrounded Buford what felt ages ago, the Mount in audience with its hills and range. By now Leviathan was sleeping again. Milo had been to the Mount, Milo had felt the dreaming, Milo had emerged resolved.

"I've been to the Mount," he told Buford.

"What did you see?"

"The truth. What would you have seen?"

"My truth. My world."

"Your world is petty and useless!" The raised voice was out of place on this empty plain.

"The parasites have been here long enough to become DNA."

"There's a cure for everything, old man."

"Not for self-preservation! Damn it, Jetstream, if your balls are big enough to do a reset on humanity go ahead and erase me. When you go back to the world it'll be as if I never left."

"No, it'll be changed because *this* battle is won. Walk," said Milo.

They walked in the direction of the Mount, Milo several paces behind Buford, until the others were distant enough not to immediately interfere.

"Stop," said Milo.

"To the death?"

Milo's eyes narrowed. A corner of his lip turned slightly upward. He would enjoy this. "What is it about so many old white men that they never want to give anything up?"

Milo unholstered his gun and leveled it at Buford's forehead.

"You'd do that then walk back to Kichi and Ramses and the young lady who kept looking at you and live your life?"

"Why did you take away my life?!" Milo blasted. The gun would be easiest. The gun would be best. Milo fired.

Fiona immediately cycled through realities until she found the one closest matching this one.

In which Milo didn't fire. She slid into herself easily and watched.

"Are you gonna make me taunt you, son? There's nothing to be gained," Buford pointed out, "in you shooting me. I'll be a body in the dust of Atlantis. You'll have a long walk back to them. The earth's rotation doesn't wobble in… the… least."

Memories. Rushing. Emotion. Crashing through him. A lifetime. A lifetime of…this. It couldn't be over. Milo faltered a step. "Raaam!" he shouted. Anguish over the plains carried like waves. He didn't lower the focum, which he had locked on the highest setting.

Ramses jumped in a rover and was there in moments. He got out, leaving the machine running and open.

Now, decided Buford, was the perfect time to gambit.

"The end of things always hurts," said Buford levelly. "Your parents were Thoom, Milo. I took you from that and made you better. Dr. King wanted to use you to forerun a new generation of egalitarian justice and civility. The illogic of waste, Milo Jetstream, sickens me."

"Shoot him, Milo."

"Shut up, Ramses," snapped Buford. "I'll get to you." He locked on Milo. "There's a good chance Count Ricky cloned me. And my closest lieutenant—"

"He's—" said Milo.

"Not that idiot! *She,* Milo Jetstream. She will be the most of your worries, I guarantee it. Know what you've got coming. Didn't I always teach you that?"

All three men were building chi.

Milo put the gun down and advanced.

"Y'know, I really hate primitive," said Buford without a trace of fear. He sized Milo up for injuries or weakness. The fire in Milo's eyes should have been molten instead of merely hot. The man was tired. Tired people were the underfill on which power was built. Buford glanced at Ramses, at Kichi in the distance with the core of the Jetstream crew, and, being the man who created the game now faced with a no-win scenario, made a decision.

Milo read Buford's body language. "If you sit down," he said, "I'll break both your knees so you never stand again."

"Fair enough."

Buford levitated two sizeable stones and shot them directly at Milo's head from different directions, timing it perfectly so that there was opportunity to direct a chi blow straight into Milo's chest when Milo raised his arms to deflect. The energy drain was horrific but the action gave Buford precisely what he wanted: first blood.

A nick on Milo's forehead was wet. It quickly coagulated. Milo noted the brief surprise on Buford's face. Milo had gotten what he wanted. Second blood: Jetstream.

"This sun must be a son of a bitch," said Buford.

"No worse than living in Texas."

"You hated that. Taught you restraint. You're in the wide open here," Buford said, nothing but empty land around them. "When's the last time you fully cut loose? Bring it, son."

Milo darted forward in a sudden chi burst, fist leaving a wavering air trail, ready to strike. At the last second he turned the burst of speed into a twisting somersault just clearing Buford's head, landing behind him and punching him dead center of his back. Buford slammed into the ground twenty feet away and rolled to a stop. He spat blood, coughed, and there were tears in his eyes. His face was dusty.

He slowly made to his knees, head hanging. "Oh shit." He grunted a foot under him. "I felt that."

Heavy elements, attracted by the chi, darkened the clouds directly above them.

Buford made of his right hand a three-fingered trident and his left a split chasm and called on Milo's fears. Shadows swirled the older man's body where there should have been no shadows, shadows that were hungry for instructions.

Ramses closed his eyes and said an incantation of peace, effectively squashing that noise.

Milo formed his own shadow, a brute of swirling light that seemed densely solid the faster colors raced its surface, which took all of a second, then the brute's car-sized fist slammed a Buford-shaped indentation into the ground.

Even with shields up that hurt. Badly.

Neon, from her far vantage, gogged. "They're using *magic,*" she said once her mouth had stopped hanging enough to speak.

"Not hardly," said Kichi. "Not yet."

Buford rolled out of the dirt and threw a gravitational pull at Milo, yanking Milo forward hard enough to dislocate a shoulder, then funneled chi into a punch that punched the hell out of the air, which in turn punched the hell out of Milo, the chest again, forcing the breath out of Milo's body a second time. Milo slid backwards, still on his feet, one hand clawed into the dirt to stop him.

He and Buford ran toward one another and met as though deciding to dance, if dancing included punches, chops, kicks, stomps, blocks, hops, spins and jabs.

"Holy fuck, it's *The Matrix,*" Neon murmured.

"I wrote that movie, you know," said Kichi offhand.

Neon glanced sharply at Malat. "Why isn't Ramses helping him?"

"He is."

A double fist strike connected with Milo's chest. Milo staunched the breath before all of it left him.

The combatants stood several meters apart.

"That's the third breath I've taken from you, boy. You had enough of me yet?"

"I have."

"Time I cheated." Buford wiped blood from above both cut eyes. He quickly reached into his mouth, pulled a tooth loose, and flung it at Milo's feet, studying Jetstream's reaction and trying not to smile.

"Microbots, Milo."

There was no way to gauge how fast the invisible swarm might spread.

"Air activated," said Buford.

"Ram!"

Ramses whipped his focum up, blasted the ground in front of Milo in two wide bursts, then blasted Milo, hoping the energy would scramble the little buggers.

Milo dropped.

Buford spat blood into the dirt, eyes narrowed on Ramses. "Young enigma. Life giver. You and your angels. All this confusion, all this strife? It's all your fault. These people would have been perfectly happy *wallowing* till the next asteroid. But you and your misguided cult of followers come in with your airs and your dreams, all your possibilities and crap about Man's potential. About *art?* Potential is a lie, Jetstream! A bald-faced, weak bit of art. Anemic hope. Irrelevant. Reality... is a son of a bitch."

"And then you die."

"You got the power to do that?" Buford said, planting his feet for another attack.

Ramses calmly re-dialed up the power. "Let's find out."

"You were *never* your brother's equal," Buford said, jabbing his finger toward Ramses. "Always in the background. You know, it was an accident I found you."

Ramses bit down on any response. This wasn't the game to play.

"Kichi filled your head with airy notions wrapped around *bullshit*, and you're standing there right now not knowing what the hell to do. Endgame, son. That takes strength. Because you know goddamn well it doesn't end with me." Buford pointed at the body in the dirt. "God*damn*, you just shot your own brother for no reason whatsoever! I did that. That's control. That's power. That, Ramses Jetstream, is why I am necessary and everything you and Milo, and all the rest of you airy-hearted fools are not!"

"And where do you go from here, Buford?"

"We both know I'm not leaving here. You're just waiting for me to give you a reason. You don't have it in you to kill a man for an ideal, son."

Ramses clenched his jaw. It was over. In all ways it was over. But Buford was trying to get in his head while, behind the action, watching, Kichi did nothing.

"And then who dies?" said Buford, eyes moving to Yvonne just long enough for Ramses to register.

Buford's chi built. He shifted his weight imperceptibly, the better to plant his foot. Injure Ramses enough and Kichi wouldn't stop him jumping in that rover and speeding away. He'd tend to his boys before anything. Even the dirt of Atlantis knew that.

"Bring it—" Buford started.

Ramses fired.

In Gaza there were bombs being lobbed for a tiny parcel of land. In Alabama police were shooting unarmed black youths. In the Ivory Coast adults and children worked to exhaustion harvesting cacoa for candy bars meant to feed the indolent around the world. The False Prophet Buford's world.

Ramses said an interior prayer for Lolita on Maseef's behalf, simultaneously with one for all the families of the dead who'd mistakenly believed they were on this earth to live long lives.

He ran to the rover, retrieved a scanner, and ran back, training it on Milo, the area around Milo, and a wider area of dirt. Nothing. No micro technology, no virals. There'd been nothing there. He picked up the tooth. It was a tooth, loosened, no doubt, by the ass whupping. He tossed Buford's last worthless gesture to the ground then knelt to his brother. "Milo?" Ramses patted Milo's face and brushed dirt from his cheek. "Wake your ass up." The others would be there momentarily. He wanted Milo awake before that.

He placed a palm gingerly on Milo's chest and chi-breathed with his brother a moment.

Milo tried to speak, coughed, and tried to speak again. Came the mumble: "Buford?"

"Not anymore."

"We know how that goes." Vampiric healing wasn't all bad. "We actually finished something, Ram. Did we win?" he asked.

Ramses surveyed the visible and invisible evidence of battles fought and to be fought. There'd been no explosions, no wanton destruction. Things began and ended with explosions. Cataclysms and drama. The way of the universe. "I have no idea," said Ramses.

"I hope so." Milo closed his eyes to gather strength for the approach of his comrades. "Gods, I hurt."

"I know." Ramses wiped tears from Milo's face.

Fiona reached Milo first. She took his hand and he was immediately suffused with everything decent about the world, the real world. Her fingers were small and pale. They entwined his as though forever meant everything.

Neon knelt. The man looked like shit. She composed herself then said, "Dude... you know Kung Fu."

He winced, which caused one of his teeth to show.

"How long you plan on being a vampire?" Neon asked.

"I think we deserve a trip, don't you?" he managed to rasp out.

"Stop talking," Ramses told him. Ramses looked into Neon's face, beautiful even—or because of—worry. "Where should we go?" he asked her.

"Maybe the moon," she said, squeezing Ramses' hand. "If you're going to be a vampire, that's a good option. You've got two space ships."

"How's your soul feel?" Yvonne asked Ramses. He made the mistake of looking up at her. His eyes brimmed.

"I can't fly," said Milo.

"I didn't say it had to be you," said Neon.

If his lips weren't two pieces of pain he'd have wanted a kiss. As it was he steeled himself not to cry out when they lifted him. Kichi was already on the comm to Asme.

"I've always wanted to know what's over the horizon," said Neon.

"Dragons," said Fiona.

"Pops?" said Milo. "We up for dragons?"

Kichi clasped Milo's hand with one hand and pulled something from his back pocket with the other. "Agents of Change can do the clean-up for a minute." He laid a book of poetry bound in singularity hide on Milo's stomach.

"Keep hold of this," said the elder. "You'll need it."

THE BROTHERS JETSTREAM

* 2016 *

THE
ADVENTURES
CONTINUE

Desiree Quicho shouted, "Move your ass!" once and only once. Anybody not clear on the concept stared at her retreating back. She whipped hell to get to the shuttle's quickly descending ramp...

About The author

Zig Zag Claybourne wishes he'd grown up with the powers of either Gary Mitchell or Charlie X but without the Kirk confrontations. The author of *Neon Lights*, *Historical Inaccuracies*, and *By All Our Violent Guides* (under C.E. Young), visit him online at *www.writeonrighton.com* or look for the grinning man in a bookstore.

His fiction and ramblings on everything ranging from science fiction to comedy to drama have appeared in Vex Mosaic, The Wayne Review, Flashshot, Reverie Journal, Stupendous Stories, and numerous other outlets.

For a good, random fun time, the blog *www.thingsididatworktoday.blogspot.com* is his place for random, fun times.

ThiS
bOOk

This goofy, irreverent, maddening book; this raucously drunk friar… would not have seen the light of day if not for equally goofy, irreverent, and gloriously generous friends:

Minister Faust, for support, tips, rips, flips, and keeping me, as a writer, from having connips;

The design team of Catherine and Nathaniel Winter-Hébert, for words, images, inspirations and the wonderful artwork throughout;

Sparkle Hayter, my glorious mofo sister, for everything after the word "Hayter";

Michelle Patricia Browne, for not being afraid to suggest major sword-play on key aspects of this tale;

Warren Bonner, for his keen eye and unerring funksmanship;

Definitely for Raffic the Mad Buddha wherever he may be.

And you. Don't for a moment think you're not part of this. You are. They might not have cloned you yet but you're still a danger. Rock on.

45802502R00236

Made in the USA
Middletown, DE
24 May 2019